Angels in the Corner

a family saga

JuliAnne Sisung

ISBN-13: 978-1544850931
ISBN-10: 154485093X

This is a work of fiction. Characters and incidences are the product of the author's imagination and are used fictitiously.

Published January 2015 by JuliAnne Sisung

Acknowledgements

Thank you to Larry Hale and Jackie Downey for their willingness to spend time on my work. They are amazing. Thanks to Larry again for making me fight for my words. One day he is going to do what I say and write his own book. Thanks to all my friends and family who do and say such interesting things! They are my inspiration.

Cover by Boris Rasin

Chapter One

1911

Kate tossed and turned for an hour or so trying to force sleep to come. She knew she'd feel it during the long day ahead if she couldn't get some rest. It was always difficult to turn off her brain during a full moon. Harley said she was half were-wolf, and maybe he was right.

But Harley was a hobo, so what did he know? He still looked like the hobo he was when he showed up at the Hughes house many years ago and had stuck around like a stray dog who won't go away and people finally learn to love. But he had incomparable, unrealistic, incomprehensible wisdom. It outstretched imagination. An unruly shock of gold curls disputed his age and grew thicker with the years, along with his girth.

Kate smiled when she thought of her old friend and wondered if he had a cure for sleeplessness as he did for most everything else.

She looked around the room where she had slept for over a decade. It was easy to see in the moonlight. There wasn't much to look at, a crude pine table grown smooth and shiny with use. It had been in the cabin when she found it and several chairs were added as needed after each of the girls were born. Two rocking chairs faced the hearth near a kitchen area with a single shelf for plates and pots, a sink and a black cook stove. Her bed was at the far end of the room.

Bug, Kate's red, long-haired dog, lay in front of the hearth snoring lightly but with one eye open, ready to leap to her defense as he had been doing for years. The other dog, Poochie, was most likely wedged in beside five-year old

Jeannie who shared a small bed with her nine-year old sister, Kat. But Poochie didn't belong to the whole family. He had adopted Jeannie at first sight and hadn't wavered since. Rachel and Rebecca, who were eleven and seven, lay near them in another small bed.

Kate tried to make her brain stop hopping about from place to place, to go blank for a moment and let sleep take over, but it wouldn't. She pulled her pillow out from under her head, turned it over to feel the cool side next to her skin and groaned when she yanked her long, blonde hair along with it.

"Damned hair. I ought to cut it off." She pulled it from where it was held captive under her shoulders, untangled it from her fingers and then lay back to try again, breathing slowly, thinking *Sleep, Kate. Go to sleep.*

They had been going to build a room, maybe even two, at the back of the cabin so the girls would have bedrooms but the dream had ended when Mark died, and for a long while after, she hadn't had the strength to care about anything except earning enough money to feed her girls and be able to live in her cabin in peace.

It wasn't really her cabin, but she felt it was. Kate had found it years before she married Mark, when it was dilapidated, filthy and covered in vines that had crept in from the woods surrounding it. It had become her refuge, even then – over fifteen years ago – and slowly she had turned it into her home. It was still her refuge.

A pair of trousers, a shirt and a coat hung by the door where they were the first time she entered the cabin. They most likely belonged to the person she called 'the man,' the real owner of the cabin. She kept them there, washed them twice a year and hung them back up on their pegs by the door out of recognition of his ownership. She was a long-term squatter.

During the first years after she had claimed the place, each noise she heard made her hold her breath in fear of the man's return. She hadn't really expected him to come back and want the place, show up one day, wander through the door and say "Hey – get out of here, squatter woman!" But

2

it was a possibility. Over time, however, it worried her less and less. She hung onto the hope that he would like it if she used his place, took care of it and loved it for him.

"Damn, Kate," she whispered to herself, "be honest. It's not for him. It's for you because you didn't want to leave this cabin since the first moment you found it, and most definitely not since Mark lived here with you." Then she added "Sorry," because she'd cussed, even though no one was near to hear it. The apology was a holdover from when she'd been a young girl with a staunchly Christian mother who was mortified by swearing, especially by ladies.

Bug heard her whispers, came over and stuck his wet nose on her cheek. "I'm fine, Water Bug," she said pulling on his long, red ears. "I think I'll go sit outside for awhile. Want to come?"

He rolled his brown eyes. 'Do you really want to? It's late, and I'm sleepy.' But he slowly stretched out his old body and went with her, waiting while she threw a couple of logs on the red embers in the hearth.

She sat in one of the two rockers in front of the cabin and looked around the clearing. Her father had made the chairs for her, and Kate never failed to think of him when she sat in them. Somehow, he still held her in the arms of the chair he'd made; he was still with her.

She missed him deeply, missed his humor, his gentleness when she was miserable. She'd never had to pretend to be anything other than exactly what and who she was with him, even when she was a little girl and wanted to sing bawdy songs, swear and climb trees. His eyes lit with humor, and he'd grin – not scold – when she exploded with news she had learned eavesdropping from behind the pickle barrel in Nestor's General Store.

Nestor's was where the men gathered in the winter around an old pot bellied stove, passed a jug of moonshine and talked about things Kate wanted to know, but shouldn't hear, shouldn't even want to hear – according to her mother. It was where she liked to linger, smell the musty wool on the men warming by the stove, run her hands over the bolts of homespun and calico, hear the laughter and grumbles of the men and women who wandered through the store, and, of course, sniff the brine of the pickle barrel where she hid from casual sight. Her hiding place had earned her the title 'Pickle Princess' from John Nestor.

That was then, a lifetime ago, and now it was dark in the woods where trees shadowed the ground. But moonlight gathered on the tree tops and spilled over, splashing into the clearing around the cabin. Kate rocked gently, enjoying the stillness. She heard the two horses, Kitty and Dusty, in the shed shuffling around in sleep and the small sounds of night creatures foraging for food.

A family of raccoons lived at the edge of the woods. She'd seen them many times over the years and knew they were not the same ones who were born the year she and Mark had married and come to live at the cabin, but she liked to imagine they were.

This year's batch of young ones had finally braved the opening of their den and scampered quietly near the entrance. Kate saw them when they strayed close to the edge of the clearing and were caught in the moonlight. She left food scraps for them when she had any, and they had become so accustomed to her presence they didn't flee from her unless she got too close.

Bug had gotten used to watching and not chasing her critters, but he was alert for any sound indicating Kate might be in danger. He was proprietary and serious about his duties and sat beside Kate, soaking up her caresses as she talked to him.

She loved the woods and, at night, didn't feel she should be doing something. She could simply enjoy the sounds, the serenity. The washing and ironing she did for the lumberjacks at the nearby camps, weeding her garden, putting up the food it produced, cooking, cleaning and taking care of the girls claimed most of the time in nearly all of her days. There was so much to be done it made her tired just thinking about it.

But in the middle of the night, she could sit and relax, think and dream whatever she wanted. At night, too, once in a while she even allowed tears to leak a bit. But only a little bit, and then she'd swipe at her cheeks like she was batting at a mosquito, take a deep breath, and say, 'Knock it off, Kate.'

"Am I being selfish, Bug?" she asked, "not letting Willie and Mel build the room for the girls?"

Bug rolled his eyes. 'Of course not, but whatever you think is probably right.'

Willie was Kate's brother who had taken over the saw mill after their father was killed helping put out one of the numerous fires that ravaged the area a few years back. Those fires drove many people from the Hersey area; sent homes, farms and dreams up in smoky flames and left despair in the ashes. They were the result of years of drought plaguing the Great Lakes States.

Willie's pockets were empty as most were in the wake of the waning lumber boom, but he did have access to scrap lumber and was willing to donate it to a sorely needed addition to the cabin. Yet, he had his wife, Mary, and two children to provide for, plus their own mother. She hadn't felt right accepting anything they might need and she hadn't earned. He and Mel tried to convince her they could do it for practically nothing, but she hadn't been ready to accept. Maybe it was time.

Kate rocked back and forth, and Bug settled in to wait, lying in the grass at her feet. She thought of Mel, the giant, the longtime friend she knew had wanted to marry her since – well – forever. He'd had no interest in having any other wife, and Kate knew it. Everyone knew it.

They'd been more than friends before Mark, and during those early years she had even considered accepting one of his many marriage proposals. For awhile, he asked every year, in the spring along with the blossoming of the crocuses, and teased saying he was as faithful and determined as a spring thaw. Mel deserved the best, to come first in someone's heart.

But she had fallen in love with Mark, immediately and passionately, and even though he had been away for a long time, she had waited—because she couldn't do anything else. For Mark, she'd known the kind of all encompassing love that brought butterflies and storms. He captivated. He took her breath away, set her on fire. Eventually, Mark returned to Hersey and they had married. They'd had a decade together before cancer took him from her just over a year ago.

She rocked slowly letting her spirit flow into the space around her, reaching out to touch him, needing to feel his presence. She knew he was near. He wouldn't leave, just die and go away. She knew better, and it helped her to go on, to do what she had to do. Love her daughters, take care of her home, live one step at a time and heal. She thanked God for her place in the forest.

In the moonlight, Kate saw the low branch that extended over the end of the path to the clearing around the cabin and grinned. The limb always reminded her of Mel because he had to duck to avoid being knocked from his horse. She allowed herself a sigh of comfort thinking of him always brought. He was a gentle giant.

Mel's family farm had grown over the years because he was unwavering and smart. He worked the land carefully and employed nurturing methods on the soil instead of abusing it. His milk cows all had names, and he used them lovingly when he sat beside them to milk, resting his head against their sides and taking in their musky scent. It was a place he loved to be.

He had quietly helped Kate through the first year of devastation following Mark's death, even made it clear in his firm, gentle way he still wanted to be her husband. But in her heart, she was still Mark's wife, and he understood.

"What do you think, Bug?" Kate asked again. "Mel will be coming out today. Should I talk to him about the addition? Maybe I should talk with Harley, but I know what he'll say. 'Don't disrespect the giver of gifts by refusing. Just say thank you.'"

Bug sat up, gave her the 'of course, Kate' eye roll and went back to watching the raccoons play and enjoying once again the attention of her hand on his head.

Daybreak came slowly in the forest because tall trees blocked the sun's rise over the horizon and filtered dawn's light. The early morning sun's rays only gradually lit the clearing with a glow not much different than the full moon had done. Kate went in to start breakfast before the sun climbed to the edge of the trees.

Jeannie heard her stoking the stove and came out rubbing sleep from her eyes. Poochie followed, never far from her side. She climbed into one of the rockers in front of the hearth, and Poochie tried to wiggle in next to her, but settled for laying his front feet and chest across her lap. He was a huge, hairy St. Bernard-type of mutt and found his size a challenge in the confines of the small cabin, but he didn't care as long as he was near and he was loved.

"Mel's still coming today, isn't he, Mom?" she asked, her face alight with eagerness.

"I believe, so, sweetie. Mel does what he says he will."

"When?"

"That I don't know," Kate said, hoping she had time to get the camps' washing done and hung on the lines first. She was doing laundry for two camps now, and if she missed a single day, it messed up her whole schedule. It was difficult keeping up, but it didn't matter. She was making it work, and they were where they wanted to be – living on their own in their forest home.

She was putting breakfast on the table when Kat and Rebecca appeared, and Kate called for Rachel to get up. Kate didn't understand her oldest child. Rachel didn't want to climb trees or run through the woods. She wanted to wear dresses, not the trousers Kate had made for the girls – against her mother's admonishments they would never grow up to be ladies if they wore pants like men.

Kate remembered as a young girl wishing she didn't have to be confined by long skirts that tangled in the briars and got in the way. It didn't make sense to her then, and it still didn't. "The ways of the world are a mystery, Kate," her father had said to her. "Understand them if you can, then don't fret about 'em." And she had. Still did. It had gotten her into trouble then, and most likely it would continue to do so from time to time.

"Rise and shine, Rachel," Kate called again. "Your mama needs you."

She heard a groan come from the tiny room at the back of the cabin, and soon Rachel came out, her long, dark curls in disarray and hanging down her back.

"I need to get started early today, Rachel, so can you supervise breakfast, please?"

Rachel gave her mother a disgruntled look, said "If I have to . . ." and ambled slowly to collapse at the table.

"I'm sorry, sweetie, but we all have to help. Rebecca and Kat, it's your day to wash up the dishes. Jeannie, feed Bug and Poochie. Rachel, please sweep up, and all of you make up the beds. Mel is coming today, and I want the place looking nice early, okay?"

That thought put a bright look on their faces.

"Does that mean no school?" Kat asked. She'd rather be in the woods looking for insects and watching the squirrels than doing her school work, than doing anything else, actually.

Kate home schooled the girls, rather than drive them into town every day to the school where she had taught until Rebecca had been born. Lately, though, she had been wondering if it was fair to keep them alienated from others so much.

She tried to take them into Hersey, the nearest small village, once a week to visit their two cousins and the rest of the family, give them a chance to be around other people, but lately she'd begun to wonder if it was enough. Maybe she was being selfish because she loved living in the woods, treasured its peace and solitude. It had become a part of her. The forest scent coursed through her blood.

Kate left the girls at the table and went to draw water for the laundry. One of the first things she and Mark had done when they moved into the cabin was to dig a well so they wouldn't have to haul water from the nearby creek. The spring fed stream was so close they could hear water gurgling over the rocks from inside the cabin when the windows were open. She loved the sound of the water, but they couldn't count on the creek's depth from season to season.

So, the well had been a godsend, especially after Kate started doing laundry for the camps.

She placed the kettle to heat over the fire pit and rekindled flames from coals still glowing red from the day before. She lugged out the wash tubs from where they lay at the side of the cabin, turned over so they would stay clean, and added the harsh lye soap that removed the deep-set grime from the lumberjacks' clothes.

She washed the whites first so they'd stay bright in the fresh water, then the colored shirts, and finally the trousers. It was rhythmic and cyclical . . . like the seasons, the days turning into weeks, like life itself. It was mechanical, but satisfying in a way, and she didn't mind the work when the weather was warm as it was today. It was sometimes even quite pleasurable.

She liked being outside, enjoyed watching the critters scamper tentatively into the clearing and then back into the safety of trees. She could picture herself running through the woods or lying in the tall grass. She could remember Mark as he had been before the cancer when they lay in the grass together.

Kate was beginning to wring out the whites when she heard hooves on the road to the clearing and then saw Mel astride his mare, ducking to avoid the low branch. She smiled. He was a large man atop an equally large horse, a horse that could take his weight without a struggle. He was easily six foot four with shoulders that grew broader each year. At thirty-nine, you'd think he would have been done growing years ago, but his work on the farm had continued to muscle his body and broaden his chest. His face was tanned from working in the sun, and the small lines at the corners of his eyes crinkled as he smiled at Kate.

He threw a leg over his mare and leaped down. "When are you going to cut that limb?" he asked with a grin. "Or are you waiting for it to knock me off my horse?"

Kate continued wringing clothes and tossing them into a waiting rinse tub. "Well, damn . . ." she said, drawing it out into two syllables and grinning back at him. "Why are you trying to hurt my poor tree? Sorry," she said under her breath, more for herself than for him. He didn't care if she cussed, but Kate had been so schooled by her mother she always felt she should apologize. She couldn't stop swearing; didn't know if she even wanted to. Cussing felt good. And she couldn't stop apologizing either.

Mel moved over to the wash tub, rolled up his sleeves, and started kneading the clothes soaking in the wash water. His huge hands squeezed water and soap through the colored shirts. Then he wrung them and washed them again.

"It's good to see you, Kate." He glanced sideways at her, saw wisps of tawny wheat escaping the ribbon tying back her mass of hair. It hung to her waist and in the sun looked like white and gold silk. She looked like a girl, like the girl he had met so many years ago, like the one he had kissed on the river bank. Memory flickered and teased.

"You're early. I wanted to have this all done before you got here."

"I know. That's why I'm early," he said with a smile.

Kate took the whites to the line and hung them. Mel had all the shirts in the rinse water and was washing the trousers when she returned.

"I'll wring," he said. "You start swishing these."

"You think I can't wring these out dry enough?" she asked, a mock frown on her face.

"Kate, you know I think you can do anything you set your mind to. You're one tough lady."

"Don't call me a lady, Mr. Bronson. I'd hate being a lady."

"Then what should I call you?" he asked.

She paused in careful thought, her blues eyes straying to the woods. "How about Queen of the Forest," she said, enjoying the playful banter.

"Just the forest? Why not Queen of Everything?"

She smacked him with a wet shirt and then cupped her hand to catch some rinse water and threw it at him. "Yes. Make that Queen of Everything."

Mel's laugh brought the girls from the house. Jeannie scrambled up his legs. He lifted her high into the air and her giggles echoed in the clearing. Rebecca waited her turn to fly around the sky, and Kat went to kiss the muzzle of his mare. Rachel stayed a dignified distance away, not vying for his attention. Elusive was her way. Mel would come to her for a hug.

Kate watched while she worked, her smile a mixture of happiness and regret. It was good for the girls to play with Mel. They needed it, and Kate was grateful he found pleasure in their company. But memory plagued her – of Mark throwing his girls high into the air to hear their screams of delight. She took a deep breath easing the tightness in her chest, willing the pain to be bearable.

"Damn it," she whispered, and scrubbed harder at the trousers in the tub. "Go away."

"I almost forgot," Mel said as he gently brought Rebecca back to earth and ambled over to place an arm around Rachel's shoulders for a reserved hug.

"I brought something." He looked at Kat who was still stroking his mare. "Why don't you get it out of the bag, Kat?"

She left off nuzzling its velvet nose to search the saddle bags, brought out a large paper wrapped package and peeked inside. "Bacon? You brought us bacon?"

"No," he laughed, "the other side. Look in there."

Kat peeked in the paper bag she found, and her face lit. "Candy!" she squealed. "Lots of it."

Jeannie and Rebecca ran over to look in the bag. "There's tons and tons of it!"

"At least eight of every kind in Nestor's famous candy counter," Mel said with a proud look on his face. "Mr. Nestor counted them all very carefully to make sure you each had two of every kind."

"You are spoiling them, Mel, and they'll get fat! Do you think I want fat little girls?" Kate asked looking at her slender daughters. "And their teeth will rot out if they eat all that." But Kate was appreciative the girls would have something fun, something she could not afford to give them.

"Then they'll have to gum their food just like Mrs. Wellington." He pulled his lips tightly over his teeth and pantomimed the old woman. Jeannie and Rebecca giggled at his antics and tried to look toothless, too.

They all knew Mrs. Wellington, had seen and heard her. She walked through the small town of Hersey each day looking for the errant husband who had long ago run off with another woman. She talked to herself, as well as everyone else who came perilously near, and cursed all men for the philandering cheats they were, but the words she toothlessly sputtered stunned anyone who didn't know her – even shocked those who knew her well.

Mel took the package of bacon, pulled his lips over his teeth again in a parody of toothless-ness, and handed the package to Kate. "This is for you, Queen of Everything."

Kate pulled in her own lips. "You're just trying to get close to me. You're definitely a no-account scum of a man like all the rest," she said, careful not to use the words Mrs. Wellington did in front of the girls.

"That's not what she says, Ma," Kat said knowingly, shaking her head.

Kate stopped her theatrics and turned to her daughter with a smile. "True, but we don't use those words, do we Miss Ramey?"

Kat wanted to know why they couldn't, and Kate didn't know what to say. She had wanted to use peppery language and sing bawdy songs. She'd heard it all as a young girl as she spied on the lumber camp, lying in the tall grass as close as she could get to them without being noticed. She had wanted to swing an axe, too, and stride into Sadie's saloon, order a whiskey and talk with the men who were in on all the exciting things going on in the world.

She hadn't understood why she should be confined to places that were just for girls simply because she'd had the misfortune to be born female. It hadn't seemed fair then, and it still didn't. Her father had agreed with her and made sure his daughters did not 'know their places' when Kate was a young girl. Now, though, she had to explain it to her own daughter, and she thought of her pa as she did.

"I'll have to think about that, Kat. Can we talk about it later?"

Kat nodded, her expression serious. "That's okay. Later is fine."

12

They finished the wash and hung it on several lines used to dry the massive amount of laundry she took in each week. Mel and the girls pulled weeds in the garden. There weren't many since it was a daily chore Kate and the girls did together. Kate made soup and added some of the bacon Mel had brought. Its sweet, smoky flavor filled the cabin and started the salivary juices flowing with the promise of longed for tastes. She raked the hot coals to the back of the hearth and hung the heavy kettle over a base of shallow, slow burning embers.

Mel and Kate rocked peacefully outside and watched the hummingbirds flit from flower to flower, the bees labor in the garden, the occasional hawk circle in its continuous land survey and the girls as they finished up schoolwork on the grass nearby.

All were doing what nature demanded, or asked of them, even the bugs and birds. All filled a personal space in their own small corner of the world. They chatted comfortably, like family. Kate sifted through a myriad of feelings, some comforting and some with an edge of concern. But it felt a little like peace.

Kate's girls were coping with their grief -- the trauma of their father's death, the horror of the rat-infested hovel they had stayed in when they were in Tennessee trying to get medical help for him. They'd been on their way south because the doctors thought a warm climate might help him. They never made it, and it had been a nightmare for all of them. Hunger and terror plagued their nights, and hopelessness cloaked their days.

Kate knew her own struggle to keep despair at bay. It always seemed just beneath the surface, ready to leap out and claim her. The thought of her daughters' sorrow increased her own, and she wished she could be in their minds, read them to know if they were healing from their wounds.

This line of thought led Kate to ask about building the rooms at the back of the cabin, what they had planned to do before Mark had become so ill.

Mel responded enthusiastically, his face alight and eager. "Absolutely! Let's do it. Let's start tomorrow!"

"Whoa, big boy. Can we talk about how I can afford it for a minute?"

"There is no 'afford'" he said, unwilling to be deterred again. "Willie has the wood, and I have the brawn. Jack Bay, too. He wants to help. Between the three of us, we'll have it up in a couple of days at the most. Oh, and don't forget Harley and Verna," he added. "I know they'll not want to miss it."

"Is Verna coming here?" Kat asked, suddenly interested in the conversation. "When?"

Kat had a bond with the strange woman who had shown up at the Hughes house one Christmas day. Harley found her somewhere, no one knew where, and brought her along. She stayed in Hersey and now worked as a bar maid at Sadie's Saloon and lived in one of the upstairs rooms.

Verna was short and stocky, cantankerous and unruly. Her small, blue eyes twinkled when she liked you and glared when she didn't. She also swore like a drunken sailor when she felt like it and openly wore trousers – every day and everywhere – without apology to anyone. Verna was also the only person who could control Harley's long-windedness, and he adored her as much as Kat did. They all did.

"Verna will come if your mother lets us add some rooms on to the cabin," Mel said, egging Kate on a bit.

"What about roofing and rafters and nails and support wood? That isn't scrap lumber," Kate said, not wanting to take what she couldn't afford to pay for. "I have a little money saved, but I need to know how much that stuff will cost first."

"What about a loan?" Mel asked. "I can lend the money to you . . . all proper, with a note and everything," he added when she immediately began shaking her head. "Kate, you can pay it back when you have the money. Think about the girls."

"Dirty pool, Mel. That's not fair."

"At the risk of getting tossed out of here," he said, "I'm going to say something you probably don't want to hear."

14

He turned to her daughters. "Girls, will you let your mother and I talk for a moment?" After they were out of earshot, he continued, looking Kate in the eyes and begging for her understanding.

"What's not fair is continuing to let your daughters live packed in like sardines in a can. They have no place that is private, no place to go where they can be alone, and that is not fair. You are selfishly letting your stubborn pride get in the way of their well being."

Kate took a deep breath and was holding it, unsure whether to be angry at his words or not. She was shocked. It wasn't like Mel to interfere in her decisions or say anything negative to her or about her, but he was honest, always. He placed a hand over hers and waited.

"I'm sorry, Kate," he said quietly. "I shouldn't have said it like that."

When she was breathing again, Kate told him to let her think about it for a moment. He waited silently and left his hand over hers. It was reddened and raw from hot water and harsh soap. The nails were broken, and palms were calloused from daily heavy labor. It hurt him to see it, to know what Kate had to do to survive, and she wouldn't let him help. It frustrated him, but he understood. He would do the same, and would do it alone as she was. He loved the strength in her, but it didn't feel good to watch, nevertheless, and nobody could tell him he had to like it.

Kate sifted through what he'd said. Mel didn't lie, ever. Nor did he exaggerate. If he thought the girls needed it, then it was most likely true. Maybe she really was being selfish, but she didn't know how she would ever be able to pay it back if she took a loan from him. "Damn," she whispered, trying to think of a way it could be done. "Sorry."

Mel smiled at her. "Apology accepted. Are you done processing?" he asked.

"Do you really think I'm selfish?"

"No, not really, Kate, just proud. And I understand," he paused, trying to find the right words, "but in this case, you might want to put your pride away for a time. Have you looked at Rachel lately? She's growing into a young woman right before your eyes. Don't you remember what that's like?"

"I'm not that old!" she spouted, taking her hand from under his and smacking his arm.

"I didn't mean you were." It was disturbing he still couldn't find the right things to say. Mel was a man of few words. He found it pretty simple to say what he meant, but today it felt like everything was coming out wrong.

"I know," she said quietly. "It's just . . . I've seen what you see in Rachel, and I've known for a long time she needs her own space, a place to dream and grow. I just hate it – and myself for not being able to give it to her – to all of them." She paused, lost in thinking about her daughters.

"It's not like you'd be taking something from me, Kate, by letting me build the rooms. It's something I want to do for you. Why do you deny me that?"

"You sound like Harley," Kate said, a small grin escaping.

"I do, don't I? Maybe he's rubbing off. God, I don't want to think I'm becoming Harley!"

"Alright," she groaned. "I'll take the money, but it's only a loan, and I want to know exactly what this whole thing costs down to the last nail. No cheating and making up stories about stuff not costing anything. Promise?"

Mel held up his hand like he was taking an oath and swore to tell the truth and only the truth, as God is his witness.

"And I *will* make payments to you until I have it paid off," she said adamantly with an emphasis on the word will and in Kate-like stubbornness. "Small ones," she added with a grin that let her get away with mulishness.

Mel counted it a win and said, "Let's tell the girls and make some plans!"

Chapter Two

Two days later, the girls danced around the clearing, raced to the road and back listening for sounds of their arrival. She'd started so early it was still night and had most of the clean, wet laundry hanging on the lines. She wanted to be finished with her work so she could help with the building of the rooms. She'd do the ironing after dark by lantern light if necessary. At the moment, she didn't care if there were wrinkles she missed. She was too excited for it to matter.

A welcoming aroma came from the hearth where a pot of stew simmered, and nearby but away from the heat sat a jug of Mark's moonshine Kate had retrieved from the outside cellar. She knew it would be called for later, most likely by Verna first who could tip it over the back of her hand and sip from the mouth of the jug as well as any man. Perhaps better.

It had been Verna who convinced Kate to make trousers for herself and her girls, not because of anything she'd said, just by wearing them so comfortably herself. Kat had admired Verna's trousers and in her matter-of-fact way had asked why she couldn't wear them, too, since they would work so well for insect and snake searches and for tree climbing – especially for climbing.

Kate didn't wear hers when people were around, but she had them on today because she intended to work, not be confined to the kitchen or stand around and watch, letting the men do it all. Whose cabin is this, anyway?

Well, it's the man's, she thought with a bit of honesty and distinctly uncharacteristic humility. "But I'm its caretaker," she sputtered to the clothes hanging by the door as she walked back outside to finish the wash.

She heard squeals from Jeannie and Rebecca before the sound of the horses and wagons. Then they were in the clearing with two large wagons piled high with lumber. Mel's hay wagon carried long joists and rafter boards, along with Harley and Verna who sat on top and stabilized the load. Harley's broad grin made her laugh. Sometimes she forgot how much she loved him; it was good to see him here again.

He'd spent long days and nights with Kate during Mark's surgery, sitting with her, being there for her. She would always remember his warm hand on her shoulder, the hours they rocked quietly in front of the fire, waiting. For probably the first time in his life, he'd been silent. It made Kate smile to think how hard holding his tongue must have been.

Verna leaped down and hugged Kat who was waiting impatiently for her. "Are you ready to work?" she asked. "Got your hammer?"

Kat nodded eagerly, wanting to emulate Verna's every move, and showed her the small hammer Kate had found for her.

"That looks like it'll do the job," Verna told her seriously. "I like your britches," she said with a grin and a tug at the seat of Kat's pants.

Willie hauled one of the mill's wagons loaded with siding boards, a keg of nails, cinderblocks and the roofing shingles. The smell of fresh cut lumber began to fill the air along with the easy laughter of friends and family. Jack Bay was with Willie, looking dashing and immaculate in his white shirt.

Jack was a slender, handsome, dark haired man who had been her husband's best friend and who helped him before and after the Landmark Lumber Company payroll theft that sent Mark to prison for something he hadn't done.

Jack had been a lawyer back east before he came to Michigan to work as a lumberjack. Few people knew why he gave up a career in law to cut trees because he never talked about it. Kate knew he'd told Mark, but her husband had kept that confidence to himself, respecting Jack's reticence. He was also married to Kate's sister, Ruthie, and was Kate's fierce guardian when she picked up and delivered laundry at the camp where he worked felling northern Michigan's tall white pines.

He walked over to where Kate was finishing the wash, rolled up his sleeves and began to wring the clothes. He looked at Kate with a grin. "You're looking good, Kate," he said, leaning back and eyeing her pants appreciatively.

"Why, thank you. You look mighty fine, too," she responded politely, but eyed his backside in the same roguish way he had looked her over.

He laughed, liking her spunk. "I deserved that," he said. "Just don't wear those when you come to the camp. Might give the boys more ideas than they already have."

He helped her hang the last of the clothes on the line as he did about once a week when he stopped to see her on his way home from the camp. Kate never protested his help, and she enjoyed his company, perhaps because he and Mark had been so close, or perhaps because he was Jack and never asked permission to help. He just did it.

They unloaded the lumber, blocks and materials and carted it to the back of the cabin. Harley measured and marked the ground, and Mel had already started digging the foundation by the time the rest had decided what job each would do. Kate came over with a shovel and began digging at the other end, opposite Mel. She felt his eyes on her, and stopped, one foot still on the shovel and ready to jump on it with both feet in order to drive the point into the dirt.

"What are you grinning at?" she asked tartly. "I can dig."

"Yup, all ten pounds of you. I know that," he answered. He raised one eyebrow; his grin widened and matched the smile in his eyes, but he didn't say anything else – just continued watching Kate and shoved his shovel into the dirt.

Kate went back to digging with a miffed harrumph and added, "Don't mess with me or you'll regret it. I've got a shovel, and I'm not afraid to use it."

Verna and Jack added their tools to the effort, and it wasn't long before they were laying the block foundation. Willie and Mel hauled the cinderblock into place, and Jack and Harley matched them up and leveled them.

Harley had an eye for architecture, as they'd learned when he had first drawn up the plans for the addition. His detailed blueprints looked like they'd been done by a professional, and he'd said "Well, of course," when they voiced surprise by the perfection of them.

Harley was an enigma with his philosophical mind and his varied talents – like when he'd made the table for the Hughes family years ago. It wasn't just a table, but a work of art and could be expanded to seat twelve people or reduced to fit a family of four. It was beautiful, burnished and polished to a shine that reflected the light.

They worked and laughed, teased and cajoled, found where they were needed and pitched in. By afternoon, they had the trusses, headers and rafters in place and were ready to begin nailing the siding boards on. It was looking like the addition they had planned; three rooms that, together, were taller and wider than the small cabin nestled in front but still maintained the charm of the original.

There were two downstairs rooms and a tiny one in the peak at the top where Rachel would be; Kat would have the smaller downstairs room, and Rebecca and Jeannie would share the larger one which could be curtained off to provide some privacy if they wanted. Kate would move her bed into the space at the back of the cabin where the girls had been sleeping.

Rachel stood back, away from the work going on around her and watched with a look of anticipation on her serene face. Every once in a while, Kate glanced at her and wondered what was going on in her mind. She was quiet, controlled, and Kate worried the scars she carried from watching her father die had permanently changed her.

Kate had been occupied tending to Mark's needs, and Rachel had quietly stepped in to take care of her younger sisters while they were on the train that took them from Nashville back to Hersey. The doctors had told Kate there was nothing more they could do; Mark was dying, and they were taking him home. Rachel held Jeannie, who was asleep on her lap, and watched her father struggle with the pain. She watched, too, as he left them and sat motionless, held Jeannie and tried not to wake her. Tears streamed from Rachel's eyes, but she tried not to sob, tried to be still in her grief.

Maybe, Kate considered, she should do for Rachel what Mel had done for her; give her a long, stout branch and send her into the woods to beat a tree in anger and grief until the branch was a stub. Maybe Rachel needs to beat a tree. *But I should have given her the branch long ago,* Kate thought, trying to quell anger she still felt over Mark's death.

"Where have you been, girl?" Jack asked. "You're holding that hammer like you're about to crack somebody's head with it."

"Nowhere," she lied, shaking her head to come out of the past. "I was just thinking how nice this will be for the girls. We're very lucky to have such good friends, you know."

Jack squeezed her arm and gave her a sad smile, knowing she lied.

"Yes, we are. Friends don't just happen, and they don't happen often." He didn't say it, but Kate knew Jack was aware of where she'd been, and he had been there with her. Jack missed Mark too, and his sorrow made him special to Kate. "Get to work, damn it!" he said, and added "sorry" like she did to see her smile.

Ruthie and their mother, Ellen, joined them late afternoon. They told Kate to stay where she was. They would handle feeding the hungry crew and left them working while they took the table outside and loaded it with bread, apple cobbler, pickles and other things they had brought to go along with Kate's stew.

When Verna threw down her hammer and loudly proclaimed, "Time for a drink," Kat copied her hero, her hammer landing on Mel's boot. He hopped around on one foot, pretending to be in pain until Jeannie came to his aid and insisted he take his boot off so she could kiss his wound and make it better. Kat ran to the cabin to get the jug for Verna. She carried the large earthenware jug carefully in two hands to where Verna sat collapsed in the dirt and deferentially handed it to her.

"You are my savior," Verna said as she took the jug and tilted it back. "You are my special little urchin."

"Is our savior an urchin?" Kat asked with an earnest, questioning face.

Harley heard her question and plopped down next to them, reaching for the jug. After taking a hearty swallow, he said "Could be, Kat. You never know who will be saving you. Could be a scamp or a scallywag, an old hobo like me, or even a mutt like Poochie. You just never know what a savior might look like."

"That's not what Gram says," Kat told him, her eyes seriously doubting Harley's words. "And don't call Poochie a mutt." No one was ever sure if Kat was pulling legs. She was good.

Ellen came around the corner in time to hear Kat and asked what it was Gram had said.

"Harley said our savior could be Poochie, and he called him a mutt."

"Are you filling this child's head with nonsense, Harley?" Ellen asked.

"No, my dear. I am opening this child up to a world of possibilities. You are well aware, given our long divinity discussions, I have ideas the rest of the world has not yet taken the time to discover. Language is a wonderful thing, as is a savior, and if Poochie here saved our Kat, say . . . dragged her from the river or even kept her from sadness, then he would be a savior, wouldn't he?"

Harley leaned back, rubbed his round belly and grinned at Ellen. His mass of curly, golden hair was a halo in the sunlight. Although Harley must have been in his sixties, no one knew for sure; his hair showed no gray even though his beard was densely speckled with it. He enjoyed the sound of his own voice, and especially loved to watch Ellen's face when he said things that shocked her. So, he did it frequently and ardently.

Ellen Hughes was a scrupulously Christian woman who struggled with ideas that might diverge from what she believed the Bible said. It had taken her a while to view Harley as anything except blasphemous, but for some strange and unaccountable reason she accepted behavior from Harley she wouldn't tolerate in others. He'd taught her to 'bend with the wind so she wouldn't break, to not be so brittle' which were his words, not hers.

He still lived in the room at the back of the Hughes' barn where he had been put ... just for the night ... after jumping off the train and following Mark like a lost puppy. But Harley was never lost. He was home wherever he happened to be. It wasn't long before he and Ellen began spending time at her kitchen table discussing religion and philosophical ideals, and Harley had put a smile back on Ellen's face, lost laughter back into her voice when they'd thought it had died.

"Wouldn't you agree, Mrs. Hughes," Harley egged her on further, "that Poochie could be our savior?"

The others had stopped to listen and waited in silent anticipation for Ellen's response with grins on their faces. Kate's hammer was still in the air where she had been about to drive a nail into the wood. Jack leaned against the corner of the new addition, waiting elegantly. Willie poked his sister in the ribs, a grin spreading over his face. "This should be good," he whispered to Kate.

"Well, I never ..." she sputtered. "You can find a way to turn words around, Harley, so that ... You are incorrigible, and I won't dignify your question with an answer." But she was smiling when she cuffed his head and told them supper was on the table. When the others let loose their held breath and laughed, she reddened, knowing Harley had baited her deliberately, again.

"What's incorrigible?" Kat asked. "Can it be a savior?" There was a collective groan from everyone as they put down their tools and fled to find supper and get away before Harley began a long explanation about the word incorrigible and anything even remotely connected to the word.

They ate ravenously after their long hours of work and rested only briefly before heading back to get more done before dark. The siding was on, and tar paper covered the roofing boards. They lit lanterns to finish and went inside to survey the new rooms. Stairs still needed to be built to get to the upstairs room, and the partitions needed to be put in, but it was beginning to look like what they envisioned. Kate's throat tightened with emotion she did not want to release.

"It's beautiful," she said quietly. "I don't know how to thank you all."

"It is we who should thank you," Harley said with a pompous, yet elegant bow, "because we wanted this for our Ramey girls. You gave us a wonderful opportunity, so I thank you, Kate."

"You old coot. Ma is right, you spin everything around," Kate said ruffling Harley's bright curls.

"That's my job. I'm a spinner."

She waved as they left and went back into the cabin, got out the irons and put them on the stove to heat. She set up the ironing board and retrieved the clothes baskets piled high with the things she had taken off the line earlier. With a tired sigh, she began ironing the first shirt.

Jack and Mel brought the table and chairs back inside and sat watching and sipping from the jug. A gentle, quiet peace descended and they talked softly. Mel's earthy good looks were a sharp contrast to Jack's slender elegance, Kate noted as she tested the iron for heat and heard it sizzle. Jack's white shirt still looked as clean and pressed as if he had just put it on . . . typical Jack Bay.

"I'll never understand it," Mel said to him, honing in on Kate's thoughts.

"What?"

"You look like you haven't picked up a tool all day, and I'm as grubby as Jeannie's dog after he rolls in the mud. I don't believe you worked at all."

Jack smiled at him. He'd been teased many times in the past about shirking work in order to stay clean. "It's just a matter of staying away from dirt," Jack told him. "Others

24

collect it quite well," he said, nodding toward Kate at the ironing board.

Kate had washed her hands before touching the clothes she had carefully laundered, but her face was smudged with dirt and her shirt and pants showed the day's dirty work. Her blonde hair had come loose from the tie at the back of her neck and long tendrils escaped around her face.

Both men watched her as she worked and grinned at the picture she made in her trousers. When she had folded the shirt and placed it on the brown paper she would wrap it in, Jack got up from his chair, picked up the trousers that went with it and the second iron heating on the stove.

"Your turn to sit, Kate," he said to her. "This one's mine."

Kate looked at him like he'd gone mad. "You're going to iron?" she asked as if he had said he was flying to the moon and would be back by breakfast.

"Well, why not? Do you think only women can handle this job? You wear pants – I can iron."

"You don't need to do this, Jack."

"Of course, I don't," he said with a wide grin. "We'll take turns til it's all done."

Mel watched them banter back and forth and saw water fill the corners of Kate's tired eyes. His own throat constricted, and with an effort he said, "Let him, Kate. He is kind of a girly guy." Then he stood to get a glass, poured some of the moonshine in and handed it to Kate. She took it and gratefully sat where she could watch Jack at the ironing board.

He smoothed the creases expertly, switching the iron back to the stove when it had cooled and grasping the hot one waiting there. His movements were fluid, not a motion wasted. He looked like he'd been ironing for years. Kate sipped her drink and felt the warmth slide down her throat and heat her stomach. She began to relax, feeling her brain mellow with the moonshine and the company of her friends.

"So, you don't like my pants?" she teased. "Why not?"

"That's not what I said," Jack answered, a wicked glint lighting his eyes.

"And you, Mr. Mel Bronson, have not even commented on my apparel."

"No, Mrs. Kate Ramey, I haven't," he said, his grin matching Jack's.

Jack folded the trousers he'd finished ironing and put them on the waiting paper, then turned to Kate. "Never has there been a pair of pants more neatly filled, Kate. But wear a dress when you deliver these clothes to the camp in the morning." Then he handed a plaid shirt to Mel. "Let's see what you can do. Promise I won't laugh."

Mel looked at the shirt like it was a foreign object, held it out away from him as if he was afraid of it.

"It won't bite, man," Jack said. "It's just a shirt. You wear them every day. Start with the collar, then the sleeves. Do the back and then the front last."

"How in hell do you know that?" Mel asked.

"I'm smart." Then he took Mel's chair and a sip from the jug.

They watched Mel struggle with the shirt, but before long he was as adept as they were. Even Bug thought the sight of Mel at the ironing board was strange enough for his attention. He sat up on his bed in front of the hearth, cocked his head and rolled his eyes, saying 'you've got to be kidding.' Then he turned around three times and lay down where he could watch Mel work, amusement in the tilt of his head and the glint in his eyes.

They took turns at the board until the three baskets of laundry were pressed and packaged. By the time they got to the last basket, they were feeling the effects of the long day and the moonshine. They cracked jokes they thought were hilarious, and in the moment they were, and laughed like school kids.

"If you tell anyone about this, I'll have to kill you," Mel whispered conspiratorially and with a glare. "I've got an iron, and I'm not afraid to use it!"

"You'll press us to death?" Jack asked.

"If I tell Harley, everyone will know, and you'll die first of embarrassment," Kate said. "But I'll keep your little secret, cause, damn, you're a good ironer. Oops, sorry," she giggled.

"I'll tell Agatha Pennington. The school board president would love to hear about your pants," Mel countered.

"I'll tell . . . Who will I tell, Jack? Help me, here."

Jack stood up and took Kate's arm, steering her in the direction of her bed. "The help you need right now, Miss Kate, is help to bed." She flopped on the small bed, grateful to lie down. He removed her shoes and covered her with a blanket. She was sleeping by the time they left.

They took the packages with them and left a note telling Kate that Jack would deliver them to the camp in the morning and collect her money. They were grinning as they walked to the wagon and shaking their heads in affection for the woman they'd left sleeping.

"How much moonshine did you give her?" Mel asked.

"It didn't take much. She's a tiny, little thing."

"Yeah, I suppose. And she's been up since before dawn getting that damned wash done. God, I hate it," Mel groaned.

"But you can't fix it for her, and she wouldn't let you."

When Kate woke the next morning, she stretched and felt the trousers on her legs. For a moment she was confused, but then she remembered being led to bed by Jack. She saw the sun peeking through the window and leaped up.

"Damn! The laundry," she said quietly and looked around for the packages. Then she saw the note on the table, read it and smiled. "Bless them both," she whispered, and went to the sink to wash the grime from her face.

When Mel arrived, she had bacon and potatoes frying and she was singing one of the songs she had learned at the lumber camp as a girl – one her mother would never have let her sing. It had something to do with camp town ladies and bob tailed horses; she wasn't sure exactly what it was all about, but she knew Ellen wouldn't like it, and somehow that made it more fun.

She heard Harley's voice adding to the chorus from outside the window, and soon they were all in the cabin looking hungrily at the food. The girls were up and eager to get started again, laughing and happy, and Kate felt wonderful, better than she had for a long time.

"Soup's on," she called. "Grab a plate and then let's get to work."

Mel drew close and whispered in her ear. "How are you this morning? Do you feel alright?"

"I feel glorious!" she said. "Never better, and thank you."

Mel looked at her, admiration leaking from his eyes. She was stunning, beautiful, and she didn't even know it. She looked rested, her blue eyes clear and sparkling. Her long, silky hair was tied back with a bright blue ribbon, and her cheeks were softly rosy from the heat of the stove. She'd changed into a clean shirt, tucked it into the same pants she'd worn the day before. They were held up by a belt cinching a small waist.

Childbirth had not altered her body. She still looked like the girl he'd met years ago. His mind strayed to a time when he'd caressed the breasts now covered by her plaid shirt, when he'd seen her wet dress clinging to them from an accidental swim in the river. A slight flush crept over his face, and he turned from her.

Kate saw the blush grow and wondered what had caused it. "Are you alright?" she asked.

"Like you, never better," he said, "but I think I'll eat your food and get to work."

"Where's Jack?" she asked. "Is he coming today?"

"Delivering laundry and collecting money. He'll be here soon."

Kate put a hand on his shoulder when he sat to eat and leaned in to whisper in his ear. "I really, really appreciated the help last night."

"With the ironing?" he asked conspiratorially.

"With everything," she said, grinning. "Don't tell Mrs. Pennington."

"Don't tell Harley," he answered.

"Don't tell me what to do," she fired back, her mischievous eyes sending sparks.

He picked up his fork and grinned back at her.

The rest of the crew arrived in time to grab hugs and breakfast before getting back to work. In late afternoon, when the addition was fairly complete, Kate left them to begin the wash Jack had brought back from camp. Harley and Mel were still building the stairs, and Verna and Willie were moving the girls' things into their new rooms. Ellen had sent two of the beds going unused in her house, so for the first time, every Ramey would have her own bed.

Rebecca was busily making hers and moving things around her room. She sat on the bed, got up and moved a small chest, then did it all over again. She helped Jeannie make hers at the other side of the room, and they sat together, in awe of all the space they had. Kat did the same, except once she had her things settled in, that was good enough, and she was satisfied. A bed was a place to sleep, according to Kat.

Rachel had to wait until the stairs were finished before she could move in, so she watched and waited patiently – well, as patiently as she could while eagerly thinking about a place all her own, away from the prattle and pester of her little sisters.

Kate stood at the wash tubs in the late afternoon sun and absently pushed the clothes around in the water. Jack showed up next to her, rolled his sleeves and started wringing. He filled a basket, took it to the lines and hung the clothes. Kate didn't protest. She'd grown used to it. She washed. He rinsed and wrung. She'd hang them – or he did, depending on who was available at the moment. Sometimes they hung them together. He was pinning a shirt to the line and spoke without looking at her.

"He's still in love with you, you know."

Kate was startled by the break in silence and stared at the shirt she'd been about to hang. She couldn't think how to respond, didn't want to. "Don't," she said.

"I just wondered if you knew. That's all."

"I know," she said. "I'm sorry. I can't."

"It's alright. I just wondered if you knew," he repeated.

He saw the tears well in her eyes and was sorry he'd said anything. He didn't want her hurting any more than she already was. Maybe it was too soon for her to think of another man; maybe a lifetime would be too soon. He wanted what was best for Kate, and Mel was a good man, one who would cherish her completely. Jack liked and respected him.

"Don't cry for him, Kate. He's happy to be your friend."

"I'm not crying, damn it!" she said swiping at her eyes. "Sorry."

"You're not either sorry. You should hang out with Mrs. Wellington," he joked. "You could learn to diversify your cussing."

She finished putting the shirt on the line and turned to him with her fists planted firmly on her trouser clad hips. "I'll have you know, Mr. Bay, I know lots of cuss words. I choose to use 'damn' because I like it. And I did too mean I was sorry. I almost always do."

He raised a dark eyebrow. "Almost?" he questioned.

She laughed then at his wicked look, "Yes, almost always."

They finished hanging the clothes. It filled the three lines completely, and waved in the warm breeze and waning sunlight. Kate was grateful she had the next day to do the ironing and could return them to the camp late in the day. She didn't think she had another long night of work left in her. Her muscles didn't ache from the last two day's labor; pain would come later, but they were tired, and she needed rest. Jack stood next to her and surveyed the neat rows of clean wash. "Looks good, doesn't it?" he asked.

Kate nodded. "Thanks for helping, again."

"Do you want to see what they've done with the rooms?" he asked.

She nodded again and headed for the cabin.

What she saw was painted in joy on her face when they stood at the door of the new rooms. Jeannie and Rebecca were scampering around their room, moving the beds an inch or two, then moving them back again to make sure they

30

were perfect. The room was bare except for the two beds and two small chests for their clothes. The windows had no curtains, but when she could afford it and could find the time to make them, they'd have curtains. Jeannie wanted red ones – Rebecca, of course, wanted blue.

"Maybe we'll do one window in red and the one nearest Rebecca in blue, how would that work?" Kate asked them, hoping to stifle a spat.

"Tomorrow? Can we get them tomorrow?" Jeannie asked, hopping from foot to foot in excitement.

Kate told them they'd have to wait a little to make it look pretty and saw disappointment in Rebecca's eyes, but Jeannie just nodded. Nothing could daunt her pleasure in the new room.

"You know, Kate," Willie piped in, "Mary could make some curtains. She has a little time to spare now that our two kids are older. She'd probably like doing it."

"Ruthie, too," Jack added. "She's always looking for something new to do."

"Right, Jack. Ruthie has an entire schoolhouse full of children to keep her busy – day and night."

Ruthie had taken over the teaching position Kate finally vacated after Rebecca was born. She'd held on to her job tenaciously after she and Mark were married and after Agatha Pennington tried to get her fired simply because she'd gotten married.

Mark could not earn enough in the smith shop, and they needed her income, but for some stupid reason the school board thought a female teacher must be single. Between Kate's stubborn refusal to leave the position and Mr. Nestor's championship of her, she'd managed to keep her job until the arrival of Rebecca. Three babies had been too many to manage along with a full-time teaching job.

"Well, you're right about that. She does keep dragging children home with her. If I hadn't finished the upstairs off, they'd be curled up all over the kitchen floor. I'd have to step over them all."

Kate peered at Jack to see if there were any signs of sorrow over not having children of his own. She knew he felt it, but it didn't show. Jack didn't wear his heart on his sleeve, and he was still smiling.

"Who's there this week?" Kate asked.

"I think it's the Tate twins. In fact," he said, his grin broadening, "I think she's teaching them how to sew!"

"Come on, you're making that up. You're fibbing."

"Honest Jack wouldn't lie," he said, crossing his hand over his heart and trying ineffectually to look angelic, but with his black hair and deep set eyes, it was impossible. He looked like a handsome, debonair but diabolical train robber.

Kate laughed at his attempts but held on to her convictions. "You look like Mrs. Wellington's slimy, runaway husband, and we'll get curtains and rugs when we can afford to," Kate said stubbornly. "The girls can wait. Sometimes waiting for what you want is a good thing."

Verna came into the room and disagreed vehemently. "Waiting is just something you do when you can't do anything else, or you're lazy," she said, the gravel in her voice adding emphasis. "What are we waiting for?"

"Curtains," Jack told her.

Kate pulled at her hair, groaning loudly. "Never mind, Verna. Let's not get into a big discussion, okay? It's nothing. Let's go see Kat's room."

They approved Kat's arrangement and then hauled Rachel's bed out of the back room and up the spiral stairway, careful not to mar Harley's workmanship on the hand rails. They didn't have another chest for clothes, but Harley had already promised Rachel he would make one for her, and it was too late for Kate to protest his gift. They left Rachel to make up her bed, as she requested, and descended to the kitchen where Kate's bed still stood off to the side of the original room.

Kate got the jug from the cupboard and handed it to Verna who toasted to a job well done with a long swig. Then she passed it to Harley. They were all tired and sat gratefully, talked about the girls and their new bedrooms, the weather, crop prices, lumber camp news, anything that popped into their heads and made its way out their mouths.

It was peaceful with comfort grown in the fertile soil of familiarity.

Kate looked around the table at her friends, cherished their banter, and breathed a long sigh of contentment. She looked at her own bed at the other end of the room, remembering nights there, in that corner, with Mark.

Harley watched her, saw her eyes cloud as she looked at the bed – an elephant in the room – and then back at the others. He saw her thoughts as they flickered across her face and knew she was struggling with memories. Now that it could be moved out of the living space and into a real bedroom . . . it couldn't. She couldn't.

Mel rose from his seat and said, "Let's get you moved into your room, Kate, and we'll be pretty much done."

Jack and Willie stood to help, but Kate sat motionless, looking at her bed, shaking her head. "No . . . not now."

Harley intervened. "You boys go on. I think I'll stay a bit. Will you take Miss Verna on home for me?" he asked. "Maybe I'll just bunk on the floor here tonight. Would that be alright with you, Kate?"

Kate nodded, grateful he had stepped in. She wasn't ready. Not right now. Maybe not ever.

They went outside, stretched and breathed in the warm night air, and left with hugs and promises to return soon and often. "You be careful at the Newton Camp tomorrow, Kate. I won't be there to protect you," Jack said, only half joking.

"I'll have Bug with me, Jack. No one will mess with me while he's glaring at them."

Bug stood on his hind legs and stuck his nose in Jack's face.

"That's right. I forgot 'death by slobber' warfare," he said, peering around the nose planted on his cheek. "This is one scary animal."

"Shhh. He doesn't like being called animal. Down, Bug," she called as she turned to leave them.

Harley and Kate tucked the girls into their beds and sat again at the kitchen table. They rested silently for a while, their breathing slow and soft in the quiet night. Then he put his hand over Kate's and gently patted it. "Some things are hard to let go," he said simply.

Kate nodded. She couldn't speak around the lump filling her throat. She heard crickets from the open window and an owl hooting from a distant tree. Sounds of the night forest drifted into the room and mixed with the smells of new lumber, leftover stew, the sweat of hard work. She needed to breathe away the lump, melt it and fill her chest with air so she could speak without tears. God, how she hated tears. She stared into the dark of the open window, then at the man's clothes hanging by the door, at the floor, anywhere but at the bed.

Harley patted her hand again. "Do you remember how everyone tried hard not to speak your father's name after he died, how the name 'Will' was avoided like it was poison because it brought so much pain?" he asked.

Kate nodded, remembered.

"Then we toasted to Will and his excellent moonshine. Remember that?" he asked, an imperceptible smile on his lips. "And before long we could speak his name with joy and loving memory; we laughed and let tears fall, and pain washed downstream with the tears. Well, the bed you shared with Mark is like that."

He paused, and Kate heard his breath in the silence . . . or maybe it was her own. She didn't know. She heard the deafening beat of her heart . . . or possibly it was the breaking of it, again. She didn't know anything for sure.

"Your memories are in your heart and soul, Kate. It doesn't matter if that bed is here in this room or on the moon. It doesn't matter if we burned it out in the fire pit tomorrow; it's all in you, Kate. It will stay there no matter what happens to that piece of furniture. It's just that, a piece of furniture and where it sits is meaningless."

"I can't," an anguished voice begged. Not hers. Hers was silent, caught in another time.

He raised the jug, said "This is to the marriage bed you and Mark shared. This is to the room you and Mark loved in, and this is to your heart full of pain and love and memories," and then he took a long swallow and handed the jug to Kate.

Kate blinked futilely at the rising pool of water that clung to her lashes and then fell to her cheeks. She took the jug from him and whispered,

"This is to . . ." She looked once more at the bed in the corner – the worn quilt – the two pillows, and then continued. "Oh . . . God . . . to what you said, Harley."

She tilted the jug over hand, tipped it up like he had done, and took a hearty swallow, then took another. She coughed, then put it solidly, determinedly down on the table.

He picked it up and raised it in the air again. "Here's to letting go of some things, and hanging on to what's worthy. Here's to breathing in the good and expelling the bad." He filled his round belly with air and deliberately blew it out, then drank again and Kate followed, repeating his words and beginning to snicker at the sight of him. She paused, breathed deeper and thought about what he'd said.

"Thank you, Harley. I'm trying. I really am. I miss him so much it's almost not bearable, not worth even trying."

"I know you do, but he's in a better place now, Kate, because he's healthy and whole again," and then shrugged his shoulders.

"Or he's here with you . . . you never know. He could be up there," he joked, pointing up at the corner of the room near the rafters. "I know, I'm just an old coot with a wagging tongue. You've told me many times, and I drove Mark crazy with my talking. I can still hear him groaning every time I opened my mouth."

Kate remembered, too, and laughed. Harley did drive Mark to distraction sometimes, even though he loved the man and had been the reason Harley ended up at the Hughes house in the first place.

"But," he said, raising his finger to make the point, "I was Mark's personal hobo, so he had to put up with me."

"And you are my vagabond, scallywag savior."

They talked long into the night, about the years she had waited for Mark when he was in prison, about the trial and the way most towns folk had called Kate a Jezebel . . . a whore . . . for being with Mark, the married scoundrel. They talked about the cancer that had taken him from her, and a little bit about the way she always felt when she saw him – even thought about him. The way she couldn't breathe because her chest filled and her throat constricted when he was near.

Kate laughed.

"Sometimes I thought I'd die if he didn't get away from me so I could catch a breath." She paused, lost in the past and then came back. "Let's move this bed."

When they were done, she gave Harley a blanket, and he curled up by Bug in front of the hearth where he had slept on other nights. Seeing him there brought back memories, and Kate tried to do what Harley had said – breathe in the good air and let out the bad.

She went to her bed, in a real bedroom. It felt large and lonely. In the moonlight, she saw bare walls and too much space. After a few minutes, she heard the soft sound of footpads on the wooden floor, and soon she felt Bug on the bed at her feet. He turned three times and lay down against her legs.

"Thanks, Bug," she whispered.

Chapter Three

The leaves were beginning to show tinges of yellow and red, and nights were growing chilly. If you stood on the tallest hill to the east of Hersey and looked down into the valley, you could see the colors of early fall hugging the village. Kate loved the smell of autumn as folks raked and burned leaves, and turned the soil so winter snow and brown corn stalks would mulch the ground and prepare it for spring planting.

Hersey looked much like it had before the lumber boom exploded the town with prosperity except for the concrete steps scattered along Main Street. They were silent monuments to buildings that were once there and had burned during the long drought that had plagued Hersey and most of Michigan. Many of the buildings, built fast and cheap when the lumber business first took hold, were now gone, and the proprietors were gone too, moved elsewhere looking for other lucrative opportunities.

The buildings left were the substantial ones like Nestor's General Store, the feed and grain supply, two of the seven saloons developed when many lumberjacks worked at nearby camps, the firehouse and post office, the Hughes and Reeves' Mill, and a small diner. Two churches stood sentry at either end of Main Street and enclosed the town in their glass stained, spiritual arms. Hersey had gone back to sleep after a few hectic, eventful years.

Kate was comfortable with the way Hersey was now even though she'd liked the hustle and bustle of those early years when the town was changing at a break neck pace. It had matured and settled down, and now the two nearby lumber camps didn't seem at odds with the town.

Or perhaps it's just me, she thought. Maybe I've matured, and Hersey is the same as it's always been. I'm getting old. How did that happen?

She made her purchases at John Nestor's General Store and chatted with her old friend for a few minutes while the girls checked out material for their curtains. It had taken Kate a couple of months to save enough to buy the fabric, and she'd had to be firm in turning down all the offers to get curtains for them. It was important to her even if she couldn't explain it and even if others didn't understand. She went to where the girls were fondling colorful bolts of cloth and mentally rechecked the yardage she would need.

Tomorrow was Sunday, and they were going to have a sewing bee, a real social event with finger sandwiches, tea cakes and lemonade. A ladies' day. Ellen, Ruthie and Verna were coming to help because the girls were going to make their own curtains, and Kate was going to need some help keeping them all on track. She looked forward to a day with the women.

"It'll be fun," she told John, "all the women together." John raised a bushy eyebrow, questioning her wisdom. With a thoughtful pause and a grin, she replied, "Well, maybe."

Jeannie found her red print, and Rebecca the blue she had her heart set on from the first. Kat chose a brown and tan check, and Rachel stewed over lilac gingham and pale green flowered chintz, not sure which she wanted. Kate watched her daughters make their decisions and smiled at their choices because she would have known what they would prefer long before they'd said it. The fabrics echoed the girls' personalities and each was so different – each unique.

John measured the cloth pieces, folded them carefully and laid them in small squares on the bolts next to each other, a line of color like the girls standing in front of them. Then he brought several spools of cotton thread over and matched them perfectly to each color.

"I think we can do with just one, John, a neutral color that won't contrast heavily with any of them."

"What kind of a seamstress are you, Kate? Thread that doesn't match is shoddy workmanship," he said gruffly, shaking his gray head at her. "Do I need to go get Mrs. Nestor?"

"No!" Kate blurted out before she could stop herself. She held up her hand in defeat, terror in her eyes. Esther Nestor was a tornado, a force of nature no one wanted to deal with. "Don't do that. Please?"

"I thought so. She is scary," he said grinning. Then he reached behind the bolts and brought out several lengths of different lace and folded them around small pieces of cardboard. "This stuff has been here so long it's never going to sell, maybe you should take it off my hands – get it out of here," he said, handing a bundle to each of the girls.

"John," Kate began, "I don't think . . ."

"Do I have to repeat myself? Mrs. Nestor . . ." he whispered, leaning in toward Kate and once again raising a goofy looking eyebrow.

Kate giggled like a school girl, and he saw the youngster who hid behind the pickles, not the mother of four beautiful daughters. "Damn it, oops, sorry, but you shouldn't threaten me."

"Come on," he said gathering up the goods "Let's see how rich you're going to make me."

He wouldn't take money for the thread or lace, and Kate was sure what he charged for the fabric wasn't even close to what he had paid for it, but she heard Harley, was painlessly grateful, and didn't argue with him.

Nestor ran his store with a firm hand, but he had a soft spot in his heart for the Ramey girls, especially Kate who he'd watch grow from a willful, spirited girl into a beautiful woman. Kate would not be bullied, even as a child, and he had admired her youthful spirit as she stomped her foot on the ground and glared at wrong doers or gave them a sweet smile that didn't match her wicked thoughts. He knew she was living on that strength now.

"Come out to see them after their done, John. We'd love to have you come for supper some time."

"I'd like that, Kate. Maybe some Sunday after the snow flies and things quiet down a bit. I might even try to catch a trout in your creek. It's been a long while since I've had that pleasure." He squeezed her arm and gave each of the girls a little hug. Even Rachel accepted it without backing up, perhaps because her hands and eyes were still caressing the lace laying on top of her lilac calico.

She loaded the girls and her purchases in the buggy next to the packs of clean laundry she would deliver on the way home. It was a tight squeeze, but they didn't care, and they sang songs all the way.

Kate taught them some her mother had sung to her as a young girl – songs Ellen had learned from her mother and were older than the tall trees lining the road. It was a glorious day, and for the moment, Kate wasn't thinking about work. Only pleasant, easy thoughts played in her mind. The sun warmed them. The breeze played with their hair, and they pulled their hair ribbons off letting the long tresses fly. Laughter rang through the air.

At the lumber camp, the girls scampered down and helped unload the laundry packages. Jack strode up, a long saw in one hand, and stood guard while they lined up the packs on the table and waited for the men to claim them. Rebecca told him about their purchases at Nestor's, and he made all the appropriate oohs, aahs, and other noises of approval.

"We even have lace and colored thread," she told him.

Jack said he'd stop by on his way home to see what they had picked for their windows, and he began calling the names on the packages and the price each man had to pay as they came into the lean-to-cook tent. Kate stood back and let him because he felt the need to do it, but many of the men had a whispered comment for her as they went by, some sweet and some a little crude, but always in good humor.

Kate acknowledged the kind spirits with a twinkle and quick retort, and ignored anything else. She didn't mind. They were harmless and good natured, and she liked them. Some missed their far away families, and some she'd known for much of her life. Some she'd been spying on since she was a girl.

But one burly man moved closer than needed, one Kate had not seen before. He stood looking from one to the other of Kate's daughters, spittle forming at the corners of his lips. He pawed his grubby beard, eyed Rachel, let his eyes roam intently and deliberately over her small breasts. Then he stumbled toward her and muttered "Where have you been sweet, little thing?"

Kate felt like she'd been physically smacked. She was enraged, shaken to the core. She bristled, threw back her shoulders and stepped in front of her daughter, glaring at the man. "That 'sweet thing' is my eleven-year old daughter. Keep your eyes off her and your head turned away or . . . you'll regret you have eyes!" she growled.

He was foul looking. His shirt was filthy, and his beard and hair were long strands of grease. Kate walked nearer to him, her chin high and her fists on her hips. She sniffed as if smelling a putrid odor.

The man mumbled something unintelligible and backed up a bit, turned his leer on Kate and then lumbered off. Some sporadic laughter had erupted at Kate's words, but the men didn't seem inclined to either console him or berate him. They made a path for his retreat with a few jeers about being taken down by a little bitty woman.

Jack saw the end of the interplay and moved closer to the girls, ready to do what Kate had threatened and save her the trouble. He hadn't heard the man's words, but he'd heard Kate's threat.

He was a recent arrival at the camp, and Jack didn't know him, but even before this day, he hadn't like his mouth or his attitude. He wouldn't have minded cracking his skull, thought it would most likely do humanity a service if he did, but he'd wait and see.

They finished handing out packages and collecting the money, and loaded up the dirty Newton camp laundry. Kate walked with Rachel as she went around to the other side of the buggy, staying close to her oldest daughter. It shocked her that a man had looked at Rachel with lust in her eyes.

She was a child. Didn't he see she was a little girl? What was happening to the world when children could be treated like tramps? Kate glared at the man's back as he disappeared into the woods, and she came as close to hating as she'd ever known.

Jack stayed nearby, waiting until Kate had the reins in her hands, then he moved closer to her.

"Where's Bug or Poochie?" he asked softly but grimly.

"There wasn't room."

"Then let them run along beside you."

Kate bristled a little, not liking to be told what to do, but she knew Jack worried about them. He didn't want to interfere; that wasn't his way.

"I won't bring the girls again," she said. "We just needed to be in town, so I thought . . . I know . . . I know, you're right," she said tiredly.

Jack patted her knee and smiled at her. "I don't want to go to prison for killing a man, Kate."

Kate nodded, and a tired sigh escaped. The man had taken the laughter from her day, maybe from more than one day. He'd awakened her to perils she logically knew existed but had spent many serene years happily ignoring, and she resented him for it. She knew, too, Jack spoke a solemn truth. He would kill without a backward glance if he thought it necessary; she had no doubt. She would not willingly put Jack in the position of having to defend her or her daughters. She would see to it that didn't happen.

Kate started the wash when they got to the cabin. It was a day early but she wanted tomorrow for the girls and the sewing bee. She asked Rachel to put away supplies, gave the girls their schoolwork, then filled the tubs with water, and set one to heat over the fire pit. When the water was hot, she remove it from the pit, put another tub of cold water in its place and started washing.

She thought about what had happened at the camp, and icy fingers crept up her spine, reached through to her heart, and hot anger followed.

"Damn it! Where the hell are you, Mark? This isn't the way it was supposed to be! And no, I am not sorry!"

Kate knew it was ridiculous to get angry at Mark, but she did it anyway. Unreasonably and in vain, she still got foot stomping, cussing mad. She couldn't think of anyone else to berate, anyone who could be faulted for the predicament they were in, and that made her angry. She'd berated God, too, and using Him as a target had been as fruitless. At times, she felt forsaken, deserted.

Mark should have been by her side raising their girls. He should be sharing all of this; the good and the bad. He'd know how to deal with it all, or at the least they'd take care of it together. When the anger had boiled down to sorrow, she talked to him quietly.

"I'm afraid. I'm afraid to do this alone and I need you."

She took it out on the clothes she was washing, beating them until they were more than clean. Then she wrung the water out until they were almost dry. It felt good taking her wrath out on the clothes! She was still at it when Jack rode into the clearing.

He rolled his sleeves wordlessly and dipped his hand in to grab a pair of trousers. He beat them against the side of the tub and then twisted them to get rid of the gray water. Kate thought he was going to tear them in two as she watched with sidelong glances. He pitched them into the clear water tub one by one, splashing them both, and then repeated the wringing process when the soap had been rinsed from them.

Kate finally stood back and merely stared because he had taken over, and she didn't know what else to do. She followed him when he picked up the basket of clean clothes and strode silently and purposefully over to the lines to hang them.

"Are you mad at me?" she finally asked, breaking the silence. When he didn't answer, she asked again. Jack at last turned to face her.

"Hell no, I'm not mad at you. I'm just mad – period," he said curtly. His hands were on his hips and his face was dark. Then he took a deep breath.

"I guess I'm not really mad, Kate. I just get afraid for you, and I don't know what to do about it – what can be done about it." A few moments later he added with the typical Jack Bay grin, "I guess I am mad that Mark had to die and that sometimes life does bad things to good people."

"Yup," she said. "I was just cussing at the world . . . at Mark, too. I didn't even apologize, and you'll be happy to know I branched out from my favorite cuss word."

"I'm proud of you. Always knew you had more in you," he teased. "I didn't mean to bark at you."

"I know that. You don't need to apologize."

"I wasn't going to, and I'm never sorry when I cuss. From now on," he said more solemnly, "when you leave this cabin, take Bug. Always."

Kate hugged him and asked if he was interested in supper, but it wasn't his usual day to come by and Ruthie was expecting him, so he declined. He looked over the curtain material and lace with the girls, made gushing sounds of awe over their choices til they were in fits of laughter, and before he left he told Kate what he had learned at the camp.

"I asked around about the man you threatened to thrash," he said, "but there isn't much. Apparently, he drifts from camp to camp, mostly the smaller, northern ones. Talk is that he doesn't leave them willingly – there's always some trouble or another, and it always seems to be about him. Stay clear of him, Kate. Please?"

"As far away as I can. I think I can still smell him," she said, grinning.

Jack grinned back, but the smile didn't reach his dark, troubled eyes. She reassured him she would be careful – and she would quickly break the man's skull if she had to.

"With what, Kate? A pack of clothes?"

"With whatever I can put my hands on at the moment," she answered. "But maybe you're right. I could use a weapon, like . . . maybe a baseball bat. I could keep it in the buggy with me."

"Now you're talking. In fact, I have one I will gladly give to you. I'll send it with Ruthie when she comes out tomorrow. Sounds like you ladies are making a day of it," he said, smiling now with all of his face and feeling better.

"Yes, we are and I'm really looking forward to it. So are the girls."

Jack finally left, satisfied, momentarily, he'd done what he could. There wasn't much else he could do short of barricading them in their cabin and locking the doors. It was frustrating because he worried so much about them, but heaven help the man who messed with the Ramey girls.

Sunday brought sunshine and sounds of laughter as the buggy rolled into the clearing. Ruthie was squeezed in between Ellen and Verna and was trying to get Verna to carry the alto part to a hymn she didn't know. Ruthie's sweet soprano rang out in the clearing contrasting with Verna's gravely, growling alto. Verna pretended irritation, but the twinkle in her blue eyes denied it. Ruthie poked her in the ribs.

"Come on, you can remember the words of the chorus if you try. It's repeated the same every time." She sang it again, and the sound of lilting voices was what Kate heard as they drove in. Kate picked up the second alto and walked out into the sunshine singing with them.

"I used to sing with my pa," Verna said, shocking them all.

They knew nothing about Verna, and for some reason they had never given thought to her having a family. She was Verna and came without benefit of having a mother and father, as if she had sprouted under a cabbage leaf or came to them fully grown for their benefit alone.

How silly, Kate thought. Of course, Verna has parents, but the idea still seemed strange.

"You have a nice alto," Kate said.

"I do not, but I can carry a tune."

Inside, they paired off in sewing teams: Ellen and Rebecca, Kat and Verna, Ruthie and Rachel, and Jeannie with Kate. They carefully measured each window again, folded, pressed and pinned the hems, and then threaded their needles. The girls watched their partners make tiny stitches, slowly pulling the thread through the fabric, and tried to mimic them. Their stitches were long and uneven, but held the hems in place and got neater as they sewed. They sorted the trims, decided which length of lace would go best with what fabric and attached the lace.

By afternoon the curtains were ready to hang, and they ran to see the real results of their work, all together . . . going from room to room as a group and standing back to admire their handiwork and the way the new curtains brightened each room before going on to the next.

In Rachel's room as the others were leaving, Kate hesitated. Another curtain. A different window. The memory of falling into Mark's arms caused an ache in her breast.

She had sneaked into the smith shop to surprise him with a curtain for the room behind his shop. She was standing on a chair, and it tilted as he walked in and surprised her, causing her to lose her balance. She reached out and he made a grab to catch her. They both fell to the floor and remained tangled there as Kate's family walked into the room and were the most surprised.

Heat flushed her cheeks now in memory of her body on his. God how she missed that feeling . . . him.

On her way down the stairs, she heard heavy hooves in the yard and looked out to see Mel sliding from his saddle. He pulled several bulky packages from the side bags and strode in the open door. Jeannie raced down and was already climbing his legs when the others got there.

"This is a pleasure," Kate said. "What brings you here today?"

"The Ramey rainbow," he said, tousling Jeannie's deep copper curls.

"Doesn't a rainbow mean there's a storm out there somewhere?" Kate asked, looking around the room at her daughters and smiling. They truly were colorful, from Jeannie's bright auburn hair to Rachel's deep, velvet brown and the two shades of silky blonde in between.

"I heard there was something going on here today and didn't want to be left out. You wouldn't leave me out of the fun would you, Copper Penny?"

Kate smiled at another tweaked memory. They were everywhere! She couldn't move fast enough to outrun them. Copper Penny was what Mark had called Jeannie the day she'd been born when he held her in the light of the window and saw the sun making flames in her bright, red hair.

"Nope," Jeannie told him, "and we had fun. I'll show you," she said, climbing down and taking his hand to drag him to her room.

"Whoa, little filly. Wait a minute. I believe I found some things you ladies will like." He untied the string binding his packages. Inside were five rag rugs of a variety of hues, two earth-toned ones, a couple woven from bright colored fabrics, and a pastel. Jeannie jumped up and down with excitement, and Rebecca raced to the table to caress the colorful rugs, her face alight with pleasure.

"So, you just found these somewhere?" Kate asked.

"I did," he said, the lie uncomfortable on his bronze, chiseled face.

"Where, might I ask, did you happen to stumble across these obviously new rugs?"

"Are they new?" he asked with feigned surprise, a look Mel didn't do well at all. "I didn't know that," he added. "Nope, I did not know that."

"Mel, you can't . . ." Kate began, but was interrupted by Verna.

"Just take the damned rugs, Kate, and quit stewing about it, geez," Verna said and pointed to the earth-toned rug. "This one?" she asked Kat who had glanced at them quickly and knew in an instant which one would look best with her brown checked curtains.

Kat nodded, and Verna picked it up and walked determinedly from the room mumbling something about stupid people and stupid pride with Kat trailing close behind.

Verna's bold move opened the door for the rest to paw over the goods and make their choices, their giggles following as they ran to their rooms and spread the rugs on the floor by their beds. After raising an eyebrow at Mel, Kate followed.

It looked suspiciously as though Mel knew what colors they had chosen for their curtains because the rugs matched perfectly. Strange coincidence? Kate harrumphed . . . crossed her arms and raised her eyebrows. They stood together at the door to Jeannie and Rebecca's room.

"Are you a mind reader?" Kate asked. "Did you read your tea leaves this morning? Check with the stars? Your crystal ball? How did you match the colors?"

"Yes. I read minds," he said grinning, "but that isn't what I did this time. I just know my Ramey rainbow. The rug I picked for your room reminds me of the forest in the fall when the leaves begin to turn."

"Hmmm, and you're getting poetic in your advanced years, Mel, and . . . that was a pretty long speech for you. And . . . I'm still waiting to hear where you 'found' these rugs. Cast offs from your mother's fall cleaning again?" she said, reminding him of the curtains and rugs he had given her years ago, when she was first trying to make the cabin livable. He'd bought them at Nestor's, given them to Mark, and told him it wasn't a Christmas present. It was just some stuff his mother was getting rid of. Kate had known better, but until now had let him have his small fib.

Mel colored, remembering the lie, and shuffled his feet. He hadn't known she knew the truth, had always thought she believed his story.

"Well, uh, it could have been. Mother could have cleaned out the cupboards . . . she does that every year," he stammered.

"Fess up, big boy. You've been caught," she said poking a finger in his chest and looking up at him.

Mel pretended fear, but his grin spread. She wasn't going to be mad, and to top it off, she was going to accept the gifts. "Sorry Ma'am. I won't fib again."

"I'll whup you if you do. Now, let's go see how they look." When she did, Kate was sure Mel had help in choosing them. "John Nestor was in on this, wasn't he? Did he help with a little 'mind reading?'"

"That's how I knew what was going on here today."

"Do you two have a private telegraph going from the store to your house? Is that how you keep tabs on us?"

"Aw, Kate. That's not the way it is. You know that."

"I'm teasing, Mel. If you can fib, I can tease. Fair play."

"John cares about you all. A lot – and so do I."

"I know that, and I'm not mad. It's sweet of you both."

Kate hugged him, and he put his arms around her tentatively, and then pulled her against him for a moment. Just a moment, but it was one he treasured.

Mel stayed for supper after the others left. He held Jeannie on his lap until she fell asleep and then carried her to her bed. *It has been a good day*, Kate thought, and it's nice having a man in the house, one who cares about all of us, a good man.

When the others went to their rooms for the night, Kate told them she'd be there in a minute to tuck them in. Rebecca and Kat nodded, but Rachel casually told her mother she didn't need to come up.

"It's fine, Sweetie," Kate said. "I'll be right there."

Rachel quietly said, "Mother, I don't need to be tucked in. Please."

Kate's head jerked back like she'd been struck and it felt like it. Mel watched her face change from contented pleasure to shock and everything in between. Kate sat back in her chair, silent, thinking about what she'd heard. She didn't know how to feel about it, or how she was supposed to feel, but bruised fit. She had been shut out of a nighttime ritual that had been theirs for over eleven years. In a single moment, it vanished.

What had just happened? Kate rose and went to say goodnight to Kat and Rebecca, walking slowly by the stairway leading to Rachel's room. She paused, grasping the handrail and looked up, listening, as if she could read in the air what was going on in her child's mind. She considered going up anyway, but dismissed it as quickly as the thought came. She'd been told not to and knew she had to respect Rachel's wishes.

Wasn't she born just yesterday? When did she stop being a little girl? Wasn't I looking? Turn it back; turn back the clock, please? But there were no clocks except the ones ticking in her children, and now Kate could hear the hours chiming away loud and clear.

When she went back to her chair in front of the hearth by Mel, her face wore confusion like a horrible mask.

"It's alright," he said.

"Why?" Kate asked. "Why is it alright that my daughter doesn't need me anymore?"

"I'm a farmer, Kate. I live by the cycle of seasons and know this is hers for learning how to be a grown up. I watched my little brothers and sisters do the same."

"But she isn't a grown up. She's a child."

"Of course she is," he said calmly, "but it's a struggle to become an adult and sometimes kids need to be on their own to do it. She still needs you, but there are times that she needs to *not* need you. I guess this is one of them." He grinned at her. "Did that make any sense at all?"

"I don't like it. Damn it, why can't anything just stay as it is, as it was? Nothing ever does! Why?" she growled. "Sorry."

Mel didn't respond, knew Kate was not just talking about Rachel. His heart was heavy, an inert mass that happened to beat at regular intervals. He didn't know how to help her, so he put his hand on hers where it rested on the arm of the chair and left it there. The fire in the hearth grew low, and Mel added a small log to keep it burning. It felt good holding her hand, and she snuggled her fingers into his palm. He wanted Kate to be happy, and if this was what she needed, then this was what she would get from him.

Kate tossed when she went to bed, slipped into shallow sleep where nightmares drifted in and out and woke her. The last one made Kate sit upright and clutch at Bug who growled at the intruder in her dream.

It was a bulky, flannel clad man who followed her from place to place, always lurking around a tree or a corner. She couldn't see his face, but somehow she still knew what he looked like. His skin was festered with sores all over, and his long nose curved down toward his chin. He didn't speak to her. He followed and leered everywhere she went. When she had the girls with her, he kept looping a rope around their hands and dragging them to him. The girls didn't fight him, and they weren't afraid, but they weren't eager to go with him either. Kate always managed to slice through the rope and pull her daughters back, but he grinned wickedly and winked at them like they shared some secret Kate didn't know.

Kate stroked Bug's head and called herself a fool. "It was just a nightmare, Bug. That's all. Want to sit outside with me for a bit?"

Bug rolled his eyes and stretched. 'Not really, but I'll go.'

It was chilly in the fall night air, and Kate sat wrapped in a quilt watching a slice of moon rise in the dark sky. The raccoons lurked near their den, and bats flitted from tree to tree. An owl said 'Whoo? Whoo?' in the distance, and Kate said, "It's not a who. It's a what."

Bug looked at her, his brown eyes round orbs in the moonlight.

"That old goblin in my dream, Bug, it's not a person. It's time dragging my girls from me. Rachel wants to grow up, and pretty soon it will be Kat, and then Rebecca, and then my Copper Penny. I'm ignoring it, and that troll stalking me in my dream is my fear for my girls – or maybe for me. They're going to leave me, Bug. And that's as it should be, but I hate it . . . a lot."

Bug stared up at her with his 'I'm sure you are right' look.

"You're very smart," she responded.

She slept better when she went back to bed, and Bug crawled up from the foot of the bed where he normally slept to lie next to her in case the troll came back. He would be ready for him and scare him off with a well-aimed wet and slobbery nose in his face.

Chapter Four

Winter 1911

Snow fell and blanketed the clearing, but the forest floor still lay as autumn had left it, uncovered except for the sound suppressing mantle of damp, brown leaves.

Her chapped fingers were numb when she hung the clothes on the line. They took a long while to get dry enough to iron. She washed inside the cabin now. It was too cold to be outside for long, especially with her hands in water up to her elbows, but there was too much laundry to hang inside where the warmth would dry it more quickly. Kate yearned for spring, but it was only December, and warm sunshine would be a long time coming.

It was warm inside and peaceful. The girls were working at the table. Kate was doing the laundry and watching them, letting her mind wander peacefully when a knock at the door startled her from quiet thoughts. She hadn't heard a horse come into the clearing as she did when visitors came by. Thinking it was probably Jack stopping on his way home and snow had muffled the sound, she opened the door with a smile that changed in an instant to surprise, then shock and anger.

It was the man she had threatened at the camp, the man who had leered at Rachel. Rage mixed with fear slammed into her, buckling her knees. She put a hand on the table to steady herself. She didn't know why her reaction was so intense, but she knew he scared her. And fright made her mad.

"You!" she hissed, regaining her strength, and putting fury in front of incapacitating fear. "What... are you doing here? What do you want?"

Her voice was low and threatening, but the fists she clenched at her sides shook with panic she refused to acknowledge.

"Just stopping by to get warm," he said looking Kate up and down. He reeked of whiskey and filthy, acrid sweat. He tried to look contrite and friendly, but it was a futile attempt, and there wasn't a chance she would let him into her house.

"Leave! Now!" she spat at him and pushed the door to shut it before he could move to enter, but he stuck his foot in between the door and the frame. She slammed it hard on his boot, but he shoved and she was no match for his strength. It opened, and Kate instinctively flew around the table to gather her daughters and put the table between them and the man.

He grinned, a malevolent look that pierced Kate with alarm. Then, once more, fear turned to anger and she became thoroughly enraged. For the first time in her life, Kate wanted to kill something. Him! And it would feel good!

Bug leapt from his rug to stand in front of the foul man, his nose inches from the man's crotch, a deep, threatening growl growing in his throat. Poochie joined him and matched Bug's growl.

"Go to Rachel's room. All of you. Barricade the door. Now," Kate said, her voice quiet and steady.

"No need to send your pretty daughters away," he said, leering at them.

"Now!" she repeated, and they fled the room looking back only briefly at their mother and the man at the door.

He held out his hands, palms up toward the dogs, and began to move further into the room. Kate saw him stop suddenly and jerk back; a harsh yelp tore from his throat as Bug's teeth sunk into his thigh. Blood spurted, and Bug held on, gripping the man's hefty thigh between his jaws and keeping him from moving. Bug's growl continued to threaten, and Kate thought he'd bitten through an artery there was so much blood spraying.

The man swung his fist at Bug's head trying to drive him away, and Poochie leapt forward, seized the flailing forearm between his teeth and bit down. A scream of pain ripped the air and Kate felt something she'd not have believed possible, pleasure in another's pain, satisfaction. Whatever it was, she wanted this man to hurt. He had threatened her girls, and for that he deserved every bit of what he was feeling.

"They're killing me!" he wailed. He tried to beat at the dogs with his free hand, but they bit harder when he moved, so he stopped, his face beading with sweat and pain. Kate stood watching, relief flooding her.

"Will you leave?" she growled through gritted teeth, slow burning hatred having replaced fear and made even harsher by it. She glared at him.

"They'll chew you up like dog meat. In fact, I'd like it if they did, damn it, so don't tempt me!" Her words were quiet, but fury left no doubt about her intent.

"Well? I won't call them off til you speak."

There was deathly silence for a moment; perhaps he couldn't talk through the pain. Kate walked to the stove and picked up a heavy iron skillet she intended to use if he didn't leave when the dogs released him.

He held up his one free hand in surrender. "I'll go. Just being friendly," he moaned.

"Get far away from here! Now! Don't . . . you . . . ever . . . come back!" Her whispered words held more threat than a scream would have done.

"Bug, Pooch," she called to her dogs. They dropped him and went to stand in front of her. She watched him limp through the door, blood leaking from his wounds and then went to the window and continue to watch, making sure he left the clearing. She locked the door, shoved a chair up under the handle, and ran upstairs.

"It's me. Let me in." The girls were huddled on Rachel's bed, their arms around each other, eyes wide with fear. Bug and Poochie had followed, but sat outside the bedroom on guard, both poised and listening for strange sounds. Kate collapsed on the bed and tried to surround her daughters in her arms, all of them at once.

"He's gone," she said. "He won't be back."

"How do you know?" they all asked at once, then "Why did he come here?"

"I don't like him," Jeannie said. "He's nasty."

"Yes, he is," Kate said, "but he's gone now and won't be back."

Ever the rational child, Kat said "You can't know that, Ma. How can you know it? He works at the camp, so he could come here anytime he wants to."

Kate smoothed her nine-year old daughter's straight blonde hair and tried desperately to find the words to reassure her children they were safe. But Kat had spoken the truth. How could she know he wouldn't come back? Sure, the dogs were still here, but things happened; horrible, unexpected things. How could she leave the girls to make her trips to the camps to deliver and pick up laundry? And she couldn't take them either. It was a dilemma, but right now her daughters needed comfort, not worry. She'd think about that problem later.

They sat on Rachel's bed for a long time, talking about what had happened. They had never been afraid of anyone before; never had reason to, and it sullied them in places that were formerly pure, untainted, untouched.

They'd known other kinds of fear, of inanimate things like the fire that scorched the earth when drought made the forest a tinder box. And they'd known fear for their father when he was so ill and of the unknown when he was dying. But they had never known an evil person before, and it was difficult for Kate to explain it to them without suspending their trust in people, without defiling their images of others. She didn't want them to fear people. It was another dilemma, one she couldn't put off solving like the others.

"Most people are fundamentally good. You know that, don't you?" When the girls nodded, she continued. "But every once in a while, you'll run across someone who is simply not a good person, and you need to be aware. You need to be able to see underneath the skin to know which person means harm."

"You can't see under skin, Ma," Kat said.

Kate laughed a little, glad she could through the turmoil racking her brain. "You're right, Kat," she said, "I'm speaking metaphorically. Do you remember what that means?"

Kat nodded, with a roll of her eyes. "It's a symbol, Mother," she said, a little miffed her language skills had been questioned.

"You're right," Kate said, realizing her error, "of course you remember. And I only meant that sometimes you can sense the goodness – and the badness – in people. You watch and you listen. That's what you need to do when you meet other people. Understand? They don't always appear to be what they really are – deep inside."

They all nodded agreement. Rebecca thought for a moment and then said, "Like Mrs. Wellington. She sounds mean, but I think she's a good person."

Kate hugged her daughter. "I believe you're right, Rebecca. I think she's a good person, too. She just sounds ornery."

"She sounds crazy," Kat volunteered.

"That, too," Kate said, "but that's not really a nice thing to say."

"True things are not nice to say?" Kat asked, her logical mind battling Kate.

"Sometimes, Kat," Kate sighed. "Sometimes it's better just to keep your thoughts to yourself." Then she capitulated, "Oh, damn it, anyway – sorry. We can say just about anything to each other, as long as we're kind. Maybe we polish it up a bit for others. Does that work?"

When Kate told them about how Bug and Poochie grabbed the man with their teeth and hung on, they were wide-eyed at first and then giggled at the idea. They laughed and enhanced the picture, had the man begging to be released, and Bug was shaking his head no. Poochie, of course, was clearly speaking, telling the man how awful, mean and evil he was.

Jeannie said Poochie could see under skin, and Kate agreed animals had a great ability to know what people struggle to see. It must go along with their powerful sense of smell. She called Poochie over to give him a hug, and he obeyed, but Bug stayed in the doorway – guarding his family.

They finally went downstairs. Kate cleaned up the blood in the doorway as casually as possible, and they went back to what they were doing before wickedness had interrupted their peace. While Kate finished the laundry, she probed her mind for a solution to leaving the girls safe when she had to make the trips to the camps.

"How would you like to drive into town?" she asked the girls.

"Where are we going?" Rachel asked.

"I think we'll visit your grandma for a bit. Would that be alright with all of you?"

They finished their work, and Kat helped hang the clothes on the line while Rachel and Rebecca straightened up the kitchen. They stacked the tubs in the corner and picked up the school books and papers.

Outside, Kate called for Bug and Poochie who weren't far away and appeared to be sniffing the air for unfamiliar scents.

"The dogs are going with us, right?" Kat asked.

"Poochie will enjoy running along beside us. He's young, Kat. We'll find a place for Bug in with us somewhere." It was obvious Kat thought they should keep the dogs with them, and she agreed with her pragmatic daughter. On the way, Kate asked the girls to say nothing about the man coming to the house to anyone, especially their grandma – so she wouldn't worry about them.

"Please let it be our secret. Okay? For now, Grandma doesn't need to know." They nodded understanding even though their eyes speculated.

When they got to the Hughes house, they were greeted by a surprised Ellen. It wasn't often they stopped by unexpectedly. Ellen made hot chocolate to warm them. Even though they had been bundled under layers of blankets during the ride, their fingers were stiff, brittle sticks and their faces rosy with cold.

After they chatted for a while, Kate asked where Harley might be. Ellen told her he was most likely in his room at the back of the barn, and Kate headed there, telling them all to stay put, and she'd bring Harley in to see them soon.

Ellen's head tilted as she watched Kate leave, and she wondered about her need for Harley but didn't ask. She'd know soon enough. She had never comprehended Kate and never would but wondered what her daughter was up to this time.

Harley was working on a thin slab of wood, rubbing it with sand paper and then running his hand over it, testing for smoothness. He looked up when she knocked at his open door, pleased surprise on his face.

"What brings you to this humble abode?" he asked. Kate didn't make a habit of stopping by to chat.

"I need your help," she said. "I don't know what to do."

He stopped his work, surprised at her words, her admission of need, and led Kate to one of the two chairs. Her face said this was serious. He was quiet while Kate told him what had happened. She berated herself for believing the girls would be safe at the cabin during the brief times she had to leave them.

"But the cabin has always been so peaceful, and it seemed so secure. I am such a fool," she said, and frustration coursed through her body and ended in tight fists banging against her thighs.

Harley didn't verbally express his anger, but his lips pulled back grimly, and his eyes squinted nearly closed. Finally, he said, "You certainly are no fool, Kate, but I can see you shouldn't leave the girls alone. Let me think on it."

Kate talked while he thought. She told him about Bug and Poochie in comic detail – even embellished by telling him what the girls said the dogs were thinking and mumbling while they held him in their teeth. She filled the moments with chatter so she didn't need to hear the silence of Harley's thoughts. So she wouldn't think.

"Just getting rid of one bad man doesn't solve the problem, doesn't keep the girls safe. You as well, Kate, and you know that. There's more than one wicked person in the world, and you need more than dogs for protection, even good ones like Bug and Poochie."

Kate watched as Harley worked out a solution.

"I don't suppose you'd consider moving to town, perhaps in with your mother?" he asked. Kate's face gave him the answer.

"If I had to do that to keep the girls safe, if there was no other way, of course, but I had a different thought," she said tentatively.

Harley waited while Kate tapped her fingers together, a staccato rhythm she used when agitated.

"Hmmm ... well ..." Tap, tap, tap, t-tap t-tap.

"Yes?"

"Well, I was thinking ... "

"I saw that. What was it you were thinking?"

"What would you think about moving in with us ... just until I can think of another way," she added quickly. "I know that's asking a lot of you, Harley. I know that ... It's just ... I don't know. I can't leave them alone now. I just can't."

Harley patted her hand and smiled.

"I didn't think you'd like me hanging around, Kate, an old man bunking down in your house," he said grinning. "But it's a perfect solution – for now." Harley was thinking of Mel and how at some point Kate would marry that fine man, and they would all be safe, but she wasn't ready. Maybe she never would be, but he hoped some day she would be able to find a special corner in her heart for Mark, lay him to rest there, and love again.

"What will I tell Mother?" Kate asked. "How can we explain this change without telling her what happened? I really don't want her to know. She'll worry, and then she'll tell Mel, and then all hell will break loose. Oops, sorry – new cuss."

Harley grinned at her new word, his face once more placid and serene. "Let me take care of that. Maybe you need some work done. Maybe I need to teach the girls some higher mathematics or science that you, my dear, do not understand."

Kate cuffed him. "Are you maligning my academic knowledge?"

"Certainly. Can you teach trigonometry? Do you fully understand the Pythagorean Theorem? Have you ever measured the height of a tree without climbing it?" he teased, enjoying Kate's look of surprise. "That, my dear, is applied physics, and I understand it."

"How do you know all that stuff, Harley?"

"Someday, I might tell you," he said.

"What, now you go all quiet on me?"

Harley smiled again. "Let's go tell the others that I'll be staying at the cabin with the Ramey girls for awhile."

The girls were ecstatic to hear Harley was going home with them, especially Rebecca who snuggled against his big belly the moment he sat down. Who knows why certain people were drawn to one another? The reasons couldn't be seen or explained. The mysterious connection we have with others is also hidden under the skin.

Kate said that Harley was moving to the cabin in order to take over their lessons. They were ready for higher math and science, and she couldn't keep up with their schooling and all of her work. Ellen was satisfied with the explanation, if saddened to see Harley go.

"You'll be good for the girls. They need to have a man around anyway." She said pointedly, careful not to look at her daughter.

Kat watched the interplay of words, her eyes moving from one to the other, watching and listening. It was clear to Kate this daughter had read between the lines and hadn't bought the story they'd given. She knew exactly why Harley was moving in, but Ellen had believed it, and her innocence was the important thing right now. Maybe Kate would explain later, but for now it would remain buried.

It was a tighter ride home, but Harley held both Jeannie and Rebecca, one on each knee, and Kat and Rachel rode in the back with Bug lying on their laps, keeping them warm. Poochie happily ran beside the buggy or raced ahead to ward off wicked robbers and errant opossums, then raced back to see if they were still following. It was a contented group; especially given the prior hours that had been fractured by fear.

60

Harley entertained them with stories about faraway lands and wood sprites, his voice a calm murmur in the night. Snow fell and brightened their way with its sparkling white, and for the first time since the man had come to the cabin, Kate felt warm.

Chapter Five

As Christmas grew near, the cabin bustled with activity. Harley had settled in easily, like he'd always been there, and slept in the small bed he'd brought from the Hughes' barn, one he'd been using for the past decade or more. It stood where Kate's bed had been before they moved it to the back room. Kate was warmed by it, comforted. It felt good to see one there again.

He helped the girls with their school work and boasted about being the best teacher ever. Kate didn't know why she believed him, but she did. Having Harley there had the added benefit of freeing up some of her time, yet she often sat at the table with them and listened to Harley describe things she knew nothing about. He was an enigma, this rogue scholar.

Rachel wasn't interested in the science he taught them, but Kat soaked it in like she'd been starving for the natural world all her life, and Jeannie loved learning about insects, wildlife and ocean critters. He speculated with them about other possibilities for the origins of life, even knowing Ellen would not approve, because he believed they should understand the issues and make up their own minds. He made math fun using objects gathered around the cabin to show mathematical relationships, and the girls blossomed under his care.

Kate relaxed. It was nice to have Harley with them, and he loved being part of the family.

The far side of the room grew cluttered as Harley stacked indistinguishable parts and pieces of Christmas presents, and the pile of wood on the floor at the foot of his bed continued to grow higher.

"I've been making mittens and scarves for the girls," Kate told Harley one night eyeing his wood pile, "but I have some other things in mind. Would you show me how?"

Since then, the number of projects expanded, and Kate and Harley spent evenings working late into the night after the girls were asleep. She was energized picturing the surprise on her daughters' faces on Christmas Eve, and she found she enjoyed working with wood. She was also learning a lot about Harley and began to treasure the time they spent quietly working.

Kate got pretty good with a saw and sandpaper. Harley showed her how to miter corners and drill holes to dowel pieces together instead of using nails.

"I don't know why my fingers are all thumbs," Kate sputtered around the thumb she was sucking after giving it a solid whack. "Why do yours work so much better than mine?"

Harley grinned at her, his eyes squinting. "You have to let the wood work for you, Kate. You can't force it."

"It's wood, Harley, not human. It can't say 'No -- don't hurt me!'" Kate said trying to force a scowl through her grin.

"It was alive with life at one time. Who knows when its spirit leaves to continue on in another form? Perhaps it's trying to help you, but you're not listening."

Kate mocked him by putting the piece she was working on next to her ear to listen.

"Hello, this is Kate," she said, a bogus look of seriousness on her face. "You don't know me, but I'd like to make a cradle out of you. Can you help? I'm listening, now."

Harley laughed at her and said, "With your hands, Kate. Listen with your hands. Don't you know there is more than one way to hear – to know things?"

"What I know for sure is that you are a crazy old coot. I still think I should fix you up with Mrs. Wellington. You'd make a great pair." But a small piece of Kate believed him. He usually made sense at some point. It was often down the road a ways, but it eventually came through. "I wouldn't want to break Verna's heart by fixing you up with another woman, though, so I won't play match maker."

Harley blushed, a phenomenon that didn't normally plague him, and he covered it by attacking the piece of wood in his hand with sandpaper, flatly ignoring her comment.

By the evening of the Christmas tree lighting ceremony, the gifts were built, ready to be painted, and sitting under carefully placed burlap. The girls were in their rooms getting ready to go, and Harley and Kate sat at the table waiting. They were both childlike in their excitement over the gifts for the girls and could hardly wait for Christmas to come. Harley went to the cupboard and pulled out the jug of moonshine. He poured a small glass for Kate and brought the jug back for himself.

"A little nip for potential frostbite and a little for the celebration," he said, then added, "Here's to us, Kate, to our girls, and to all the love in this house." He lifted the jug to her raised glass and then took a long sip. "Thank you for including me in making these Christmas presents."

Kate took a sip and raised her glass again. "Here's to you, Harley – my friend, the angel in our presence disguised as an old coot. You have been one many times in the past, and you still are." She clinked her glass against the jug, and suddenly felt her eyes water. She had no idea why, and swiped at her eyes in frustration.

"Damn," she said. "Where did that come from? Sorry."

"So, I'm an old coot, and many times over, huh? Well, you're a sentimental, cussing, hundred pound, foot stomping piece of work."

"No . . . no, no, Harley, not the old coot part many times over, although old coot's true, too. I meant that for all these years now, like it says in the Bible, in you . . . we may have been entertaining an angel unaware."

"Who's wearing an angel's underwear?" Jeannie asked as they came into the room dressed and ready to go.

"Probably Harley, he's bizarre," Kat said with a wide grin. "Are you wearing angels' underwear, Harley?"

"Oh, good Lord" Kate said in exasperation. "Let's go, or the candles will all be lit before we get there!"

Harley rose, stretched and sipped again at the jug, his eyes alight with joy as he peered over the top of it. Oh, how he loved these girls. "Come on, let's light up a tree!"

Harley piled blankets around them and climbed in. Kate handed him the reins. She wanted to sit back and enjoy the ride. The evening air felt warm on her cheeks, and she closed her eyes for a moment to embrace more fully the contentment around her. She breathed deeply, slowly, savoring the taste of happiness on her tongue, then opened her eyes to mammoth snowflakes drifting lazily in the air. She stuck out her tongue to catch them.

They sang carols in the beginning dusk and arrived at Ellen's after the others were already there, bundled and ready to go. When they piled out of the buggy, Kat looked around.

"Where's Verna?" she said, planting her feet like she wasn't moving a step until her friend was there.

"We're picking her up at Sadie's," Jack said. "Don't worry. We're not leaving her behind."

Kat nodded approval, and they started out. A large group moved down the road and into town. Jack and Ruthie were there, along with two of her students who were spending the holidays with them; Willie and Mary, with their two children; and Mel with his mother.

It was like a dozen other Christmas tree ceremonies all rolled together, identical, yet unique. Carols, friends, family. People had been added and it blossomed each year with new arrivals. At the same time, it was diminished through loss, and shadows followed them down the street.

Kate knew her mother remembered Will, and the many, many times she and her husband took this walk together, kissed as they put their candle on the tree together. Kate could see it reflected in her eyes. But Ellen, like others who suffered losses, didn't talk about it, about how nightfall brought longing for days that went before. About feeling the touch of his hand on her neck and turning, expecting to see him there, and then remember he was gone. Knowing with certainty he was with her a moment ago – she'd felt him touch her -- and the other painful certainty of knowing he was not. At Christmas, especially, but other times, too, his presence was in her every pore, every element of her being.

Kate remembered her father this night, too, and the mixture of feelings in remembrance filled her spirit, the good and bad, the grief and delight. It mingled and tangled with memories of Mark until Kate couldn't separate or define the pain, the joy, the emotion.

Harley put his arm around her shoulder and squeezed. "Angels are everywhere," he whispered with a wink. "Some you can see, and some you're better off just feeling, like a piece of wood. Let the angels give you peace and joy."

She smiled at him; hadn't known it was on her face. She'd have to work on her face, for her girls.

"You sound like a Christmas carol. Which one of the wise men are you?"

"The fourth one. Bet you didn't know about him, did you? Not many do."

Kate grinned at Harley's efforts to lighten her mood, but didn't respond. He was right, Christmas should only be about peace and joy, and she'd see to it that it was happy, damn it! Oh, God, did I say that out loud . . . and on the way to the nativity scene? With angels, everywhere? "Sorry."

Mel, walking by her side, heard the last single word and leaned toward her. "Who are you cussing at now?" he whispered.

Kate was embarrassed. "No one. Nothing. I didn't mean to. Really, this time I didn't."

"Don't worry about it, Kate. I'm fairly sure you won't get struck by lightening cuz it's winter. Thunder storms are pretty rare right now."

Kate glared at him. "You shouldn't have been eavesdropping."

"You should be glad it was me. Ellen would dress you down but good if she heard you cuss right now," he said, raising his eyebrows toward her mother.

"I'll do worse than dress you down if you tell."

"No dressing allowed at Christmas time. I think there's a Christmas moratorium on dressing."

"Really? We're all to go naked? Hmmm . . . interesting."

"You know ... I mean ... you know what I meant, Kate. You brat!"

They sang carols with the folks from town as they walked to the tree, and like they had been doing for years, the rest waited to hear a hymn from the Hughes family. Ruthie's sweet soprano filled the air and then was joined by Kate and Ellen's harmonies. Willie made hearts break with his solo chorus and then Jack and Mel joined in the harmony. Verna even knew it and lent her voice, a full octave below the other altos.

One by one, each Hersey family added an ornament they'd brought with them, and one by one, each person old enough to hold a candle lit another one already tied to a branch on the tree. Some went to the tree alone, some with a loved one, and some were children sitting on their father's shoulders to reach the high branches. Each of the girls had a candle, and the Ramey family went together for their lighting – along with Harley, still connected by hand to Rebecca, and Verna, dragged along by Kat, and Mel who still held Jeannie – now on his shoulders.

Kate smiled when she saw the extended family group, and her mind drifted back to where it had been during the walk. Families diminish and they grow. Harley would say it was the cycle ... or the season of things, or something similar. Or was it Mel who said it? She chastised herself for getting old and forgetful.

In her musings, she saw the girls with children of their own lighting the candles and herself standing off to the side with the widows, watching. It looked like the Hughes-Ramey family had grown even given the absence of her father and her husband. Kate hoped Mark was smiling nearby, that Harley was right about the angels.

She lit her candle by herself standing next to Rachel. Her eyes were bright and clear, and she whispered, "Merry Christmas, Mark. I love you. I always will." One tear escaped, and then she took a deep, cleansing breath that led to peace and a smile.

On Kate's other side, Mel had given his candle to Jeannie who was trying to light the highest candle on the tree. Mel steadied her with both hands as she put her feet on his shoulders and reached even higher. Jeannie didn't falter. She was unafraid of the great distance to the ground – first, because she wasn't afraid of anything, and secondly, because – well, Mel was holding her, wasn't he? When she was done, Mel eased her to the ground so she could stand back and look at her accomplishment. He pointed to the candle she had lit and Jeannie spun around with a squeal.

"Mine is the highest of them all! Look!"

"It is, Copper Top! You did it," he said, grinning at the pride suffusing her freckled face.

"Show me yours, Mama, and Rachel's and Rebecca's. Where are they? Where's Kat's?"

Kate pointed them all out to her, and Jeannie wouldn't quit until every member of the Hughes-Ramey-Bronson-Benson troupe had shown her where their candles were on the tree.

Ellen stood behind the group with Mel's mother, Laura. They talked quietly, contented smiles on their faces. Each woman had a long history of different trials and joys, but they were united by those, by their widowhood, and by their motherhood; and because of that, there was connection and understanding, sisterhood. No explanations were needed for their brief comments, no details necessary. It was all displayed in front of them, in their offspring and in their friends.

Laura watched her son intently, warmed by the glow on his face, his joy in the child on his shoulders obvious, and she wondered about his relationship with the mother. She prayed for his happiness and hoped the Ramey family would provide it. There had been a time when she had been angry with Kate, could have hated her for turning away her son . . . as much as she was capable of hating, anyway. But her anger had gone long ago, after she had resigned herself to the fact that Mel would remain a single man, and no children would run through their large farm house. She asked Ellen about Kate and the children.

"They're doing alright," Ellen told her. "The girls seem happy. She's a stubborn girl, my Kate. Always wanted to do things for herself, and she hasn't changed."

A small smile played around Laura's mouth. "I raised one just like that. I never could tell Mel what to do – or when to do it. Only his pa could do that."

"I understand." It was that way with Kate and her pa, but he usually didn't tell her what to do, anyway. Will was a free spirit, and Kate's a lot like him. He taught her that -- against my wishes, darn him -- and he loved it in her.

Laura nodded, memory flooding her with pictures of Mel's father. It was so long ago and it seemed so fresh, so new. "Christmas is a time for reflection, isn't it?" she said quietly. It was Ellen's turn to nod silently.

They went back to the Hughes' house to warm up, drink hot chocolate and, for some, sip at what was left of 'Will's famous moonshine.' Kate could remember a time when Ellen would not allow the moonshine in her house. If Will had wanted a drink, he had to slip out to the barn to do it.

That was a long time ago, but it still startled her a bit to see her mother lift the jug from the pantry and bring it to the table with a smile on her face instead of a scowl. She handed the jug to Harley.

"Ah, my lovely Mrs. Hughes," he said. "You certainly know how to bring a smile to my face. I thank you with all of my heart." He raised the jug, about to make one of his long toasts, when Ellen uncharacteristically interrupted him.

"I have all your heart, Mr. Benton? Shouldn't you save some piece of heart for Miss Verna?" she said, a sly smile tweaking her lips.

That stopped his words, and they all watched Harley work to find his tongue again. His lips puckered, then opened. Nothing came out.

Verna helped by grabbing the jug from him. Unruffled by Ellen's teasing, she said gruffly, "You can keep your heart to yourself, Harley, 'cause I've got one of my own, but you're gonna darn well share the moonshine! To Ellen Hughes and

Will's moonshine," she said, and without added ceremony, she took a long swig and passed it on to Jack, who with a devilish grin deliberately bypassed Harley and handed it to Willie who passed it to Mel.

Harley stood empty handed and looked forlornly at the jug as it went around the room. When it finally stopped at Mel, Harley puffed his chest out and reached for the jug.

"None of you know how to make a proper toast."

But before he could begin, Kate said "What about the rest of us? There are other adults in this room!"

Harley ran his hand through the mass of curls on his head. They were all in cahoots to keep him from a sip of the jug.

"My apologies, Miss Kate. I have seen you sip like a sailor from this jug, and you are certainly part of this celebration." He went to the cabinet, retrieved several small glasses for the ladies in the room and was about to pour small amounts in each when Ellen stopped him. He turned to her, looked her squarely in the face, bewildered.

"Are you trying to keep me from a drink, Miss Ellen?"

She shook her head and laughed with the others. "Would I deny you anything, Harley? Never. I just remembered the blackberry cordial I made from some of Will's moonshine and thought the ladies might enjoy that more."

She brought the jar to him, and he poured a little in their glasses. Then he raised the jug. He looked around the room at everyone, drawing out his time in the limelight, making sure each person was appropriately attentive.

"Here's to all the generations in this room, from our youngest – Copper Top Jeannie – to our oldest – me," he said, puffing out his chest again and pausing for effect. They waited, knowing Harley was long from finished.

"Don't you want to get up on the chair for this, Harley?" Willie teased. Harley had climbed on a chair long ago when he was desperate to be heard. Laughter erupted from those who had been there and remembered Harley on the chair bellowing, "Look at me, damn it!" with a grin on his face and his eyes sparkling.

"Let him finish – please," Mel groaned, "or we'll never get this done."

Harley cleared his throat, loudly and intentionally, regaining his position at the center of attention, and then he completed it by taking Willie's advice. He pulled a chair out, stood on it, and raised the jug again.

"I was toasting to the generations represented here," he repeated. "We have mothers, fathers, grandmothers, and children. We have a man in the milling business, a farmer, a lawyer turned lumberjack, a laundress, a school teacher, a most excellent barmaid, and me – a hobo. We are an entire world here in this room. But I toast not to what you do, but who you are under your skin, as Miss Kat and I have been talking about lately." He nodded his bushy head at Kat. "I credit her for this eloquent toast because it was she who brought the idea to me."

"I'm getting thirsty, Harley. Are you about done?" Jack asked, leaning back against the wall. He was settling in for a long wait.

"I toast to the beauty under your skin, every one of you. And" he quickly added before he could be interrupted again, "to the angel in you and around you." He finally raised the jug to his lips, drank and passed it to Mel. The ladies raised their glasses and sipped in agreement with the toast, and the jug made the rounds of the men.

"Thank God, I thought I was going to die of thirst," Willie said, loud enough to tease Harley. "I'm gonna change your name to Windy."

"Pass it on, Windy," Verna said to Harley. "I'm getting parched again."

"My name is Pretty Eyes. Miss Kate named me years ago, and she was exactly right." Ruthie, Ellen and Kate all had something to add because they had been there and remembered the laughter filling the room the first time Kate had seen Harley. He was grubby after jumping from a train and spending many days without a bath. The only nice thing she could think to say after they'd been introduced and he had complimented her beauty so profusely was, "And you, Mr. Benton, have . . . pretty eyes."

Harley had grinned, said, "I do, don't I?" and looked at each person one by one to show off his pretty eyes. He had them holding their stomachs in laughter at the incongruity of anything pretty on that ragamuffin man.

They told the story to the rest, and soon they were laughing much the same as on that day. Other tales were told, and the room was warm in Christmas spirit.

Kate said, "We need to go, Pretty Eyes. It's a long ride home."

They gathered the girls and said their goodbyes. Mel asked if he could ride out on Christmas Eve for awhile, and Kate agreed with the girls that they would enjoy his company. She had planned on a quiet day with the girls and Harley but Mel was family.

The ride home was serene. The girls, snuggled deep in their blankets, were asleep before they started off. A light snow was falling, and moonlight threw diamonds on the narrow road ahead. The buggy crunched its way up the long drive, into the clearing and stopped. They carried two sleeping children into the cabin. Poochie followed quietly, understanding the night peace. Rachel and Kat awakened enough to follow on their own steam and stumbled to their beds.

Harley rekindled the hearth fire, where Bug waited patiently on his rug, and they were soon warmed. He and Kate sat for a little while in front of the hearth and watched the flames, comfortable in the silence of the room.

"I'm a bit tired, Harley. Do you think we can finish the presents tomorrow night?"

"We'll just have to, won't we?" he said, patting her hand.

Kate nodded sleepily. The long day, the night chill, and the cordial all came together to make her feel pleasantly fatigued.

"I appreciated your toast tonight, Harley. It was multifaceted, and don't think for a moment that I didn't get what angels you were talking about. When did Kat ask you about this 'under the skin' thing? I know where she got it from – me."

"She mentioned it a couple of days after I moved out here."

"Was she concerned or scared?"

"Kat? No, she just wanted a second opinion," he said smiling. "You know her. She has a scientific mind and wants just the facts. She can't see under her skin, so it doesn't exist for her. I merely explained that while science and evidence are fine things, much that matters most can't be seen or even explained, like happiness, for instance. We can't see it or touch it, but we know it exists. We feel it. She thought about it for a few days and came back to me, said she agreed with me, and that I was telling the truth."

Harley laughed a little. "It's odd. I felt privileged by her acknowledgement."

"Yes, Kat has a way of keeping you on your honest toes, doesn't she? I'll see you in the morning, Pretty Eyes."

"Good night, Kate."

Harley stayed up late working on the projects, happy to be doing something for her and his adopted family. He put on the final coats of paint and waited for it to dry before covering them with the burlap. When he fell into bed towards morning, sleep came instantly, but it always did for Harley.

The days before Christmas flew by in a flurry of activity. They were to have their Christmas dinner and presents on its eve and would go to Ellen's house for dinner on Christmas day. The girls were so excited they couldn't concentrate on school work, so Harley declared a holiday until after the festivities.

He, Kate and the girls went into the woods for a tree, and while Kate was tweaked by memories, happiness trickled in when she wasn't paying attention. The day was winter warm so they didn't freeze completely, and the sky was clear and sunny. Snow covered the pine trees, and the forest was magical. Kate was at home in it. She cherished the mystical serenity of the woods and its creatures; the squirrels, raccoons, deer and other critters that remained in the north and braved the winter with her.

They cut and hauled a tree out of the woods, and were decorating it when Jack knocked. He came in with a hearty stomp of snowy boots and hugs for everyone -- even Harley. He helped string popcorn and cranberries, hung mistletoe, and dragged each of the girls and Kate under it for a kiss. Kate pulled Harley under it, too, and planted a kiss on his cheek which he promptly returned. When Jack left for the evening, they repeated the kissing process . . . just to get it right.

They were finally ready for the big day. Kate had a pot roast in the oven, with potatoes and carrots from the cellar, and pumpkin pies cooled on the counter. The table was set with the best tablecloth, and decorated with pine boughs and candles in the center.

Harley had found a holly bush and arranged its branches on the hearth shelf. In the center was a small nativity he had carved from pine. It was only the baby Jesus and Mary as yet, but more would be added over the years – "when I'm not being worked to death and have more time."

He complained with a huge grin so there would be no misinterpretation of his jest. He had never been happier and never considered teaching the girls a job. To Harley, a job was something you did only when it didn't interfere with pleasant pastimes.

The presents had been wrapped and lay under the tree, periodically drawing Jeannie and Rebecca to touch them in awe. The cabin looked, smelled and felt like Christmas when Mel knocked on the door. He came in with a flurry of snow and arms full of more wrapped presents.

Bug stood on his hind legs to put his nose on Mel's cheek, saying 'Are you friend or foe behind all this stuff.' He moved his wet nose long enough to share love and Bug slobber then satisfied, went back to his rug. Guarding this family was hard work.

"Thanks, Bug. I needed that," Mel said with good humor.

Jeannie circled Mel's legs, jumping up and down.

"Are you after me or the presents?"

She held out her arms to take the packages from him.

"You're an honest rascal, aren't you?" he teased.

But after she helped him put them under the tree, she climbed into his arms for a hug.

"I like presents," she whispered in his ear, and then quickly added, "but I like you, too."

Mel hugged each of the girls and then Kate, and told her he could smell her dinner all the way from his farm.

"Sit," she said. "We'll eat in about half an hour. Harley is about to tell a Christmas story." The girls gathered around him by the hearth, and Mel held Jeannie on his lap. Kate gave the men a small glass of eggnog laced with whiskey and made one for herself. She sat at the table to listen.

They were all entranced by Harley's tale, especially the way he told it. By the end, they were all sitting spellbound, eager to hear what happened to the orphaned child in the story who had been turned away by almost everyone in town.

He described a poor mining town where the people had little to eat and were afraid if they shared what they had, they and their own children might go hungry. Their fear had made them stingy and mean. Harley embellished the boy's sorrows until their hearts were breaking for him.

"In the end, a poor, sick, old woman gave the boy some food, and a single star grew brighter in the sky, right over the old woman's house. As she continued to help the boy, the woman grew well and strong, even younger. She took him into her home and made him her son. One night the woman saw a white circle around the boy. It hovered around him, and then it drifted into the sky toward the bright star." Harley paused, sipped his drink, looked around at his wide-eyed audience, and continued.

"The boy was happy to find a home, but every day he tried to make a star get bright over another family's house, to help them, too. One by one, he would ask for food at their doors, and those who gave him a morsel, made stars grow brighter over their houses, and they were happier.

He continued asking for kindness. In fact, even to this day he asks in order to help those who are mean spirited. Some thought the boy was an angel. The woman thought he was simply a wise and kind boy. I think," Harley added, "caring and compassionate people might be angels, in a way, because they make the world a much brighter place. What do you think?" he asked the girls, whose eyes were wide with wonder at the special boy in Harley's story.

"I think he's an angel," Jeannie said with certainty.

"Maybe," Rebecca said, not sure about a boy angel.

Kat, pondered before making up her mind, and asked, "Where are his wings? Angels have wings, and he'd have to have a halo, too. Maybe under his skin . . . I'll have to think about it."

"I think," Kate said, "that dinner is ready, and we should eat and then open presents."

Everyone was in agreement about that. It was a quick meal because the girls' eyes were on the brightly wrapped presents under the tree. Kate had lots of help with the clean up, and they moved to the gifts.

Rachel and Becca carefully removed and neatly folded the wrapping paper from their presents before examining their gifts. Kat and Jeannie ripped the paper off theirs, not willing to waste time trying to keep it in one piece. They were in awe and immediately wanted to use them, to take the tables to their rooms, to find the doll who would use the cradle, to take the trap into the woods.

"My turn," Mel said before they could run off and handed Jeannie a large package. She tore off the paper and found a red-haired doll wrapped in two receiving blankets. Under the doll lay two nightgowns carefully stitched by Mel's mother.

"It's me!" Jeannie squealed. "Mel, she looks like me. Thank you. I love her!

"So do I, Copper Top, and you are welcome."

Rebecca was next. Her present surprised them all. It was a tractor, complete with a wagon, a barn, and two cows. She immediately set it up and busily rearranged her farm.

"I wouldn't have guessed Becca would enjoy playing with a farm." Kate told him. "I wouldn't have dreamed it."

"I'm just trying to lure you all to mine," he teased. "I thought I'd start with Rebecca."

Kate smiled and reminded Rebecca to thank Mel, which she briefly did and went quickly back to her farm.

Mel gave Kat a book on Michigan insects and woodland creatures – complete with pictures for identification of all the species. Kat flipped through the pages quickly, and ran to hug Mel. "I will use this," she said. "Thank you."

"I know you will, and I expect you will teach me a thing or two."

Kat nodded seriously and sat to look at her book.

Rachel's gift was a brush, comb and hand mirror, all with lilac colored handles inlaid with pearl. Nestled in the package with the rest was a pearl hair comb that would look magnificent in Rachel's dark hair.

Kate looked at Mel, a mixture of curiosity and respect on her face.

"How did you manage to choose such perfect gifts for the girls?" she asked. "Look at them. They love what you gave them."

"I hope that goes for the last of the Ramey girls," he said and handed a package to Kate and one to Harley. Harley's held a small carving knife with a fine blade for making intricate designs in wood. It had a sheath to keep it protected when it wasn't being used. Harley beamed and thanked Mel for his thoughtful present. "Like Kat said, I will use this. Thank you."

Inside Kate's package was a small box, and inside that was a gold locket. It was attached to a long piece of black velvet ribbon. She sat looking at it. It was beautiful, and she wanted badly to put it around her neck, but it was expensive. Was it a commitment she couldn't make? She stared at it in her palm.

Mel watched her, wanting to see her eyes shine, her face to light with happiness.

"It opens, Kate, so you can put things in it, things you love, like pictures of the girls." She still hesitated, and his heart was sinking into his stomach. "That's why it's a heart. That's all. I hope you like it, that you'll wear it."

Kate held it up by the ribbon. The heart glistened in the fire light. Harley got up to look at it, and then took the locket from her. He walked behind Kate, put it around her neck, and tied it at the back. He went to stand in front of her, leaned in and looked her in the eyes.

"Say thank you, Kate," he whispered, as if she were a child who had forgotten – much like she had said to Rebecca.

Kate gently fingered the locket where it rested above the gentle rise of her breast and looked at Harley for a few moments and then said, "Thank you, Mel. It's truly beautiful."

She heard a small explosion of breath escape his chest, like he'd been holding it. Relief was written on his face and when Kate saw his eyes, it touched her. She stood to get the gift she had made for him. It felt insignificant compared to the gifts he had given.

Inside the package was a deep blue, knitted scarf and hat. She'd been careful to choose small needles so the stitches were tightly woven and he would be warm when he wore them in the winter cold as he worked outside. She told him what she'd been thinking while she made them.

"I wouldn't wear these to work in, Kate. They're too beautiful, too fine. I'll save them for special times, like when I come here. I love them. Thank you."

Harley had an identical set, but in deep red. He immediately put them on and pranced in front of the girls, demanding they look at him in his new hat and scarf. They looked briefly, nodded their approval, then their attention zipped back to their own gifts until Harley shouted and stomped his foot.

"Hey, I said look at me. Don't I look grand...?" He danced around the room, preening and modeling his gift. Harley's hat had a ball on top. It bobbled when he nodded his head, and he looked like an elf with a Santa belly. His round button nose matched the hat.

Before Mel left, he hugged the girls, shook Harley's hand, then hugged him warmly. Kate walked him to the door, thanking him again for the wonderful presents, and Mel waved her words away.

After a moment, Kate said, "Mel, I'm sorry if I seemed unappreciative of the locket. It's just that it must have cost a lot, and . . . well . . ."

He stopped her with a kiss on the cheek. Kate was shocked, and then saw the girls all pointing over her head and laughing.

"Mistletoe," he said, looking at the decoration and laughing with them at Kate's surprise. He said goodnight and went out into the snow.

Chapter Six

1912

The winter was kind. Snow fell frequently, but not the way old folks talked about Michigan snow storms, the kind that barricaded you in the house for days, the ones that made you peer through frost glazed windows and stare at swirling snow with something close to fear. Authentic northern Michigan winters piled snow a foot higher with each of Mother Nature's north wind furies, and window panes were caked with ice. Those were real winters and made her feel trapped, insignificant, at the mercy of a force she couldn't control. During the winter of 1912, those days were few, and Kate felt blessed.

When spring came, it effortlessly eased into warmth without threatening to flood the Hersey and Muskegon rivers and without the usual spring storms with snapped trees and roaring wind.

Robins returned and rejoiced, letting everyone know spring was officially here. Kate and Jeannie watched them building nests, carrying sprigs of straw they found scattered near the horse shed to the trees at the edge of the clearing. Later, they all listened for the sounds of baby birds to come from the nests. They were rewarded when tiny, demanding chirps filled the air and beaks opened wide above the sides of the nests when the adults returned with food.

"I think they're hungry," Jeannie said. "Can't we help feed them?"

"No, we can't interfere, Jeannie. Their mommas and daddies are taking good care of them. Besides, do you want to chew up worms?"

Jeannie's face said yucky, but she still thought the baby birds might be too hungry without her help.

Two beavers built a dam in the creek by the cabin, preparing a home for their offspring. Kat was interested in the construction of their dwelling and often hid quietly nearby to watch how it changed from one day to the next. Harley sat with her and told her what they would do next.

"How do you know?" Kat had asked.

"If you take note of nature," he'd said, "you'll understand how we all work – birds, beavers, even people."

She looked up beavers in her book, and then compared what the book said to what she saw with her own eyes. It was close, but she believed her eyes more and waited to see if what Harley told her would happen actually occurred. It always did.

Deer came to drink at the creek each morning and had grown used to seeing Kate at her wash tubs. They chose to ignore her and grazed at the edge of the clearing where the wild grass grew and was plentiful.

She was glad to be working outside again. Mornings were still chilly, but when the sun cleared the tree tops, it quickly warmed the air. By the time she was ready to hang the clothes she'd taken off her sweater and felt its rays massaging the muscles in her neck and arms like warm fingers. Bug lay nearby in the sun and alternately watched Kate, the deer and whatever creature scampered into the clearing.

Trilliums laced the forest floor, trout lilies were close to blossoming, their buds snug under the cover of their own thick, protective leaves, and tiger lilies sought light near the edge of the clearing waiting for the perfect warmth before opening their flowers. Kate loved Michigan springs. The sights and sounds called to her, and she eagerly watched for each new sign spring had come for good.

She longed to toss the wash into the tubs, abandon it and run through the woods, climb trees and spy on the lumberjacks like she had as a girl. Or lie on her back on a mossy bed under a huge oak tree and find faces in the shadows of the leaves.

Harley had helped Kat set her new insect trap the day before, and they headed to the woods to check on it with Jeannie in tow. They came back a short time later with an obviously ill, tiny field mouse. Jeannie had tears in her eyes, and Harley was telling her the mouse would be fine in a few days.

"We could take it to the doctor," she told Harley. "Can't we, Momma?" she begged as they neared Kate.

"No, but maybe we could make a little house where he could stay while he gets better," Kate told her. "Would that be alright?"

They took Kate's sewing supplies out of an old hat box she used to store buttons, needles and thread, lined it with a clean rag, and punched some holes in the top to let the air in. Jeannie carefully placed the baby mouse in and watched as it lay still in the center of the box floor. "Will it be okay?" she asked.

"We won't know until later, sweetie."

"How will it eat?" she asked.

"We'll have to feed it," Harley said. "Let's look in Kat's book to see what they like. Then we'll grind it up with some water and give it to him in an eyedropper."

Kate watched them go, hoping the little mouse survived, and Jeannie's heart wouldn't be broken, but she thought she knew better. They crushed some grain between two spoons, added water until it was gruel-like, and managed to get a couple of drops into the mouse. In a few days, it was moving around in the hatbox and then standing up with its front feet on the side of the box waiting for food. It was soon crawling around on Jeannie's arm and snuggling in the crook of her neck.

Not too long after, she dragged home two young birds that had been tossed to the ground in a spring thunder storm. They were young enough their down had not yet turned to feathers, but not so young they didn't know how to open their beaks wide when they were hungry and Jeannie came near. She was kept busy trying to make sure she had food prepared for them and the mouse.

Harley made a small cage out of screen and thick wire for the birds, and they put in a nest they'd found on the ground near where she'd found the birds. They were content to be back in their nest and flourished.

"You're going to have to let me know in advance," he teased, "if you're going to bring any more critters home, or should I just start making more cages now?"

"Are they going to fly?" she asked.

"You're going to have to teach them," he told her, "because you're their momma now."

"But, I don't know how to fly," she said tilting her freckled face, concern written all over it. Harley grinned at her troubled look and ruffled her copper curls.

"When the time comes, you'll figure how to teach them even if you don't know how to fly, and I'll help if you need it, okay?"

Jeannie nodded and went to talk to her birds. Kat was sitting by the cage with a tablet of paper on her lap. Every now and then, she'd stop watching and write on her tablet. She wished she could tell the two birds apart. How could she study them without knowing? When she went to Harley with her problem, he suggested they tie a small piece of yarn to one's leg and assured Jeannie it wouldn't hurt them. They'd take it off when it was ready to fly. Kat and Jeannie spent hours with them; Jeannie feeding and petting; Kat watching and writing. They were a team.

Spring moved on. Kate was content; the girls were blossoming under Harley's tutelage, and he was happy, too. Kate worried she was keeping him cloistered in the forest, but when she brought it up, he grinned and told her he was exactly where he wanted to be and doing what he wanted to do. Periodically, when Kate was home all day, he'd take the buggy into town and be back at the cabin before evening fell. She was glad he went. It gave him a break from the girls, even though he claimed not to need it, and he was happy to be back with them when he returned.

Toward the end of May, Kate told them she would be a bit late coming home from the camp. She wanted to check to see if the mushrooms were up. She knew a spot near the river where she picked baskets full of the tasty morsels each year.

"We'll all go tomorrow if they're ready," she said, looking forward to the taste of Michigan morels. "My mouth is watering already!" she said with a slurp and a grin.

It was early afternoon when she finished the ironing, packed the clothes, and headed for the camp. Jack was waiting for her when she arrived, and helped unload the packages and collect her money. Bug jumped down and ran around, sniffed each man, stood to Bug slobber a couple he liked better than the others, or perhaps they tasted better, and then moved off to see what critters were in the area. She bantered with the men, gently cuffed one of the Thompsons, as she usually did, and scolded them for getting their clothes so dirty. It was comfortable, even enjoyable, but a small part of her was alert, tense, as it had been since the unwelcome visitor had come to the cabin.

She scanned the area, as she always did now, to see if the man was nearby, but since she had refused to do his laundry, he had no need to be at the cook tent and was most likely in the woods somewhere, chopping down trees. Kate's hair prickled at the back of her neck, and it made her angry she felt fear because of him.

This was her woods, damn it! she thought to herself as she walked back to the buggy to leave the camp. She waved goodbye to Jack when she headed her buggy down the narrow lane through the woods and heard him say he'd be by later, after the day's work.

Kate enjoyed the way the sun filtered through the leaves in the woods. The air was warm, and she relaxed against the seat back, letting the mare move at her own pace. Kitty knew the way, and Kate could let her mind wander while she searched the undergrowth for signs of the tender spring morels and elephant ears. She spotted an area where tall oaks spread their limbs and gave the perfect amount of shade for mushroom growth, pulled the mare to the side of the path, tied the reins to a near tree and walked off to search for the tasty treats. Bug jumped down and followed, sniffing the ground, helping her look.

She found several near the path and left them to go a little further into the woods. She was on her hands and knees, wishing she had her trousers on while she crawled through the underbrush, when she heard Bug growl and felt someone behind her.

"I been looking for you girl. We got some business."

Kate turned and saw him standing there with a sinister smile on his face and an axe handle in his hand.

It happened so fast, it was a blur. He moved towards Kate, and she saw Bug leap through the air and sink his teeth into the man's arm before he could react. She jumped to her feet, brush clawing at her hair and clothes, quickly looking for something to hit him with, but couldn't find a limb heavy enough. She heard him howl as Bug's teeth bit further into his arm, and then he flung the dog to the ground. Kate raced to the buggy to get the bat Jack had given her. It took forever to get there even though the buggy was close by. Her breath was ragged with rage and fear.

She got back in time to see Bug flung to the ground again. Before the dog could rise, the man swung the axe handle hard across Bug's head. Kate heard the blow as she ran, saw it crush his head and his body go limp.

Kate screamed her rage, raised the bat and swung it as hard as she could. It thudded against his forearm and he dropped the handle, but he caught the bat as she pulled back to strike again and pulled it from her hands. His face broke into an evil leer, and he tossed it away. Then he leaped forward and grabbed Kate by the hair. She scratched at his face, and he backhanded her, letting her fall to the ground. He bent forward and grabbed at the front of her dress, and Kate tried to kick him hard between the legs as her father had taught her to do, but only managed to connect with his thigh.

The man howled, further enraged, and fell on top of her, ripped at her clothes and tried to free her breasts from the shreds of her dress. Kate twisted and turned, trying to get him off her, but he was heavy and intent on what he wanted. He managed to bare her breasts and had his mouth over one; then he ripped her skirt up and pushed her legs apart with his knees.

Kate was screaming and thrashing, but she was no match for his brute strength. He placed his forearm across her chest just below her throat, and Kate struggled to breathe. She felt him between her legs, pushing at her, and her mind fled from what he was trying to do. Her arms flailed over the ground, frantically searching for something, anything she could use to hit him with.

Her hand closed around a rock, and for a brief moment she held it motionless, praying he would not look up, would stay attached to her breast while she lifted the rock. It came down on his head with a muted crack. He groaned and jerked up. She swung again, smashing the rock against the side of his head and felt his body go limp on top of her. She pushed at him, trying to get out from under his dead weight and finally heaved and rolled quickly, then ran. She didn't know how long he would be out, was even surprised she'd hit hard enough to knock him out.

She ran to the buggy, tears coursing down her face because she was leaving Bug, but knowing she had to run, get far away fast. She grabbed the reins where they were looped around the tree, jumped in and slapped the mare with the ends. They raced down the path as fast as the buggy could take the bumps and the curves.

Minutes later, she pulled the buggy into the woods near a creek that ran through a small clearing and was hidden from the path. She sat shaking, her mind screaming in rage. She tried to tie the reins to a branch, but her hands trembled so badly she gave up and sat down next to the creek. She sobbed and raged, damned the man to hell, cried some more, and then sat silent.

When she grew quiet, she listened carefully for long moments to hear if he had followed her, but all she heard was the forest and creek. She sat with her arms wrapped around her legs, pulled up tight to her chest, her chin on her knees. She stared at the water and saw water bugs scamper across the ripples. She cried again. Bug had gotten his name from the leggy insects – because he loved to leap out into the river to swim, and his long red hair spread out over the top of the water like the legs of a water bug. Deep sobs racked her as memory played over her years with Bug – her defender – her companion, and she curled up in a tight ball, a mindless sphere of flesh and pain.

She didn't know how long she'd been there when she heard the rustle of leaves behind her. Her heart pounded painfully, a drumbeat she was sure could be heard by whoever was coming toward her. She moved as stealthily as possible into the nearby underbrush and held her breath, hiding, waiting. Time crawled by. She felt like her chest would explode when she heard, "Kate? Are you here? Answer me, please."

Her breath rushed out in an explosion of relief. Jack heard it and rushed into the undergrowth to find her huddled behind the brush. He took in her disheveled state, the swollen, tear-streaked face, and then sat and took her in his arms. He held her for a long time silently, waiting for her to speak. When Kate moved to get up, Jack took off his shirt and wrapped it around her. Then he went to the creek and dampened his handkerchief. He wiped her face, smoothed her hair with a comb from his pocket, and retied it in the back. She tried to fix the front of her dress, but it was shredded and the buttons were gone.

"Who did this to you, Kate?" he finally said.

"That filthy man," she hissed, grief and rage alternately vying for dominance in her heart and mind.

"What man?"

"That man at the camp ... the one who looked at Rachel. The one who came to the cabin."

"Son of a bitch!" Jack growled. His voice was a harsh whisper and contained more venom than any loud expletive could convey. "He came to the cabin? Why didn't you tell me?"

"Harley came to stay. I thought we'd be safe."

"Where's Bug?"

"Dead ... protecting me," she said in a voice too lifeless, too devoid of emotion. "I need to go to him."

Jack paused, trying to think clearly, to understand it all, but his fists clenched into tight balls. That filth would pay for what he had done to Kate and Bug. He would see to it.

"You tell me where Bug is, and I will get him after I take you home."

"No. I'm going."

He looked at Kate, searched her eyes. Her spine was stiff, her eyes blank and dry. He didn't want to leave her while he went to find Bug, but didn't want to take her back there again either. He didn't know what to do. He finally tied his horse to the back of the buggy, helped Kate in, and took the reins. The man was gone when they got there.

They wrapped Bug in a blanket from the rumble seat and laid him in the back. Kate was still dry eyed, her tears stuffed deep and dry inside her chest.

"Are you . . . okay?" he asked carefully. Kate nodded.

"We need to get you home, Kate. Are you ready?"

She nodded again, climbed up the step of the buggy and sat erect, brittle, her movements stiff and mechanical.

When they got to the clearing, the girls were outside with Harley doing their schoolwork. Jack told Kate to go on in the cabin, and he walked over to where they worked on a blanket near the woods. He sat with them for a while, keeping them there while Kate changed and tried to compose herself.

"Where is Bug?" Kat asked, looking around for the red dog that was always by her mother's side.

Jack took a deep breath. They hadn't talked about what to tell the girls. He looked at Harley, at a loss for words and shook his head. Jack's face said it all, and Harley knew Bug was not coming home.

"You girls know that Bug is a very old dog, don't you?" Harley said. When they agreed it was true, he explained Bug was most likely with their pa in heaven, and with their grandpa. "Is that right, Jack?"

Jack nodded, wiping a hand over his grim face.

"Are we going to have a funeral?" Kat asked, her eyes filling with tears.

"Of course we are," Harley said. "Bug deserves the best funeral anyone ever had."

When he could keep them outside no longer, Jack went in too, hoping Kate would be ready to face them. She was composed, even had a ghost of a smile and hugs for her daughters. She explained she was sad because her friend, Bug, had died. They needed to hear it from her and to know she was alright, just sad. Jack stayed until late, watching Kate pull on some incomprehensible well of inner strength to get her through the rest of the day. She fixed supper, set the table, and pretended to eat by pushing her food around on the plate. Jack stayed to eat with them, then hugged Kate and left.

He tied his horse to a tree near the path to the camp and crept quietly through the darkness toward the river. He skirted the camp, intending to wait where he could watch the man's tent until he came out, but as he silently neared the river's edge, he came upon him squatting near the water, alone.

He and the man went for a long walk, well into the woods and away from others. Then Jack went home. A grim look was on his face; it would take a long time until he felt good, but he was satisfied.

Kate went to bed and laid awake, feeling Bug at her feet. She couldn't cry anymore; the pain was too deep for tears to wash away, too harsh for the healing kind of sorrow. She got up to sit outside in the moonlight. Harley joined her, and they sat silently, watching the moon slide across the sky.

The next day, they dug a grave for Bug at the edge of the woods near the place where the raccoons played so he could hear them scamper and romp. Harley lifted Bug from the back of the buggy, and Kate quickly made sure the blanket covered his wound. She didn't want the girls to see his injury, but Harley saw and raised his eyes to Kate, a question on his face she did not answer. They put him in the wooden box Harley had spent the morning building and laid him in the ground. Kate tried to read from the Bible, and when she faltered, Harley took over.

When they were done, they sat on a blanket near Bug's grave and talked. Kate reminded the girls how funny Bug was, like when he stood on his hind legs and gave people the 'Bug slobber' when they came too near the people he loved.

Jeannie held Poochie tight against her, afraid to let go of him, and said "Yeah, remember when he bit Poochie for chasing chipmunks?"

"Yup," Kate said, trying for lightness. "He had to teach this youngster a lesson. He knew he was the boss. He was older and wiser."

It helped the girls to talk about him, to share the grief, but Kate wanted to sleep the pain away, to wake up and have the world right again. But it never happens. Life isn't a fairytale. You move forward . . . one foot at a time. Because you must.

Harley went into the cabin and came out with lemonade for the girls and two small glasses of cordial for him and Kate. Then he made a toast to Bug.

"Let this toast be for Water Bug, who shared his life with us and made our lives richer. He lives on in all of us because he gave so completely and unselfishly. Bug, who was an amazing dog, will surely be with us forever. Look around you, and someday you will find him." He raised his glass to touch Kate's, but she stopped him, her hand raised.

"He doesn't like that," she said.

"What?" Harley questioned.

"Dog," she whispered. "He never liked to be called a dog."

"I'm sorry," Harley said. "Let me rephrase. Bug was amazing and will surely be with us forever." Then they toasted to Bug.

Later, when the girls were occupied with their schoolwork, Kate went into the woods to be alone. She looked for a long branch, one she could use to beat against a tree, one strong enough to withstand the anger boiling in her. She had beaten a tree in anger and pain when her father had died. She had done so for Mark. She would do it again for Bug and for herself, for something inside of her the man had damaged. Had killed.

She found a stout one and carried it further into the woods. When she reached an old scarred oak tree, she sat, leaned against it and looked around, remembering. She didn't see him watching, hadn't know she'd been followed. He crouched in a thick growth of brambles, hiding, far enough away that she couldn't spot him. But his sharp sight still allowed him to watch her.

He was large and thin to the point of gaunt. His fur was mangy and matted. One eye was blue and the other was brown and dotted with yellow flecks. His pointed ears perked to listen as he watched her. The wolf part of him made him wary, stealthy in the forest, and gave his voice a timbre that kept would-be predators away. Part of him wasn't wolf, and the puppy in him wanted to go sit by her.

Kate finally got up, took a deep, choked breath, and smacked her branch against the oak tree. The tip broke off, and she whacked at the tree again, harder, then harder. She swore. Then she swore again, and then again and again. Tears streamed down her face, and she raged loudly against everything and everyone, against the world and Mark and God.

She heard his mournful howl and momentarily stopped, but then continued. When she yelled again, he howled. She raged, and he responded. She soon came to unconsciously expect the howl. It suited her grief.

When there was nothing but the stubble of a branch in her hands, she stopped, stared at it, and thought of the other two she still had in a small box under her bed. She'd keep this one, too. It would have to hold her pain, because she couldn't. She sat again, drained; her rage spent, and she looked around. Only then did it occur to her to wonder about the voice that had joined hers while she'd been beating the tree. It had been a part of her grief, had made her mourning whole.

He had moved closer, but was still a distance away. And then she saw him, a huge but scrawny animal sitting there watching her.

"You don't look any better than I feel," she said to him.

He stared, rigidly still.

"Are you just going to sit there and look at me?"

He didn't answer.

"Well, I'm going home. Thanks for your help."

When Kate started back to the clearing, he followed at a distance, his eyes on her, his nose sniffing the air. She turned to look back every now and then and didn't see him. She felt him, though, and it didn't occur to her to be afraid.

In the clearing, she turned to look one last time and spotted him a few feet into the woods. He stood tall, ears perked, watching. Kate went into the house and brought out food and water. She left it at the edge of the woods and went into the cabin. She fixed a quick supper, with Harley's help, and they ate quietly.

"Do you feel better now, Ma?" Rebecca asked, her eyes wide and hopeful.

"I do, Sweetie. Did Harley tell you I would be better when I got back?"

She nodded. "He said if you hit a tree, it makes you feel good."

Kate gave her a smile and told her it did. "Well, something like that. So, when you are sad or angry, you should try it, Rebecca. It works, sort of."

"Doesn't it make the tree sad?" Jeannie asked.

Kat told her trees didn't get sad. "That's silly."

"Are you sure about that, Kat?" Harley asked, smiling at her and trying to divert attention and get them thinking about something other than their mother's hurt eyes.

"Well, no, but I've never heard one cry," she told him.

"Sometimes you don't always hear when people cry. They do it inside – under the skin," he teased. "Maybe trees are like that."

Kat stared at him, trying to figure out if he was teasing or serious. Then she saw his eyes crinkle, and poked him in the stomach.

"Okay, you got me. And trees don't have skin or they'd be sunburned being outside all day. That's why they have bark instead." But she still wasn't sure about the trees having feelings. They were alive.

Kate was glad the attention was off her, even if briefly, and then she remembered the animal that had followed her in the woods and told them about it. They listened eagerly, half excited and half fearful a wolf might be near.

"Is he still out there?" Kat asked. "I want to see him."

"I don't know. I gave him some food and water because he looked like he was starving, but I don't know if he ate it or if he just went back into the woods. We'll have a look after supper."

They cleaned up quickly so they could check the animal's food and water bowls and found them both empty. They refilled them, hoping he would come back, but Kate didn't see him again until later, after the girls were asleep.

Kate and Harley sat outside, rocked quietly and watched night creatures flit through the air and scamper over the ground. A crescent moon gave enough light to form shadows in the clearing. Young resident raccoons played at being stealthy hunters near Bug's grave and a hitch caught in Kate's chest, blocking breath. She swallowed and struggled with the anger that threatened to overcome the evening peace.

An opossum bumbled out of the woods at the other side and began digging at the ground with its sharp claws, his nose pushing at the loose dirt, hoping for grubs to be tumbled from the soil. Bats darted from tree to tree, sure of their paths through the forest dark, seeing in ways no human could know. After a long while, Harley broke the silence. "Are you gonna talk about what happened?"

Kate thought for a while, and then shook her head.

Harley nodded, not pushing. "If you ever do, I'm here," he said. "But just answer one thing. Are you . . . okay?"

"Yes, as good as I can be without Bug. I loved him," she said.

They both saw him at the same time standing just inside the clearing. His full voice filled the air with a long, mournful howl.

"He seems to have followed you home," Harley said.

Chapter Seven

Spring and summer, 1912

Kate hauled the laundry out from where it had been left in the buggy. She was a day late getting it done, but she didn't care. She couldn't ... no, she wouldn't allow herself to feel anything right now because pain would seep in around the crevices of thought and she'd crumble. She put one foot in front of the other and mechanically moved through the morning doing what had to be done. She was stiff and aching, both inside and out, and trying not to continually look over her shoulder for Bug.

"Get a grip, Kate," she berated herself. "He's gone. He was old. You had to lose him sometime."

She rekindled still glowing coals in the fire pit, put a kettle over the fire and filled it with water, set up the wash tubs, filled one with rinse water and then kicked the other . . . hard.

"Damn, damn, damn!" she bellowed, hopping around and holding onto one foot. She finally plopped down on the ground, still holding her wounded toes and then giggled.

"Kate Ramey, that was stupid," she said, looking around her and then remembered the animal that had followed her from the woods. She looked but saw no wolf-like creatures lurking nearby, and it occurred that she was losing it -- her mind. "Were you real?" she asked him.

She got back to work and was rubbing the whites vigorously over the washboard, when he appeared. She continued her work, every now and then glancing up to see if he was still there. At one moment, he'd be near the bowls of food and water, and in the next, she'd see him at the other edge of the woods. Like an apparition, he materialized here and there without seeming to make an effort. He was there one instant and not there the next.

She tried to ignore his presence, but once in a while she'd talk to him. "You're going to get scrawnier if you keep running around like that," she told him. But he didn't respond. "Maybe you can't speak wolf, Kate," she said to herself. "You speak horse and dog, damn well, too, but maybe not wolf."

She was putting the trousers into the wash when Jack rode in.

"Hey," he said as he slid off his mare. Then he rolled up his sleeves and plunged his hands into the water. They worked quietly for a few minutes and were ready to hang them on the line when he finally spoke.

"You don't need to worry about him anymore. He won't be back to bother you."

Kate stopped, immobile, her hand clutching the pants she was about to attach to the line. She was frozen in place like the ice crawling up her spine.

"How can you know that?" she said. "How can we ever know what people will do?"

The deadness in her voice scared him. Kate had been badly shattered, he knew, and her empty voice spoke the horror. He turned to her and took her shoulders in his hands. His face was hard, his deep brown eyes black in the shadows.

"I just know, Kate. That's all I can say, and you have to believe it."

She looked at him for long moments, searching his face for validation of his words, and she saw it, the truth, and the certainty. Her eyes watered in relief, but she swallowed and stood tall, like she'd been pulled up by the string her mother always talked about when she was a girl. The string that was attached to her head making her stand tall and straight. Then it was to learn posture; today it was for strength and power.

She nodded and didn't ask any more questions. Kate trusted Jack, knew his compassion and his power. If he said she was safe from that perverted monster, then she was safe. It was done. She would never have to see him again. He was gone. Her breath came easier and her shoulders settled back, unwinding from the fight they had been posed for.

She turned and raised her eyes to the sky, breathing deep, seeing her surroundings with clearer eyes, and saw the wolf-dog had moved into the clearing. He was crouched low and inching toward them. His ears were laid back and a low growl came from his throat. Jack saw the animal at the same time.

"What the hell?" Jack gasped, stepping back, and then in a burst of fear, he ran to his mare for the revolver he always carried.

"No!" Kate screamed when she saw the gun. "It's Wolf." She wasn't sure what his intentions were, but she knew he was hers and she would protect him. She walked slowly and cautiously toward the animal, her hand held out in supplication and talked.

"You must not growl," she told him. "Shh, it's just Jack. He's a friend," she murmured softly over and over, her voice like velvet, sliding over the animal and begging him to live, to not force Jack's gun.

For a long while, Kate talked and soothed and watched. Eventually and amazingly, he quit growling and sat back on his haunches. His ears tipped forward and his eyes flickered back and forth between them. Kate knelt down a distance from him and continued her slow patter. He cocked his head, still listening and watching. Then he stood, circled Kate where she kneeled, watched Jack who kept the gun in his hand and aimed at the animal. He couldn't decide what to do. If the creature was going to attack Kate, surely, he would have done so by now, but he didn't trust that it wouldn't.

After three slow circles around her, Wolf sat down between Jack and Kate who was still wooing him in a musical cadence, a vocal waltz for lovers and wolves. He must have liked it because he lay down, put his head on his front paws and rolled one brown eye.

Jack could see the eye roll from where he was standing and he chuckled. He wasn't going to mention it, but it was exactly what Bug used to do.

"So much for the fearsome wolf." He put his gun back in the saddle bag and walked slowly near them. "Where did you find this?" he asked, pointing to the critter.

"In the woods. He howled with me and then followed me home."

"Hmmm . . . you know he's part wolf, don't you?"

Kate nodded. "That's his name – Wolf."

Jack walked closer and knelt about ten feet from the animal, his hand outstretched. "Come on and sniff me, big boy. I'm not Kate's enemy."

Wolf looked at Kate and then did as he was told. He sniffed the hand, then put his paws on Jack's shoulders and stood there, his huge head hovering over Jack's. 'I'm the boss here,' was the statement, and Jack could do nothing except agree. Then Wolf got down, walked over to Kate and sat next to her.

He stayed, slept on the hearth rug and went in the buggy with Kate during the day and camped on Kate's bed at night. He tolerated Poochie, and after a few days, he let the girls give him a bath and comb out the mats in his black and silver coat. He looked more wolf than dog, except for his eyes. One was blue, and one was brown with yellow speckles. The brown one markedly rolled when he was thinking or talking. He filled out and his muscles began to ripple in his strong legs. Wolf was home.

Kate did the ironing, packed the clothes and put them in the buggy. She told the girls and Harley she was leaving and called to Wolf. Harley came out and put a hand on her shoulder.

"Are you sure you want to go alone?" he asked, positive something had happened to Kate, not just to Bug, on the last trip to the camp. Kate told him she'd be fine, but it was a bald-faced lie. She didn't feel fine. Nerves fluttered in her stomach, and she thought she might throw up. Fear made her irritable, angry, belligerent.

"Wolf will be with me."

"So was Bug," he said firmly. Then he saw her eyes cloud, and she looked like she'd been struck. "I'm sorry, Kate. That was harsh . . . but I'm afraid for you."

Kate didn't respond. She couldn't at the moment, and silence lay heavy in the air and in both their hearts. He laid a gentle hand on Kate's arm, wanting so much to make her do as he asked. Knowing he couldn't.

"Look," he said, pleading with her. "You wanted to pick mushrooms, why don't the girls and I go with you. We can stop and gather them on the way back."

"No," she said. "We'll hunt them nearer home. Harley, I need to do this." She jutted her chin, threw back her shoulders and squinted her eyes.

He knew better than to argue with the eye squint, even applauded Kate's resolve. It wasn't what he wanted for her, though. He would have liked to make it easier, make it all go away. He wished she would talk with him, talk about what had happened and get it out where it could be dealt with. Air it and beat it like a musty rug at spring cleaning. He suspected but wasn't sure, and he kept putting his foot in his mouth because he didn't know how not to – what not to say . . . what to say.

She hopped into the buggy, called to Wolf who easily leapt onto the seat beside her like he'd been riding in buggies all his life, and they left. Jack met her on the road close to the camp, climbed in and sat next to Wolf as they drove the rest of the way to the cook tent. Wolf gave him the honor of a wet nose on his cheek, and Jack felt like he'd been accepted into the pack.

"Are we brothers now?" he asked. Wolf rolled his brown eye.

Kate's heart was in her throat and cold fingers crawled up her spine, raising the hair on the back of her neck as they pulled into the camp. She couldn't help but look around at the faces and search the woods around the cook tent for the one who tormented her in dreams. She knew he wasn't there, but she couldn't stop herself. Her muscles were tight, her back was stiff, and she thought when she moved to climb down, she might break. He could be hiding anywhere. He could be behind any of the trees, waiting for her. Then she scolded herself. Jack said he was gone – wouldn't be back. She trusted Jack. The man is gone, damn it!

Wolf leaped down and made the rounds sniffing at each man, giving them the two-colored eye stare, and then sat near Kate's feet as she sorted the packages on the table. He watched while the men paid her.

"That's some dog you got there, Kate," Tommy Thompson said. "Where's your red dog?"

Jack fixed him with a stony glare that quickly shut his mouth. "Sorry," he said, and he was but didn't know why.

"Don't call him a dog. He doesn't like it," Kate said, and Wolf stood to give Tommy a more meaningful warning. Tommy backed up, his hand in the air palm out towards Wolf like he was warding off an attack, and Jack laughed at the look on his face. Kate was in good hands.

Wolf settled back on his haunches, a satisfied wolf-smirk on his face that said, 'Pretty good, aren't I?'

"Yes, you are, Wolf."

Kate and the girls turned the soil in the garden and raked it smooth, then planted seeds and the small shoots they had grown in the house during late winter when eagerness for spring made you hold your breath in anticipation.

Growing seedlings when snow was still flying helped them all hang onto the promise of sunshine and warm air. Pickles, tomato and pepper plants were already a gangly six inches high, and they carefully placed their roots in tiny holes and patted loose dirt around them, tenderly planting hope and faith in fertile soil. Poochie helped by digging frantically in the newly turned soil and then rolling in it until Wolf nipped at him and flattened his ears. He decided to make his own garden, outside of the enclosure, and stayed happily engaged in digging there.

Their needs had outgrown the area Mel had enclosed with protective chicken wire, so they cultivated a second patch near the edge of the woods to plant the pumpkin, squash and other viny plants that spread and smothered anything in their paths. There it wouldn't matter what they crawled over.

Rebecca carried buckets of water, and Jeannie ladled enough to dampen the soil around each plant and seed mound. Kat dug the holes and Rachel planted. The sun was high and warm, and Kate mindlessly hummed a tune while she worked. She looked up to see Harley nearby working on another cage for Jeannie's wildlife collection. She felt his eyes on her before she noticed him. He was smiling.

"What are you grinning at?" she asked.

"Nothing," he said, holding his hands up in defense of an attack. "Really."

"Are you making fun of me, Harley?"

"No ma'am. Never. It's good to hear," he replied, meaning it more than Kate could know. It had taken her a while to come back to them, but she was on her way, and he'd missed her. "How about a little Ramey harmony, girls?"

"Good idea, Harley," Kate said. "How about a lullaby?" She started singing and the girls joined in – a song Kate had learned as a girl – another Ellen hadn't let her sing in the house. One she had taught to her girls . . . just because she could.

I was just thirty-five and no longer a bum.
My girl was so sweet and Lord was she fun.
She'd go out on the town and leave me behind.
But oh lucky me, I had babies to mind.
Ain't I a happy man?
Sleep, babies, sleep.

Harley laughed. "That's quite a lullaby! Where'd you learn that one?"

"At the camp."

"When you were spying?" he asked.

Kate nodded and went into the second verse while she worked. It felt good to sing again, and the mood was catching. When the song ended, Kate stretched and looked around her. It had been a while since she'd enjoyed the moment, been happy in her surroundings, and it hit Kate she'd been so entrenched in anger and fear her daughters had suffered. Harley saw the look pass over Kate's face and wondered what had changed in a quick moment in time.

"Don't ever bet big in a poker game, Kate," he remarked.

"Why? What on earth would make you say that?"

"Your face is a road map."

"What? It has lines all over it? Are you telling me I have a wrinkled face?" she said, phony anger pouting her lips.

"No. It is simply readable, like a chart or a map, silly girl."

"Hrrumpf and bah to you . . . I think it's time we had some company," she said, "before I get too old and decrepit that no one will visit. What do you think about a party?"

The girls looked up from their work, their faces eager, their eyes wide with expectation.

"A real party?" Kat asked, "With cake and everything?"

"Yes, a real one. We have worked hard and deserve it."

Harley thought it was a fine idea and they should stop what they were doing and plan it right now.

"We work first and play later," Kate reminded him.

"You've got it all confused, Kate. The real work of life is to find as many pleasures as possible, to fill all of your days with sunbeams and smiles and as many days of play as you can. When are you going to figure that out, young lady?"

Kate grinned at him and wondered how he had survived for so many years. "And who is going to plant the garden while I'm walking around smiling in the sunshine?" she asked.

"The trick is to figure out how to fit in a little work around the edges of enjoyment – just enough, mind you, to allow you to fill your belly."

"That's quite a trick, Harley." Then she stuck her shovel in the ground and raised her eyebrows at him. "I think I've got it! Here," she said, offering him the shovel. "I think the girls and I will go find some of life's pleasures while you finish the garden. Is that how it's done?"

Harley laughed out loud and got up, shaking his head at her. "I think you've got it." He went into the enclosure and took her shovel. "Go on, get out of here. I'll finish."

Kate and three of her daughters left, grinning at Harley and feeling like they were playing hooky from school. Rebecca stayed to help him because she loved gardening, and because she loved Harley. She went inside for a blanket, paper and pencils. They sat in the sunshine and planned a summer party. Rachel wanted it to be elegant, with invitations and planned games. She also thought they should invite other folks from Hersey, too, instead of just family and the friends who usually came to the cabin.

"Like who?" Kate asked, wondering where her daughter was headed. "I don't know how refined this will be, Rachel, we're not fancy, and do you have some people in mind?"

Rachel fidgeted, "Oh, you know, just people, like maybe the Tates. They're nice." A flush began to grow on Rachel's cheeks, and she looked down, embarrassed.

Kate nodded, still watching her daughter and visualizing the Tate's brood of young sons. *Damn, why do I continue to see her as a little girl? She's growing up*, she thought, and mindlessly added 'Sorry.'

They made lists of people, food and games they'd play. Wolf joined them on the blanket, and Jeannie laid her head on his belly and fell asleep. Kate smiled at the picture they made – wolf and child. A wonder, two miracles snuggled together.

They added the Nestors, Reeves and Tate families to their list, and Rachel volunteered to make invitations. When Harley was done in the garden, he sat with them and reviewed the plans.

"It sounds like a party," he said. "When the invitations are ready, I'll deliver them personally."

Kate was anxious about the cost of all the food, but Harley said "Make it potluck. Everyone brings a dish. It's easier that way, too. Less work" he said, grinning broadly. "See how that's done, Kate?" he asked, leaning back and patting his substantial belly. "You took a baby step today, my lovely friend, but you've got a long way to go."

In the week before the party, they cleaned the cabin, gathered branches and limbs from the forest for a bonfire, and made pies. They raked a gigantic circle at the edge of the clearing for the fire, and piled the wood nearby. They brought an old door from the Hughes barn and set it up on saw horses to use as a table. When Mel learned about the party, he said he wanted to roast a pig.

"I've got Clyde who is ready to donate himself to the cause. I'll dig the pit and do the roasting."

Her face scrunched up at the idea of seeing a whole pig cooking, one with a name! But he said she wouldn't have to look at it. All she'd have to do was eat it – after it was sliced.

"You eat pork, Kate. It's no different. It all walked around on four legs at one time."

"I know it's silly, but somehow it is different to me. And don't call him by name. I can't eat anything with a name."

"Sweet, but some farm woman you'd make," he said, tugging on her hair.

Kate finally agreed, but told him she definitely would not look at it until it was on her plate, and he was on his own with the roasting.

"I'll have to start it the day before, you know. It'll take a long time to cook Clyde, oops, sorry, and that means I'll be here over night. Is that alright with you?"

Kate blanched and stomped her foot. "No name! I said no name!" She thought for a moment. This detail hadn't occurred to her. She'd never roasted a pig before.

"I can toss a blanket on the floor or sleep under the stars," he said. "I enjoy doing that once in a while."

"If you promise no more names, then that's fine, Mel, wherever you are comfortable."

"Well, I hadn't mentioned *that* place," he said, giving her a wicked grin and raising an eyebrow, "but if you don't take up too much space, that'll be just fine with me."

He watched her. It took a moment, and he could tell when she understood. She flushed pink and punched his arm, once, then again harder.

Harley walked up just then, and his face lit with enjoyment in seeing them having fun with each other.

"Is she beating you up, Mel? Do you need me to come to your aid?" Harley asked.

"Yes, she is, and no, I think I can handle her."

"I don't know about that. There's a spark in that little firecracker."

"Well, if she gets too fiery, I'll just dump her in the creek before she burns up." He paused, a twinkle in his brown eyes. "I've done it before, and I can do it again. In fact . . ." but he didn't finish. He scooped her up and strode to the creek. Her legs and arms thrashed and she screamed, "Put me down! Mel, put me down, damn it!" But he hung on.

When he got to the creek, he waded in and dumped her gently but firmly into the water. It came up to her neck where she was half sitting, half laying, and it flowed and swirled around her. The girls came running to watch and were jumping and shouting with delight at the picture their mother made sitting in the middle of the creek. Mel stood over her, pushed at her shoulder, and she tipped under. Kate came up sputtering and splashed him with her hands and feet.

"Do it again," Jeannie cried. "Do it again!"

But Mel ran to her, scooped her up, and placed her next to her mother. Jeannie screamed and splashed – both Mel and her mother. Kate sent a spray of water Jeannie's way, and then they rolled together in the water and came up gasping for air.

Mel caught Rebecca as she tried to run away, sensing she was next. Rachel merely stood still. Mel wouldn't really toss *her* in. But he did, and her gasp of affront and shock at the cold was not as ladylike as she'd hoped for. Mel tried not to laugh out loud.

Kat just walked in and sat down knowing at some point she was going to end up there anyway. "Saving you the trouble," she told him. It wasn't long before all the girls were in the middle of the creek. Harley stood on the bank holding his stomach and laughing, harder than he had in a long time.

Mel saw him and walked over like he was going to watch the fun with him. He stood a moment by Harley's side, his arms crossed in relaxed ease. Then he turned and tossed Harley over his shoulder. With a groan, he carried the kicking man into the creek and dumped him next to the girls. "Heavy load . . ." he moaned, holding his back.

They laughed, doused each other and sent sprays of water toward Mel where he sat, a satisfied peacock perched carefully out of harm's way, watching. When they got out, Kate nodded subtly, and they charged him and dragged him into the creek. It took all of them, but they did it. Then Jeannie sat on his stomach, so he couldn't get up, and Rebecca on his legs. Kat walked to his head and slowly, very deliberately pushed it under the water. She let him up before he drowned completely and said, "Give up? Say uncle."

"No! Never!"

She pushed again and repeated it. "Say uncle, Mel."

It took several near drownings, but he finally said it. "Uncle Mel," he teased, and they let him sit. "I've been whipped by a bunch of scrawny girls," he added, squeezing the water from his hair and wiping his face.

"Scrawny?" Kate asked. "Do you want another bath?"

"Sorry," he said, trying for a look of fear, but it didn't work well on him. "And you owe me an apology, too, for swearing at me earlier," he told her.

"Well, I'm not a bit sorry, so I'll wait to see if I have a change of heart."

They were shivering and blue when they wrapped themselves in blankets, but they were still laughing and talking about the near drowning of the giant.

Mel rekindled the embers in the fire pit, and they dried off in its warmth. Harley brought out the 'frost bite medicine,' and passed the jug to both Mel and Kate who had hot chocolate beginning to simmer at the edge of the fire for the girls.

"Is it your work in life to continue to drench me in water?" Kate asked Mel.

"Could be, but I wouldn't call it work, and if there wasn't such a fire in you, I wouldn't have to keep trying to douse it."

"Give it up, Mel," Harley teased. "You can't quench the flame in Kate."

"I wouldn't want to do that. It's just a lot of fun dumping her in water." He pulled off his boots and poured the water out, then took off his socks and wrung them. "You might want to take yours off too, girls. Warm your toes so you don't catch cold."

He pulled Kate's off, wrung the socks, and then gathered them all and spread them on the grass near the fire to dry. He rubbed each of their feet between his hands until he felt warmth return and then sat, satisfied he had done what he could to keep them well.

Kate watched, amused by his mothering. There was a tender side to Mel, incongruous with his size. But she'd always known that about him. Jeannie climbed on his lap and snuggled there. He stroked her still damp copper curls and looked around him at the bedraggled group. They meant so much to him.

The sun was high in the sky, and between it and the fire they dried out and grew warm.

Harley passed Mel the jug, and he sipped from it, felt the heat of the moonshine slide down to his belly. "You're quite the mother hen," Harley said, a smile in his eyes.

"Just call me Mother Mel. No, better make that Uncle Hen. Does that work for you, Copper Top?"

Jeannie giggled sleepily from her cocoon on his lap. "I like it, Uncle Hen."

Chapter Eight

In the morning on the day before the party, Mel drove his wagon into the clearing. It was loaded with wood for the fire pit; the pig, cleaned and prepared for roasting; extra plates and silverware sent by his mother; and blankets for his night under the stars. He set to work digging the pit, checking the wind direction to make sure wood smoke wouldn't drift to Kate's laundry.

Kate washed and hung the clothes early so they would be ready to iron and returned to the camp that day instead of the next. Nothing was going to interfere with tomorrow. There would be no work allowed that wasn't party work. By the time the last load was hung on the line, the first ones had already dried in the warm breeze drifting through the clearing.

She set up the ironing board outside and heated the irons at her fire pit, periodically watching Mel work. Hair fell around his face and clung to a brow damp from perspiration in the heat of the fire. He brushed the hair out of his eyes and left ashy smudges on his face. Kate could see it from where she worked across the yard.

He looked good, strong and supple, and Kate admired him from the distance. The blue flannel shirt stretched across his broad, tapered back as he reached to add wood to the fire, and his long legs swung gracefully from the wood pile to the pit. For such a large man, Mel moved without effort, even gracefully.

Kate's mind wandered from her ironing to other places as she watched him work – to the first time Mel had caused her to fall into the river. She had been a young woman then, a girl, and it had been the first time Kate felt the awakenings of physical passion as they lay on the river bank in the warm sun and they had kissed and caressed each other. She grew warm and flushed with the memory.

Kate packaged the clean and ironed clothes. She loaded the bundles in the buggy and hitched up the mare, Kitty. As she was finishing, Mel asked if she wanted company – other than Wolf.

"I can leave Clyde for a short time . . . I mean the pig," he said. "I've got the coals just right so it will be fine."

Kate scowled deliberately at his slip but said, "That would be nice. I'll just tell the girls we're leaving."

Harley watched Mel give her a hand up into the buggy and pick up the reins. He smiled when he saw Kate lean against the seat back and release a soft sigh of contentment. Harley's sigh was more a wish than one of momentary satisfaction, but it was there nevertheless.

Kate relaxed and watched white wisps stretch across the sky and curls of smoke from the fire pit meander upwards to merge with the delicate clouds and then disappear. She saw Kat and Jeannie feeding the birds, now growing feathered and active, almost ready to fly, Rebecca pulling weeds from around the pumpkin and squash plants near the woods, and Rachel reading in the warm sunshine.

There's very little more one could ask of a late spring day, she thought. It was almost perfection.

Kate called for Wolf who glanced at Mel and then leaped up to the seat and planted himself next to her. He was taller than Kate when they were both sitting, and Wolf eyed Mel over Kate's head. He gave Mel the two-colored eye stare which caused Mel to grin and wonder just how safe he was in the buggy with this animal.

Yeah, Kate had to move closer to make room for Wolf, and that was nice, but Mel was fairly certain Wolf merely tolerated him and would have his jaws around his arm in an instant should he suspect anything untoward going on. Great for Kate – not for Mel, but he was glad she had him.

When they got to the camp, Wolf jumped down and stood stiffly alert, swinging his lupine head at each man as he moved toward the cook tent to retrieve a package and pay. None were totally comfortable with Wolf's inspection

Angels in the Corner

but tolerated the animal's stare knowing better than to complain. Kate giggled watching the big, burly men grow chicken wings.

Jack strode up to help and was surprised to see Mel with her. He helped her unload and collect her pay, and Mel noted how easy they were together. They'd done this before. Jack was Kate's protection. He made sure she was safe at the camp. Wolf leaped back up on the seat, satisfied his work was complete.

"You're coming tomorrow, right?" Mel asked Jack.

"You couldn't keep me away. In fact, I thought I'd come by later today to see if Kate needed anything. But I see she's already got some brawn to help," Jack responded, punching Mel lightly on the arm.

"We still need the brain to go with the brawn," Kate teased.

"Hey! Am I being unfairly maligned?" Mel asked.

"I think you've been fairly maligned," Jack responded with a playful smirk. "What do you think, Wolf?" he added, leaning against the buggy and scratching Wolf's ears.

Wolf stuck his nose against Jack's face for a friendly bit of Wolf slobber and then turned to give Mel the two-colored eye stare.

"Look at him. He loves your attention. What does he have against me" Mel asked. "He looks at me like I'm supper, and he's hungry."

"He's smart, and you're a whole smorgasbord," Jack answered with a crooked grin.

Kate looked into the woods around the cook tent, searched behind the trees, while Jack and Mel bantered. She couldn't help it even though logic told her the evil was long gone. Her spine still tingled and the hair on the back of her neck prickled whenever she was here, and it made her angry.

Mel noticed the changing reflections and didn't understand. He cocked his head, looking at her and then at Jack. Something was going on, but he didn't have the slightest idea what it was. "Are you ready?" he asked Kate.

109

She nodded, came back from wherever she had been, and the anxious look was gone. She hugged Jack and invited him to stop by later.

On the ride back, Mel pondered what he had seen. It made no sense to him. Kate was frightened or at least apprehensive, and showing fear wasn't like her at all. She wasn't afraid of anything, so what could have caused the look he had seen? After a time, in the only way he knew, he just asked. "Is everything alright, Kate?"

"Everything is perfect," she answered. "Why?"

"You seemed sort of . . . I don't know . . . uneasy back there at the camp."

Kate was startled. "No, I was just thinking about everything that needed to be done before tomorrow," she lied, then paused in thought. "I'm fine, just a little tired."

Mel nodded, not believing her at all, but he didn't want to push it. If something was wrong, she would tell him in her own time. Or not.

When they got back to the cabin, Harley was outside nailing boards together. Several other long pieces of wood were stacked beside him.

"We forgot chairs," he said. "We have no place for people to sit unless it's on the ground."

"Oh, my God, I didn't even think of that. Is that a bench you're pounding on?" she asked.

"Is there any problem you can't just fix, Harley?" Mel asked.

"Nope. I'm a fixer. I'm a fixer, a spinner, an angel, and I have pretty eyes," he said with a smile.

"Okay, Pretty Eyes, what can I do to help? I'm just going to check on Mr. Pig, and I'll be right back."

After a light supper, they all joined Mel at his roasting pit. Jack joined them for a few minutes, shared a sip of the jug Harley had retrieved from the cellar and passed around, and left saying he and Ruthie would see them in the morning, maybe with a stray kid or two in tow. He never knew who or how many would be at his house when he got home.

Kate had put the girls to bed and soon Harley left, too, saying he'd had a long, hard day and wanted to be bushy-tailed for the big day tomorrow. He smiled as he walked to the house and hoped Wolf would leave Mel alone if he managed to put his arm around Kate while they tended the fire.

The iridescent glow of a half moon rose over the tops of the trees and shadows stretched across the clearing. Kate pointed out the raccoons when they emerged from their den, and Mel watched Kate's face as she watched them. He loved how her eyes danced with enjoyment. He put his arm around her shoulders, and Kate rested her head against him. They stayed that way for a long time, comfortable and content.

Mel caressed the back of her hand lightly, and she moved hers in response. He wanted to kiss her, but wasn't sure if it was time, if she was ready, and it frustrated him to be uncertain. He was used to conviction, certainty – except where Kate was concerned. When she finally stood and said good night, that she needed to get some sleep, he cursed himself for a fool.

Schoolboy. Damned chicken, he said to himself as he stood with her.

"Who's a damned chicken?" Kate asked.

"Nobody. Did I say that out loud?"

Kate laughed loudly. "Now you sound like me! And surely you're going to apologize for cussing."

Then Mel laughed with her. "Not unless you do. You still owe one."

"Okay, I'm sorry – almost."

"Ditto."

"That's not good enough. You have to say it."

"You're a tough woman, Kate, but alright. Sorry."

Kate stood on her tiptoes, put her hands on either side of Mel's face and gently touched her lips to his. She heard the rough intake of breath, and his lips parted to taste hers. His hands still hung at his sides, motionless, and Kate could feel the pounding of his heart against her chest. Mel was immobile except for the movement of his lips and the solid pulsing of his heart. It would surely leap from his chest at any moment.

Her lips left his, and she looked down to see Wolf standing beside them, glaring at Mel. Mel sensed Wolf's presence before he saw him; he always appeared out of thin air, never having to take the time to get somewhere like other earthly creatures. Kate turned to leave and Wolf followed after a satisfied, momentary look back at Mel. It was a sneering look-- a self-satisfied one.

"Good night, chicken," she whispered into the night.

He whispered back, "damned brat."

A giggle wafted back to him.

Morning brought bright sunshine and clear skies. The girls were up early and eager to finish breakfast and get the party started. Jeannie ran outside first to see if Mel really did sleep on the ground by the roasting pig. She found him already up and tending to the fire. She dragged him in for some breakfast and commented on how much he could eat.

"He's a big boy," Kate told her. "He has a lot to fill up."

"He's not a boy, Ma," Kat said.

"You're right, sweetie. He just acts like it sometimes," Kate teased.

By noon, everything was ready and they were outside when the first of the guests arrived. Jack and Ruthie were first and brought Verna with them. They were soon followed by Willie and Mary, their two children and Ellen. John and Esther Nestor brought Mel's mother in their automobile. They were the attraction of the moment. Everyone wanted to sit in it and pretend they were driving. John looked like a proud papa as he showed them how it worked.

"Would it be alright if I took the girls for a ride – just down the lane and back?" he asked.

"Sure, if you promise to keep them for a day or two," Kate said with a grin.

"Mama," Rebecca asked, "don't you want us?"

"She's teasing," Kat said, shaking her head. "Can Verna go?"

"Nope," Verna said firmly. "I don't trust anything that doesn't have four legs."

"I only have two," Kat told her.

Verna tousled her blonde hair, and added, "Maybe you, Kat."

"We're roasting Clyde," Kat whispered to Verna, taken with the idea of cooking a whole pig. "We're not supposed to call him Clyde."

Kate rolled her eyes and grimaced. "That wasn't a very good whisper, Kat."

Verna raised her eyebrows in question. "And who is the unfortunate Clyde?"

"Mel's pig. We're roasting it, and Ma doesn't want to see it, but I did."

Verna laughed at Kat's words and Kate's expression of disgust.

"Well, you go for your ride, and I'll go check out . . . Clyde." Verna whispered the last part in Kat's ear.

They piled in and drove off with shouts of excitement.

The Reeves and Tate families followed the automobile when it came back up the lane and piled out of their buggies. Tom and Millie Reeves, with their three boys brought plates of cookies and a jug of moonshine Tom explained had been made by Kate's pa and stashed at the mill. He told them it had been there since long before Will died and should be fairly stout by now.

He held it out to Harley who gingerly took the jug from his hands and caressed it. "This is gold, Tom. You don't know how priceless Will's moonshine is. I'll just put it in the cabin where it's safe."

Leo and Martha Tate had twelve children, but only five were with them; the others were grown and married with children of their own. Leo was a hulk of a man who looked even bigger next to his tiny wife. Kate was always amazed she could have born twelve children and still look like a child herself. They had kids spread out from ages fourteen to thirty. Martha and several of the little Tates had stayed with the Hughes when fire claimed their farm house years ago, but those were the ones who were now grown and married.

Kate suspected the youngest boys were the 'other people' Rachel made sure were invited to the party, and she looked them over with a mother's critical eye when she greeted them.

Rachel stood off to the side when they piled out of the buggy. She'd taken a long time at the mirror fixing her hair. It was pulled back from her face and held in place with the pearl comb Mel had given her for Christmas, spilling down her back in long, dark waves. Her sea-blue eyes were sparkling, and there was a rosy glow on her cheeks.

She's stunning, Mel thought as he watched her, like a fragile, exotic flower, and except for the color of her hair, she was a copy of Kate when she was thirteen. He walked over to Rachel and told her how beautiful she looked. The flush on her cheeks grew rosier, and she whispered a thank you.

"Let's go say hello," he said, taking her arm.

After taking the food to the cellar to keep cool, they carefully unloaded their surprise. The Tates were a musical family. Everyone played an instrument of some kind; a banjo, fiddle, mandolin or harmonica, depending on what they felt like at the moment. They set up some stools near the roasting Clyde, and got out the instruments.

Leo's fiddle sang in the summer air; Lenny strummed the banjo; Martha joined them on the mandolin; and Charlie, the youngest boy, filled in on the harmonica. *Red River Valley* soon filled the clearing.

John Nestor dragged Esther out to dance, and before long, the rest were either tapping their feet to the rhythm or shuffling to the music. Kate danced with Harley, and then Jack. Mel claimed not to know how, but she convinced him to just move his feet when a slow song was played, and he couldn't resist the opportunity to hold Kate close, so he complied. Harley coaxed Ellen into a dance with him. She was as light as air on her feet, and he told her so.

"You're a sweet-talker, Mr. Benton."

"You're a feather, Mrs. Hughes. Your feet don't even touch the ground. Are you a woodland sprite?"

"You're a flatterer."

"You told me I was a spinner."

"You are. You're both of those, and many more things; some we haven't even discovered yet," she said. "I bless the day you came to our home, Harley."

He was startled by Ellen's words of praise and for just a moment at a loss for words. He continued to move his feet and watched Ellen's serene face.

"Now who's the flatterer?" he asked, wondering where this complex woman's mind had wandered.

"I don't flatter. You know that about me, Mr. Benton."

"True. That is quite true," he murmured and left off musing to enjoy the dance.

When Charlie gave up the harmonica to his brother, Alf, he moved to Rachel's side and stood watching the dancers.

"I don't suppose you like to dance," he said without looking at her.

"I like to dance," she said, not taking her eyes from the dancers.

Charlie kicked at the dirt and stared at the toe of his boot. *That didn't go well*, he thought, kicking himself, too. After a moment, he tried again.

"What I meant was . . . I mean . . . uh, would you like to dance with me?"

Rachel nodded without speaking and wondered why she felt so stupid around him. She said the wrong things. She tripped over her feet. She wanted to sink into the ground, live with the worms she abhorred.

He took her hand and led her to where the others were dancing, placed his arm around her back and held her well away from him. She looked down at their feet and stumbled a bit.

"I'm sorry," she said, an embarrassed flush creeping from her neck to her cheeks.

"My fault," he told her. "I'm clumsy."

He held her a little closer, and they soon moved effortlessly with the music – only stumbling when he spun her around.

Kate, standing next to Mel by the fire, watched her daughter dancing with the Tate boy. A smile played at the corners of her mouth, but it was tinged with sorrow.

"It's too soon," she mumbled, musing. She'd been only three years older than Rachel when she had fallen in love with Mark. Would Rachel do the same? Would she give her heart the way Kate had? She was of two minds about it. She wanted her daughters to experience that kind of consuming love, but knew it could be detrimental, too. It could cause all consuming pain. She shook her head and tried to brighten her weak smile.

Mel watched, not knowing what she was going through, but still understanding it a little. "Lighten up, Lucy," he teased, patting her head.

"My name's not Lucy. I'm Kate. Remember me?"

"Uh, Kate . . . Kate who? Not sure I recall, but I'd like to know you better," he teased, wiggling his eyebrows up and down and leering at her.

"Kate, Queen of Everything, Ramey," she told him and planted her fists on her hips and puffed out her chest. "And if you call me Lucy again, I will toss you into the woods for my minions to eat."

"Come on, Queen. Let me try to do this dance thing one more time."

They danced again, several times, and Mel improved with each dance, even got to be pretty light on his feet. They looked a little like the Tates with Mel's huge frame towering over Kate.

Wolf sat off to the side and watched, his eyes roving around the clearing, checking it for evil, and coming quickly back to watch Kate with the tall man. He wasn't sure he liked them so close together, but the tall man didn't seem to mean her any harm. As Wolf watched Kate, Kate watched Rachel, and her thoughts were similar.

Clyde was a success. Kat and Verna helped Mel and his mother put him into shapes that were not recognizable as an animal with a name.

"Will slices offend your very tender sensibilities?" Mel asked, getting in a good tease with the opportunity.

The rest of the food was brought from the cool cellar and set out on the door-table. Clyde was moist and tender, and the variety of side dish specialties caused smiles of delight along with stress when the hungry guests piled their plates high and then tried to eat it all.

After so much exercise, laughing, dancing and making music, everyone looked for a place to settle in. Some found Harley's two new benches; some took their plates to the blankets spread on the ground. People congregated by age groups, and the level of laughter followed chronological age; the higher the number, the lower the sound.

After supper, the sun still lit the clearing, but it was beginning its slow slide behind the trees. The younger children played at the woods' edge, within sight, or at the creek with John Nestor who had dropped in a line to see if any trout would bite.

Kate looked for Rachel and saw her sitting on the cabin steps with Charlie. She could see them talking and wished she could hear what they were saying. *You didn't have any troubles spying before,* she thought to herself. Why now? But she couldn't do that to her daughter. She would have to trust, and that was hard.

The Nestor and Reeves families, with Mel's mother, packed up to leave before dark, and Willie's family, with Ellen, followed soon after. When the Tates left, Kate invited them to visit, knowing Rachel would like to see them again. Charlie told her he and Lenny would be back soon. They were going to give music lessons to Rachel and Rebecca.

"If that's okay with you," they both blurted in embarrassing afterthought.

Kate looked surprised. "I didn't know you wanted to play," she said to the girls, but after a moment, she understood. "That's a wonderful idea. We will enjoy it. Maybe you can teach me, too?"

The boys didn't look excited about the last part, but they were too polite to refuse, and a bit of a smile creased the corners of Kate's eyes. Mel's too, knowing exactly what Kate was up to.

They sat by the fire pit, now empty of Clyde, as the night fell; Harley, Verna, Kate and the girls, and Mel. He stoked the fire so the chill of the night was kept at bay. They talked about the day, each person bringing something from it that was special for them. They shared their moments and each person's pleasure was multiplied by another's memory. Voices grew quieter and thoughts were absorbed into the flames.

Jeannie leaned in total repose against Mel, sure in the knowledge of his care and love, her youthful heart serene, her eyelids drooping, her breath growing slow and deep. He patted her back, feeling the child's trust through his fingertips, soaking in her peace.

Kat sat near Verna, their arms just touching. Every once in a while, Verna patted Kat's hand, and Verna found contentment she hadn't known existed. Would have blustered loudly against the possibility it could exist had someone told her she'd love a child. She merely borrowed the girl every once in a while, just because . . .

What the hell, she thought. I can give it back when it gets ornery. But she never felt like giving Kat back. She adored this extraordinary, sensible child.

Rebecca, next to Harley, soon had her head on his lap. He stroked her blonde hair in rhythmic pleasure, purring in comfort. Kate watched the adults' slow slide toward blissful lethargy, the result of a busy, pleasant day as well as the small people snuggled at their sides. Rachel, sitting next to Kate, was quiet. Periodically, Kate looked her way and watched her daughter's eyes follow the flames. Kate knew her thoughts; crossed her fingers -- and her heart -- then asked silent blessings for Rachel.

When the girls grew sleepier and it was time, she led them to their beds and Harley drove Verna home in Kate's buggy. This night, in the minds of many, could not be duplicated. It was treasured.

She was alone with Mel. They sat on a blanket near the fire and leaned back against a log, talking quietly about the day, the music, the people. He put his arm around her, and she relaxed against him. Taking his cue from Kate's kiss the night before, he tilted her head back and kissed her softly. A small, contented sigh escaped her lips. It was a long, slow kiss that warmed them both. Kate's lips responded to his, and she melted against him. She felt so safe, so cherished. She was in a warm cocoon of his strength and allowed herself the pleasure of snuggling into him.

Mel's lips tasted her closed eyes and brushed lightly at the side of her face where fine whispers of hair fell, and then his lips slid down her neck. When he pulled her against him, Kate was suddenly trapped by his arms, by his male strength, and terror flooded her, wrapped her in iron shackles. She jerked back, shoved frantically at his chest. The look on her face screamed at him.

"I'm sorry," he said, unsure what he had done to cause this reaction. "I didn't mean to . . . I thought . . ."

She crumpled and put her hands over her face. For a long moment there was silence. He couldn't think of anything to say that would erase what had just happened – didn't even know what it was. All he knew was overwhelming sorrow. He had allowed himself hope.

Kate didn't understand either. She just knew in the brief second when his arms had surrounded her, pulled her against him, she panicked. She saw the face of the monster who had attacked her, felt his mouth on her, tearing at the tender skin of her breasts, and alarm invaded the warm place she'd been enjoying.

She didn't know what to do or say to explain, to wipe away the hurt on Mel's face. She didn't know how to rid herself of feeling violated. Loathing and repulsion filled her when she thought of what that man had done. She tried not to think about it at all, but every once in a while, the picture flooded her brain and crippled her. She couldn't control it, so she pushed it down – deep into a place inside where she could keep it hidden and it couldn't touch her – hurt her.

"Kate?" Mel said softly, trying to peek under her hands to her face. "I'm sorry if I did something to make you uncomfortable. I'm sorry," he repeated, clueless about the cause of her discomfort. What he had done.

Kate finally peered at him, and her heart broke at the distress in his eyes.

"You didn't do anything wrong, Mel. It's me."

"If you don't feel that way about me, I understand, but I thought . . ." Then he saw the way she was holding herself, her arms wrapped tightly around her chest, her legs pulled up tight, and the nagging remembrance of Kate's face at the camp niggled at his brain. "There's something else, isn't there, Kate?"

She shook her head forcefully, not wanting to talk about it, not wanting Mel to know the horror of what had happened. "But it isn't you. Please know that."

"How, Kate?"

"I don't know. Will you let me work through it, please?"

"And how can I do that if you're hurting?"

"It isn't you . . . or us. Try to accept that. Please?"

Mel thought for a moment, wondered whether to push her to talk with him or give in to the privacy she asked for. He wanted to help, wanted to hold her in his arms and make her safe from whatever demons she was battling, but he knew, too, Kate would first and always want to fight her own battles, needed to. So, he nodded. "Would it be alright if I put my arm around your shoulders?"

"Please," she said, and nestled into him, putting her back against his broad chest. After a few moments, her breathing slowed, and she grew comfortable being held.

Mel relaxed and watched the fire. He brushed his cheek over the top of her head and wondered what was going on in there.

"If you have demons, Kate, fight them with angels. They're the good guys, and you have plenty of those in your corner," Mel whispered into her hair.

"Yes, I do, Mel. I have many of those."

Chapter Nine

1912-1913

Mel threw his long leg over the horse and rode off in the direction of the camp. He'd watched Kate over the months since the party. At times she was easy, laughing and teasing as she'd always been, but in brief, unchecked moments, distress flickered in her eyes. It was bothersome, and it wasn't Kate.

Mel thought a lot about her distressed reaction the night of the party, and it disturbed him. He remembered back to when they delivered the laundry to the camp together, the way her eyes searched impossibly behind the trees. For what? He'd made a point of going with her to the camp on another day when he *just happened by* her place at the right moment. He saw it again and knew he hadn't been mistaken about the agitation he'd seen the first time.

The more he thought about everything, the more Mel began to put two and two together and came up disturbed, angry. He didn't know who to be mad at, but, damn it, he was.

Once, when Mel had stopped by to visit, Kate had reacted unreasonably over what he thought was typical, innocent teenage behavior. Lenny and Rebecca were still practicing mandolin, and Kat was busy with the birds. It was early evening, and the sun was still warming the earth when Rachel and Charlie went for a walk in the woods after her lesson and left the others behind.

Kate was fine while the two were in sight, but as soon as they left her field of vision, she stood up and walked to the pumpkin patch near the edge of the woods and pretended to pull weeds, her head cocked, listening. Finally, she gave up the pretense, looked at the sun and then at Mel.

"They've been gone a long time. Maybe we should go look for them. Maybe they got lost."

"Kate, Rachel has lived here all her life. She knows these woods," he said, trying to calm whatever had ruffled her.

"I know but . . ."

"But what? What's wrong?"

"Nothing. You're right," she'd said, but she didn't relax until Rachel broke through the forest darkness and walked into the clearing.

He hadn't probed further, but Kate's unusual reactions prompted him to question the nature of her nervousness, and that was why he went to see Jack. He found him in the woods leading two huge horses as they hauled a load of logs to the river. He waited until Jack had the logs floating down the current and heading toward the mill before he asked if Jack could take a break for a few minutes.

"Sure. It's almost noon, time for some lunch."

It took Mel a while to get to the point of his visit, and Jack waited. Finally, Mel just said it. "Something is wrong with Kate, and I think you know what it is."

"Why do you think so?" Jack asked.

"Because she's afraid of something, and that's not Kate. And you know her, better than anybody."

"Have you asked her?"

"Yes. She says 'Nothing.'"

Jack pondered the problem, wishing he could confide in Mel so he'd understand, but if Kate wanted him to know, she'd tell him herself. It wasn't his place. "Then I guess it's nothing," he said not unkindly.

Mel took a deep breath and blurted out what he suspected. He did so because if what he thought was correct, he was going to have to do something about it. He had to.

"I'll tell you what I think. I think someone hurt Kate – or tried to, and I believe it was someone at this camp. The look in her eyes when she's here. She's looking around trees for someone or something. I don't know who or what, but she's afraid of something in the woods, like when Rachel went for a walk with the Tate boy. Kate has loved these woods since she was a girl. Loved the camps, too, and something has changed how she feels about them."

Jack listened quietly to what was a long speech for Mel and knew he was getting close to the truth. He also knew Mel wasn't the kind to give up. He would do whatever it took to protect Kate. How could he reassure him she was safe without giving out information that wasn't his to give? He finally decided he could tell about his own role. "Look, Mel, Kate will have to decide what she wants you to know, but I will tell you this. A man upset her, and I saw to it that he is gone. That's it."

"Son of a bitch!" Mel exploded. "What man? Where did he go? What did he do?"

"I told you. I won't go into that. He's gone."

"Where? If he hurt Kate, I'm not done with him, and he could come back."

Jack rubbed his hands over his face, wondered how to deal with Mel's need to avenge Kate. "No, he can't, and Kate is our concern now. Just be patient; give her some time."

"That's all you'll say?"

"Yes. That's it."

Mel was quiet for a moment, thinking, but his agitation was evident.

"She has Harley with her when she's at the cabin, and Wolf when she's not. She's in good hands – or paws." Then he smiled at him. "Even if they're not yours at the moment."

"Does this have anything to do with why Harley suddenly decided to go live with Kate?"

"You'll have to ask her."

When Jack wasn't smiling, he could look menacing with his dark eyes and hair. He was as slender as Mel was brawny but had an agile, muscled body from his years as a lumberjack.

Even so ... Mel thought, and his anger grew as he looked at Jack for long, strained minutes. "You're a damned hard man to talk to, Jack."

"True." Then he grinned.

Mel admired Jack's silence, his regard for Kate's privacy, even if it frustrated him. "But I guess you're right. I'd do the same."

"You would. I know that."

"But if anything happens to Kate, I'll have to kill you," he said, finally grinning back at Jack.

He shook Jack's hand and got up from the cook tent bench. The rest of the men were just coming in from the woods, and Mel couldn't help but scan the faces looking for something in their eyes. He didn't know what and knew, too, that he wouldn't find it here any longer. Jack had said the man was gone, and Mel had a high regard for Jack's word, but like Kate, he looked anyway. He couldn't help himself.

He took a few steps and then walked back to Jack. "Is Kate going to know I was here asking questions?"

"Sure. Is that a problem?"

"I guess it can't be. I was here, wasn't I?"

It was Jack's usual day to visit, and he thought carefully about what he would say to Kate as he rode there. He understood Mel's desire to protect Kate, and Jack thought it would be best if Mel understood what had happened, especially if she was still emotionally impacted by what that vile piece of crap had done to her. He didn't know if the man had completed his violation, but that was Kate's business, not his or Mel's, or anyone's. He couldn't force her to talk about it if she wasn't willing, and Kate was a stubborn, private woman.

When he rode into the clearing, Kate was wringing the last load of laundry and tossing it into a tub. He hefted it to his shoulder and walked over to the lines already three quarters full of half dry clothes flapping gently in the light breeze. Kate's hair was tied at the back, but loose strands wisped around a face tanned from hours in the sun each day. She wouldn't wear a hat. She liked the feel of sun on her face. A few freckles sprinkled her nose, and she looked like a comical elf in her worn, baggy trousers. She'd taken to wearing them frequently, except when she had to go to town or the camp.

She followed him to the lines and grabbed a pair of pants from the basket. "Good to see you," she said, a little weariness mixing with the affection in her voice.

"Why don't you plop down right there on the ground and let me hang these? Rest your trouser clad legs for a minute."

Kate did what he asked. She flung herself on the grass and leaned back on her hands to watch. Wolf spread himself across her legs. "You're a good man, Jack Bay."

"That's what I like to make all the pretty ladies think," he teased, wiggling his black eyebrows dramatically, "before the real Jack corrupts his damsels."

Kate laughed at his antics and turned her face to the sun. "It will be fall soon. I hate to think of winter coming."

Jack nodded.

"We have a new critter, a woodchuck with a broken leg. Harley made another cage and put the leg in a splint."

"I'm surprised the animal didn't chew his hands off while he was doing it. It can hardly be a baby at this time of year, and full grown chucks can get mean."

"You know Harley. He has a way about him critters just trust. Besides, I think the poor thing was starving. It looked like he'd been caught in a trap. He got himself loose, but the leg is pretty mangled, and he probably couldn't forage for food too well."

"I'm sure Jeannie will have him fattened up in no time," Jack said. "That girl loves her critters almost as much as her momma."

Around mid-summer, Jeannie had taught the two birds to fly, with Verna and Harley's help. They were still in their cage, but the door was left open so they could leave and come back for food if they needed to. They flew in and out as they pleased and appeared to be comfortable with the arrangement. Her mouse was still in its cage, a permanent member of the Ramey family.

After Kate updated Jack on the welfare of all the strays, Jack finally asked, "Is Kate doing as well as all of them?"

"Sure, why wouldn't I be?"

"Just wondered. You sound a little tired."

She picked a piece of grass and stuck it between her lips. "Being Queen of the Forest is a lot of work, and even the queen gets tired now and then. She needs more minions."

Jack nodded and continued to hang the clothes. "Maybe you should get one of those machines, the kind that wrings the water out of clothes between two rollers. Have you seen them?"

"Yes, you turn a crank and the clothes magically come out almost dry. I've lived most of my life under a rock," she teased, "but not all of it. Maybe I will one day."

"What? Live all your life under a rock?"

"Silly . . . no, buy a magic machine."

"You should. Mel came out to the camp today."

"You're kidding. Why?"

"To see me."

"You two sweet on each other?" she giggled. "That's gonna surprise Ruthie quite a bit."

"And what do you know about those dark things, young lady?" he said, turning to her and planting his feet squarely in front of her.

"Again . . . the rock thing. I didn't just crawl out from under it."

"I'm not so sure. Sometimes I think you like it there."

Kate sat up, the blade of grass sticking out of her lips and pointing at Jack. He couldn't help but grin at the sight of her, but what he wanted to say wasn't at all that funny.

"Well," she drawled, "you obviously want to tell me why Mel went out to see you so I'll ask. Why did Mel come to see you, Jack?"

"He's worried about you. He's noticed a couple of things that make him think you're afraid, but he doesn't know why, so I'm thinking you haven't said anything about what happened."

Kate nodded but didn't respond.

Jack finished hanging the clothes and sat on the ground next to her. Wolf gave him the obligatory 'wet nose wolf-slobber' and then reclaimed Kate's legs.

When she didn't speak, he continued. "Have you been able to put it behind you? I'm thinking no."

Silence hammered the clearing.

"Do you think it might help both you and Mel if you explained a bit?"

"What did you tell him?" Kate blurted.

"Nothing except someone upset you, and that person is long gone."

Tears welled at the corners of her eyes, but her face was set like a stone wall. "I can't think about it, can't talk about it. You don't understand."

"No, I can't fully understand, Kate. I just know that Mel loves you to distraction, and he is concerned for you."

"I need to bury this, Jack... but I promise to think about it."

"Don't go back under the rock, Kate. There's all kinds of grubs, centipedes, and creepy things there."

"I like creepy crawly things, even snakes like you." She took a deep, cleansing breath. "Let's go see the girls and the woodchuck."

They found them all at the back of the cabin. They were watching the new critter chomp away at a carrot Harley had brought from the cellar. He sat awkwardly, his splinted leg stuck out at an odd angle, but he held the carrot firmly in his paws and happily gnawed at the end of it. When that was gone, he grabbed a piece of rutabaga, tried a bite and tossed it aside for another carrot.

"Picky little devil, aren't you," Harley said to him.

Jeannie said he probably thought he was a rabbit.

"If he wasn't so skinny, he'd look a bit like you, Harley" Jack told him. "Look at that scruffy hair sticking up all over his head."

"Well, he is a she, and she does have pretty eyes, even if they are brown, so maybe you're right," Harley said. Then he turned sideways so Jack could see both faces. "What do you think? Are we twins?"

127

Jeannie giggled at him. "You'd look funny with wood-chuck hair, Harley."

Rebecca thought the woodchuck would look even fun-nier with gold curls like Harley's.

"Do you think he'd look better as a blonde, Becca," Har-ley asked, "or with coppertop curls like yours, Jeannie?"

They laughed more at that picture, and Kate wondered what their lives would be like without Harley. She mildly scolded herself for the hundredth time.

Look beyond the looks, Kate. When hobos come to the door, you must always remember what wonderful souls they may be, what treasures they might have hidden be-neath their frequently odd exteriors.

Summer turned to fall, and Kate was busier than ever trying to make use of every last bit from the garden. She had the fire pit going all day, either washing clothes or putting up vegetables that otherwise wouldn't keep during winter. She already had dozens of jars of stewed tomatoes, peas, green beans and pickles, all preserved at their peak of ma-turity.

Now, she canned the kale, soft shelled squash and pumpkin. Root vegetables, like carrots, potatoes, rutabagas and beets were stored in crates packed with straw to winter in the cool cellar. She was concerned and didn't want to waste a morsel that might keep them through the snowy season when camp laundry diminished along with the money she earned.

She picked apples growing wild in the woods and turned them into applesauce, adding a few crabapples so it would be pink and tart. Wild grapes were plentiful as well, and she smashed them into juice, then sieved and canned that, too. Whatever was available for picking, she used, and she was exhausted, yet she frequently wrapped herself in a quilt and sat outside at night when she couldn't sleep.

There was nothing she could do about the number of men who worked at the camps during winter, and fewer men working at the lumber camps meant fewer dollars in Kate's pocket.

"Damn," she whispered. "What in hell can I do?"

She heard Harley chuckle behind her. She hadn't known he was there. He appeared wrapped in a quilt, too, all the way up to his curly head, and sat next to her.

"I'm waiting for two sorry-s," he said.

"Sorry. And you're only getting one cause I'm not even close to almost meaning it twice."

"What are you cussing at, Kate?"

"The trees, the owl who keeps hooting at me like I'm funny or something, the fat raccoons who get to wander into the creek to find dinner. All of them."

"So, you're just pretty mad at the world, huh?"

She nodded, and Harley patted her hand. "Do you want to tell me why?"

She nodded again, fighting back the tears his tender touch had produced. When she could talk without flooding, she explained.

"The camps are getting slow, Harley. Without men and dirty clothes, I have no money to feed my family. I'm not sure what to do, and I guess I'm afraid, and God I hate to be afraid – almost as much as I hate to cry!" She blinked to stem the flow and turned away.

"Tears are just kisses glistening on your cheeks, Kate, wet sloppy angel kisses. Kind of like angel slobbers. And," he continued, "you're not afraid of anything. You'll know what to do when the time is right. You always do."

"I might have to move," she said. "I might have to leave our home, find work somewhere, and that worries me."

"Well, then you'll move . . . and if worrying helps in some way, then by all means continue, but does it really do any good?"

Kate shook her head.

"If it doesn't make you feel good, then don't do it."

Kate ran a hand over her face just like Mark had done so many times before when he heard Harley wind up for a long discourse. Harley waited to hear if she'd groan like Mark too, then he continued.

"Worry just incapacitates people, keeps their minds occupied with things that get in the way of working stuff out.

It also makes funny lines on your face. Do you see any on mine?" he said, turning to her with a grin.

She looked at him and shook her head, amazed to see he was right. There weren't any lines, and she knew he had to be close to seventy, but no one knew for sure because he kept changing his age.

"I don't worry," he said, a bigger grin spreading over his chubby face, his eyes squinting to slanted slits.

"You are ageless," she said, "and no, you do not have worry lines on your face – devil man."

"I thought I was an angel, and a spinner, and flatterer? I'm a lot of pretty snappy things, aren't I?"

"No, I've changed my mind. You're a devil man." She paused, once again lost in thought about what she might have to do. "What if I have to move, Harley? I don't want to leave here. I'd hate it."

"Well, that's pretty simple, too. Don't hate it. Find the adventure in it. You can enjoy where ever you are if you look for the fun, Kate."

"Damn it, Harley! Why do you have to make everything sound so simple? It isn't. Some things just aren't simple!" She jerked herself upright and stomped a circle in front of him, angry that he thought life was that easy. Solutions that straightforward.

"I think they are, but possibly I'm just simple minded."

"I'm mad right now, so just let me be mad."

Harley closed his mouth and sat quietly, watched Kate stride with heavy steps around the clearing. She finally stopped in front of him.

"You're not simple minded, Harley, and you know it. Your brain is complex and strange. Thanks for listening."

"Are you over your mad?"

"Yes. Sorry."

They sat in the quiet night watching stars blink on in the sky, pin pricks of gold light through black satin. There was comfort in the silence, like a soft, wool scarf on a winter day, and Kate felt swaddled in the warmth of Harley's odd strength.

Late in the fall, Mel drove in with his wagon. He jumped down and walked over to Kate, who was surrounded in steam as chilly air met the hot water her hands were in up to the elbows.

"You must be just about ready to move this stuff into the cabin for the winter, huh? It's getting a bit cold for playing in water."

"You're the one who likes playing around in water. Well, let me adjust that. You like throwing other people in and making them play in water," she said with a scowl.

"I do. It's always entertaining."

"What are you doing here on this fine, fall day? Trying to escape farm work, you shirker?"

"Nope. I brought a present you might like. Well, I think you'll like it. I'm not positive, never am with you."

"You didn't steal from your mother's cupboards again?"

"No. But there are too many deer stealing from my corn fields, and I've had to cull the herd a bit. Our larder is full, so I brought one out. Thought you might be able to use it."

Kate paused, thinking. They certainly could use some venison. The idea of eating those gorgeous creatures was always difficult. She kept seeing big brown eyes, but she knew better than to let her silliness get in the way of their bounty.

Mel read her briefly indecisive looks. "All meat has eyes at some point in time, Kate," he said, remembering the pig roast.

"I know, damn it! Sorry. Thank you, Mel. We appreciate your gift."

"You won't have to look at it in one piece, Kate. I'll cut it up for you."

"It's my meat. I'll help. Kat and Rebecca will want to help, too. Kat will study the structure, and Becca won't think anything of cutting up a deer to eat. She's a farmer at heart – thanks to you and the farm set you brought her," she added, grinning at him.

Mel hauled out the door they had used as a table during the party and set it up on the saw horses while Kate finished the laundry. He quartered the deer in the wagon and had one quarter on the makeshift table ready to carve into steaks and roasts when Kate came over to help.

Kat and Becca had followed her out of the cabin and were already sticking their fingers in heart valves and searching for organs they could identify. Kate shook her head at them, but was pleased they could ignore the fact the animal had been alive and walking through a corn field mere hours ago. Kate tried to resolve her issues with a prayer of thanks to the deer.

After wiping a damp cloth over a hind quarter to remove the stray hairs, she began slicing thin steaks from it. Mel carved the tenderloin from the back and held it up.

"I'm not sure how you want this. It's the best part of the whole deer – the tenderest."

"I've never done this before, so I don't know. Just slice it, I guess," she said.

He handed the long slender strip of venison to her, and Kat ran to look at it. "That's the piece that goes by the deer's spine, isn't it?" she asked Mel.

He nodded and asked how she knew.

Kat shrugged her shoulders. "I don't know. I just pictured its pieces – like a puzzle."

"Pretty clever," Mel told her.

"Pretty strange," Kate added. "Not a puzzle I'd want to do."

After the first two quarters were cut up and stacked in piles, Kate retrieved a small, wooden barrel from the cellar, salt from the kitchen, and began packing the meat in tight layers with salt in between. She wasn't sure how it was supposed to be done, but Mel and his mother had processed meat many times, and he told her she was doing fine. She would can the rest of the meat. That she was sure of.

She avoided the carcass in the wagon bed, steered clear of the head of the deer where the eyes watched her and tried not to think of the doe walking through Mel's corn or drinking from her creek. She hoped it wasn't one from her woods who had traveled to Mel's farm. It was silly, not rational she should care which one it was, but she did.

"I don't have to be rational if I don't want to," she told herself.

"No, you don't," Mel said.

"I did it again! I said that out loud, didn't I? God, I'm going looney."

"No more so than usual," he teased.

Mel watched her avoid the wagon bed and got a burlap sack from the shed and tossed the hide and head into it. "It's gone," he told her. "All we have here is meat. The rest is gone."

"Thank you and I do appreciate having the meat for winter. Thank you for that, too."

"You are welcome, Queen of the Forest. It is my pleasure to bring you bloody gifts, and I get to spend a little time with you to boot."

Harley came out with Jeannie when they were finishing packing the meat into the barrel. "Is this like Clyde?" she asked.

"No," Mel said. "This is like meat you buy at Nestor's store. No names, just little pieces of delicious meat. Is that alright with you, Jeannie?"

She nodded and looked into the barrel to make sure Mel was telling the truth.

"How about putting some of this in a frying pan for dinner?" he asked Kate. "Can I invite myself?"

"I don't know if I can cook this today," Kate said. "I think I might need a day or two. Sorry."

"I can cook today," Harley volunteered. "Why don't the two of you take a rest outside and enjoy the evening. I'll let you know when it's ready."

"Great idea. Get Rachel to help. She didn't watch any of the butchering. Ooh, bad word. I don't like it."

Harley and Rachel set the table, made potatoes and beets with the greens still on, and then fried some of the venison. Kate could smell it from where they sat by the door, and her mouth watered. "It smells good," she said to Mel.

"Well, yeah!" he said. "Would I bring you venison that didn't smell good? And . . . it's corn raised venison, the best corn, from my private stock!"

The addition of venison to her larder helped reduce some of the worry, and Kate was grateful; she even relaxed a bit. The last of the garden vegetables had been canned; the potatoes, beets, rutabagas and carrots were pulled from the garden just before the ground froze and were stored in the cellar. They could survive for a long time on what they had, and maybe the camps would be full of dirty lumberjacks wanting clean clothes by spring. You never knew, and you could always hope.

Christmas came and went with the tree ceremony and all the festivities that accompanied the holidays. Charlie Tate managed to walk beside Rachel down Main Street and held his hand around her candle flame when she lit one on the tree. Kate watched them walking side by side and noted Rachel's flush.

"Maybe it's just the cold," she said and knew she was lying to herself.

During the afternoon of Christmas Eve, Mel, Jack, Ruthie, and Willie drove out to the cabin towing a wagon with a large, covered object in it. Verna was already there, invited to join them for the evening. Kate and Jeannie ran out to greet them, surprised since they weren't expecting anyone except Mel.

Mel lifted Jeannie high in the air, excitement lighting his face. Jeannie squealed her delight. Flying through the air in his hands never failed to thrill her.

"Go on inside, Copper Top. You too, Kate. We have a surprise for you."

"What? What's the surprise?" Jeannie asked. "Candy?"

"Nope. This surprise is for your mom."

Kate gave them all a quizzical look and did what he asked.

With Mel and Willie on either side of a large wrapped object, they hauled it into the cabin and put it down in the center of the cooking area. Kate's eyebrows rose in question. She couldn't think what the thing under the canvas wrap might be, try as she might.

"Well, it's obviously bigger than a bread box," she said, "and smaller than a house. I give. What is it?"

"You get three guesses, and you have to make them," Jack said, visibly delighted in the surprise.

Willie and Ruthie were clapping their hands together like kids who couldn't wait and would rip the covering off themselves if she didn't hurry and guess. Jack leaned against the cupboard, grinning. Poochie backed up to stand next to Jeannie and growled at the strange thing in the kitchen. Wolf put his front feet on it, head high, and sniffed the air, gave one good howl, then grew bored and walked over to Jack to give him a Wolf-slobber. His cheek was too clean.

"I have no idea," Kate said. "I truly don't."

"You have to guess," Jack demanded with a grin.

"Okay, how about a barrel of pickles? Wolf, did you smell pickles?"

"Nope, guess again," Jack told her.

"A huge bird cage with a very quiet owl inside."

"Nope. Try again."

"A very small silo," Kate said quickly and immediately attacked the covering that was tied with twine around the sides.

"Oh, my God. It's a washing machine – with rollers to squeeze out the water!"

Kate stared at it in awe. There were two tall tubs on a platform with wheels so it could be rolled wherever Kate needed it. The large one was for washing the clothes, and a smaller one for rinsing. Attached to the top was a set of rollers that swung over either tub to allow the water to stream back into the appropriate place.

"Before you start saying it's too much and you can't accept it, Kate, this is your Christmas gift from all of us including Verna, Ellen and John Nestor, so don't even start," Mel said, grinning at her evident pleasure in the machine.

Kate beamed and nodded. "Let's try it! We need dirty clothes. Can I have your shirt, Harley – oh! Not that yours is dirty," she added when he looked affronted.

Harley stripped down to his long johns and gave Kate his shirt and his pants, grinning at the gasps from Ruthie and Rachel. "I can give you my long johns, too, if you want. . . just wait here in all my natural glory."

"I don't think that will be necessary, Harley." Kate said. "These will do."

"Your mother used to wrap me in a sheet when she wanted me out of my clothes. She didn't seem to mind," he teased, but he added "for washing," when he heard Rachel gasp again.

Jack and Willie went out to get water from the well and brought in four buckets, enough to at least partially fill the two tubs. They heated the water, but just a bit because they were too excited to wait, then filled the tubs and put in Harley's clothes. Kate shaved some soap into one and began rubbing his shirt on the wash board clipped to the inside of the tub. Then Jack showed her how to fold the shirt and stick the end in between the two rollers. She cranked, and the shirt rolled through, squeezing the water back into the tub. Kate shook the shirt and held it up for them all to see.

"Look how dry it is!" she cried out. "I could almost iron it now!"

"You might want to rinse the soap out first," Jack told her. "We don't want to give poor Harley's tender skin a soap rash."

"Oh, I got so excited that I forgot that part." She dipped the shirt into the rinse water, swished it around, flipped the rollers over the rinse tub, ran it through the rollers again, and showed it to them. Then she flung it aside and attacked his trousers, but when she tried to get them between the rollers, they wouldn't fit. Jack showed her how to adjust the tension between the rollers for different materials, and soon the trousers were squeezing through and coming out the other side.

"This is so great! Look how much water went back into the tubs! I won't have to constantly refill them! And no more wringing! Look!" she demanded like a toddler wanting everyone's attention.

Mel peered compliantly into the tubs and responded with suitable awe at the amount of water left in them. They grinned at Kate's enthusiasm, enjoying the eagerness lighting her face, as she dragged Harley over to look, and then Verna and each of the girls.

"I think this calls for a celebration sip, don't you all?" Harley said.

"It's about time," Verna said. "All this fun has me dry as a bone."

Harley brought the jug from the cupboard and a smaller one with blackberry cordial which he poured into small glasses for Kate and Ruthie.

"This is Will's good stuff, some Tom brought to the party." He raised the jug high and said, "Here's to a Merry Christmas and to the wonders of machinery, and the wonders of friendship, and to presents."

When Kate started to touch her glass to Ruthie's, Harley said, "Not yet. I'm not done."

Kate's groan harmonized with Mel's, and the rest waited silently knowing they would not drink until Harley was ready. They had come to believe Harley never really wanted the moonshine, probably didn't even like it; he just wanted an opportunity to talk – on and on and on.

"Don't make me stand on the chair for your attention again," he said with mock ferocity. "Here's to Kate's work, honest work, and even better to honest fun, and here's to just plain honesty. Here's to a grin instead of a frown, to a happy heart and not a heavy one . . . and here's to . . ."

Verna grabbed the jug from him and had it tipped over her hand with the clear brew draining into her mouth before he could react. She took a long sip and then handed it to Mel. "Here's to a drink," she said brusquely.

Mel passed it to Willie who passed it to Jack, and it finally landed back in Harley's hands.

"You folks just can't wait for a good toast, can you? Good ones take time, just like good food." But he was grinning because Harley had the kind of heart he'd toasted to, and he didn't even know how to frown. He lifted the jug and said, "Here's to me . . . Pretty Eyes."

They emptied the water from the wash tubs and rolled them to the side of the room where they would stay for the winter, and then took seats around the table before heading back to their homes. Kate walked outside when they left and hugged them all.

"I can't begin to thank you. This will make things so much easier."

"It was Jack's idea," Ruthie told her, her arm around her husband's back. He patted her bottom, and Ruthie blushed.

"If you're going to tell tales, I've got a few I can tell about you, sweet thing," he said leering at his wife.

"It probably was your idea, Jack. I think you were getting tired of wringing," Kate teased.

"Yeah," he said. "It was chapping my hands."

Mel stayed, as they had planned, and Christmas Eve with him and Verna was as good as Kate could have asked for. Kat had her Verna, Becca had her Harley, and Jeannie had her Mel. Kate wondered if Rachel was wishing Charlie was with them, but she wasn't going to ask. The time wasn't right. Rachel was too young.

Kate looked around her. Color wrestled with the dark green of the pine tree, and brightly wrapped presents nestled underneath, waiting for eager hands. Comforting aromas slid from the oven, scenting the air, teasing hungry senses. The room radiated Christmas and warmth, comfort and love. The hearth fire crackled and drew eyes to watch the dance of flames.

Kate breathed deeply, her spirit serene and smiling. She imagined Mark suspended contentedly in a corner, healthy, free of pain, loving them, and this year the thought wasn't as raw, as bitter on her tongue. She still yearned for him, still ached, but it got easier each year to put the pain aside like a broken treasure to be fixed at a later time, to not let it consume her. Maybe someday she would not bleed, but have a heart as light as Harley's. Not yet . . . not today, but someday.

Winter was quiet. With fewer clothes to wash, Kate spent time stabbing a needle through frayed socks, britches and dresses in need of mending, neglected during busier times. She patched the girls' trousers and mended tears in their dresses. She turned the collar and cuffs on Harley's shirts so the frayed material would be hidden underneath. She let down hems on dresses grown too short. She was glad she had put in good sized hems in the first place, otherwise they'd have to pass them on to the next younger sister, and she'd have to make an entirely new one for Rachel.

She wished she could buy fabric now, wished they could each have a new dress, but they couldn't. By summer she'd probably have to make one for Rachel – but not right away, thank God. She'd worry about that later – or not. Maybe she'd learn to be more like Harley and not worry at all. What good did it do?

Kate wiped white frost from the window pane, making a circle she could peer out. The whole world was white; the clearing around the cabin and nearby branches were layered with weeks of heavy snowfall. Three deer were drinking from the creek edge where a spring kept a small patch from freezing.

She watched for a while, and her breath steamed the cleared circle. She wiped again. The deer drank their fill and then stood on their hind legs to nibble at the lowest branches of a tree. A jack rabbit race across the clearing, its long rear snowshoe feet skittering across the top of the snow, leaving long streaks in the fresh layer fallen during the night.

The sun was just rising, trading places with the moon and sliding over the edge of the forest canopy to land lightly in front of her, brightly tinting Jack Frost's art work shades of orange and yellow.

The moments just before dawn were her favorite parts of the day. The girls and Harley were still asleep, and it was so quiet she could hear her own breathing, maybe even her own heart beat. A woodpecker flew to the trunk of an ancient oak and drove his beak into the wood looking for breakfast. Its bright red head was a bold streak of color in the stark black and white world of winter. Its rat-a-tat as it drilled into the bark cracked the heavy silence.

Wolf stood and put his paws on the window sill beside her, and she stroked his head as he rested his chin on her shoulder, staring at her. Then he turned to look outside, and his nose made a wet print in the rime of the window pane.

"Are you trying to draw pictures in the glass like the girls do?" she whispered to him and stroked the side of his face with her cheek.

"Draw spring," she told him. "It would be nice to see spring."

Chapter Ten

Spring 1913

Kate stretched under her warm patchwork quilt in the early morning chill, dressed quickly and left the cabin. She slapped at her arms to warm them, blowing white breath as she murmured unladylike words. She hitched Kitty to the buggy and piled the clean clothes packs in the back. The camp had moved again, and it took longer now to drive back and forth to pick up and deliver the laundry. The hills nearer Hersey had been cleared of the tall, straight pines prized by the lumber companies, and they followed the trees.

She had made up her mind. Today, she'd talk with Landmark's foreman to find out where they were heading next and how much work she would have throughout the coming summer. She'd stop by Nestor's before going home if what she learned meant she wouldn't have enough work and had told Harley she might be longer getting home. Wolf was perched on the seat. He knew the routine and didn't have to be told what his job was.

Jack wasn't waiting for her when she arrived because she was so early, but Wolf accompanied her as she looked for Matt, the foreman. She found him at the river's edge supervising the men as they hammered Landmark's stamp into the ends of the logs before rolling them into the water to float down stream.

She waited, not wanting to interrupt. She knew one bad move could throw several men into the freezing river. And that might be the least of their pain. Landing underneath huge rolling logs, either on the bank or in the river meant certain death. She watched, in awe of their combined skills and strength, their work as a team. They moved in a ballet, silent, communicating only with a single word, signal, or nod.

When they had the logs moving down the river, Matt turned her way. "Can I talk with you for a few minutes, Matt?" she asked when he spotted her.

Matt nodded, spoke a few words to the men, and walked over. "What can I do for you, Kate?"

"I need to know how long the camp will be here, how many men you'll have, and where you'll be going next," she told him.

"That's a lot of questions this early in the morning. Would you like a cup of coffee to go with the answers?"

Kate said, "Sure," and moved off in the direction of the cook tent.

"It's not as good as yours, I'm sure, but it's hot."

When they were seated across from each other, Wolf sat on the bench beside her and stared at Matt. "Is he wolf or dog?" Matt asked.

Wolf rolled his brown eye, said, 'Really?'

"Neither. He doesn't like to be called either."

"Where'd you find him?"

"I didn't. He found me."

They chatted about nothing for a bit and then Matt asked her why all the questions.

"I need work, Matt, and I need to know if I'll have enough to get me through another year."

Matt nodded understanding and let her continue.

"I also need to know it won't be so far away that it takes half the day to get there and back."

"Well, I'll tell you what I know, but they don't always keep me informed. They just point the direction one day, and I go there the next."

Kate understood, but anything he knew, even a guess, could help her decide what she had to do.

"We'll probably be here for the next six months or so, maybe into the fall, and the way I see it, we'll probably have about the same number of men we had last year, maybe a few less. I don't know where we'll be going next, but I suspect it will be north and west of here. How far, I don't know."

Kate nodded, thinking and sipping at the thick, bitter coffee.

"Does that help at all?" he asked.

"It does. Thank you, Matt."

He was quiet for a few moments and then said, "Look, I know things have been tough for you since Mark died. If there's anything I can do to help . . ."

There isn't, Kate thought to herself. Can you bring him back or magically make the trees grow tall in the hills closer to home?

"Thanks. I appreciate that, Matt," she said. "And now I think I'd better collect my money and dirty clothes. Love those dirty clothes!"

Wolf glared at each man as usual, just enough to make them uncomfortable. He stood on his hind legs to glare into Tommy Thompson's eyes just to scare him.

"He's harmless, Wolf. He just likes to pretend he's a big, scary man," Kate said.

"Why doesn't he like me?" Tommy asked.

"You called him a dog. He never forgets an insult." But Wolf was a bit of a tease and would terrify Tommy every chance he got. It was fun, as good as hunting rabbits which he couldn't do because Kate wouldn't let him. But he could intimidate Tommy. And so, he did. It was a game.

"Well, he . . . never mind. I won't say it," Tommy stuttered.

"That's probably a good thing," she teased. "He could rip your arm off and toss it around like a stick. Then you'd be out of work."

He backed off, his hands raised in surrender, grinning at Kate. It was a game they played, but Tommy wasn't convinced it was all a joke.

"And be careful how you smile at me, too. He's possessive," she warned. She piled the clothes in the back and called to Wolf.

"See you next time, Tommy."

Kate stood in front of Nestor's and looked in the dusty windows as she'd done when she was a girl. She could see several men seated near the round, black stove, driving out the spring chill with the warmth of its fire and the jug by their feet. Two were bent over a checker board, and Kate imagined their banter as one swooped in to steal the other's wooden disks.

She looked down the sidewalk to Sadie's Saloon where Verna worked. She'd still like to stride in there and order a beer, just to see the looks on their faces. She didn't like it that a lady shouldn't be in a saloon . . . or that a woman in a saloon wasn't a lady.

"Who'd want to be one, anyway," she griped to herself.

She took a deep breath and strode into Nestor's. John greeted her warmly, and Kate told him again how much she liked the washer he'd helped to buy.

"What are you doing out and about on this beautiful spring day, Kate?" he asked.

"I just came from the camp, and I wanted to talk with you, John."

"This sounds serious. Is there a problem?" He leaned forward, put his elbows on the counter, chin on his folded hands.

"No, not really a problem . . . well, yes, I guess there is. I'm not making much sense, am I? Damn. Sorry."

John smiled, "Are you really?"

"Nearly," she said, smiling back at him.

"What is it, Kate?"

"I might need to find some work. I wondered . . . if you needed any help here . . . or . . . well, if you knew anyone who needed help. I'd do anything."

"Well, I'd be careful about advertising that, Kate," he teased.

"You know what I meant," she bantered, lightly tapping his arm in protest. "I'm strong, and I don't mind hard work."

"I know that. Are you going to quit doing the camp laundry?"

"No. It's just that there's less than when I started doing it, and it's getting further and further away. I plan to continue this season, but I thought I could supplement it with some work here in town."

"Have you thought about doing laundry for some folks in Hersey – those who have the money to pay for it and either can't or don't want to do it themselves?"

John fiddled with the licorice jar as he talked, bent to rearrange the candy containers on the shelf below, and wished he could hire Kate so she wouldn't have to worry about money. He wished, too, that she would just marry Mel and not have to work at all, outside of her home, anyway.

Kate said she hadn't thought about that.

"Who would not do their own laundry if they had a place to do it?" she said, amazed by the thought. Would anyone actually pay her to do their laundry just because they could?

"People might," he said, "like Agatha Pennington. She has plenty of money, and she'd like nothing better than to get someone to do her work for her. She could lord it over them, too. She'd like that. Probably even pay more for the lording," he said beaming at her. "Or what about cleaning their homes? I'll bet she'd pay for that, too, and what about old man Woodward. He's got the money, a big house to keep, and no wife."

Kate thought about what he was saying, and a spark of hope lit her eyes. "You know, you might just have a good idea here."

"You sound surprised that I could have one, Kate. Are you disparaging my mental abilities?"

"No. Did you want me to?"

"Very clever, Kate. You're still a smarty pants. What do you think about making up a few signs and putting them in different places around town? You could leave a place at the bottom for someone to write their names if they're interested in hiring some help, and then you could go visit them and see what their needs are."

"I think that's a great idea!" She reached across the counter and planted a solid kiss on his cheek. "Thank you. I'll be back with some signs."

"Have them stop in here, if you want, Kate. Leave a message with me."

"Thanks, John. Really, Thanks a lot." She left with a little skip and her head held high. "I can do this, damn it!" she said as she opened the door to leave and passed Bessie Dunn on her way in.

Bessie's head jerked back when she heard Kate cussing, but she gave her a warm smile anyway. She'd always liked Kate and had hated the way she'd been treated by Agatha Pennington when the old biddy tried to get Kate fired from her teaching position. It was a long time ago, but Bessie had been on the school board and a part of the whole mess. She'd resigned her board position shortly after.

"Bessie," Kate said, reddening from Bessie's involuntary reaction. "Good to see you."

Bessie nodded and Kate fled, calling unnecessarily for Wolf who waited for her outside the door.

The drive home was lighter. The sun was high in the sky and warm on her face. Spring in Michigan was amazing. Freezing cold before the sun was up, and sixty by midday. Kate took note of her surroundings, sniffed the musky aroma of damp earth. Saw the riot of color that had sprouted so fast you could hear the growth, Mother Nature's egocentric exhibition of spring.

She planned what she would write on the posters, and calculated what she would charge if someone actually wanted her to clean their house. She mentally bought new shoes for the girls and some material for new dresses – even new pants for all of them.

When she drove into the clearing, Harley and the girls were squatted on the ground in a circle. She walked over before unhitching Kitty and saw what they were looking at, three tiny critters, hairless baby raccoons. They were so young their eyes were still closed, but their tiny mouths made hungry sucking motions.

"Where on earth did you get those?" she asked.

"Mel brought them," Harley told her. "He said the mother had been killed, and these sweet babies were starving."

"Well, that's just dandy. More stray critters. Thanks, Mel" she moaned, but grinned at the squirming babies. "I wonder how Mildred will get along with raccoons."

Mildred was the wounded woodchuck they had taken in. Her leg had healed, and the cage door was left open now, but she hung around the clearing, limped to her cage when she was hungry, and went back into the woods when she wanted woodchuck company. Kate hoped she would not give them a nest full of little woodchucks, but it wouldn't surprise her if nature had its way. It usually did.

They took the babies inside and found a basket they lined with a layer of clean toweling. Kat got out her book and read up on what raccoons eat, and Harley set about making a milk concoction for them. He found an eyedropper and managed to get a little of the liquid into each of their mouths. Wolf and Poochie stood side by side staring into the basket, and then Wolf nosed them, pushed them around on the towel with his big black nose and then lay down next to the basket. Poochie whined a little, snuffled and walked away.

Jeannie was in awe, her blue eyes wide in wonder. "They're so sweet, Ma. Let's name them."

"I guess they should have names, but honey, they're really tiny, and you need to understand that they might not survive. They need their mother's milk, and they're so young. Can you try not to get too attached just yet?"

Jeannie nodded, but her eyes filled with tears. "They can't die. We can't let them die."

"We're going to do our best," Harley said, and Kate knew if anyone could save them, it would be Harley and Jeannie; Harley because he just knew things; Jeannie out of sheer determination born of love for critters, especially baby critters.

She unhitched Kitty, brought in the laundry and started supper. When they were eating, Kate explained her plan to find some work in Hersey.

"I need your help, girls, making up some signs to put up around town."

Rachel volunteered to write them, and Becca said she'd draw some pictures so they'd be pretty. Kate was glad Rachel would do the writing – she had a good hand, and accepted Becca's offer of decorating them because she couldn't say no.

Squeals came from the raccoon nest by the hearth. Wolf stuck his nose in the basket, and then looked at Harley, his eyes scolding. 'When are you going to do something about this? They're hungry again.'

Several times in the night over the next couple of weeks she heard the raccoons squeal and then Harley shuffle around the kitchen. He fed them every two or three hours, and before long, their eyes opened, and they were crawling around in the basket.

Then their fur changed from the tawny down over pink little bodies to the dark, raccoon hair she recognized from watching the den of coons by the clearing. They no longer looked like little rats and were getting to be a handful, crawling to the edge of the basket and deliberately falling over the rim and onto the floor to escape.

Mel came to visit one day and laughed when one fell out and Jeannie ran to pick it up. She sat with the coon on her lap and stuck the end of her little finger to its mouth to let it suckle at the tip.

"He thinks I'm his momma," she said proudly. It certainly quieted the animal.

"See what you've done?" Kate said to Mel. "This was already an animal paradise; Wolf, Poochie, Mildred, two fully grown birds who would rather be waited on than find their own food, and now, thanks to you, a basket of raccoons."

"Mildred?" he asked. "Who is that?"

"The woodchuck. You know her."

He nodded, trying to hide the developing grin.

"I believe I've had the pleasure. Just didn't know her by name." Then he asked how the quest for work in Hersey was going.

"John was right. Agatha Pennington would like her laundry done, and Mr. Woodward wants both his laundry and his housework done."

"That's great, but I wish you didn't have to."

"I don't mind Woodward. He's a quaint, comical old man, but it sure galls me to do anything for Agatha Pennington, the old stick," Kate told him. "But I will."

"Old stick?" he queried. "What does that mean?"

"Stiff, ornery, other things I'm too polite to say."

Mel raised his eyebrows, questioning. "Hmmm, Kate? Too polite?"

"I can be nice," she said sulking for show. "Sometimes I can."

"Sure, and I'll remember the term stick for when you use it on me."

"Do you want to help feed Max?" Jeannie called to Mel. "That's his name," she said pointing to the raccoon on her lap.

"I'm not sure how good I'll be at it with these clumsy old hands, but I'll try."

Mel sat on the floor next to her, and Jeannie held Max out to him. He held it gently in the palm of one hand and cupped the other around it so it wouldn't fall out. It looked so small in Mel's huge hand. They had graduated from the eyedropper to a small bottle. Mel held the nipple to its mouth, and the raccoon gripped it in his hands, its dexterous fingers grasping the bottle as if it was born to it. When the milk was gone, Jeannie put her finger out to him, and Max pulled it to his mouth, once more contented.

Kate and Harley watched from their places at the table. Mel was good with Jeannie – with all of the girls. There was gentleness in the huge man and tenderness. He was perceptive with both the child and the animal.

The other two coons began squealing and crawling out the basket, and soon Kat and Becca brought them to join the feeding circle on the floor. Harley refilled the bottle, and they began the process all over again.

"Can you tell them apart?" Mel asked.

149

"Of course," Kat said, slighted by the question. "This one is Jenny," she said, pointing to the one on her lap. "And that's Winnie."

"How did you pick the names?"

"Well, Winnie is mine," Kat told him. "And I picked that because she chews all the time and scolds when she's mad, so I asked Ma what Mrs. Wellington's first name was. It's Winnie."

Mel nodded and laughed, picturing the old woman in a raccoon face.

"How do you know which ones are boys and which are girls?"

Kat looked at Mel like he was from the moon and shook her head. "You're kidding, right?" she said.

Mel blushed, quite a feat given the deep tan of his weathered skin.

"You are a farmer, aren't you?" she continued, still sounding amazed he had even thought the question, but Kate saw the gleam in her daughter's eyes. Kat had a way of baiting a person, and you never knew for sure when she was teasing or not. She was a straight-faced comic in a child's body.

Harley grinned at the conversation and at Mel's discomfort.

"Have you not had the birds and bees talk yet, Mel? If not, I will certainly have to set aside some time to have a conversation with you."

Kate made the trip out to the camp each Monday, went into Hersey to clean house for Mr. Woodward and pick up his laundry every Tuesday, and stopped by Mrs. Pennington's on the way home to deliver and pick up hers. Wednesdays and Thursdays were wash days, and on Fridays, she ironed. Somewhere in between, she planted the garden, cooked and cleaned her own house, with the girls' help.

She had a routine that worked, even if she was exhausted, and she was saving enough money to do some of the things she couldn't afford to do before the additional income. Soon she would have enough to buy some shoes for the girls and fabric to make dresses. The problem was she didn't know when she'd find the time to make them.

Eldon was a pleasure to work for. He told Kate to take her time and do what she could accomplish in one day. "Don't worry. Let the rest go for another time, Kate," he'd said. "It'll be there next week." He told her jokes and was constantly under foot, but he had coffee made when she needed some, and for that she was grateful.

One day while they were sitting on the long, covered porch with their coffee he said, "Kate, if you'd marry this old man, I'd make you a happy lady of leisure. I'd hire someone else to clean this house – for you."

"You're much too young for me, Mr. Woodward," she'd responded with a sparkle in her eyes.

"Ah . . . my heart is young. I do feel like a boy."

"You act like one," Kate bantered.

"The rest of me is youthful, too," he countered, the glint in his eyes matching Kate's. "At least that's what Sadie's ladies tell me."

"You're a rascal, Mr. Woodward, a rogue," she said, picking up her coffee cup. "And I need to get back to work."

"Call me Eldon," he said, and before she knew what was happening, he'd smacked her on the bottom as she turned to leave.

Kate whipped around to him, fist raised, ready to round house punch him until she saw the merriment on his heavily creased face and knew he was just a harmless old reprobate.

She grinned back and told him he was lucky Wolf, who was waiting on the porch for her, hadn't sunk his teeth into his arm. But then she looked at Wolf lying in the shade, and he rolled his eye at her, 'He is a harmless degenerate, Kate. Deal with it and don't bother me.'

She took pleasure in helping Eldon. His house was huge, but it wasn't dirty, and his clothes were made of fine fabrics that were a pleasure to iron. Almost. She took special pains to make sure they looked perfect, were crisp and wrinkle free. Kate grew fond of him, and he enjoyed the time she spent there. It was dramatically different when she went to Agatha Pennington's.

The bitter old woman found fault with everything Kate did. There wasn't enough starch in the sheets, and there was too much in the pillow cases. Her shirtdresses had wrinkles Kate knew didn't exist. She counted every penny into Kate's hand like she was handing out pennies to a beggar. Kate hated every moment she had to spend with the odious old biddy and wished she could tell her to go jump in the Muskegon River when the current was rampant with spring thaw.

During the ride from Mr. Woodward's to Agatha's house, Kate conjured up all the ghastly and unspeakable calamities she could think of that might befall the insufferable old woman. She pictured her being dunked in a horse trough, at least three times, until she came up sputtering and choking, saying "Uncle, uncle, I give up. I promise to change. . ." The picture made Kate smile, so she continued playing with others until she pulled into the driveway.

When she knocked on the door, Kate was smiling, and that always galled the woman. She handed her the package of clean things and took the bundle to be washed. Then Kate slowly recounted the money Agatha had given her, just to further needle her, and said, "Have a good day, Agatha. See you in a week," and she skipped down the steps, happy to be gone.

The work was infinite, but the new washer helped. The whole process was much quicker having the rollers to squeeze the water out, and her hands weren't always in pain from twisting and wringing. It saved refilling the tubs so often, and the clothes dried as fast as she could hang them on the lines.

Kate cranked the rollers over the last garment and threw it in the basket, glad to be done with wash for the day. She hung them and then went to call Harley and the girls to help plant the seedlings they had started in the window sills when it was still winter. Mel pulled into the clearing as they came out of the cabin with their plants.

The raccoons scuttled out with them and chased around the yard. They were roly-poly fur balls now and the world was their plaything. Mel watched the train of people and coons. It was a great picture. He threw a leg over his mare and went to take a tray of seedlings from Kate. "Want some help?"

"Just try to get out of it," she said grasping a hoe leaning against the cabin.

They were in two lines; one person in each row dug a small hole, the next separated and dropped in the seedling, and the next gently patted the ground around its tender roots. When they reached the end of the garden and turned to go down the next row, they saw the coons. They had pulled out every carefully placed plant and thrown them on the ground to die in the sun.

"No! Max! Jenny! Winnie!" Kate screeched. "Damn it, stop!" They all looked at the devastation; even the raccoons had halted in their tracks and stood looking around. She sat in the tilled dirt and looked again. Defeated tears sprung to her eyes and threatened rivers on her cheeks.

She sat motionless, staring at the wreckage, too tired to move, and then she giggled. Once started, she couldn't stop. It bubbled out. Gurgled, like lava from a volcano, giggles spewed from her. She cried and laughed at the same time, and somewhere in the deep, dark, recessed logic part of her brain, she wondered if this was hysteria.

I could be crazy, she thought. Probably am.

The girls chuckled tentatively, then louder, and soon they were holding their stomachs and rolling in the dirt. Harley joined them. When the hilarity finally died, someone would snort, and it would start all over.

When he could stand erect, Harley gathered the plants and put them in a bucket with a little water. Kat, Becca and Jeannie each caught a raccoon and took it outside the garden enclosure, and Mel walked over to where Kate still sat on the ground. She wiped the tears from her face and left dirty streaks.

"You look like a homeless waif," he said, and handed her a handkerchief.

"This is your fault," she told him with an accusing finger pointed at his chest, "You and your big heart. Here Kate, have some baby raccoons. They're so cute. I know you want them."

"Sorry, but they are cute little monsters, aren't they?"

"Yes, they are, but they are going to have to learn where they can go and where they can't."

"Do you think they'll hang around much longer? They'll be grown soon."

"I don't think they'll ever leave, ever, ever, and forever," Kate sighed. "They were so young when they came they think the girls are their mamas. Have you seen the way the cute little fiends follow them around?"

Mel nodded and smiled, not at the critters she was describing, but at the picture Kate made sitting in the dirt. "Come on," he said, standing and holding out a hand to help her up. "Let's fix this mess you've made."

"Me? The mess *I've* made?" she said, grabbing his hand and a bunch of loose soil. She bounced up, pulled at his open shirt and dumped in the dirt.

"There. Now, I've made a mess," she said, smiling wickedly as she watched him untuck his shirt and try to shake out the dirt.

"Brat!" He bent, grabbed some loose dirt and flung it at her. It landed in her hair, and she grabbed some more and tossed it on his head.

"Ha!" she said as she watched it trickle down his face. Dirt was flying everywhere before long. Kate felt her teeth grind with grit, and didn't care. It was a battle to the end. The girls heard the commotion and came running to see their mother and Mel in a dirt fight, laughing and shouting at each other.

"Look out, Ma," Kat yelled when she saw Mel leap forward to grab Kate.

He scooped her up, then put her on her back and straddled her middle, holding her hands above her head. "Surrender?" he asked.

"Never! To a confounded, brute of a scoundrel like you? Never! Never!"

He positioned both her hands in one of his, scooped up more dirt, and held it above her head. "Are you sure? Say uncle."

"Damn it, Mel, if you do . . ."

"Shut your eyes" he said, and he trickled a little of the dirt onto her face. "Oops. Your mouth too, I guess."

"You'll be sorry for this. I'll call Wolf," she threatened menacingly, spitting dirt.

Mel unconsciously glanced around for the animal, not trusting him. "Wolf is right there watching. He doesn't care."

She felt a little more dirt drop, and she turned her head so she could open her eyes and look for Wolf.

"What the hell . . . Why are you just sitting there watching when I'm being killed?"

Wolf just rolled both eyes at them, saying 'I've played in dirt before – when I was much, much younger and sillier.'

"Say uncle – and while you're at it, say you're sorry for the cuss word."

Kate couldn't budge him no matter how much she bucked and squirmed under him, so she crossed her fingers under his hand, and pretended to give up. "Uncle, and more or less sorry."

He helped her up and tried to brush some of the dirt off of her. He peered into her face, searching, because something didn't feel just right and immediately knew Kate hadn't surrendered. She was plotting revenge, and he wouldn't know how or when it would come. But it would come. That he knew, and he felt something close to fear . . . well, uneasiness sweep over him. Kate was a force to be reckoned with. With quiet, feminine wickedness, she was saying exactly the same to herself. Sometime, somehow, he would pay for his play.

They replanted the seedlings –restricting the coons to the other side of the fence. Most of the plants hadn't been harmed; they'd just been pulled out and tossed aside. Mel brought buckets full of creek water, and Jeannie and Becca ladled some over the soil around the roots. Then they stood looking at the neat rows that would soon produce fresh vegetables for the table and the storage cellar.

"Did I earn supper?" Mel asked, trying hard to look inoffensive and contrite.

"I guess, but don't be surprised if you taste something peculiar in your food."

They heard pounding and followed the sound. Harley had begun constructing an outside cage for the raccoons, a large one so they had plenty of space to run around, he told them. "And I'd like to put a couple of big tree limbs in so they have something to climb. They like that."

"I know," Kate said, "have you seen the scratches on my legs?"

"No, but I'd like to. I'll bet they're quite nice; the legs, not the scratches," Mel teased, ogling Kate's legs.

"Don't give me any more reasons to thrash you, big boy. You're already on my list." Kate was surprised by the tenor of Mel's teasing, but in an odd way it pleased her.

He was growing more and more comfortable with her and the girls, or 'maybe it's me who's getting more comfortable having him around,' she said to herself. 'Maybe he has always been at ease, and I've just begun to.' She shrugged her shoulders and went into the cabin to wash up.

She put water on to heat, and when it was ready, she poured some into the bowl in her room and stripped out of her clothes. She soaped and rinsed her hair and then washed the rest of her body. When she was toweling her hair dry, she turned to look in the mirror leaning against the wall of her bedroom. Her hands were stilled for a moment as she looked at her naked body. Then she turned and looked again. She saw long, firm legs and a round bottom. She lifted her breasts and tilted her head.

"I'm not so old," she said out loud. "I could look worse." Then she blushed and shook herself.

"What in hell are you doing, Kate? What's wrong with you?" She quickly turned away from the mirror and pulled a dress over her head, her nice one, then ran a comb through her long hair and let it hang to dry.

She put more water on to heat, took some outside for Mel and Harley and some to her daughters' rooms. She called the girls in to wash up.

As she was preparing supper, she glanced out the window over the sink. Mel had stripped off his shirt and was rinsing off the dirt she had dumped inside. Kate paused, watching muscles bunch across his shoulders and taper down to narrow hips. The skin under his shirt was white compared to the brown of his arms, and appeared cool and smooth, unblemished.

She watched silently, unaware she was doing it until Mel turned to put his shirt back on. Then she blinked and twice in less than an hour, shook herself. "Good God, Kate. What is the matter with you today?"

She finished putting food in the kettle, set it on the stove to simmer, and went outside to sit in the diminishing sun. The air was still warm, and lay like feathers on faintly damp skin. Kate ran her fingers through her hair, lifting it and letting it fall to her shoulders to help it dry.

Mel turned the water bowl over to Harley and came to sit by Kate. It was his turn to silently watch, a voyeur, hoping to hold time, enjoy each sweet, scented moment. Her long hair shimmered in the sun's low rays, and was streaked with different hues of summer's golden wheat. He reached to touch a strand as it fell from her fingers like soft silk. A few light freckles sprinkled her nose and cheeks, and the tan on her face brightened the sapphire of her eyes. The sight of her made his breath catch in his chest.

"You grow more beautiful each day, Kate," he whispered hoarsely. "Do you even know how you look?"

Kate was startled by his words, remembered looking at herself in the mirror a short while ago, and felt blood rush to her face in embarrassment.

What was going on today? Is there something in the air? she wondered, then took a firm hold of her thoughts and turned to him.

"You're a scoundrel, Mel Bronson, a womanizer with your fancy words."

Mel laughed at the idea of himself as a womanizer. Nothing could be further from the truth. He'd been a one-woman man his entire life – even when that woman had spurned him for another she had loved more.

"That's me," he said leering at Kate, "a rogue, a scala-wag, a dirty old man."

Harley walked over, and Kate was glad. He saw Kate's flushed face and wondered what he had interrupted, hoping he had broken up something good. His curls were damp falling over his forehead, and he looked like a wet cherub.

"I hear there's a spring dance in town this Saturday," he said. "Are we going?"

"Are you asking me for a date, Harley?" Kate asked. But Harley was hard to tease. He always had a response that made quick work of the effort and plunked the teaser into the hot seat.

"Miss Kate, I'm too much of a man for your tender sensibilities. You wouldn't know what to do with me, but I'm thinking I can get a date for you. What about Tommy Thompson? Will he do? Or I hear old Woodward is kinda sweet on you. How about him?" he said, grinning at Mel.

Wolf, who had come over and stood next to Kate, peered over at Harley like he'd lost his mind. "I swear that animal understands English," Harley said. "He just glared at me."

"Don't call him an animal. He doesn't like it, and I'll consider Tommy."

"You're a witch, woman," Mel said with a grimace and a groan, then added, "Will you please go to the dance with me, Miss Kate?"

Kate put a finger to her chin like she was thinking about it and waited a few moments.

"I don't know" she said in feigned solemnity. "Eldon has made a proposal of marriage, and I haven't given him an answer yet, so I'm not sure I should be dating other men until I decide."

"Eldon proposed?" Harley and Mel sang out in sync.

"Yes, Eldon Woodward. He's quite rich, you know, and a manly kind of man."

"So it's Eldon, now, instead of Mr. Woodward," Mel said. "And he proposed to you?"

Kate nodded. "He sure did – said he'd give me a life of leisure and luxury."

"I guess you might want to think about that. He is rich," Mel told her, going along with her game. "I can imagine him carrying you across the threshold and to your marriage bed. Can you?" he teased.

Kate shuddered. "Ohhh . . . I think I just made up my mind," she said laughing at the thought. "Let's go get some supper."

Chapter Eleven

They took their time getting ready for the dance, bathed in lilac water, put on their best dresses and took extra time with their hair. Rachel wore the pearl comb, and her dark curls were a thick, ebony river flowing down her back. Kate tied Jeannie and Becca's hair with red and pink ribbons, and Kat's straight blonde flowed over her shoulders in long strands of corn silk. She didn't want ribbons in her hair. They were much too fussy for Kat's taste.

Harley wore his good blue shirt, the one Kate and Ellen had made for him several years ago and he saved for special occasions. He put on his red suspenders and fluffed his own curls with a brush.

Mel drove his buggy out to pick them up, and when they heard it in the clearing, they were ready and eagerly waiting. He knocked on the door and gave a low bow before he entered.

"Your carriage awaits, ladies," he said with mock formality. Then he gave a long whistle and spun around. "You all look beautiful, like a spring garden in full bloom."

"You look beautiful, too," Jeannie told him as she took his hand.

"It's handsome," Kat said. "Men are handsome."

"This old horse face?" Mel asked.

"I like horse faces. They have pretty eyes," Kat said, "like Harley."

Mel laughed, but wasn't quite sure if it was meant to be funny or not. It was hard being taken in, totally flummoxed by a child, but he was. Most people were. Harley stuck his thumbs in his suspenders and pushed out his round belly proudly. "I truly am something to behold."

"Yeah, we just haven't figured out what yet," Mel said and pulled out one of the red suspenders to let it snap back at Harley's belly.

Harley drove Kate's rig with Becca and Kat on either side. They were picking up Verna at Sadie's. Kate, Rachel and Jeannie went with Mel. Wolf stared forlornly at them as they drove away, then he turned three times and lay down in the grass by the door. Poochie flopped down next to him, but not so close he would get nipped if he growled in his sleep.

When Verna climbed in, she heard a grumble from Kat. "I didn't hear you, Urchin. What'd you say?"

"I told Ma I could wear my pants. You are."

Verna chuckled. "That's because my Ma isn't here to tell me I can't."

"That's not fair."

"Life isn't," Verna said, her blue eyes sparkling at Kat. "And you look very nice."

"Clean is good enough. I don't need nice," Kat said.

Harley listened to them and wondered when Kat would learn to like being a girl and start to care that most boys, not all by any means, but most of them liked girls in dresses. He hoped it wouldn't happen soon. He liked her just the way she was. He wanted all his Ramey girls to stay just as they were for a long time, yet he couldn't help but tease her.

"The way you look, I'm thinking you'll have a lot of boys standing in line to dance with you, Kat. You, too, Becca."

Kat frowned and Becca smiled and asked if Harley was going to dance with Verna. When he said he most certainly was, Kat mumbled, "And she's wearing pants, so it doesn't matter, see?"

The Hersey Town Hall was filled with folks who had driven for miles to celebrate the coming of spring. They greeted people they hadn't seen during the long winter when they were cloistered and confined to their homes. It was a family reunion with handshakes and hugs for everyone, even for people they didn't like all that much, just because it was good to be out and about, see other faces.

161

Jack and Ruthie pulled up about the same time as they did. Ellen was with them and they all went in together. Mel couldn't define the crowding in his chest, right next to his heart, when he walked in with Kate on his arm and the girls around them, but it was powerful and heady. He saw eyes turn on them appreciatively, and he knew soaring pride that they were by his side. Not some other man . . . him. He stood tall, an expression on his face that said it all. They are with me. These ladies are with me.

They were surrounded by people wanting to say hello as soon as they walked in the door. John Nestor lifted Kate off the floor in a big bear hug and told her she was the most beautiful woman in the room – except for her mother and her daughters, he added quickly.

Tommy Thompson shook Mel's hand and asked if he could have a dance with Kate. "One," Mel said, grinning and feeling good he'd been consulted. As it should be. They're with me, he thought with pride. He'd have snapped suspenders had he been wearing them.

Matt Keller, Landmark foreman, strode up in time to hear Tommy ask and told Mel he was claiming the next dance; and Jake the jailer asked for one, too. Mel held up his hands and said, "Hey! When do I get to dance with her?"

"First and last," Kate said with a determined grin, and then eyed the suitors with a pseudo-frown.

"And since when do you ask Mel Bronson who I can dance with and talk about me like I'm not even here? I decide and I choose you." She pointed a finger at them all one by one.

John Nestor slapped Mel's back, laughing at the sheepish look on his face, and the rest joined him. They'd all known Kate a long time, and she hadn't changed a lot since she was a girl. She had never liked being told what she could do.

"She's still Kate," John said to Mel, patting his shoulder in fatherly fashion.

Kate took Mel's hand in hers and squeezed gently, then stood on tiptoes to kiss his cheek. "I still like you," she said softly and the group of would-be suitors laughed and applauded. They were all saved further decision making by music from the back of the room.

The band had gathered on a small stage and was tuning instruments. Soon the sweet, whining warble of a fiddle filled the hall, and Kate turned to see two of the Tate boys and their father, Leo, getting ready to play.

Gordon Tilmann from the hardware store was with them, his stooped shoulders bent over an old, now colorless guitar. Gordon's bushy, gray head shook with palsy, but his fingers were steady and sure on the strings of his instrument. He'd been playing at hall dances for as long as Kate could remember, most likely as long as anyone could remember. It was hard to watch him, though, because of the quaking and quivering of his muscles, but if you closed your eyes and just listened, his guitar sang like a harp from heaven's orchestra. It pulled at the strings of your heart and lifted your spirit.

Kate looked for Rachel to see if she had noticed who was playing in the band, saw her eyes search the room, and knew Rachel was looking for Charlie Tate. It was quite obvious when she spotted him because she heard Rachel's small intake of breath, a sigh of relief and anticipation. Her face lit. Then the music started, and Mel led Kate to the dance floor. They glided easily around the room to a slow two-step, and Kate relaxed in Mel's arms.

Harley watched with a smile. "They have no idea how good they look. Kate's a china doll next to him," he said to Verna. "And he's a colossal, handsome storybook hero, our Lancelot."

"Aren't you the poet," she said with a grin.

"Would you like to dance, Miss Verna?"

"Not until I've had a nip of that jug I know you brought."

"Now how would you know that?" he asked, his elfin face a perfect picture for the blarney stone.

"Because you invited me, not some old stick."

He grinned, wondered where he had heard that term before, and led her outside to the buggy where they sipped a few times on Will's good moonshine. Then they went in, ready to dance.

While Tommy, Jake and Matt claimed their dances with Kate, Mel took each of the girls out on the floor. He held Jeannie in his arms while they danced, but Becca wanted to do it the 'right' way since she wasn't a little girl anymore. Kat shrugged her shoulders when he asked her, but went with him saying, "I guess I could do that."

It was all too perfect, and for a brief moment, Mel felt like an interloper, a thief, as memory of his friend, their father, drove a wedge into his contentment.

But I love them, Mark, was all he could say.

When he looked for Rachel, she was already dancing with Charlie. He watched and felt something akin to concern. *You're getting as bad as Kate,* he thought. She's a young lady dancing with a boy she likes. There's nothing wrong with that. But he still watched; then he saw Kate on the dance floor with Matt, and knew she was looking at Rachel, too.

Eldon Woodward shuffled out to the dance floor, his long, thin frame bent with age. He tapped Matt's shoulder, and Kate grinned at Matt's frown, but he dutifully held out her hand to Eldon, giving up his dance with her to the old man as propriety insists is appropriate. It was dance floor etiquette.

Eldon was surprisingly graceful as he swung her around the floor, his arm firmly around Kate's back. She saw Harley and Mel grinning at them and recalled Mel's comment about Eldon and the marriage bed. She blushed at the thought, and determined to have a second dance with Eldon just to teach Mel a lesson.

When she and Jack danced, he held her away from him for a few moments and looked at her. "You're having fun, aren't you?" he asked, looking at her flushed cheeks and the sparkle in her blue eyes.

Kate nodded. "I really am."

He pulled her closer for a proper waltz, and they glided easily around the room. Jack reminisced while they danced and wished Mark could see her. He thought of Lorraine,

Mark's first wife and compared her dark, wicked beauty to the woman in his arms. He knew from the last time he'd seen Lorraine she would not wear her dissipation well over the years.

Yet, Kate had a fresh loveliness that increased with time. Her face was tanned and unlined, her eyes clear, healthy and sparkling. She emanated strength in his arms, but Jack knew her fragility. "If wishes were horses," he whispered to Mark, "you'd be here."

"I'm sorry," Kate said, looking up at him. "I didn't hear you. What about a horse?"

"Uh . . . nothing. I just said I dance like a six-legged horse."

"That, you know full well, is nonsense. You float. Are you angling for a compliment?"

He smiled, knowing what she said was true. "You're right. I am good."

Jack handed her back to Mel, and they all danced to the rousing Virginia Reel, after which, they walked outside into the night air to cool off. Harley invited them to sip at the jug he'd squirreled away in Kate's buggy. Jeannie, Becca and Kat had been left in John Nestor's care for a few minutes, and Rachel had been dancing with Charlie. They toasted to a good time and to feet that wouldn't hurt in the morning.

They were just about to stash the jug and go back in when Mel saw two figures slip out the side door. He stared into the dark, trying to see who it was, and a prickling began at the back of his neck and crawled down his spine.

"Go on in," he said. "I'll be there in a few minutes. I know there's a long line of men waiting to dance with you, so you won't be lonely."

Kate tapped him on the arm, a devious grin on her face. "Jealous?"

"On the contrary. I'm grateful that they are saving my feet."

When they had gone, Mel quietly walked to the side of the building. He wasn't positive he'd seen Rachel and didn't want to disturb two people who obviously wanted to be alone. But he needed to know for sure. When they heard him coming, they sprung apart from the embrace, embarrassed.

Charlie stammered, "We were just getting some air . . . we're going back in now." Rachel didn't say anything, but her hand went to her hair as she reset the comb that had come loose.

"Why don't you go on in, Rachel. I want to talk with Charlie a minute," Mel said.

Her face flushed with self-conscious, unreasonable anger. "You can't tell me what to do, Mel! You're not my father." Her back was stiff, her arms crossed firmly across her chest.

Mel took a deep breath and thought about what to do. He was lost. How do you deal with young women? He had helped raise his younger siblings, but he'd not run into anything like this with them, and Rachel was apparently not going to take advice from any man . . . who was not her father. The thought was oddly painful. Finally, he said "Your mother is looking for you."

Rachel spun on her heels and sprinted in.

He and Charlie stared at each other for a few moments. Charlie shuffled his feet in the dirt and studied the toe of his boot. Mel stood as if he'd been planted in concrete with his hands clenched, wondering what he could say that would do any good, letting the silence stretch. He wanted to punch him but knew that was stupid. Charlie was a kid – just a normal kid. He finally found his voice, but it came out a low growl.

"I don't want to see anything like this happen again. Rachel is thirteen."

"She's almost a woman . . . and she's right. You can't tell her what to do," Charlie said with bravado inconsistent with his shuffling feet.

The youngster was right. He couldn't, but that just made him angrier. He grabbed Charlie's arm and drew him up to glare stonily into his face. Fear lit Charlie's eyes as he peered up at Mel who stood a foot taller and was twice as wide. At the moment, it felt to Charlie like he was up against Goliath, and he wasn't sure what the giant was going to do.

"No, I can't tell Rachel what to do, but Kate can. And right now, I *am* telling you what to do, so if I were you, I'd listen. You will not treat that girl with anything but respect or do anything that will hurt her! Do you understand what I'm telling *you*?"

When Charlie didn't respond, he gripped harder, his hand circling the boy's bicep. "I said, do you understand?"

Charlie nodded because he couldn't speak. When it felt like his arm was about to break, he squeaked out "Okay, I get it."

Mel dropped him and strode off, running his hand through his hair in frustration. He was angry, and it scared him that he had wanted the boy to take a swing at him so he could knock him to the ground. That had never been his way – to use physical force, but he had wanted to plant a fist in the kid's face.

He stood by the buggy for awhile to cool off and saw Charlie slip back in the side door. He hoped the boy had been scared, or at the very least anxious enough to behave himself with Rachel. He thought about what she'd said, remembered the look on her face. It saddened him, and he wondered what he should say to Kate. When he went back in, she was dancing with Jack. She looked so happy he didn't want to say anything that would spoil it for her.

Maybe later, he thought.

It was late when they left. Jeannie quickly fell asleep, and Rachel was silent beside her. Kate leaned against Mel, contented, and talked about the night. Every so often she asked Rachel a question, to which Rachel gave brief responses.

"Is everything alright?" she prodded, wondering what was going on in her daughter's mind.

"Sure, I'm just tired from all the dancing."

And she's angry at me, Mel thought but didn't say. Or afraid I'm going to say something.

Mel carried Jeannie in to her bed and went outside to sit while Kate tucked her in. He remembered the night Rachel had told Kate she didn't need that anymore. She was growing up fast, and he wondered if her rush toward adulthood was connected to her father's death. Did the loss of him impact her intimacy with Charlie?

He was still pondering his dilemma when Harley drove in with Kat and Becca. When Harley sat next to him, Mel asked if he could throw a question his way. He told Harley briefly what had happened and laid out his concern over keeping it from Kate – and about telling her. Neither was good.

"You're right about that," Harley said, rubbing his hand over the stubble of his beard. "Rachel said you're not her father and you can't tell her what to do? Those were her words?"

Mel nodded. "I don't think I've ever tried to be that – have I?"

"Only in good ways, by being here for them, helping out like the rest of us. But Rachel was older when Mark died, and she saw it all. Maybe she's resentful that you're here and her father isn't. Or maybe it doesn't have anything to do with you at all, and she's just trying to be an adult with a thirteen-year old brain. She got caught doing something she shouldn't have been doing, and took it out on you because you were the one who caught her."

"I almost wish I hadn't seen them, but then . . . I don't know. Maybe I overreacted because Kate's been worried. I've seen her reactions and haven't understood. Still don't."

"Kate wouldn't like being kept in the dark about this," Harley said.

"I know. I just hate to add to her worries."

Harley stood, saying he would leave them alone and that Mel would figure out the right thing to do.

"Kate's strong, Mel. Don't make the mistake of underestimating her. And remember this. You can't make good decisions about the future if you don't understand the past. If there's a hole in Kate's knowledge, you've hampered her – and perhaps hurt Rachel." With that, he left and said goodnight to Kate as she left the girls' room and went outside. She sat with a tired sigh.

"This was a good night. Thank you for spending it with us." She rested her head against the back of the chair and looked up at the stars. The moon was rising, full and round, and lit the clearing.

"It is always my pleasure," he said. "Do you mind if I stay for a bit, or are you too tired?"

"I'm tired, but I feel so good I'm not ready to go to bed. I couldn't sleep yet."

"I need to talk with you about something, Kate. Can I get you a small glass of cordial?"

Kate's senses pricked at her, and apprehension crawled up her back. "What's wrong?" she asked, contentment on her face replaced by concern.

"Nothing's wrong. I just need to tell you something. Let me get that cordial first."

When he came back, she was sitting erect, feet firmly planted, hands folded in her lap, waiting. "What is it?" she asked bluntly.

Mel told her what he had seen, leaving out the part about Rachel's hair needing to be fixed and her words to Mel. He merely said she and Charlie had been outside in an embrace and he thought Kate should know.

Kate's reaction was as intense as he had feared it would be, but it took a turn he hadn't expected.

"What did he do to her? Was she afraid? I need to teach her how to kick a man. I haven't done that." Tears had sprung to her eyes around exploding anger.

Mel sat back, stunned. "Kate, it wasn't like that. They were two kids who like each other – kissing. That's all. I just thought you'd want to know."

"If he hurt her . . ."

"He didn't, Kate. Listen to me. He didn't hurt her. Rachel wanted to be kissed."

Kate folded her arms tightly across her breasts, her hands clenched around her biceps. Her head was bowed, and Mel could see spasmodic trembling in her shoulders. "I'm sorry. Maybe I shouldn't have said anything. I just . . ."

He left it there because he didn't know what else to say. They sat for awhile letting silence fall around them. Darkness in the shadow of the cabin was warm, a safe place blanketing them from the outside world. It was them and no one else. He gently put his arm across her shoulders and left it there while she was quiet. He pondered Kate's immediate reaction to what he'd told her and found it strange. Did all mothers worry about their daughters being forced into compromising situations? He didn't know, but it niggled at him.

He remembered the look on Kate's face when Rachel went into the woods with Charlie, and they were out of her sight. He thought about Kate searching behind trees when they were at the camp, her unaccustomed angst in the woods and the reason he'd gone to see Jack.

"Do you want to talk about it?" he asked softly.

She didn't answer immediately, so he waited. She sipped her drink and followed the warm burn as it trailed down inside her chest. He listened to her breath, could feel the pulsing of her heart in the quiet of the night. And he waited. He was good at that. When she finally spoke, her words came out in a flood of tears and whispered wrath.

"He tried to rape me! He violated me! My clothes were torn ... That bastard had his mouth on me! On my skin! My breasts!" Kate pounded her fists on the arms of her chair, enunciating each horrific, appalling word she spoke.

"That wretch put his ... He killed Bug," she sobbed. She put her face in her hands and sobbed, long wrenching sobs that tore at Mel's guts. "He killed my Water Bug ..."

It took everything he had to sit there quietly. A fury he had never known filled him totally, and he wanted to smash something. Anything. The hand on the arm of his chair clenched into a tight fist, and his muscles twitched with rage.

When Kate's sobs subsided and her breath came slower, he asked, "Who did this?" His voice was a harsh, whispered growl.

"I don't know. A filthy wretch of a man. He came here once, but Bug and Poochie stopped him from coming in – bit him."

Mel nodded, the pieces coming together. He got up and kneeled in front of her, took her face in his hands. "Did he rape you, Kate?"

She slowly, almost imperceptibly shook her head. "No." Then added, "He nearly did. I hit him with a rock."

"I'll kill him," Mel said in another whispered growl.

"He's gone. Jack saw to that."

Mel nodded again, more pieces of the puzzle fitting into place. He wished the man was still around so he could have the pleasure of killing him – slowly, but his guess was the man was already dead. Knowing Jack, Mel didn't believe he would have been allowed to live and prey on other women. Jack Bay would have meted out punishment swiftly and surely.

Kate leaned against Mel's shoulder and rested there quietly, glad Mel finally knew, glad she didn't have to keep it hidden any longer. Some of the pain had been leached away with the sharing of its horror.

"I'm so sorry about Bug," Mel said softly.

More tears trickled from the corners of her eyes, and she tried not to see Bug as he died defending her. That torture was the hardest to deal with. Wolf, who had been lying by Kate's chair, alert and watching, got up, squeezed in front of Mel, and put his head on her lap. She stroked him and thought about when he had found her in the woods and followed her home right after the attack and Bug's death.

"I know this will sound trite," Mel said, "and I know that he can't replace Bug in your heart, but you have a great dog here."

Wolf spun around, looked at Mel and rolled his brown eye, then put his nose on Mel's cheek for an intentional Wolf-slobber and stared at length into Mel's eyes. Kate chuckled, relieved to laugh, even a little. Then Wolf got down, went to the side of Kate's chair, made three circles and lay down.

"Don't call him that. He doesn't like it," she whispered.

Mel sat again and held Kate's hand. He gave her the glass of cordial, and she sipped, then sipped again and began to relax. She took a deep breath, feeling drained and limp. Another breath brought fresh air and a tangible sense of freedom -- from worry and fear and hate. It felt good. It felt damned good.

"I think I reacted badly to what you tried to tell me about Rachel. Sorry."

"Did you cuss?" he asked, hoping she was ready to be teased and wanting to lighten her mood.

"Probably. If not, I should have."

"I asked Harley about telling you. I hope that's okay. He said something about history helping make decisions about the future, and I believe that is true."

"He's pretty smart, and in this case, I think he's right. I need to talk with Rachel, but it's hard. She's distant, so self-contained."

"She's growing up. And that, all by itself, is hard."

They sat quietly for a few minutes, and then Mel took his leave. Kate walked him to his buggy and stood on her tiptoes to hug him. He asked if it was alright if he kissed her, and she nodded. "You don't have to be afraid of me, Mel, or ask permission to kiss me."

"That, my sweet, is very good," he said, pulling her against his chest and touching his lips softly to hers.

"You're right," she said, tasting her own lips and grinning. "That's very good." And then she added more seriously, "Thank you, Mel, for everything."

"Why, Madam, you don't have to thank me for a little kiss."

Kate smacked him on his bottom and walked to the cabin.

Chapter Twelve

Summer 1913

Kate opened the door and two raccoons scampered in. One leaped on Harley who was still asleep on his bed at the side of the room, and the other climbed up the chair and into the middle of the table. When Kate tried to push her to the floor, Winnie stood on her hind legs and chattered at Kate.

"Don't talk to me like that, Winifred. Get down. Now!"

Kate picked her up and put her outside, but she ran back in before Kate could shut the door. Winnie climbed up and onto the cupboard, grabbed an apple out of the bowl on the counter and began dunking it in the water in the sink. She heard Harley chuckling behind her, watching her futile efforts to control the coon. Max, the male, was sitting on Harley's pillow rubbing his paws over Harley's scalp and through his hair.

"You think this is funny, don't you?" she said to him.

"Pretty much," he said. "Max gives a great scalp massage, and Winnie just wants a breakfast apple, but she wants it washed first. Where's Jenny?"

"I don't know, outside, and these two need to go out with her."

"I'm betting Jenny's inside snuggled up with Becca."

"These critters are making me crazy. Why won't they go hunt in the woods like normal coons, damn it? Sorry."

"Because they're not normal," he said, grinning.

"Well, I'm going out to start the wash and leaving them to you, Harley. If they get into anything, I'm blaming you. You are now responsible."

Kate made flames out of the coals in the fire pit, put the buckets of water on to heat, and stretched. It was going to be a warm day. She looked around, saw three deer grazing in the woods and smiled. A gray squirrel climbed up a post she'd attached a corn cob to. It was designed to feed the squirrels – to lure them into the clearing so she could watch them. This year she was determined to save enough corn to feed them during the winter when snow covered much of their food.

Wolf watched the squirrel scamper down the post and another one climb up. Then Max ran out the door and leaped on Wolf's back. Kate shook her head. She didn't know why he put up with them, but he did. He turned his head to look at the coon and let him climb over him. All of the coons had snuggled with Wolf, especially when they were small. They nestled against his belly like he was a surrogate mother.

"You are pretty amazing, Wolf," she told him.

Wolf's eyes agreed, 'Of course, and see what I have to put up with?'

"Yeah, I know. It's tough. I'm going in to get Rachel. Keep demon coon here."

Rachel moaned when Kate woke her, but dragged herself out of bed and dressed. "It's too early. Why can't we start later?"

"Because it's cool now, and later it won't be. Come on, sleepy head. We have lots to do," Kate said, tossing a brush to her. "Tie that gorgeous hair back, and let's get going." Kate waited, watching her daughter brush and tie her hair back, wishing she could find a way to penetrate Rachel's reserve, and they went downstairs together.

Outside, Kate dumped the hot water into the tubs, shaved soap into one, and Rachel started rubbing the whites on the washboard. She knew the routine by now. Kate ran them through the wringer, rinsed them, and ran them through again.

After the incident with Charlie, Kate wanted to spend more time with her daughter and having Rachel help was the way she sought to do it. She'd been quiet since the dance, and she wasn't any more garrulous at the wash tubs. It took Kate a few days to figure out how to bring up the subject. She couldn't put off talking about Charlie any longer.

"I think you really like the Tate boy," Kate said and then waited for some reaction, anything. Rachel blanched, flushed red and kept rubbing the white shirt against the washboard. She didn't look up and didn't respond.

Kate watched from the corner of her eye, and then added, "Did you know I fell in love with your father the very first time I saw him? I was sixteen."

Rachel looked up then and kept scrubbing the shirt.

"I did. He didn't know it then, but I did." Kate kept up the quiet flow of one-sided conversation.

"He was the most handsome, elegant man I'd ever seen, and I was such a silly girl. The first time he came to supper at our house, I was so nervous around him that I did really stupid, clumsy things and wanted to slide off my chair and fall through the floor boards – live with the woodchucks under the house."

Rachel grinned and finally spoke. "How did you know?"

"What? That I loved him? Butterflies. They invaded my stomach, and made me say and do dumb things. Your grandpa understood butterflies. He had them all the time. Over so many things. He was quite a man..." Kate persisted, feeling anxious and rambling. Thinking if she just kept talking, at some point her daughter would understand, would come back to her. Rachel nodded, and Kate continued.

"Sometimes, though, we confuse real butterfly feelings with other things, like the way we feel when a boy holds our hand or gives us a little kiss."

Rachel blushed again and looked down, stared into the wash water. "Sweetie, I know that you and Charlie kissed. That's normal when two people like each other, but you're too young. It's not time. Do you understand what I'm saying?"

"I knew Mel would tell you," Rachel said, resentment infusing her words with venom.

Kate took the shirt Rachel was still washing and reached into the water to hand her another one. She ran the shirt through the wringer.

"Of course he told me, and he should have. Why are you cross with him?"

"It's none of his business. He's not my pa."

"Rachel, Mel is a good friend, and he loves us, all of us. Is this really about him or something else?"

"He doesn't need to love me. I had a father, and he loved me," she said, rubbing harder at the washboard, not looking at Kate.

"Yes, your father loved you very much, and I am so sorry he is not here for you now, but he isn't Rachel, and we all miss him terribly. He's here, in our hearts."

"You're trying to replace him," Rachel said angrily, "and you can't. Ever! It's not fair!"

Kate stepped back like she'd been slapped. She rubbed the throbbing in her temples and tried to find the right words, ones that would help her daughter understand and ease her pain. But there were no magic words. No peace offerings. Finally, she repeated softly, "Mel is our friend. He was your father's friend, too."

"Well, he isn't mine, and he doesn't need to be here all the time, butting in, doing things for us, and pretending to be our pa!" Rachel's thoughts spilled out in a torrent of bitterness. She dropped the shirt and turned to face Kate.

"I love Charlie and he loves me! Mel had no right to interfere with us. I know what he did to Charlie. He told him to leave me alone, and he can't do that. He can't! And neither can you! I hate him, and I hate you!" she said stomping her foot.

Kate's hand came up instantly and met Rachel's cheek, the sound a sharp crack in the silence around it. Her hand stilled immediately, frozen in the moment of contact. Kate's shock exploded. She watched the red stain grow on her daughter's cheek and felt the sting as if it were her own.

"I'm sorry, Rachel. I'm so sorry," she whispered, her voice choked with the horror of what she'd done.

"Why? Did you cuss again?" she sneered sarcastically, staring at her mother with livid, hate-filled eyes. There was

176

no hint of humor in her voice, no affection that usually accompanied that question. Instead, there was derision. She pivoted on her heel and walked away.

Kate sat on the ground, her face in her hands. Too stunned to cry, too bereft over what she'd done. Where was her baby girl? What had she not done that she should have? What now? Wolf came over and put his wet nose on her cheek, nudging Kate to look at him. She put her arms around him and just sat there, numbness a heavy weight filling her chest.

Harley came out of the cabin, walked over to where Kate sat, and started scrubbing the clothes against the washboard. He ran the rest of the whites through the wringer, rinsed them, and began on the dark ones. Kate picked up the basket he'd thrown the whites in and took them to the line. When they were hung, she went back, rinsed the darks, ran them through the wringer, and went to hang those. Harley followed her to the line and broke the silence. "Rachel looked pretty mad."

"Yes. She hates me. I slapped her. What kind of a mother am I?"

"A good one, and she doesn't hate you. She's simply thirteen."

"She thinks I'm trying to replace her father with Mel."

"Are you?" he said, looking at Kate, waiting for an answer.

"No! I'm not. Mark can't be replaced by anyone."

"Well, then," he said, patting Kate's arm. "Like I said, she's thirteen, and if I read her correctly, she thinks she's in love."

"What should I do? Tell Mel to stay away?" Kate asked, jamming the clothes pin hard over the trousers she was hanging and snapping it in two. "Damn! I'm . . . damn!" She couldn't say sorry just now.

"I can't tell you what to do, Kate. No one can do that," he said, a slight sparkle lighting his eyes, "but sending Mel packing wouldn't be right for anyone, not even Rachel, I'm thinking."

"Well, how do I help her? Damn it, I don't know anything right now."

"Give her some time, and give yourself some, too. Nothing is broken that patience and love can't mend."

Since then, Kate continued to rouse Rachel from her bed on wash days. The first few times were pretty quiet, and each time Kate tried to broach the subject, she was met with stony silence, but eventually they were able to engage in conversation, however reserved it was.

When Mel visited, Rachel fled to her room. She would not be enticed to do anything with them except when Kate demanded she join everyone at the supper table or for work in the garden -- even if Mel happened to be there. She maintained silence unless asked a direct question, and as soon as allowed, she left for the privacy of her room.

Mel was uncomfortable and distressed. He had told Becca he'd take her turn washing the dishes and had his hands in sudsy water up to his elbows. The little girls had run off to play with the three coons, and Harley was outside with Kat.

"Maybe I shouldn't have said anything to Rachel or Charlie," he said. "Maybe I should have just gone in to get you."

"You did what you thought was right," Kate told him, putting the last plate away after drying it. "It isn't really about you, Mel. I've been thinking about everything, what they've been through, especially Rachel. She had to sit in that horrid train compartment and hold her sister so she wouldn't wake and have to watch her father die. Rachel was ten – old enough to understand what was happening and not old enough to know how to cope with it."

"Are we ever old enough?" Mel said, a statement of fact rather than a question. He thought of his own father, handed the clean kettle to Kate and dried his hands.

"I don't know. It seems like I've been a hundred all my life, so I should be old enough, but I sure miss my father."

"Well, you look about twenty to me," he said with kind of a sad smile, and then added, "Do you think it would help if I talked to her, tried to explain?"

"I just don't know. Would that make it better or worse? It could go either way."

"Is Charlie still staying away?" he asked.

Kate nodded. "And that's too bad. They were really enjoying learning to play the mandolin, and it was nice for all the girls to have friends out here."

Mel looked defeated. He tossed the towel he was holding onto the counter and turned to watch Jeannie and Becca through the window.

They were playing tag with the coons; they'd chase and then turn and run; then the coons chased them. It was all so simple when they were younger. Then it was patching up scrapes and kissing little wounds; it was something you could clearly see and fix. He didn't know how to deal with something he couldn't see, and it frustrated him. He put his hands on the counter and leaned closer to the window, his shoulders hunched, and his back taut.

Kate put her hand on his back and gently rubbed the knotted muscles at his spine. She heard his breath ease. "I didn't mean for Charlie to stay away, Kate, just . . . you know."

"It will be alright. Maybe I can take Rachel into town more often, let her visit with friends more. Come on. Let's go outside where it's cooler."

They sat in the chairs her father had made for her, and she thought of him as she did every time she sat in one. She wished for the hundredth time that he was here to talk with. He'd know what to say – what to do. Harley plopped down on the ground near them, took out his carving knife, and started whittling on a piece of wood.

"What are you making?" Mel asked him.

"I'm not really making anything," he said. "It's already made, and I'm just looking for it. What it is, is already there and waiting to come out."

"And you're going to let it out?" Mel asked with only a bit of a tongue in cheek edge.

179

Harley ignored the satire and nodded, continuing to take thin, curling slices from the piece of wood.

"I think you're a bit crazy," Mel said, grinning. "You know that, don't you?"

"Some people do. And some people have a hard time looking inside things, get stuck on what they see in front of them instead of what can only be felt or sensed."

He held up the wood and looked at it. "There's something beautiful inside here, and I'm just trimming away the stuff that covers it up. If nobody looked inside, it would be wasted, probably rot on the forest floor and end up compost."

Mel drove a hand through his hair and groaned, "Are you getting ready for a long speech, Harley?"

"I could. Would it do any good, young man?" he said with a grin.

"Is all this really about a piece of wood?"

Kate laughed, knowing Harley well enough to understand he wasn't talking about wood at all. Well . . . she thought so anyway. She was never sure where he was heading, but it was always interesting to find out.

"Sometimes, if I don't go slowly, I might make too deep a cut and damage what's inside. But if I'm careful and tender with my knife, let my hands sense what it needs, it tells me. It wants to come out, and I need to be ready to help by looking at it in many different lights, seeing it through different eyes, and carving away all the superfluous stuff around it."

"And if you make too deep a cut and damage it, what then?" Mel asked, playing with Harley's story.

"Then I toss it away. It's just a piece of wood," Harley said, standing up with a silly grin and then walking away, his gold curls picking up the last rays of the sun as it crept into the trees.

Mel looked at him and shook his head, a confused expression on his face, and Kate laughed hard, a good belly laugh, at both of them.

"What was all that?" Mel asked, incredulous.

"That was Harley being Harley."

"He wasn't talking about wood at all, was he?"

"No. Well, yes and no, but mostly no. I think he was talking about Rachel and you, or Rachel and us, or just Rachel. Or a piece of wood..."

"Does he read minds, or does he just have extra good hearing?"

"I don't know. I'm never sure. I think, though, that Rachel will be coming to town to help me clean Mr. Woodward's house."

"Did you get that out of what Harley just said?"

Kate nodded, and Mel looked at her the same way he'd looked at Harley. "You might be a little crazy, too," he said.

"Yes, I know."

Chapter Thirteen

Rachel went to Eldon Woodward's with Kate and helped her clean. He enjoyed having Rachel around, and tried to entice her to skip the cleaning and just sit on the porch with him. Sometimes Kate encouraged it. Rachel liked the old man and blossomed under his teasing. She made iced tea, set up a tray with a doily on it and a single flower from his garden in a vase. She poured for him, and he fawned over her. But she helped with the cleaning, as well, and didn't mind it too much.

Rachel ran her hand over the beautifully burnished cherry wood table after she dusted and polished it.

"Wouldn't you love to have a table like this and a fine cloth like the one Mr. Woodward has for it? Don't you want this, too, Ma? Don't you love it?" she asked, her voice soft and echoing reverence

It saddened Kate that her daughter was so taken with Eldon's home and the things in it, and she wished she could give Rachel what she needed or wanted. But she understood, too. It was all new and exciting for her to be around such fine things.

"I wouldn't say love, Rachel. That's a little strong, but you're right, I do admire Mr. Woodward's home."

"Well, I love it. It would be nice not to be poor."

"We're not really poor, Rachel. We have a wonderful home in the woods and our critters and our friends and family."

"I know, but that's not the same as having nice things," Rachel said wistfully.

"Well, I have a secret that might cheer you up. Want to hear it?"

Rachel looked up expectantly, her dust cloth momentarily stilled. "What?"

"I've saved enough to buy you girls each a pair of new shoes and material for new dresses. What do you say about that?"

Rachel clapped her hands together and her face lit up. "When? When can we do it?"

"Why don't you let me finish up here, and you go on down to Nestor's to look things over. I'll join you there when I'm done. I won't be long."

Rachel was out the door before she'd completed her sentence, and Kate smiled. It was good to see her daughter happy, and she hoped it would last for a while. It took another half hour for Kate to change the sheets on Eldon's bed and collect the dirty laundry. She stopped as usual at Agatha's, and headed for Nestor's, but when she got there, Rachel was not to be found.

Kate looked down each aisle, went back outside to look up and down the street, and then asked John if he'd seen Rachel. John raised an eyebrow and nodded. "She was here looking at the bolts of material."

"When did she leave? Do you know where she went?" Kate asked, growing uneasy.

"Two of the Tate boys came in, and Rachel left with them. They headed off that way," he said, pointing north.

"Damn! Sorry."

"They're probably just taking a walk by the river. It's a beautiful, summer day – a great day to stick your feet in the Hersey River," he said, trying to coax away the worry he saw growing on her face.

"Thanks, John," Kate said, and flew out the door and down the sidewalk toward the edge of town where the Hersey River ran under the Main Street bridge. Wolf followed. The river was across the road from Jack and Ruthie's house and just behind the smith shop where Mark worked before he became ill. Kate passed them both on her way and left only a brief sigh as she passed the smithy.

She heard them before she saw them. Their laughter sifted through the leaves of the tamaracks and willows lining the banks of the river. When she grew nearer, she saw them sitting with their feet in the water, gently splashing. Kate stood where she was for a few moments just watching.

Rachel was in the middle of the two boys, the edge of her skirt drawn up to her knees. The sun trickled through the leaves and shot red sparks into her glossy black hair. She heard Rachel giggle and saw her poke Charlie in the ribs with her elbow, then raise her foot and dribble water over his leg. Charlie leaned forward to cup water in his hand and then tossed it at Rachel whose scream didn't sound at all like she was mad or afraid.

Kate remembered back to a time when she and Mel had played in the river – and the embraces afterwards. Warmth flooded her chest and neck from the vivid pictures the memory evoked.

Not now Kate. Definitely, not now, she thought to herself, and kicked at the ground. Wolf looked up at her, 'Did I do something?' She patted his head and pointed.

"Go, let them know we're here."

Wolf vaulted through the air and crossed a quarter of the distance in one bound. He gave a wolf howl midway through the leap, and between the leaves of the undergrowth she saw Rachel turn her head in Wolf's direction. Then Wolf was standing behind Charlie with his wet nose on the back of his neck.

"Get back!" Rachel yelled. "Sit, Wolf!"

But Wolf rolled his eyes heavenward. 'You should know by now that I will when – if I feel like it.'

"I know you're there, Ma. Come on out."

Kate moved through the brush to where they were, sat next to Lenny Tate and took off her shoes. "Nice," she said after sticking her toes in. Then she pulled her skirt up a little and scooted forward to dip her feet in further.

"This is very nice."

The boys were mute and red from the neck up, their shoulders hunched, and their eyes pointed at the river as if there was something of great import about to surface there. Rachel stole sidelong peeks at her mother and waited for a clue to her mood.

Silence hung in the air, a heavy hammer about to drop. Kate let it settle slowly over them, a small but noticeable smile playing at the corners of her lips.

Good, I hope you are uncomfortable, she thought as she waited for one of them to say something. She watched water bugs scamper over the ripples and thought of Bug, missed him. And she waited. She heard woodpeckers drilling holes in the white pines across the river and the rustle of dry underbrush as field mice and squirrels shifted it with their burrowing. And she waited.

Finally, she heard a deep, slow intake of breath from Lenny beside her. "It wasn't Rachel's fault," he said, and then came the expulsion of relieved breath.

"Really? Whose was it?" Kate said lightly.

"Well . . . I mean . . . we were in Nestor's and she was waiting . . . and we just asked her to come."

"I guess that means Rachel is blameless – and mindless, as well, huh?"

Lenny looked at Kate and was once more speechless, unsure where he should go from there, so Kate just waited. The silence stretched into long awkward minutes, and Kate saw her daughter's shoulders twitch and the muscles of her jaws clench and relax, clench and relax.

When she thought they'd had enough, Kate said to them, "We've missed seeing you both at the cabin, missed the mandolin lessons, too."

She heard a second explosion of breath, this time from Charlie, a painful puff of air as if he'd been holding it for many long minutes. "I thought . . ." he said, but he never finished because Kate finally let him off the hook.

"Why don't both of you come by on Friday afternoon? You can pick up where you left off. Becca really wants to learn more." She began putting her socks and shoes back on, and Rachel followed suit. When they were on their way back to the buggy, Rachel finally spoke.

"You took a long time getting to Nestor's, so I thought I'd just go with them for a few minutes."

Kate nodded, said "Hmmm..."

"I didn't do anything wrong," she added, unsure how to combat Kate's calm. She'd rather her mother scolded her. "We just wanted to put our feet in the water. It's a hot day."

Kate nodded again. "If they come out on Friday, Becca will be getting the lesson. You'll be in your room," she said quietly. Then she added, "Just for this Friday. It was wrong of you to leave Nestor's without my knowledge or permission."

"That's not fair. Charlie will think I'm being punished, like I'm a baby!"

"Yes, he most likely will, and maybe he'll understand that you're thirteen and you're being raised to be a lady." Kate heard her mother's words and flinched.

"I hated those words when I was young and my mother said them, Rachel – and they still rankle me, but your grandmother knew what she was doing most of the time."

Some respect, no . . . a lot of respect for her mother grew in that moment, and she wished Ellen could be there along side of them to bask in the glory of being told she'd been right. She deserved that and more. Kate had put her through many trials, most likely worse than Rachel had ever done.

"It's still not fair," Rachel said, pouting.

"It's done. But I'm not. Charlie and Lenny can come to the house, and we will all enjoy their company, you too, after this Friday. But Rachel," Kate said turning to face her, "you will not wander off alone with Charlie. Is that understood?"

Rachel kicked at a small stone and sent it flying down the path, her face furrowed with annoyance.

"Do you understand?" Kate repeated.

She waited, and when Rachel nodded agreement, an imperceptible acknowledgement, Kate put her arm through Rachel's and smiled at her.

"I know you feel a bit cloistered out in the woods, sweetie, and I promise I'll try to take you into town more often to see people – maybe have some folks out to the cabin more often. I do understand, you know." Then she added, "Did you find any material you like at Nestor's?"

186

Rachel told Kate about the different fabrics she'd looked at, and slowly her excitement grew. She prattled on about a green calico she thought would go great with her eyes, and Kate felt the bunched muscles in her neck begin to ease. She looked up at the clear sky and said a silent prayer of thanks for green calico, a strange prayer -- for fabric of all things.

"What about shoes?" Kate asked.

"Mr. Nestor has a catalog with all kinds of shoes he says he can order for us. Do you think we could take the catalog home so we can all look at them and decide?"

"I think John would let us. That's a good idea."

Wolf ran ahead, clearing the way for them. His head swung from side to side looking out for pirates, brigands and bandits . . . bad things in general. He leaped to the seat of the buggy still standing in front of Nestor's, watched them approach and go into the store.

John looked up when they entered and was glad to see smiles on their faces. He gave them the catalog and pointed out a pair of shoes he thought Rachel might like. They were light colored suede with a little heel and pointy toes. Rachel fell in love.

"They're not too practical," Kate said, "and they don't look very sturdy."

"But they're beautiful, Ma, and they'd really look good with a light green dress."

"Take the book with you," John told them. "Look it over and take your time."

"We will, John. Thank you. I'll bring all the girls in to pick out some fabric soon."

When they got to the buggy, Rachel tried to scoot Wolf over so she had a place to sit; he objected by rolling an eye at her. "Why did you have to find such a big dog, Ma? He takes up too much room."

"Don't call him that. He doesn't like it."

Rachel rolled *her* eyes.

After supper, they gathered around the table and went through the catalog page by page. It had things in it that drew exclamations from all the girls, from frilly petticoats to winter coats to shoes, and that was just in the girls and women's section. So much was available it boggled their minds. How could people use all this stuff? Where would you put it all, and how could anyone have enough money to buy it?

Becca was awestruck with the choices and possibilities. Jeannie wanted everything she saw and pointed out something on each page. Kat wanted a pair of shoes that didn't pinch her toes and a new pair of trousers.

They decided to mark their choices with pieces of paper stuck between the pages and sleep on their decisions. They'd look again tomorrow and make sure.

Harley said sleeping on decisions was a good thing, but waiting for something wasn't all it was cracked up to be.

"Waiting's just a procrastinator's way of elevating putting things off," he said. "It's his way of making himself feel good about not doing anything or making a simple decision. And I only used the masculine pronoun because it's simpler. I could have used the feminine 'her and herself' and it would have worked just as well."

Kate groaned and got up from her chair.

"What's a pro . . . craskinater?" Jeannie asked.

"That's procrastinator," Harley said, drawing the word out for her. "Let me tell you about procrastination. It's usually not a good thing because if you think too much about something, it probably isn't even the right thing to consider," he began and looked at Kate when he heard her groan again.

"I'll just do the dishes myself tonight," she said with a grin. "You girls look at the catalog with Harley and let him give you every definition he can think of – or make up -- about that word. Sometimes procrastination even gets you out of doing the dishes."

Charlie and Lenny rode out to the cabin Friday afternoon, doubled up on their father's mare. They tied the horse to a limb and shuffled their feet in the grass. Kate saw from the window and smiled, imagining their words. 'You go in. No, you go first. No, you.'

When they finally knocked on the frame of the open door, they looked for Rachel and were surprised she didn't greet them. Kate carefully explained to them that Rachel was unavailable for lessons today, but would be free next week if they came. She didn't say why, but she didn't have to. They understood, and it showed in their shifting stances.

Wolf stood on his hind legs to give Charlie an eye-to-eye stare and then followed them outside, turned three times and lay down by the steps with a groan that might have been interpreted as a growl if one was uneasy.

They sat on a blanket in the grass, and Becca practiced what they showed her on the mandolin. Her slender fingers touched the strings expertly, like they had always known where to move on the frets, and the sweet sounds of *Red River Valley* floated through the open window.

Kate looked at them periodically from the garden where she and Kat worked picking beans and smiled. "Wouldn't you like to learn, Kat?"

"No. I like this better."

Jeannie joined the boys and Becca on the blanket, and soon she was holding a mandolin and strumming a three-chord song, her sweet voice filling in where a chord was missing. Kate saw Charlie and Lenny laugh at Jeannie's efforts, and Kate breathed a little sigh of relief.

They'll be back, she thought, *and I don't know if that's a good or bad thing.*

Harley came through the gate of the garden enclosure with an empty basket and started filling it with the lush, slender yellow beans. The vines were full, and picking was easy. He held the stalk with one hand and pulled at the beans with the other, each time coming away with a handful.

"You've got a good crop of vegetables, Kate. You've nurtured them well."

Kate continued to work, stopping now and then to pull an errant weed. The sun was hot on her back, and sweat trickled into her eyes. She wiped her hands on her skirt, and then pushed back the hair falling over her eyes. She stretched, easing the muscles in her back, and looked into the clearing to watch them laughing as they practiced on the blanket.

"Only a bug or two," Harley said, "finds its way into your garden. You should be proud."

"Thank you, Harley, but you've all had a part in this vegetable patch."

"True," he said, "but you've led the way, known when it needed water, commanded the weeding, driven away the violators, protected the tender shoots so they could grow, made sure all was safe from harm. It's your nurturing that has provided us with this almost perfect bounty." Harley's face was tucked into the tangle of vines and beans as he talked.

Kate watched him for a moment, his golden hair an aura lit by the afternoon sun. Sometimes she couldn't help but wonder where he'd come from, who he was. She'd come to consider him part of the family a long, long time ago, but every once in a while she pondered his past. He was so different than anyone she'd ever known. Where he had come by his knowledge was a mystery, and periodically his wisdom was a little uncomfortably prophetic.

"Are you being philosophic right now, Harley?"

"Could be," he said.

"Would you like to be a little more concrete?"

"See this?" he said, holding up a long yellow bean. "Not a blemish on it that you can see. It appears perfect. Now this one," he added, holding up one with a small dark spot on its end, "is slightly marred, but it's still good. It will still fill our bellies and taste wonderful, but if you left it here untended, that mark would most likely invade the bean further, and it would be lost to us."

Kate stood there listening but not really thinking about what he was saying. Sometimes it was just too much, especially on a beautiful day when other things crowded your mind.

"You old coot," she said, laughing. "What are you talking about? It's a yellow wax bean. Some have spots. Some don't."

"Ma," Kat said from under the vine where she was picking beans. "He's talking about us – Rachel, Becca, Jeannie and me. He just called us beans, and we have dark spots, but you tend to them."

"Is that really what you're talking about?" Kate asked him, a quizzical look on her face.

Harley smiled at Kat. "You're pretty smart," he said. "Why do you hide your light under a bushel basket?"

"I like it there. It's nice," she said and threw a handful of beans at him.

Summer progressed with ease. A pattern had been set; Rachel helped with the laundry and with Eldon Woodward's house cleaning; Kat cared for the horse and cleaned the shed, plus worked the garden; Becca and Harley weeded, picked vegetables and helped Kate prepare them for canning; Jeannie fed the raccoons, cleaned the cage, and did what she could in the cabin to keep it clean. They were content in their work, and they played when they could.

Jack stopped by less often than before because the camp was so far away, but he still came frequently. He visited one Friday afternoon when the Tate boys were there and commanded a performance by each of the girls.

"You are talented, my extraordinary nieces!" he told them. "I knew there was musical ability in the Hughes family, but I am duly impressed!"

"We would do better if we could practice more," Rachel said, "but we can only play on Fridays."

"And why is that?" he asked.

"Because we're using Charlie's mandolin. We don't have one."

Jack thought a moment and then said, "What if I could find a guitar for you? Would that be as good?"

Rachel nodded, and Becca's eyes lit up.

He'd seen one floating around the camp. Every once in a while, one of the lumberjacks would pick it up, strum a tune or two, and then put it away. The owner had tried to sell it a couple of times when he needed money, but he

191

thought the man might still have it. Maybe he still needed money and would part with it.

The next Friday, Jack rode in, and strapped to his saddle was an old six string guitar. He slid off his mare, untied the instrument and slung it over his back. When he got to the blanket where Charlie and Lenny sat with the girls, he placed it lovingly in front of them.

"There you are. Your wish is my command," he said. The guitar was faded, had scratches on the body and burn marks on the neck, but it was in one piece and all the strings were there.

"It doesn't look like much, but when I heard it played, it sounded pretty sweet," Jack said. They sat there staring at it until Jack finally grinned and said, "Well, somebody pick it up! See if it makes music!"

Lenny reached for it and strummed a chord, then turned the ivory pegs to bring the strings into tune, strummed again and smiled.

"This is a good one. Nice sound," he said, and continued to strum. Becca asked to try it, and he showed her how to make the three chords that would play a waltz they all knew. She did it effortlessly, and soon they were singing along in harmony.

Kate came out of the cabin when she heard them singing, and stood watching from a distance. "They're good," she said to Harley when he joined her.

"Yes, they are, and I'm betting you'd like to be playing with them." After a moment he said, "You miss your piano?"

"I do, Harley, but I wouldn't have time for it anyway."

"You'd have to make time. Music soothes the troubled soul."

"My soul is just fine, untroubled and serene, thank you very much."

For once, Harley didn't expound on his theories. He merely grinned and raised an eyebrow at her.

"Why don't you go get the jug? We'll sit a bit and listen." she said.

Harley came out with the jug, a glass of cordial for Kate, and an extra chair for Jack who joined them by the steps of the cabin. They passed the moonshine, and Kate sipped from her glass. They heard Charlie tell Becca she could play a lot of songs with the three chords she'd learned, and they moved into *Home, Home on the Range* and then several others.

"Becca has a really good ear," Jack said.

Kate nodded. "I think they all do. Thank you for bringing the guitar. Where did you find it?"

"A lumberjack who needed money and didn't need a guitar."

"Thank you, Jack. Again."

"Wow. You're not going to protest a gift? Not going to try to pay me for it? I'm impressed."

Kate kicked his chair and stuck out her tongue.

They watched and listened as the sun worked its way down and tried to peer under the trees. Kate and Harley rocked in rhythm, both content in the moment.

Harley was always content it seemed to Jack, but he wondered about her. He missed his weekly visits when he helped hang the last of the wash with Kate, and worried she hadn't completely recovered from the ordeal she'd been put through. Not knowing how to ask, he simply said, "How have you been, Kate?"

She didn't look at him, but knew what he was asking. "I'm okay, Jack. I'm doing alright."

"What would you say to a fall hayride? Ruthie and I will plan it. You won't have to do a thing – just bring the girls and the old coot," he said, grinning at Harley who smiled back.

"That's Mr. Old Coot to you, son," Harley said, puffing out his chest.

"Bring the guitar, too. Becca can entertain us while we roll along in the hay wagon."

"Hmmm, I didn't know a roll in the hay was part of this. Do you really think we should bring the girls along?" Kate said, strumming her fingers on the arm of the chair and looking at Jack with mock concern.

"You're right," he said. "Harley, you'll have to baby sit. It's just Kate and I who'll be going for a hayride. Wear your pants, Kate. You look fetching in them."

"In just about anything, I'd say," Harley said, getting in on the game.

Kate finally blushed at the banter and told Jack it was a great idea. They planned the festivity, and Jack left. Charlie and Lenny said goodbye soon after, and Kate told the girls about the plans for the hayride.

"Can Charlie and Lenny go?" Rachel asked.

"We'll see," Kate said. "It depends on how many people Jack and Ruthie invite, I suppose. How do you like your new guitar?"

"I like it. We can practice now, but I still like the mandolin best." Rachel said. Becca added that she'd wanted to play guitar all along and loved it.

"We'll keep our eyes open for a mandolin. One might show up." Kate said. "Let's go make some supper."

Mel loaded his biggest wagon with hay, and stashed two jugs of cider at the front along with several thick blankets. A lantern hung from one of the posts. He hitched two of his work horses and was ready. Folks started pulling into his farm just before dusk.

Jack and Ruthie brought a basket of freshly made doughnuts, along with Ellen and Verna. Willie and Mary brought a jug of Will's famous home brew and their two children, who looked like they didn't really want to be there. They thought this kind of thing was for little kids or old people, and they thought they were neither. Kate's buggy was full, with Harley, all four girls, and Wolf who would not be left behind. The two Tate boys showed up last with a guitar and a mandolin.

They piled on the wagon with a great deal of jostling for position and laughter. Verna was by Harley next to the jug and immediately tipped it in salute to a wonderful adventure.

"I'm not waiting for a toast from Harley," she said to the group and patted Harley sweetly when she sent the jug on its way.

Mel took the reins and they pulled out of the yard. The sun finished setting as they drove down the road toward Hersey. Charlie began strumming on his guitar, and soon Becca strummed along. Lenny picked at the mandolin, and everyone sang. Doors opened when they got to town, and people came out to listen and wish them a good time. John Nestor stood leaning against his door, a wistful look on his face. "Wish I'd thought of this. Looks like fun."

"Come on along," Mel told him. "Jump on."

"Got room?" he asked.

"Sure. We'll squeeze you in."

He ran back in to tell his wife and then climbed on the wagon, a bag full of penny candy in his hand. His lap was quickly full of Jeannie who had her face in the bag, ogling the pieces and then handing them carefully out to the others, counting each one.

The night was still warm for a Michigan fall, and stars glittered in the black sky. Bats darted across the road in front of them, and Wolf's head spun back and forth, following movement, ready to leap on intruders and save his charges from bats with evil intent.

Kate leaned against the back of the wagon and watched the night and her family and friends. A smile lingered on her lips as she saw Verna pat Harley's thigh and say, "Behave yourself, old coot."

The smile stayed there when she saw Rachel look at Charlie with something close to adoration. She breathed a contented sigh when she looked at Willie with his arm around Mary, and Jack as he whispered in Ruthie's ear, causing her to nudge him gently. It looked to Kate like love was pervasive, contented and wonderfully, slightly mischievous.

Outside of town, Mel turned the wagon around to head back, and Harley spoke up. "Verna and I'll take the reins now if you think we can handle your team."

Mel agreed they could, and Harley helped Verna up to the seat. Mel climbed on the wagon and looked for a place to sit. He wanted to be next to Kate, to hold her hand or put his arm around her, but he was concerned Rachel would be upset, and he didn't want anything to spoil this night.

Kate saw his dilemma and moved over, patting the hay next to her. She would take the bull by the horns this time -- Rachel would have to adjust. He questioned with his eyes and then shrugged and sat. Wolf walked over, put his nose on Mel's cheek and stared into his eyes.

"Why? Why, for heaven's sake, doesn't he like me?" Mel asked, exasperated but patting Wolf's head in an effort to erode the critter's contempt.

"He doesn't dislike you," Kate told him. "He just loves me. He has a one-woman heart."

Mel leaned close to whisper in Kate's ear. "Both of us do."

Rachel looked away.

Harley asked for another song, and they gave him a rousing version of *Camp Town Ladies*. What they lacked in knowledge of the words, they made up for in volume. Ellen smiled through her frown, wondering where on earth her girls had learned such a bawdy song. It certainly wasn't in church where they had come by most of their music.

They passed around the doughnuts, cider and moonshine, and Kate sipped without choking. The warmth spread to her belly, and she snuggled back and leaned against Mel.

'To hell with what Rachel thinks. I'm a grown woman, and this isn't wrong,' she said to herself. Then added, 'Sorry, and God I hope I didn't say that out loud.'

"Is it alright if I put my arm around you?" Mel whispered.

"I'll be mad if you don't," she answered.

Harley turned down the lantern and let the moon and stars light the way home.

Chapter Fourteen

Fall 1913

When Kate and Rachel went to Eldon Woodward's house on Tuesday, they found him in the kitchen on the floor. His back was propped against the cupboard; his face was ashen and racked with pain. A broken dish lay beside him, and shards of pottery were scattered across the floor. The fire had gone out in the stove. It was cold in the room, and Eldon was shaking with chill and pain.

"Find Doc Chess, quickly," Kate said to Rachel, and then went to Eldon. "My God, what happened?"

"I fell," he gasped. "Last night. I can't move."

She ran to find some blankets, threw them on the floor, and turned him so she could lay him down. She rolled a blanket, put it under his head, and covered him with another. "Where do you hurt?"

He nodded and touched his leg. "I think I must have broken it," he said, grimacing in pain.

Rachel raced into the kitchen with Doc puffing behind her. She stood at the end of the room, her face pale and frozen.

Doc kneeled down beside Eldon. "What have you done to yourself?" he asked gruffly.

"I fell. That's all."

"Stupid thing to do. Did you have any chest pain before you fell? Did you feel dizzier than you usually are?"

"Bastard," Eldon groaned.

"Yup. Answer my questions, please."

"No, I didn't feel dizzy or have any pain. I just tripped and fell."

Doc felt along Eldon's leg, and when he moved to the knee, Eldon cried out.

"Damn it, man. Are you trying to kill me?" His face grew grayer as Doc continued to probe his leg.

"It's broke," Doc said. "Looks like a couple of places. You're going to be laid up for a spell."

"How could I break my leg just by falling down?" Eldon asked.

"You're older than a redwood. You're ancient. That's how. You have ancient bones."

"Find some whiskey, Kate, and give him a good swig." She did as she was told, and Eldon gratefully drank.

After a few minutes of letting the whiskey do its work, Doc took a swig for his own medicinal purposes and began putting the broken bone back in place with a grim scowl on his face and a great deal of cursing from Eldon.

Kate tried to keep him still. Eldon was a skeletal man, but Kate struggled to hold him while Doc was pulling on his leg. She finally asked Rachel to help, and between them, with one of them sitting on his chest and one on the good leg, they kept him from thrashing around while Doc set and splinted the leg.

They carried him upstairs to his bed, put him in it, and sat with him after Doc left saying he'd be back with crutches and something to help him sleep.

"Well this is a fine howdy-do," Eldon said when he could speak through the pain.

"It is," Kate said. "How will you make do around here?"

"I don't know. I really don't know."

"What about family? Don't you have anyone who could come to stay with you?"

Eldon shook his head. "No. No one near enough. I'll have to hire some help, damn it, maybe a live-in house-keeper."

Kate looked forlorn. That meant she'd lose her job cleaning his house. She chastised herself for thinking only of money when he lay there incapacitated and in pain.

He saw the look flit briefly across her face and said, "Sorry, Kate. I know you need this job. What else can I do?"

Rachel moved toward his bed then and stood quietly for a moment. Then she put her hand on his shoulder and said, "Will I do? I could be your housekeeper."

Startled, Kate stared at her. "What are you talking about – moving in here? Do you know what a live-in housekeeper is?"

"I think so. I would cook and clean and take care of Mr. Woodward while he gets better. I'm strong. I can cook and clean. Then we'd still have the cleaning money."

Rachel's chin went up. Determination grew on her face as she talked. "I'd like living here," she added.

Eldon gave her a grin devoid of pain. "And I'd like having you around. It's a splendid idea. You have the job."

Kate spoke before she thought. It was an instant reaction to his words.

"You can't just hire my daughter without my permission, Mr. Woodward. Some things aren't yours to buy even if you do have more money than Midas."

"Yes," he chuckled and then grimaced with the movement. "I do."

"Sorry. I didn't mean to snipe at you." Kate looked down at her hands twisted together in her lap, her mind struggling with the idea. Mr. Woodward was a good man, and she had known him all her life, but she didn't want her daughter moving in with him . . . away from her. "I need to think about this," she said.

Minutes went by while a hundred thoughts went through her brain. She knew Rachel wanted to be in town and hated living in the woods. She also knew Rachel wanted people around her, friends besides her sisters. But she wasn't even quite fourteen, and Kate was concerned about her.

She got up and went to the window that looked out on Eldon's garden. She saw humming birds; their tiny bills thrust into vivid orange day lilies, and then they nearly disappeared into the nearby trumpet vines. A tufted titmouse flew to the bird feeder and stayed there until a blue jay drove him off, chattering angrily as he went.

"Your gardens are beautiful, Eldon," Kate told him, avoiding a decision she didn't want to make. Then she turned to face her daughter.

"You may stay for the night, Rachel. Tomorrow we'll talk about whether or not you'll take the position. Is that okay with you, Eldon?"

Eldon smiled and said he would like that. "I hope you'll decide to let Rachel take care of this old man. We get along, don't we, Rachel? We see eye to eye."

"Yeah, like two peas in a pod," Kate said under her breath and went down to the kitchen. Rachel followed, telling Eldon she'd be back up in a few minutes to see if he needed anything.

"Are you sure about this, Rachel?"

"Yes. I am."

In that moment, she understood being with Eldon -- living in this house -- was what Rachel wanted, and tears threatened. Kate turned away, needing to leave.

"I'll be back tomorrow then, and I'll have my decision. Do you know where everything is that you'll need?"

"I do, Ma, and everything will be fine."

"Grandma is nearby if you need her. Willie and Ruthie, too."

Kate left the house, climbed in the buggy and Wolf leaped up beside her. He looked back like he was waiting for Rachel and then laid down next to Kate. She sat for a moment, her hands on the reins, unable to leave, wanting to go back inside, grab Rachel and run. Then she slapped Kitty's rump, harder than she meant to, and they drove to Agatha's house to pick up dirty laundry and deliver the clean package.

They were surprised when Kate pulled into the clearing with just Wolf beside her. Kate tried to put on a good face when she told them what had happened to Eldon and that Rachel would be staying the night to take care of him.

"Yuck," Becca said. "She's going to take care of an old man?"

"That's not kind," Kate told her. "Mr. Woodward is a very nice person, and he needs a little help. We all do at some time."

"He's still really old, and it's yucky."

"Was it yucky when you had to take care of the raccoons? And Mildred?" Kate asked.

"No, but the raccoons were babies, and they're animals. That's different."

"To each his own," Harley said. "Some people are natural nurturers, and some aren't, but I must admit I'm surprised to see our Rachel in the role."

Kat agreed with Becca that animals were better to take care of than people, but in her mind, animals were just better than people, period.

"Well, some animals and some people," Kate said, grinning at Kat. "So tomorrow, I'll need some help at the laundry tubs from you, Kat. You can take Rachel's place there. Becca, Jeannie, pick up Kat's work, okay? Harley will help if you need it. Everybody on track? And when we're finished, we'll all go see Mr. Woodward and Rachel."

"And after that," Harley asked, "what happens to Eldon?"

She hadn't said anything yet about the possibility of Rachel staying longer than tomorrow. Kate set the kettle down on the cook stove with a thud and started cutting venison into small chunks. She rolled the chunks in flour and threw it in the pot. When it began to sizzle and brown, she stirred the pieces, added some cider, and stirred again.

He waited until Kate chopped the onions and added them to the meat before he spoke again. "Rachel wants to stay there, doesn't she?" he asked.

Kate nodded, "He's going to need help for a couple of months, and she wants to stay. She likes him – and she likes it there."

"What did you tell her?"

"I said I'd think about it," Kate said, a look of distress making a slow journey from her eyes to her brow, raising furrows of concern there.

"And have you thought about it?" he asked.

Kate peeled carrots, and Harley took potatoes from the bin and began washing them. When the carrots were chopped and the potatoes quartered, she added them to the kettle with a little water and covered the pot. Harley found the cordial jug, poured some in a glass and handed it to Kate.

"Get your wrap, and let's sit outside for a spell."

Kate did as she was told.

Harley sat quietly for a moment and watched wildlife frolic in the woods. A young white tail nibbled at a quince bush growing wild where the trees met the clearing. The older deer were too smart to be out this time of day and were likely deeper into the woods, hidden but watching from a distance. They would come nearer the grassy area just before dusk began to fall around them.

Finally, Harley asked the question he knew Kate was fighting. "What exactly is it that you are struggling with?"

"Rachel's not a nurturer."

"So it has seemed," he said. "Maybe she's been hiding it."

Kate shook her head and looked at him with raised eyebrows. "I don't think so."

"So why does she want to care for Mr. Woodward?" he asked.

"I think she loves his house. And," she added thoughtfully, "she wants to be in town."

"Is that wrong of her? Is her fondness for town living necessarily bad?"

Kate thought for a moment, wrestled with scenes sliding into her brain, like kaleidoscope pictures changing before you could comprehend them, before there was time to get used to what they were and figure them out. She sipped at the cordial. Its bitter sweet bite soothed and warmed her from the inside out. She shook her head again, and Harley continued.

"I think there's more to your discomfort with Rachel's choice than her nurturing abilities and abode preferences. I think you know it, too. Rachel has been unsettled lately, and you've been concerned. I also think it had its beginnings when something happened to you last summer and was rekindled after the Hersey dance. I'm not going to pry into any of that, but I'd like you to think about what I'm saying."

"I just don't want anything to happen to her. She's so young, and I don't want to lose anyone else. I want my family all together – where I can see them." Tears began to fill the corners of Kate's eyes, and she struggled to hold them back, not let them win. She took a deep breath, filled her chest with clean air and pushed away the sob lurking there.

"So, what else are you afraid of?" he asked.

"That she'll like it too much to ever want to come home, that I won't be there to help her make good decisions, that . . . Charlie . . ."

"Kate, you've taught your girls well. You can't be at their sides forever. You know that." When Kate nodded, he continued. "If you tell her she can't do this, she will resent it – and you. What then?"

"I know. I know. There isn't a right ending to any of this, and it makes me angry. Why did the old coot have to fall and break his leg?"

"Hey, I thought *I* was the old coot?"

Kate smiled and ran a hand over her face. Harley was reminded of Mark. It was what he used to do when he was frustrated, and she had picked up the mannerism from him. She even groaned like he used to when he thought Harley was talking too much.

"You know, you can still give her rules even if she's not in this house, and you can still drag her back here if she disobeys the rules."

"How will I know if she disobeys?"

"You'll know. Mothers always know. It's the umbilical cord that's never really cut. It's just unseen, and it telegraphs messages from the child to the mother." Harley paused for a moment. "Plus, you'll have spies," he said with a chuckle. "Trust, but check it out anyway."

"Would you go into town and see her when I can't?"

"It will be my pleasure. I'll take one of the girls with me to visit with their sister. They'll enjoy that."

Kate smiled for real then and patted his arm. "Then I guess it's settled. Thank you, Harley, for understanding."

The next day, Kat helped with the laundry. *Good thing I have a ready supply of daughters*, Kate thought with a giggle. She enjoyed the quiet time with her second daughter and learned some things she hadn't known before, like the fact that Kat wanted at least twelve children even though she didn't much like other people's babies and a place in the woods where she could raise them. Also, Kat thought Bessie Dunn's boy, Daniel, wasn't entirely stupid even though boys in general were pretty dumb.

Kate vowed to spend alone time with each of her girls. Maybe she'd take one with her each time she drove out to the camp from now on. That would be fun.

They all drove into town together when the wash was done and hanging on the line. Rachel invited them into the Woodward house like it belonged to her and made coffee and lemonade for them. She served it elegantly on the front porch – so they wouldn't disturb Eldon.

"I brought some of your things," Kate told Rachel when she had finished pouring the coffee and sat down.

Rachel jumped up and clapped her hands together. "Does this mean I can stay?" she asked, surprise and happiness lighting her eyes.

"Yes, it does . . . but there will be rules, and when we're finished with our coffee, the girls will walk to Nestor's to choose fabric for their new dresses and we'll go over the conditions of your stay. Okay?"

Rachel wasn't happy about the rules, which meant she would not see Charlie at Eldon's house or go anywhere alone with him, but she agreed to that and the minor stipulations.

"I'll still pick up the laundry and wash it at home," Kate told her. "And I'll still collect the money for doing his washing. Whatever else Mr. Woodward pays you for his care will be yours to keep."

"I don't need to keep any, Ma. You can have it," but Rachel was already thinking about what she would buy with money of her own, and it gleamed in her eyes.

204

Kate smiled at her daughter and looked at her; looked with a keen eye, like she'd never seen her before. Rachel was extraordinarily beautiful and at home in this elegant house, much more so than she'd ever been in the woods.

"No, it's yours. You'll be earning it. This will be a lot of work, Rachel. Have you considered that?"

Rachel nodded. "I don't mind. I like taking care of Mr. Woodward's house. It's so nice."

"Yes, it is, Sweetie," Kate said softly, thinking of all the things she hadn't been able to give her daughters.

"Don't get too attached to it, okay? I want you back at home as soon as your charge is well. I'll miss you. So will your sisters."

Eldon Woodward's home had lots of visitors; some to see him, and many to spend time with Rachel. When Charlie learned where she was staying, he went to see her. She dutifully told him his presence at the house was not allowed, but she would be doing the shopping at the same time twice each week. He grinned and asked when that might be.

Since Ruthie lived nearby, she stopped by to see Rachel most days after school let out. They discussed recipes Mr. Woodward might like and what Rachel was going to buy with her earnings. When Eldon was settled comfortably, they walked to Nestor's and looked at fabrics for a Sunday best dress Rachel wanted and picked out a pattern that could be used several times and altered to look special for different occasions.

"When you save enough to buy it, I'll come and help. It will be fun," Ruthie said.

"Mr. Woodward has a machine that sews. Do you know how to use it?" Rachel eagerly asked.

"I'll bet I can figure it out. That'll be fun, too."

Near the end of the month, Rachel bought her green material, and Ruthie helped cut the pieces. Together, they figured out the machine and the dress materialized. She tried it on and modeled it for Eldon who whistled and told her she was a vision of loveliness.

"But you've got to get rid of those old black shoes," he said. "They just don't work with the dress."

"I know. That's what I told Ma."

"Get some different ones – maybe light beige. Tell Nestor to put it on my bill."

"Really? Are you sure?" she asked, her face glowing with pleasure.

Rachel wore the new dress and shoes to church the next Sunday. Her dark hair was pulled back and held in place by a pearl comb and flowed down her back in soft shining curls. The sash at her waist boasted eighteen inches, and the dress was just the right length to show off her new beige shoes. She lingered at the entry, talking with folks, so she could be there when the Tate's came in and was satisfied by the look in Charlie's eyes when he saw her.

"You look . . . wow!" he told her, his face aglow in embarrassment at his outburst.

"Thank you," she said, suddenly shy, the adult of a moment ago having fled and left her a young girl again.

"Can I sit with you?" he asked.

"I need to sit with Grandma, but you can sit with us."

When Ellen got there, she eyed her granddaughter up and down. "Where did all this come from?" she asked.

"Aunt Ruthie and I made the dress," Rachel said. "I earned the money for it, but Mr. Woodward bought the shoes."

Ellen looked stunned, and her eyes widened. "You must pay him back. It isn't appropriate for a young girl to take gifts from a man, especially not something as personal as apparel. It's not fitting, Rachel, and he's your employer."

Rachel looked chastised, like a little girl again. "But he wanted to. He said my other shoes weren't good with the dress."

"No matter. I'll pay him if you don't have the money, and you will pay me back when you do." She took Rachel's arm and led her to the Hughes pew.

Harley brought her schoolwork and spent an hour, sometimes two going over lessons with her a couple of times each week. "I don't think you're giving much attention to your school work," he told her. "Your mathematics is slipping."

"I don't like it. Why do I need to know this stuff?"

"How will you ever measure a tree without climbing it?" he asked with a grin. "And I know you don't like to climb trees."

"No, I don't, and I don't care how tall a tree is, either." Rachel was silent, petulant. "I think I'm done with school. I know how to read and write, and I know more history than I'll ever, ever need."

Harley looked at her across the kitchen table, tried to think of some way to make her understand how important knowledge was, even if you didn't think you'd ever use it.

"You like all the things money can buy, don't you?" He looked around the huge kitchen and waved his hand at the shiny enameled stove, the sink with its gleaming faucets, and the ice box that kept food cold without being in a cellar. "How will you earn money for all this if you don't have skills and knowledge?"

"I don't plan to earn it. I want to get married. My husband will have money."

Harley nodded. She meant what she said, and he shouldn't have been surprised. That was what most young women wanted – a home and family. He just didn't believe women should be tied to the house. They should explore options and be prepared to make their own way if necessary.

"And what if your husband doesn't have money?" he asked.

"He'll earn it," she quickly responded.

"And if, God forbid, you lose your husband, if he should die?"

Rachel looked down at her hands folded in front of her on the table, and he cursed himself for his crude comment.

"Rachel. That was obtuse of me. But it is a reality you must think about before you make a decision to quit learning."

"I don't want to think about that. I hate it that Pa died! And I hate it that Ma has to work so hard and that we're so poor! I won't be poor like we are!"

"Maybe not," he said, not knowing how else to respond. "But I think you should talk with your mother about all this before making a decision." He patted her arm and watched Rachel as she went through multiple facial transitions that followed her words; from sorrow to anger, and then on to settle in stubborn clenched jaws.

He looked for signs of Kate in Rachel's face. Long ago, he'd thought they could have been twins, except for the difference in hair color. And even now they shared memorable blue eyes when they were lit with fire, but there was little else. He wondered how one's offspring could grow to be so different from the parents – from their siblings. He thought it might be more a countenance born of attitude or manner, maybe mindset. It was something new to ponder.

When he got back to the cabin, Kate was just finishing up the wash and hanging the last of it on the line. She smiled and waved; the chilly November wind had tousled her hair and turned her nose red. She looked like she was twelve, not forty.

"How did it go?" she yelled to him. "How is Rachel?"

Harley walked over to her before answering, and it occurred again how much Kate meant to him – how much he didn't want to say anything that would cause her grief.

"She's fine. She's a regular little housewife to that old man."

Kate smiled again. "She's doing a fine job, isn't, she?"

Harley nodded and let it go for the moment. "Can I help?"

"Sure. You can empty the tubs, and then I'm done. We're having company for supper tonight, so I'll just scoot in and get some started."

"Mel?" he asked hopefully.

"And Jack and Ruthie."

Good, he thought, *a worthy reason to put off saying anything about Rachel.* He grabbed the clothes basket to carry as he went and then turned back. "Don't you ever get tired?"

"Not until I sit down," she said with a grin, and skipped toward the cabin. "Til then I just put one foot in front of the other and keep on chugging. I'm a choochoo train."

Kate put a venison roast in the oven and called out to Harley to get more potatoes and onions from the cellar. Wolf watched, after making three circles on the rug in front of the hearth and lying down. When Harley came in, the raccoons quickly followed before he could close the door. Kate screeched at them, but they leaped up to the chair and then onto the table and stood there, looking at her. 'You don't scare us,' they said. 'This is our home, too.'

"Jeannie, Becca, get them out of here. Put them in their cage, please. Wolf, help."

Wolf rolled both a blue and brown eye at the coons, clearly telling them what obnoxious creatures they were, then stood and slowly stretched. He walked to the table, stood on his hind legs and nosed them one by one until they leaped to the floor. Then he moved in a circle around them, herding the critters until they were at the door. Harley opened it for him, and Wolf nosed them out.

"Well, that was pretty clever," she said to Wolf when he came back in. "Why haven't you done that before?"

'You never asked,' he said and curled up on his rug.

Mel came in with a freshly baked apple pie, a sack of dried apple slices and Verna.

"I invited myself," she said, taking off her coat and hanging it by the door next to the man's.

"You are always welcome, Verna," Kate told her.

"I ran into Verna at Nestor's on my way here. She followed me home, I mean here, just like a lost puppy."

Verna reached up to cuff Mel's head.

"I've never been lost in my life, just in some place I haven't been before." She sat down at the table and crossed her legs; one ankle over her knee like a man, and somehow it suited Verna. "What does a girl have to do to get a drink around here?"

Kate laughed. "You know where the jug is. Help yourself."

"I'll get it. Stay put," Mel said, and with Jeannie in one arm, he grabbed the jug from the shelf and put it on the table in front of Verna who sighed with pleasure as she uncorked it.

"Ah, sweet nectar of the gods," she said after taking a long sip from the jug and holding it out to Harley. But when he reached for it, she thought twice and abruptly pulled it back. "You can have it if you promise not to make a toast."

"Not even a little one?" he asked. "I'm hurt. I'm wounded to the very core."

"Your core is full of babble," she said. "Do you promise no toast?"

Harley nodded and reached for the jug. When he had it in his hands, he grinned slyly and said, "For the moment, wicked woman. For the moment, only."

Jack and Ruthie came in with a gust of November.

"It smells wonderful in here – like good home cooking," Jack said, giving Kate a bear hug.

"It sounds like you're starved for good, home cooked food, like I don't feed you properly," Ruthie said, pouting at him.

"Well, he is a little on the scrawny side," Mel teased. "He could use a bit of beefing up."

"I'm elegantly slender," Jack said, "not coarsely muscled."

Ruthie put an apron over her head, and Jack whispered in her ear, "I love your food," as he tied her apron strings.

"I know. You're a little pig. All men are pigs . . . at least once," she teased.

Verna hawed loudly and grabbed the jug again.

"At the risk of being like Harley, this calls for a toast. Here's to Ruthie's words of wisdom. All men are pigs . . . at some time in their lives."

"But sweet little pigs we love, at least some of the time," Kate countered, laughing with the rest.

Harley put on an expression of deep, aggrieved pain. He looked around the room at each person.

"Once again, I am wounded, mortally injured by the comparison to pork. I do understand the nature of man is one of animalistic tendencies, however ... Clyde?"

He was interrupted by Kate and Mel's synchronous groan and the laughter of the rest. Kate noted Mel's comfort and knew at least some of it had to do with the fact that Rachel was somewhere else. She had made it difficult for him to feel at ease, and her absence, while hurtful to Kate, made it easier for Mel. Life was complicated.

Kat and Becca cleared the table after supper, leaving the rest to drink their coffee or sip at small glasses of cordial. They talked about the predictions for heavy snow during the coming winter, the waning lumber business, and Rachel's new job with Mr. Woodward.

"She seems to really like it," Ruthie said. "And I certainly enjoy having her nearby. I get to see her almost every day."

Kate nodded, unsure exactly how she felt about it, but knowing she wasn't completely comfortable with the whole thing. "She's learning a lot," Kate said.

"And she's doing a good job," Ruthie added.

Harley listened as Kate and Ruthie talked, and an idea began to grow that might help keep Rachel at her schoolwork.

"You've become pretty close since she's been there, haven't you?" he asked.

Ruthie told him about the time they spent together after school was out for the day, about making the dress, and sometimes shopping together. Harley asked questions, and it was clear Rachel admired her aunt. Finally, he broached the subject.

"How would you feel about taking over some of Rachel's lessons?"

Kate was stunned. Was Harley tired of home schooling her girls? She had never asked if he wanted to continue teaching them. She had just assumed, and now ... 'damn, I shouldn't have assumed. What an idiot I am,' she said to herself.

"You mean after school?" Ruthie asked.

"After – or maybe she could get a couple of hours off when the old man is comfortably settled for a while and go to school for lessons."

Kate listened for a while longer and then interrupted. "I'm so sorry, Harley," she said. "I didn't know."

"Didn't know what?" he asked.

"That you didn't want to school the girls any longer. I should have paid attention, should have asked."

"My sweet girl, that is not the case at all" he said, reaching out to put a hand over hers and letting it lie there. "Teaching them is one of the lights of my life. It's just that Rachel may need more than me right now, and Ruthie might be exactly what she does need. That's all."

"Why do you think that?" Kate asked.

Harley thought for a moment. He hadn't meant to tell Kate like this, knew it would distress her, and it wasn't fair to bring it up in company. He had messed up the evening.

"I believe Rachel is tired of learning from me. I've been her teacher for quite a long while, and she doesn't seem to be interested in school any longer. Ruthie might be able to spark her interest, give her a different way to look at the world."

Ruthie watched Kate's face and then quietly said, "I'd like to try, Kate, if that's alright with you."

Kate told them she'd think about it and talk with Rachel the next day. "Damn! How did I not know? Why didn't I see this?" she said, and then added, "Sorry," and grinned sheepishly at them.

When Jack and Ruthie put on their coats to leave, they offered to drop Verna on their way, but Harley told them he wanted some fresh night air and an opportunity to sneak a kiss, so he'd drive her home. Mel knew differently. Harley was leaving in order to give him some quiet time with Kate, but if he wanted to claim the blame, that worked for Mel. He was happy to have a little more time with Kate.

She put the girls to bed, and Mel stoked the fire in the hearth. Wolf sat up while Mel was adding wood to the fire and put his nose on Mel's cheek for a brief, surprisingly tentative Wolf-slobber.

"I know," Mel told him. "You're here and watching everything. I get it."

He had a glass of cordial sitting by Kate's rocking chair and the rekindled fire spread new warmth into the room. He sat rocking in the chair next to hers and was staring at the flames when she returned from Jeannie's room.

"Jeannie would like to say goodnight to you. Would you mind?"

"Not at all," he said, beaming in delight that she had asked for him. "It would be my pleasure."

Kate sat, saw the cordial and smiled. She leaned her head against the back of the chair and breathed a contented sigh. She would not think of Rachel right now. Not tonight. There would be time for that tomorrow.

Before Mel came back into the room, he stood in the doorway and watched Kate staring into the fire. Its glow turned her hair to crimson gold, and her face in repose was clear, unstained by worry. A small lump grew in his throat as he looked at her. He waited for it to leave before he moved to take his seat.

"Thank you for doing that. She really loves you."

"I love her too. I love all your girls."

"Even Rachel?" she asked with a grin.

"Yes, Rachel, too."

They talked quietly and sat in comfortable intermittent silences while they sipped their blackberry cordial. Kate felt the glow of both the companionship and the cordial as it relaxed taut muscles. A flush rose on her cheeks, and her bones melted into the chair.

Mel lifted a tendril of her hair and one finger traced the line of her chin. Her skin tingled under his touch and sent a small shiver down her back. He saw the tremor and felt his stomach tighten. He leaned across the arm of his chair and kissed the line his finger had traced. Kate lifted her head to give his lips more room, and they moved over her exposed neck. A small moan escaped, and he groaned hearing her pleasure.

When he kissed her, she opened her lips to taste his tongue, and Kate's pulse beat more rapidly in her breast.

Mel pulled her tightly against him and felt the pounding of his own heart, a primitive drumbeat in his veins. He stood, picked her up and sat with her on his lap, his arms wrapped around her. Kate ran a hand through his thick brown hair and pulled his lips to hers, eager to feel his tongue push into her mouth again. She gasped when she felt his hand on her breast and then arched into his touch, quivered with desire and need. Her breath caught in her throat, and all thought was gone. Her mind flooded with simple, deep yearning.

Mel's ragged breath warmed her throat as his kiss moved down her neck. His lips moved to the opening of her dress and traced the skin where it swelled at the top of her breasts, and Kate wanted to rip the dress open and give him access to all of her. But Mel took his lips from her and sat back in his seat, breathing long, slow gulps of air.

"I want to love you, Kate," he whispered hoarsely.

Seconds turned into minutes, and she tried to form the right words, ones that meant exactly what she felt. When she took too long, he added, "Marry me, Kate."

"It's not time, Mel."

"That's a yes, then, and it's just time that is the issue?" he said in a kidding way, but lightly pushing, too. "When would be a good time?"

"When I can let it go."

Mel was quiet, tried desperately to understand, to continue to give her what was important to her. He needed to do that for her as much as she needed it from him. That was hard for some folks to get. They didn't understand the nature of giving was receiving, too, and it was reality for him.

His hand played with the loose hair at the side of her face. Her head rested on his shoulder. She was small curled on his lap as they sat staring into the fire. He wanted to stay this way forever, circled around her, cherishing her.

"I love you. Always have. Wolf and me. We're one-woman animals, remember?"

Kate smiled a little. "I truly am getting there. I'm letting it go little by little."

"Yes, you are, Kate. Wolf waited in the woods for you, and so can I – well, not in the woods."

They were laughing and talking about nothing when they heard Harley drive back down the path to the clearing. Kate sat across Mel's lap and didn't care if he saw them, knew he'd even be pleased. Harley sat in Kate's vacated chair and they talked about the night. Mel asked if he'd sneaked that kiss from Verna, to which Harley responded he didn't kiss and tell. He was a gentleman.

Then Kate surprised them by asking if they thought the girls would enjoy spending a night with their grandma or Ruthie. They hadn't done that before, but now that they were older, maybe they could even be some help to Ellen.

"Is something wrong with your mother? Is she ill?" Mel asked, concern written on his face.

"No, she's fine. It was just an idea. I always thought they were too young to stay away from home. Ma always wanted them to sleep over for a visit, but I was waiting until they were older. I think I've waited long enough," she giggled.

Harley grinned broadly. "I think that is a splendid plan. How about next Saturday? I think I'd like to bunk in my old room at the barn, too, just for old time's sake. And in case Ellen needs my help."

Harley got up and went to the cupboard. He retrieved the moonshine jug and the jar of cordial from its shelf and brought it back to them. After pouring a little more into Kate and Mel's glasses, he raised the jug.

"Here's to spending a night in different beds. May we all have wonderful adventures and return home late Sunday, say about five o'clock, no sooner, with a renewed heart. Here's to friends and family, and here's to love, and here's to ..."

"Harley," Kate groaned.

"Okay, okay, just one more thing. Here's to living life to its fullest. I've always said that waiting is not what it's cracked up to be. Now you can drink," he said, tipping the jug for more than a single sip. "This is good," he said, and he didn't mean the moonshine.

Chapter Fifteen

Still fall, 1913

Kate packed the clean, pressed clothes and linens in brown paper and tied the packages with string. She hummed a tune and wondered where the song had come from. She didn't remember learning it. It was just there in her brain, waiting to spring from her lips.

The raccoons raced inside when Becca went out to get wood for the stove, and Kate didn't care. She even smiled at them as they leaped around the room, flew across Harley's bed and stopped to rub his scalp before taking off again.

Harley scratched at Max's head, and Winnie butted in to get her share. Jenny, the smallest coon, curled up in Jeannie's lap in the rocking chair and was content to lie there getting her belly rubbed. She wrapped her paws around Jeannie's hand, holding it there to ensure continued rubbing.

"You're getting an early start today," Harley noted over the top of a ball of raccoon fur on his chest.

Kate nodded. "Places to go. Things to do. Who wants to ride out to the camp with me today? We're going to stop and see Rachel, and Grandma, too, on the way back."

Both Jeannie and Becca leaped at the invitation, but Kat said "No. I'd rather stay here. Is that okay?"

"Sure," Kate told her. "You can take care of Harley."

"He's too old to need taking care of, Ma."

Harley laughed and pretended to be insulted. "Hey, I'm not too old for anything."

"Yeah, you are," Kat said. "You just don't know it."

The growing gleam in Kat's eyes was the only indication she was teasing. Harley watched her face. You never knew what was going on in her head. Her words spoke the

216

obvious, and her quick mind understood things people didn't immediately catch. When Kat made a joke, you had to listen carefully to what was between the lines to know if she was kidding or not.

"Okay, you two, Jeannie, Becca, oatmeal's on the stove. Eat up and get ready to go."

Jeannie put the coon down in the curve of Wolf's belly, and it snuggled in. Wolf rolled an eye, but stayed put and let Jenny crawl in closer.

Kate watched and wondered again how Wolf knew what to care for and what to scare away. Since the day he'd followed her from the woods, Kate would swear he'd always known the Ramey family. And he could be fearsome with his steely two-colored eye stare and menacing growl, or he could be goofy and sweet, Bug like. She was grateful he had adopted them.

"I'm going out to hitch up," she said, picking up a load of paper-wrapped packages. "Meet me out there in five minutes if you're going with me."

Wolf stood, dumped Jenny to the floor, said 'thank God,' with his eyes and followed Kate. He leaped to his place on the buggy seat, and when Becca ran out, she shoved him over to make room for herself. Jeannie climbed in the back next to the packages, and they drove off. Kate hummed a tune, and soon Becca joined her.

"You're pretty happy today, Ma."

"I am, Sweetie. It's a beautiful day. Are you warm enough?" Becca nodded.

"There are blankets under Jeannie if either of you get cold."

When they got to the camp, Jack met them, swung Jeannie high into the air and hugged Becca.

"Glad to see you have company," he said. "And thanks again for the supper last night. It was wonderful."

"You are most welcome. I had a great time."

"You're looking cheerful today. Any special reason?" he asked, his eyes twinkling at her.

"Nope. It's just a beautiful day."

Tommy lumbered up to claim his package. "Sweet Kate," he said. "I've missed you. I liked it better when you came twice a week."

Wolf put his front paws on Tommy's shoulders, and Tommy stumbled under the weight.

"I know Tommy. I've been pining away for you, too," she teased, "but as you can see, Wolf has other ideas."

"Why are his eyes two different colors?" he asked, his nose just inches from Wolf's.

"Because he's of two different minds. One wants to give you a friendly slobber, and the other wants to eat you for dinner."

"I can see that. Will you tell him to get down?"

"Naw" she drawled, taking her time. "He's just checking you out cause he's not sure about you. As a matter of fact, neither am I."

"Kate . . ."

Kate left him there and moved off with a grin. It's good to be queen.

Wolf eventually moved from Tommy to sniff the legs of the rest of the others. Satisfied all was as it should be, he leaped to the buggy seat and sat watching.

"Ruthie's excited about teaching Rachel her lessons," Jack remarked casually. "She talked about it all the way home last night. Have you thought about it yet?"

"I need to talk with Rachel first. I'll be doing that to-day."

Jack was quiet for a few moments, thinking, and Kate saw the thoughts flit across his face as he pondered. "What is it, Jack?"

"She loves all her children in school, but she's missed not having any of her own. I think Ruthie's beginning to feel that Rachel is the child she didn't have."

Kate nodded. "I understand. She's spending a lot of time with her, now. They're bound to grow closer." She put her hand on Jack's arm and gave it a little squeeze.

"I'm sorry for her, Jack – and you. I know you wanted babies. And if it seems right when I talk with Rachel . . . I have to do what's right for her. You understand that, don't you?"

"I do, Kate. It's just . . . damn it, I want everything for Ruthie."

"It's alright," she said, then added with a grin. "Aren't you going to apologize?"

He put his arm around her shoulder and kissed her cheek. "No, that's your specialty. I'll leave that to you."

"Hey," Tommy yelled loudly from a distance. "Why isn't that animal chewing you up?"

"Don't call him that," Kate yelled back. "I've told you before, he doesn't like it."

"Stupid dog," Tommy said, more to himself than to Kate.

Wolf gave a low growl and leaped off the seat toward Tommy who turned and ran. Kate knew Wolf was just playing. He was lupus grinning when he turned, raised his head proudly and leaped back into the buggy.

Jack chuckled and patted Wolf's head. "You are something else."

"He is, isn't he? But what?"

Kate and her buggy full of two daughters, one Wolf and lots of dirty clothes, headed to Hersey. Rachel met them at the door, surprised to see them on a Monday. She had a dish towel in her hand and wore a long apron over her dress. Her hair was tied back in a ponytail, and she looked a little frazzled.

"Are you alright?" Kate asked.

"Sure, I'm fine. It's just that Mr. Woodward wants constant attention, and I have to get some work done, not just sit in his room entertaining him."

"Why don't we let Jeannie and Becca go see him for a little while? Maybe they can read to him or something."

Rachel looked relieved and went to ask him if he would like to visit with her sisters. When she came back, she told them he would love the company, and Kate said, "Sit for a bit. I'll make some coffee."

They talked about Mr. Woodward, the housework, hauling in wood for the many fireplaces, and trying to do it all while taking care of his countless, immediate needs. Rachel began to relax and told her everything she did for him, things which simply had to be done.

"Is this all too much, Rachel?" Kate finally asked.

"No. I don't mind the work. I just feel like I need to get away from him sometimes – that he doesn't like it when I'm not right here to come running when he calls."

"Well, you need to talk to him, and you need to be clear. He doesn't need you around constantly. It's not like he's sick; he's just got a broken leg."

"You're right. I should tell him that."

Then it came to Kate. She knew how to deal with Rachel's schooling. She needed to go for a couple of hours each day, get her lessons, and see other people. When she asked her how she would feel about it, Rachel leapt at the idea.

Kate went with her to tell Mr. Woodward their plan, and he agreed it would work.

"You'll be fine alone for a couple of hours," Kate said. "Rachel can leave whatever you need right by your bed or chair, which ever you prefer."

"Yeah," he said with a grin. "I'm a selfish bastard. I just want a pretty girl around me all the time. I like it."

"Yes, you are, Eldon, but at least you can admit it," Kate said and gave him a kiss on the top of his balding head before she left.

Rachel was excited. They planned the timing of her lessons, talked a little longer, and then Kate gathered the rest of her family and left with only a smidgen of sadness that her oldest daughter wasn't going with her. She was content to see Rachel excited and happy, and that was the important thing.

They stopped at Ellen's house, and after covering the weather and other inconsequential and banal topics, Kate finally asked if she would like to have her granddaughters stay for the night on Saturday.

"Harley could bring them in and stay, too, in his old place in the barn. Just to be here in case you needed help with them."

Ellen looked at her quizzically; an unasked question hung in the air. *Since when do I need help with my grand-daughters?*

Kate fidgeted, sure her mother could read her mind. Ellen brought a canister of fresh oatmeal cookies to the table and arranged them on a plate, then poured milk in glasses for them all and sent the girls off with their snacks.

"Do you want to tell me why you're getting rid of your family?"

Kate stuffed a cookie in her mouth and choked trying to chew the whole thing at once. She looked at the plate of cookies, at her shoes, at anything but her mother.

"I'm not getting rid of them," she said when she could form words around the cookie that had turned to dry oatmeal dust, actually more like sawdust in her mouth.

Ellen nodded at her, but her eyes said, 'sure you are.' A full minute of uncomfortable silence later, she asked, "Are you having company?"

Kate bent to retie her already tied shoe so she wouldn't have to look at her mother. How many times would she beg to live with woodchucks under this floor?

"Well . . . Mel might come out . . . to visit."

"Might?" Ellen smiled a little then. She had wanted Mel to be her daughter's husband since Kate was a young woman, long before Mark appeared to sweep her off her feet, but she was still concerned – the two of them, alone together. It wasn't fitting.

"Do you know what you're doing?"

"Yes, Mother. Of course."

They skirted around the edges of what was in Kate's mind because they didn't talk about things like love and passion. That wasn't Ellen's way. It had never been. And Kate wasn't even sure what she was planning, didn't know and probably wouldn't until the moment came. What she did know was her heart was lighter than it had been for a long time, and it felt good.

Ellen picked up the empty plate and took it and the glasses to the sink.

"I will be happy to have the girls and Harley here. I look forward to it." Her mind was in confusion, though. She wished she could talk with her headstrong daughter, but knew it probably wouldn't do any good. Kate's father could. He understood her, could talk with her about anything, and Ellen wished he was here to do it now.

"Thank you, Ma. Do you want me to give them supper first?"

"No. I'll feed them. It will be nice to have company for supper."

Kate hugged her mother, said thank you again, and called to the girls who had gone outside with Wolf. Ellen followed her out, hugged Becca and Jeannie, and told them she'd see them on Saturday.

"Wolf is staying home, isn't he?" she asked with a little un-Ellen-like smirk. She wasn't sure Kate was doing the right thing, but it was good to see her happy. The glow in her eyes was real, Ellen thought, and it had been a long time since it had been there.

Kate nickered to the mare, and they headed home.

The week flew by. She saw Rachel briefly when she stopped at Mr. Woodward's to pick up and deliver laundry, but Rachel was excitedly heading for her two hours at school. She was nervous, never having been to a real school, and she'd dressed carefully for the occasion.

"You look beautiful, Rachel," Kate told her when she saw Rachel patting her hair and checking it in the long mirror for the third time. "You'd better get going. I'll check in on Eldon before I leave, so don't worry about him." She watched Rachel skip down the steps and wave goodbye, obviously happy to be free for a while.

Even going to Agatha's didn't bother Kate. She smiled at the old biddy, recounted the money again, just to irritate Agatha, and skipped down the steps of the porch much like Rachel had.

The sun was shining, and the air had a cold bite, but she didn't care about that either. She stopped at Nestor's, and John noted her fresh look with approval. When Jeannie, who had made the trip with her, stuck her nose against the glass of the candy counter, Kate told her to pick three. "Just one for each of you."

Jeannie looked at Kate with wide, surprised eyes. It wasn't like her mother to spend even a penny on sweets. Nestor held up three fingers and winked. "Times three," he said. "Do you know how many that is?"

Jeannie was appalled and raised her eyes toward the ceiling. "Of course. I'm almost eight now," she told him. "And three times three is nine."

"You're pretty smart. Do you know what five times three might be?"

"Fifteen."

"Well, because you're so smart – and almost eight – I think you should pick out fifteen."

"I know what ten times ten is," Jeannie said coyly.

John laughed loudly and picked her up for a hug. "Just fifteen because the smarter you get, the broker I'll get."

Kate shook her head at his generosity, but didn't say no, so Jeannie studied the candy seriously while her mother gathered what she needed.

"I need some brown sugar and cinnamon, John, and a pound of butter."

"You making something special, Kate? Is someone having a birthday?"

"No, just some apple cobbler. I thought it would be a nice treat for a cold November evening."

"I also need some lye for soap, and that's not nearly so fun, is it?"

"Nope. It isn't. How's the laundry business going? Is Agatha treating you alright?"

"She is just Agatha, and she always will be. My job is to do her laundry, and hers is to complain. It all works out," she said with a chuckle. "It's a symbiotic relationship. She grouses. I listen and let Wolf slobber on her skirt. It's an agreeable trade."

223

The door slammed when Winnie Wellington came in, and they both looked up. She wore two sweaters, maybe more, two coats, one over the top of the other, and a furry cap with ear flaps that flopped when she walked. Her wrinkled face peeked out from the fur like a ferret coming from the womb. She walked straight up to Kate, her jaws working as she chewed, and started talking.

Kate ignored her words and said, "How are you, Mrs. Wellington?"

"I know you," Winnie said. "You're the bad one. You married that dirty jailbird, the one that was already married."

"That's me, Mrs. Wellington. I'm that one." Kate smiled and added, "It's pretty cold out today, isn't it? Feels like winter is on the way."

"They don't care about winter or spring or summer. It doesn't matter. Screw, screw, screw." Chew, chew, chew . . . "They'll screw any time, even winter. Have you seen my husband around?"

"No, I'm sorry, I haven't lately." He'd been gone for so long Kate couldn't remember ever seeing him, but she didn't say so.

"Bastard," Winnie growled and chewed some more. "They're all alike."

John stepped in to sidetrack the old woman. "Do you need something, Mrs. Wellington?"

"No. I'm just looking for my husband."

Jeannie watched and listened, her face split in a grin. She'd known Winnie Wellington all her life and was used to her, but she still thought the old woman said funny things.

When John went around the candy counter, Jeannie told him her choices, and he put them in a bag and handed it to her. Mrs. Wellington had moved to the three men who were gathered around the stove and was repeating her denunciation of all men to them, pointing to each man in turn.

Jeannie peeked in her bag, pulled out a chewy piece, and walked over to Winnie. She tugged on her coat to get Winnie's attention and handed her the piece. Winnie popped it in her mouth, chewed and left without another word.

"For that little kindness," John said, "you get two for the one you gave away."

He took two from the case and dropped them in Jeannie's bag. "You are a sweet child."

"I'm not a child. I told you, I'm almost eight," she said seriously.

By Friday, Kate had all the laundry done and was ironing inside where it was warm. The cook stove where the irons were heated kept the room too hot, and Kate opened the window a little to let in the fresh, brisk air. The girls were doing their school work at the kitchen table. Wolf and Poochie were curled up on the rug in front of the hearth. The coons were outside.

It was peaceful, and Kate's mind wandered. She had ironed so many shirts and pants and linens the work was mechanical. She didn't need to think about what she was doing because her hands moved automatically. She looked out the window and saw leaves whisk across the clearing. They were no longer red, and most of them had already fallen from the trees.

I should rake them and put them on the garden, she thought. And dig the rest of the root vegetables, get them stored in the cellar, and cut more wood for the winter.

Kate's thoughts roamed wide, some about the work she needed to do and some much more fanciful. She thought about Saturday, and the flush already on her face from the heat in the room grew deeper. Then she stopped, her iron stilled in mid air.

The sudden cessation of her rhythmic movement caused Harley to look up. "What is it?"

"Nothing . . . I just . . ."

"What did you just . . . ?"

"I forgot to do something."

Harley got up from the rocking chair and went over to her. "Can I do it for you?"

"I don't think so," she said, her flush increasing. "Damn. Sorry."

"Well, maybe if you told me what it was, I could help. You're looking a bit unsettled."

Kate beckoned to him with a tilt of her head, and he moved closer.

"I thought it might be nice . . . you know . . . to have Mel for supper when you and the girls went to town tomorrow. . . but I forgot to ask him if he could come," she whispered, total embarrassment flooding her face.

Harley tried not to grin, but wasn't successful. "I see. Yes, that might be nice for you. Oh, well, perhaps another time."

He moved to go back to his chair, and when his back was turned, he let the grin grow. His eyes sparkled.

"Harley!" she growled in a whisper. "You're not funny."

"I don't know what you mean," he said in mock seriousness. "I'm sure you'll enjoy the solitude, as you so rarely have any."

"Well, damn!" she repeated.

What seemed to Kate a long while later, Harley said, "I'd like to take the rig into town and see Verna for a bit. Would that be alright with you, Miss Kate?"

"Sure," she said, despondency clouding her voice.

"I thought I'd stop and see Mel on the way – just to visit, you know. Would you girls like to ride along?"

Kat jumped at the opportunity to visit her idol, Verna, and slammed her book shut. "Absolutely," she cried.

Kate gave him a foolish little grin and said, "six o'clock, and thanks, you brat."

"I don't understand why you would call me that," he said, putting on his coat and getting Kat's from the hook by the door.

"When are we going to get rid of the coat and trousers hanging there that don't belong to any of us?" Kat asked when the removal of her coat revealed them.

"We're not," Kate told her. "They belong to the man who lets us live here."

"But we've been here forever and don't even know him."

"True, but I feel like we do, and that's where they stay." Kate had explained the coat and pants many times before, but the girls still found it curious their mother washed the clothes and hung them back on their hook by the door. Somehow it made living there fairer to him if she kept them clean and on the hook. It was a small charade she played with herself; that he could come back at any time, and his cabin would be returned to him.

Kat shrugged and put her coat on. Harley winked at Kate when they left, and she threw the damp rag she used to steam out wrinkles at him. He ducked like it would hurt if it hit and then slammed the door. "See you later," he yelled through the open window.

After they left and Kate's ironing resumed its mechanical mode, she thought about the next day – and the next night. She shivered a little and then lectured herself.

'You're acting like a schoolgirl with a first crush,' she told herself. 'What's the matter with you? You don't even know what you want. Well, you do, but . . . well, maybe . . . and what would that mean? Damn it, Kate. You're a mess, and no, you're not even close to *almost* sorry for cussing, and you know you'll do it again -- soon more than likely.'

Saturday finally came. She packaged the clean laundry, raked the leaves and piled them near the garden. The root vegetables that had needed to be dug filled several baskets and sat lining the fence just inside the garden, safe from the coons. She stretched her tired back, and then one by one, she hauled them to the cellar, climbed the ladder for the last time and closed the heavy door.

It was quiet with everyone gone. She'd forgotten the sound of the woods without the background of the girl's voices. She stood still listening to the leaves rustle as chipmunks scampered through them and the sound of a woodpecker drilling into the bark of a nearby pine. When the three resident whitetail deer came to the edge of the clearing, Kate realized dusk was soon to fall and ran into the cabin.

She dragged the bathtub to her room and filled it with five buckets of water she'd drawn from the well and heated on the cook stove. It smelled of lavender from the dried leaves she'd sprinkled in. Then she removed her clothes and gratefully sank into the water.

"Ah, heaven ... "

She let the warmth soak into her body, dipped further in so her head was under the water and then washed her hair. She lay back, soaked in the silence and the warmth of the water until it began to cool, and then got out and wrapped up in a fluffy towel. She couldn't remember the last time she had spent so long just taking a bath. It was a luxury she never took time for.

"You need to do this more often, Kate," she said.

She toweled dry and looked at herself in the mirror. She put her hands on her flat stomach and sucked it in further just to see if it would go. It did and she turned from the mirror with a satisfied smile.

"You're being really, truly stupid, Kate . . . vain," and heard Wolf whine at the closed door.

She threw her good dress over her head and opened the door to let him in. Wolf leaped on her bed and sat looking at her, his head cocked to one side and his ears perked forward. Then he got down and went to her, sniffed at the side of her hip, and cocked his head again.

"Is it too much lavender?" she asked him.

Wolf dipped his head and looked up at her, 'Any is too much.'

"Well sometimes it's nice to smell pretty," she told him.

He followed her out of the room and lay on his rug watching as she combed her hair in front of the fire. The room smelled like venison pot-roast and cinnamon apple cobbler. It was warm and cozy, and she relaxed as she ran her fingers through her hair, letting the heat from the hearth fire warm it. When it was dry, she tied it at the back of her neck and then put on the locket Mel had given her for Christmas. It lay just above the swell of her breast in the 'V' of the dress neckline. She went to her room to check it in the mirror.

"Mel will like it, I think."

She took two small glasses from the shelf and poured some blackberry cordial into each, and then took them to the chairs in front of the hearth. She sat sipping hers and thinking. Her hand trembled slightly as she lifted the glass to her lips.

"I think you're afraid, Kate. Why?"

Wolf made a low growl and stood up, then went to the door. She hadn't heard the sound of a horse come into the clearing and was surprised at the knock on the door. When he walked in, Wolf stood on his hind legs, put his front feet on Mel's shoulders and gave him a long, hard stare. Then he got down -- without being told -- went to his rug, turned three times, lay down and closed his eyes.

"You look beautiful," Mel said when Kate got up to greet him. "And you smell a whole lot better than Wolf," he added after giving her a hug and kiss on the cheek.

"So do you, smell good, that is, not that you're beautiful. Not that you're not, too . . . but you are very handsome tonight. Sorry for the short notice. I hope it didn't interfere with any plans . . ." Kate stopped talking and looked at Mel who was grinning at her. Embarrassment flooded her face.

"I'm babbling. Sorry," she added, and took the box he held out to her. "What's this?"

"Chocolates, to sweeten you up."

"So, did your mother clean her cupboards again, and these were just going to be tossed out like the rugs and curtains?" Kate teased.

"No, I cannot tell a lie," he said with a smile.

"Thank you and, yes, you can too tell a lie. I've heard you. I remember that one time when you were . . . wait. Am I not sweet enough?" Kate stopped herself once more, put a hand to her forehead as if in pain. "What's wrong with me?"

Mel walked over to her, took the box from her hands and laid it on the table. He tilted her chin up with one finger and bent to kiss her. Kate stood on her toes to reach his lips and let him pull her up against his chest.

When he released her, he said, "Nothing's wrong with you – nothing at all. There, now that's out of the way."

"What is? What are you talking about?"

"What was worrying you – making you babble, not that I don't enjoy your babble." His hand went up to ward off an attack.

"Can we just go sit for a bit and drink some cordial? I've poured some for you already," she said more confused than she'd been in a long time.

Kate relaxed as she rocked in front of the fire. Mel threw on a couple more logs, nudged them with the poker, and then sat next to her. He picked up his glass and touched it to hers.

"Here's to our second first date," he said and added to himself with a smile, 'and to Kate's jitters.'

They talked quietly for a long while. Kate told him about her week and what she'd been doing putting the garden to bed for the winter. Mel refilled the glasses, and they talked some more. He offered to help restock the wood pile when she expressed concern that they didn't have enough for the winter, and she gratefully accepted.

"Maybe I can start tomorrow," he said.

Kate suddenly stopped the slow rocking of her chair, wondering if Mel would still be here in the morning.

'God, I don't know. I just don't know. This is just too damn hard,' her silent words screamed.

Mel turned and put his hand on her arm. "Look at me, Kate," he said.

When she did, he took a deep breath and quietly said, "Whatever happens is alright, Kate. You know that, don't you?"

"Did I say all that out loud?" she asked.

"No, but I heard you."

"Are you reading my mind again?"

Mel sat back in his chair, a smile on his face. "It's not hard to do. I know you so well," he said, "and your face talks."

"Is it really alright, I mean wherever . . . *this* . . . goes?"

"Yes. It is." He added softly but determinedly, rocking slowly and looking at the flames leap in the fire, "I know we will be together, and I will wait for as long as it takes because you are all I've ever wanted. Ever. And you are all I ever will want."

Kate could only nod because his words had brought a lump to her throat. This time, Kate refilled the glasses, taking time to regain her ability to speak. She checked on the pot roast in the oven, and then brought the glasses to their chairs. She felt the effects of the first two glasses, wondered if she was getting tipsy, and asked Mel if he thought so.

He grinned a little and nodded his head. "That's alright, too," he said. "You deserve it."

"Are you always so damned good? Oops, sorry," she added with a giggle.

"Nope, but maybe we should put the food on the table?"

"That might be a good idea."

He helped set the table, got the roast from the oven, and they ate, Mel ravenously and Kate pushed the food around on her plate. He washed the dishes and Kate dried them and put them away. Wolf opened his eyes and watched as they moved around the room. When they came back to the chairs in front of the fire, Wolf half closed his eyes in watchful sleep.

Kate finished the rest of her cordial while they talked about nothing, and she grew sleepy. She was exhausted from her long day, and even more so from the emotions that had been running rampant through her body and mind. Her eyes wanted to close, and she tried to keep the lids from drooping, but struggled.

"I don't know what's wrong with me," she said again.

Mel repeated, "Believe me, Kate, absolutely nothing is wrong with you."

He took her hand, pulled her up from the chair, and led her to her bedroom. Kate followed reflexively. She stood where he placed her until he pulled back the quilt and she fell gratefully on the bed, her face buried in the pillow. Mel stood motionless looking at her.

You couldn't possibly know what you mean to me or how beautiful you are.

She felt his weight on the mattress and his hand on her back as it gently stroked her. He kneaded the muscles at the base of her neck and ran his thumbs down the firm muscles lining her spine, taking his time and lingering where his touch caused her to quiver. Kate moaned with pleasure as he massaged her back, felt her body tingle under his hands as warmth spread from her toes to her finger tips.

He ran his hands through her hair and massaged her head, then her arms, all the way to the tips of her fingers and returned to her back. She moaned again and turned over, reaching for him. Mel kissed her lips softly, then more deeply, and rose from the bed.

"I'll be back in the morning, Kate," he whispered, covering her with the quilt. "Sleep well."

She heard the door close when he left and luxuriated in the softness of her bed. She stretched, felt the memory of his hands on her, and the warmth spread throughout her again. She fell asleep smiling.

She was adding wood to the stove and humming a tune when he rode into the clearing the next morning. She watched him leap gracefully from his tall mare and stride to the door. She had it opened for him before he got there. He smiled at how good she looked, picked her up and kissed her, holding her there for a long moment.

"Sausage and pancakes?" she asked when she caught her breath.

"Absolutely, lots of them." He poured coffee and sat at the table watching Kate turn the sausage in the pan and pour batter into the iron skillet.

"You must have been milking in the dark this morning."

He nodded, "I don't think I slept at all. I didn't feel like sleeping."

Kate smiled remembering that she had slept wonderfully. She had never felt better and told him so.

"You probably needed a good sleep," he said. "You were pretty tired. Can I do anything to help?"

"I don't think it was because I was tired, and you did all your helping last night," she teased. She came over to where he sat sipping his coffee, took the cup from him and set it on the table. Then straddling his knees, she sat, which she could do easily because she was wearing pants in readiness for cutting wood for the wood pile. She put her arms on his shoulders and stared into his eyes.

"You were wonderful – in all ways," she said. "Thank you. I really mean that."

"And so were you wonderful – and beautiful in your sleepy state," he said, then added in a mock whisper, "or shouldn't I say that out loud?"

She kissed him then, grew warm in his embrace, and it felt comfortable and exciting and exactly right, just as it was. Whatever came later would happen when it felt right, just as this had.

Kate jumped up and ran to the stove. "I'm burning the pancakes," she yelled. "Damn!"

"I like char-cakes. You can burn them all, just come back and do that again."

"You'll have to wait or you won't get any breakfast, and I'll be thinking Winnie Wellington thoughts," she said, flipping the pancake, and then turning to him with a fake scowl. She put one hand on her hip and pointed the spatula at Mel. "She might just be right about all you men."

"Right now, I'm thinking she probably is," he said, grinning and leering at Kate.

They ate breakfast and baited each other, enjoying the companionship and the lusty teasing developed over night. Her apprehension was gone, and while the thought of his touch brought excitement as before, it was accompanied by anticipation instead of fear and anxiety. They washed the dishes and headed for the woods with Wolf and Poochie running ahead on the lookout for those marauding brigands they were sure lurked nearby.

Mel led his mare, and Kate led Kitty so they could drag back full logs and cut them in the clearing. Wolf and Poochie ran ahead, scouting the territory. The closest downed trees had been taken long ago, so they had to walk some distance before finding them plentiful. They trimmed the branches from them and tied the logs to the horses to drag back. Mel's huge mare could drag several at once, and using both made the trips many times fewer than it would have if Kate had been doing it alone.

"This is really good of you, Mel."

"I'm enjoying it – and you," he told her.

They sat on a log to rest and he put his arm around her shoulders. When he kissed her, she leaned in further, then further until Mel slid off the log and fell backwards. Kate quickly straddled his chest, his legs still over the log at the knees. She picked up a mass of damp leaves and dangled them over his face.

"I never got you back for dripping dirt on me and making me say 'uncle.' It's long past time. Say uncle," she told him "or you get nice wet leaves all over your face."

"Don't do it, Kate," he threatened, trying to rise, but his legs were in the air, making it difficult for him to sit up.

She pushed his shoulder down with one hand and wiggled the leaves. "Say it. Say uncle."

"Don't you dare," he said, grinning.

That was the wrong thing to say. She dropped the wet mass on his face and rubbed it in. He rolled and flipped her on her back, pinning her to the ground as he did, and then with a face still wet with soggy leaves, he kissed her face, rubbing in the leftover mess as he went.

Then he kissed her for real, and felt her stop fighting. She kissed him back, unconcerned about the dirt between them. His breath grew rapid, and his heart beat so hard he thought it would burst through his chest. Kate ran her hands through his hair and pulled him closer. He felt Wolf's wet nose on his cheek and didn't care. Then he rolled again and pulled her on top of him.

He put his hands on either side of her face and looked up at her. "You love me, don't you?" he asked with a grin.

She nodded and slid down to rest her head on his chest. They lay that way for awhile. She listened to his rapid heartbeat, felt it slow down as he rested under her. Then she stood, held out a hand to him, and laughed as she tried to pull him up.

"You're kind of a mess, Kate. You have stuff all over you."

"It's entirely your fault, and you never said 'uncle,' either."

"I never say 'uncle.' That would be giving up, and I don't do that, do I?"

"No, thank God," she said with a smile.

They hauled the logs to the clearing and took a long, pleasant lunch break before heading back for a second and third load. They worked the saw together, and while Kate could handle it alone, Mel was much, much quicker at it. His long, muscled arms sent the blade through the seasoned wood like it was butter.

Kate sat and watched him as he worked. He'd removed his coat, and the flannel shirt stretched across his back as he pushed and pulled the saw back and forth. His pants were tucked into tall black boots and showed off his long legs. A stray curl of brown hair hung over his forehead, making Kate want to push it back for him and wipe the sweat from his brow.

He is such an amazing, peaceful man, she thought, *and so damned fine.* What did I ever do to deserve him?

Kate was stacking the split logs on the growing woodpile, and Mel was swinging the heavy splitting axe when Harley and the girls drove in. They jumped down from the buggy and ran toward them, all talking at once. Kate hugged each of them, glad they were back. She'd had a wonderful day alone with Mel, but she had missed them, too. Poochie leaped around like an overgrown pup, getting in on the excitement, his long, gray hair flopping in the air. Wolf sat regally, his eyes shifting from one to another, ignoring the high spirits.

"We slept in your loft, Ma" Becca said. "Grandma said it was where you used to spy on them all the time."

"I did not spy," Kate said. "It's not nice to spy."

Mel grinned at her discomfort. "I'm thinking you probably did."

"She did," Kat said. "Grandma doesn't lie."

235

Mel put down the splitting axe and squatted on one of the logs to listen to them chatter about what they'd done at their grandma's house. Jeannie sat next to him and showed him the pot holder she'd made. "Grandma helped me, and I picked the colors."

"I can tell," he said, looking at the strange object in his hand. What should have been a square was long at one end and short at the other, making more of a trapezoid than a square. The threading was uneven, crisscrossed tightly in places but with wide gaps in others, and Mel tried not to smile as he admired her work.

"How can you tell?" she asked, and added, "Did you cut all this wood? It's a lot."

"Because I know you like red and orange, and your mother and I cut it together."

Becca and Kat showed off their potholders, and Kate told them they were good little weavers. Kat shrugged and said she didn't want to be a weaver, "but Grandma thinks ladies should know how to do all this silly stuff."

"Well, ladies can do just about anything they put their minds to," Mel told her.

The sun had set, and the November chill drove them inside. Mel said he'd finish splitting before going in, but Kate told him absolutely not. Another day. "It's time for some hot chocolate and a rest," she said.

"I guess I've been told," he said, grinning. "Your mother is pretty bossy," he whispered to Jeannie, ruffling her copper curls.

"It's good to be boss," Harley said, "and I'm thinking a sip of the jug might take the chill off me a bit better than hot chocolate."

Inside, Mel accepted the jug from Harley and warmed for a few minutes by the fire, then said he had milking to do. He hugged them all, shook Harley's hand and said, "Thanks."

Harley just nodded, but the twinkle in his eyes told everything and more. Mel blushed a little under his tan and said goodbye.

Kate followed him out to his mare, wondering how she could kiss him goodnight with the girls right there in the cabin – maybe even watching out the window. She stammered a little, not knowing quite what to do, but Mel took over. He hugged her, kissed the top of her head, and got on his horse grinning.

"For such a strong woman, sometimes you're just a little girl, Kate."

"Sometimes, I feel like one."

"Goodnight, little girl," he said, and then leaned over to whisper, "I love you."

Harley saw the flush on Kate's face when she came back in but was still. They ate supper and settled in front of the fire and talked about their day. The girls weren't even curious about why they'd gone to their grandma's house, and even said they'd like to do it again sometime. Kate agreed it was a good thing to do, and Harley smiled. He thought so too. Kat said she'd go if she could visit Verna at Sadie's again, and Kate looked up in surprise.

"You went to Sadie's?" she said with a little gasp.

"Well, just during the daytime on Sunday when it wasn't full of rowdy drunks. Verna had to work, so we visited her there for a bit," Harley quickly explained.

"Yeah," Kat said. "It was fine, Ma."

"But," Kate stuttered, and then laughed at herself. "I guess it's just that I've always wanted to go there and never did. I think I'm jealous! What did Ma say about that?"

Harley winked at Kat who grinned slyly at him. "It was a secret," she whispered conspiratorially.

"I think it should probably stay a secret. I'm not quite sure how Grandma would take it – Kat in a saloon."

"It's just a place, Ma. That's all."

Kate agreed and said it was time for bed. She tucked them in and then sat by Harley in front of the fire for a while. She was tired but felt a serenity she hadn't known for a long time. He saw and was careful not to mention it. When she said goodnight, she hugged him and added, "Thank you."

"You are very welcome, little girl," he said.

Kate walked to her bedroom wondering again if Harley had exceptional hearing or extrasensory perception. She cautioned herself to be careful what she was thinking around him.

Wolf leaped on the bed to lie next to her after she snuggled under her quilt. She stroked his head, and he wiggled closer. She watched his eyes close and his breathing slow in contentment. "I think you're purring like a cat," she told him.

He opened his eyes, two narrow slits, and peered sideways at her. 'Don't insult me.'

"Sorry," she whispered.

Chapter Sixteen

Spring 1914

In the warm April sun, Kate hung laundry and vividly remembered longing for this day when warm sunshine melts the tightened muscles in your shoulders and thaws the knots at the back of your neck. Budding trees showed tiny sprigs of green that shouted 'winter's over,' and the robins were back, busily building nests soon to hold hungry babies. Squirrels tripped enthusiastically, clawed the ground in search of forgotten acorns buried in the fall and until recently covered by snow.

A hard winter had left them more than ready for spring. Kate's hands had been red, raw and cracked from hanging wet clothes in the freezing cold air. They never thoroughly dried on the line, but were frozen stiff when she brought them in and melted them in the heat of the cabin. She looked at them hanging in the sunshine now and thanked God again for spring, a renewal, a promise. Winter had been a nightmare she remembered too well, but today she breathed in the sweet nectar of sunshine.

It would be time to plant the garden soon, and she looked forward to digging in the dark loam and replenishing her larder. Food was growing sparse and the cellar would soon be empty.

Two deer were digging at the ground looking for new growth. Kate wondered where the third one was and hoped it had survived the long winter. The two she saw looked thin, with sharp, spiny backbones, and the fur was patchy over their backs.

"We're all getting a little hungry, aren't we," she said, commiserating with them.

Kate's supplies had dwindled more than expected, even with one less mouth to feed. Rachel had stayed on at Eldon Woodward's, more because she liked it there and he liked having her than because she was needed. It was an agreeable situation for them both, and Kate had to admit Rachel was a help to him.

He was able to get around without crutches after a couple of months of being in a splint, but he still had to use a cane, and it wasn't easy for him to haul in wood and carry groceries from the store, all of the things that took two hands or a strong back. Rachel had begged to be allowed to stay for the winter, and Kate had reluctantly agreed – as long as she continued to go to school.

Of equal concern to Kate right now was her need for money. She was fairly sure Landmark lumber camp would be moving again, and she still didn't know how far away. The number of lumberjacks working at the camp had dwindled as winter progressed, and so had the money she collected at each trip. She still had Eldon and Agatha's wages, but she needed the camp money, too.

She and Becca had put up signs around Hersey again, looking for more work, but no one had signed their names on the posters. She had to see Matt Keller again, ask him to find out, if he could, what Landmark's plans were. She had to know. Had to make some hard decisions, some plans of her own.

Kate looked up when she heard the sound of horse hooves and smiled when she saw Jack. He leaped down and ambled over to her.

"Hey," she said. "It's good to see you. Isn't this a glorious day?"

"It is, Kate, and you look glorious, too."

"Charmer," she said, grinning at him. "What are you doing out this way?"

The smile left his face, and Kate was suddenly afraid. She stood fixed, holding a white, frilly blouse, Agatha's. "What's wrong? Is Ruthie okay? Did something happen to Rachel?"

"No, no, everyone's fine. It's just that . . . can we sit down for a minute?"

"Just tell me, Jack. What's wrong?"

Jack kicked at the ground, irritation in his hard stance. When he looked at Kate, his dark eyes softened, and he touched her arm as he spoke.

"The camp is leaving, going north, Petoskey."

"When? How long do I have?"

"As soon as the snow leaves the woods they'll be hauling out the equipment. Snow is a little deeper up in the Petoskey area, so they'll have to wait for it to melt there, but it won't be long. I thought you'd want to know."

"Damn! I knew it!" She threw Agatha's blouse on the ground and watched it soak up the damp dirt. She glared at it for a few moments, walked to it and stomped on it, over and over again until it was as brown as the ground under it. Then she turned, walked to a patch of grass, sat down, and stared at Agatha's blouse.

Tears came to her eyes, and she didn't even try to stop them. They rolled down her face and fell onto her lap. Jack watched her cry and then kneeled next to her, his arm around her shoulder. She looked up, saw Agatha's blouse lying in the dirt and started to laugh. She giggled at it lying there, a sodden, muddy mass, then giggled again, and couldn't stop. A river of tears, frustration and laughter ran down her face. She swiped at them but couldn't stem the flow, and Jack watched until she was quiet, exhausted and spent.

"What am I going to do?" she asked, her voice flat and empty.

"I don't know, Kate."

She stood and looked again at Agatha's blouse. Jack stood, too, and picked it up. He walked with Kate back to the wash tubs and dropped it in the soapy water. He rolled his sleeves and started rubbing it on the washboard.

"You did a pretty good job on this," he said with a grin.

"I'm glad, damn it! It felt good, too. Sorry."

When they finished the last load of wash, along with Agatha's almost-clean blouse, he helped her hang it all and went into the cabin with her. The girls were in their rooms, and Harley was in town, so they had the room to themselves. Kate poured stale, hot coffee and they sat at the table looking at each other, not having words for what they felt. Then she took a long, deep breath and straightened her back.

"It's time for a change," she said. "I've known this was coming for a long time, but I've been avoiding it. Hoping. Pretending. I can't any longer." She looked around the cabin, and her eyes misted, but she would not allow tears again. "I've loved this place so much," she whispered, more to herself than to Jack.

"I know," he said.

"And I've loved so much in this place."

He nodded. If there were words that would help, he couldn't find them.

Early on Saturday before the sun rose, Kate loaded the wrapped packages of fresh laundry into the buggy and hitched up the mare. She'd drop the camp laundry off on the way, maybe for the last time. Wolf waited on the seat and nudged her with his nose when she got in.

"Yeah, I know," she said to him. "I'm feeling kind of blue about all this, too."

She arrived at the camp just as the men were gathering for the day's work, and Matt Keller confirmed what she'd been told by Jack two days before. Landmark would be moving north – too far for Kate to reasonably travel back and forth each week. She'd have to look for other work. Matt shook her hand after paying for his laundry, and Tommy Thompson hugged her and said he was going to miss seeing her every week. Wolf didn't even move from his place on the seat. He merely rolled an eye, 'Alright, just this once, and then get a move on.'

As she drove out of the camp, Tommy yelled to her, "Marry me, Kate, and you'll never wash dirty clothes again." Wolf turned his head and gave him a menacing growl.

Kate laughed. "I guess you figure he meant that, huh? Or has your measure of tolerance just run out?" She patted

his head and didn't even bother to turn hers to respond to Tommy. She was not looking back any more. It was time to move forward.

It took three hours to get to Big Rapids, and when she got to town, she pulled the buggy up to the rail in front of Taylor's Emporium, a large general store, much bigger than Nestor's, and big windows filled with dresses, pots, tools, anything you could want or need.

She sat looking around, getting a feel for the town. On one side of the street, she saw a clothing shop, a newspaper office, a diner, two saloons and a huge Presbyterian Church, plus several shops she wasn't sure about. At the end of the street sat the school house. Knotted ropes hung from a nearby tree, and Kate imagined children swinging on them when they were outside playing. On the other side, she saw numerous undetermined buildings, another diner, two more saloons, the firehouse, a jail, and the town hall. A couple of automobiles were parked along the street and several buggies.

People strolled the wooden sidewalk, going into the shops and out, carrying packages and talking with the people they passed. It felt strange not to recognize anyone. Some folks nodded at Kate when they passed by her buggy, but no one stopped to chat and pass the time of day. No one said, "Hey, Kate." A strange loneliness overcame her. She stiffened her back and lifted her chin.

"You can do this, Kate. Come on Wolf."

She got down and headed for Taylor's Emporium. When she went in, Wolf stood sentry outside, like a living, motionless gargoyle decorating the entry. It was a huge place but had the same pot-bellied stove in the center, just like Nestor's. Sorrow gnawed her stomach seeing unfamiliar men gathered around it – men she didn't know and who would not be making the same old comments she was used to, looked forward to.

She searched for the owner – or anyone who looked like they belonged there besides the men around the stove.

Spotting a rotund, balding man wearing an apron, she figured he had to be the one.

"My name is Kate Ramey," she said, holding out her hand. She shook his hand firmly and continued. "I'm looking for work."

He looked at her appreciatively. "Curtis Taylor and what kind of work would you be looking for Miss Ramey? Or is it Mrs.?"

"It's Mrs. Ramey," Kate told him and noted disappointment flicker in his eyes.

"You just move to Big Rapids?" he asked. "I haven't seen you around, and I pretty much know everyone around here."

"Not yet, but I'll be moving here if I can find work. I'll need a place to live, too, for my daughters and me."

He nodded, happily noting she didn't mention a husband, and his spirits lifted. He told her he didn't need any help and asked what kind of work she could do.

"I can learn to do anything," she told him. "I taught school for several years before my third daughter was born, and I've been cleaning house for a gentleman and doing laundry for many people. I can cook and . . . well, I can learn what I don't know."

"I wish I could help," he said, "I really do, but right now I don't know anyone who's looking for help. I guess all you can do is stop in and ask." He kept on making small talk as Kate tried to leave, like he was a man starved for affection. His round, pale cheeks flushed with the effort, and he huffed as he followed her to the door. But she was a woman on a mission and had other stops to make, other people to meet.

Kate was disappointed he didn't need help, but she thanked him, shook his hand again and moved on, determined to find something before heading home. When she was just outside the door, he spoke again.

"Hey, you know, there's a house available on Fourth Street. The people moved out a couple of weeks back. You might check with old man Johnson who owns the place."

Kate brightened a little and asked where she might find Mr. Johnson, but it wouldn't do any good to find a house if she didn't find a job.

She stopped at every business on that side of the street and then started down the other. She was growing despondent, and her feet were complaining about walking on hard sidewalks instead of her own grass.

"I wasn't meant to wear shoes," she said, and the man walking past her said, "Me neither."

She looked up at the tall man, surprised to hear someone speak to her on the street in this town full of strangers. She stared blankly at his friendly face until he spoke again.

"I don't like shoes either. I like the feel of grass and dirt under my feet."

"Sorry, I didn't realize I was talking out loud."

"I do that, too," he said and added, "I'm Frank."

"Yes, you are."

He looked at her blankly, confusion written on his face. "How do you know?" he asked.

"Know what?" she responded with just as blank a stare.

"That I'm Frank. You're perplexing me. Can we start this again?" he asked.

"Sure," Kate said. "Where would you like to start?"

"How about this? Hi. My name is Frank."

"Just Frank?"

"That's me, just Frank."

Kate laughed. "I see. I thought you meant you were frank -- like outspoken or forthright, not that you were Frank somebody or other." She laughed again, shook his hand and introduced herself. They chatted for a few moments, and then Kate said, "I'm looking for work, Just Frank. Do you know of any?"

He told her to check the diner at the end of the street, "Tessa's Diner. Her girl, Letty, just had a baby, and I hear she's not going back. Well, I didn't just hear it; she told me, so it must be true and you might get work there."

Kate's face brightened. She started to race off to the diner, and then turned back to him.

"Thank you, Just Frank" she said with the second real grin of the day. "You don't know how much this means to me. Thank you."

The diner was small, noisy and cheerful. Bright yellow walls, red checked table cloths and wonderful aromas made Kate feel at home the moment she walked in. She spotted a thin, gray haired woman behind a counter lined with red, upholstered stools and walked over.

"I'm your new cook, waitress, whatever it was Letty did for you."

"You are? And who else are you?" the woman asked, liking Kate's bold attack and the open, warm face she saw in front of her.

"Kate, and I really want this job."

The woman stared into Kate's eyes, looked her up and down, and then held out her hand. "Letha Cross. I'm your new employer. When can you start?"

"Is Monday alright?"

Letha paused for a moment then said she'd make do until then and asked her where she lived. Kate told her she was looking for a Mr. Johnson who she'd heard had an empty house. Letha gave her directions to his place, and Kate left saying she'd be there by seven on Monday morning.

With Wolf by her side, Kate practically ran back to the buggy. He leaped to the seat and stared hard at Kate's face as she climbed up. "Let's go, Kitty," she told the mare. "We're going to see a man about a house. And yes, I said house not horse."

Harold Johnson lived in an outrageously mammoth home at the end of Third Street. Kate hopped down, told Wolf to stay, and ran up the path and onto the porch. She lifted the brass knocker and rapped several times and then waited. She tried three more times and was about to leave when she saw him through the stained glass. It had taken him awhile to hobble to the door, and Kate understood when he opened it and peered at her through the screen.

"What?" he barked.

"Mr. Johnson?" Kate asked, a little taken back by his abrupt bark. When he nodded, she continued, saying she was interested in his house on Fourth Street. He opened the screen door then and motioned for her to come in. Kate looked back at Wolf, hoping he would stay put and went in. The man had to be at least ninety and was bent over at the waist, shuffling in front of her. The cane he used wobbled, and Kate was afraid it was going to break each time he put weight on it. When he got to a chair, he dropped heavily into it, coughed repeatedly and spit into a handkerchief he dug from his pocket.

"You got money to buy it?" he rasped.

Kate shook her head slowly. "I'd like to rent it from you."

"No! I'm not doing that!" He coughed once more, spit, and when he had breath again, said, "Fool renters don't take care of it."

"My daughters and I would take very good care of it, Mr. Johnson. I promise," she answered, still standing, her hands held together like a school girl because she hadn't been invited to sit.

He eyed her, a look on his face that said she was a vile bug about to be crushed beneath his feet, and Kate squirmed under his penetrating gaze. She shifted uneasily and prayed to find the words that would change his mind.

"Daughters. Humph," he growled. "Silly, no good females."

His condemnation of her daughters made Kate angry, and she forgot they needed his house. She straightened her back, that old string pulling her upright.

"My daughters are not silly females, Mr. Johnson, and you don't even know them," she spat at him. "They are bright young ladies, and I would thank you to not make disparaging comments about them."

When he just squinted at her and remained silent, she continued, anger clipping her words and plunging her into what could be a rash move.

"Would you be willing to take a small down payment for your house and sell it to me on a land contract?"

He nodded, after moments of intense scrutinizing, and she said, "Then I'd like to see it, please."

He gave her the key and told her how to find it. Kate breathed in a gulp of fresh air when she left, got in the buggy and hugged Wolf. "That is a hateful man, Wolf. I'm glad you weren't in there with us. You would have attacked him, I think."

Wolf put his nose on Kate's cheek and then sat down and glared at Mr. Johnson's house. She didn't know how she would come up with the down payment, but if the house was decent, she was prepared to borrow from whoever would lend it. It was unsettling to think of being in debt to anyone and most of all to Mr. Johnson.

It was a short ride to Fourth Street, just one block over, but nearer the center of town. It was two stories, was covered in brown shingles, and sat at the top of a hill. There were neighboring houses on both sides and at the back, and Kate wondered how she would deal with being so close to other people.

"Well, you don't have much choice now, do you? Come on, Wolf, let's see what you think."

Mothball odor smothered she when she opened the door, so she left it open for fresh air and began looking around. A decent sized living room led straight through to the kitchen, and off that was a bathing room with a sink and porcelain tub. She liked the tub – and the room, and came close to smiling when she saw it. At one side of the living room was a small bedroom off to the right, just before the open stairway that led up to two other small bedrooms. It appeared to be big enough for them all, but the girls would have to share rooms again.

She looked it over carefully, and then went outside to check out the porch and yard. She wondered how Poochie and Wolf would take to living in town – how Kat would.

"Damn," she said. "How will I?" She sat down on the steps of the wooden front porch and looked around. "Sorry, Wolf," she said and put her face in his fur, hugging him against her, "for dragging you from the woods, not cussing."

Kate returned the key to Mr. Johnson and told him she'd take it. They settled on a price, after thirty minutes of haggling, and she asked if she could come back tomorrow with the down payment.

"If someone comes with cash before you get back, I'm taking it, young woman," he barked at her.

"I'll be here early," she told him as she walked determinedly out of his house.

During the long ride home, Kate's mind was a torrent of questions. Fifty dollars was a lot of money, and she couldn't think who would have that kind of cash just sitting around – certainly not anyone she knew well enough to ask. Mel could get it, she was sure, and knew he would do it, but it would take time she didn't have and it didn't seem right to ask him. It wasn't right. It might seem like she'd be using him, using their friendship. She thought of Jack, then Willie, and shook her head. They wouldn't have it either, and her mother certainly didn't have money lying around.

She was close to Hersey when a thought occurred to her ... Eldon Woodward ... but did she have the guts to ask him for it?

"Hell, yes you do, Kate," she said out loud, and nickered at Kitty to move her along a little faster.

Kate pulled up to Eldon's house and leaped to the ground. Wolf followed and sat by the door when Rachel opened it and Kate went in.

"Is Mr. Woodward up and around?" she asked. "I'd like to speak with him for a bit." Rachel questioned with her eyes and pushed at the swinging door that led to the kitchen. He was eating dinner, and when she entered, she got right to the point.

"I need fifty dollars, Eldon, by early tomorrow. Could I borrow it from you?"

"Are you in trouble, girl?" he asked through a mouthful of potatoes.

"Not really trouble," she said, pulling out a chair and sitting across from him, "more like I have to make a change and don't have the money to do it."

"Would you like to tell me a little more about this change you're making?"

Kate told him about the camp moving, the need to find work, the job she took in Big Rapids, and the house. It was all too monumental to her when she said it out loud, too big and unreal, and she rushed over the words, trying to get it over with – have it done.

Eldon listened without interruption and finally resumed eating his supper. "I assume you have looked for work around here?" he asked in between bites.

Kate nodded. "Everywhere. There isn't any."

"And this job you found, is it enough to live on and make payments on your house and to me?"

Kate had been wondering the same thing, knew she'd have to supplement her salary doing laundry, and told him so. "I'm not afraid of work, Eldon, you know that. I'm more scared of not working, and I will pay you back, with interest."

Eldon got up and left the room. He was gone for only a short time, and when he came back into the kitchen, he had a bundle of bills in his hands. He held it out to her, and Kate stared at the money. She'd never seen so many dollars all together at one time.

"I don't know what to say. Thank you."

"You said you'd pay it back, and I believe you, Kate. But there is something, and it's not a condition of the loan mind you, just something I want." He paused while he sat back in his chair. "I would like Rachel to stay."

Kate was stunned. That though never occurred to her, never once crossed her mind. All four of her daughters not go with her? Ridiculous.

"I can't leave her," Kate said absently, wondering where she'd find someone else with money just laying around. "She's my daughter, Eldon, and we'll be too far away."

"I think she's happy here. I need her, and her presence makes me happy, too. Why don't you ask her?"

Kate ran a hand over her face and rubbed at her creased brow. She struggled with the thought of leaving her oldest daughter, and knew Eldon was right that Rachel liked being here, loved living in town in Eldon's beautiful home. But to leave her here, so far away . . .

"She needs her mother," Kate said inaudibly, not believing her own words. Rachel hadn't needed her for a long while, and she knew it. "Damn it, I don't want to leave her. Sorry, Eldon. Is the loan truly not conditional, dependent on Rachel?"

He smiled at her and patted her hand. "No, I told you. The loan is yours. And you've been cussing since you were a little girl. Do you still think you have to apologize for it?"

"No, I just do. It slips out all by itself." Kate pondered the situation, warmed a little by Eldon's smile and words. He was a good man, even if he was an old coot. Rachel would be safe with him, and he obviously cared about her welfare – along with his own.

"She has her Aunt Ruthie and her grandmother nearby. She sees them all the time, you know, and she has her friends at school, people around who love her. Think about it, please."

"I have to take this money to Mr. Johnson in the morning," Kate told him. "When I come back, I'll have a decision about Rachel. Will that be alright with you?"

Eldon nodded. "You'll make the right one, Kate. I'm sure about that."

Kate thanked him for the loan and left without telling Rachel about her plans. She needed to think first.

Chapter Seventeen

Harley and the girls were making supper when she got to the cabin, and Kate said a quick hello and went back out to unhitch Kitty and rub her down. She worked slowly, taking time to soak in her surroundings, absorb the years and days and hours spent here; the shed her family and Mark had made for their first mare, the cellar they had built to hide in when fires had ravaged the area during several years of drought. They'd never had to use it, thank God, but it meant they didn't have to move from the forest. The gardens, the woods, the cabin. God, she loved the cabin. Now they were moving to town anyway, not because of fire, or desire to be somewhere else, but because of money, and she hated it.

The sun was beginning to set, and the woods around her grew dark. Kate watched the deer move into the clearing, remembered feeding them the first winter she and Mark had come here and snow had piled too high for them to find food.

They had lived in town during the first winters, behind the smith shop, until they'd dragged a road through the woods so the horse and buggy could get in and out. After that, other than for work, they'd not had to go into town unless it was for supplies or because they just wanted to.

That's the way it should be, she thought. People shouldn't be forced from places they love.

She didn't know how she was going to leave, and tears stung her eyes when she thought of packing up and closing the door for the last time.

"One foot in front of the other," she said to Wolf who sat watching. "It will be an adventure. And I'll smile because I must. There's no choice." She put one on and went in to tell them.

Harley sat listening to Kate's tale, his face expression-less, thinking. He had never considered being apart from this family; they had become his. This was a new thing for him – an attachment that tied him tightly to others and controlled what he desired. Deep down, he had known for a long time he belonged with the Hughes and Ramey families, but he'd not considered exactly what that meant, how it might impact him.

Kat was horrified she would have to leave the woods, and Kate assured her they would be back to visit as often as they could. Becca took it all in stride, but Jeannie cried that the raccoons would be alone, and how would Mildred get along without her help?

"I could stay on here," Harley finally said. "I could keep the place up."

"How will you eat?" Kate asked. "What will you live on?"

"I will manage," he said with a little grin. "I always do, but what about the girls' schooling?"

"They'd go to a school. I saw it today. It's a nice building right at the end of the main street in town. They'll make new friends."

The girls were both horrified and excited about going to school with other children. Kate told them about Letha Cross, the owner of the diner where she would work and about Mr. Johnson. She mimicked his stooped walk, making them laugh a little, and described their new house.

"It's at the top of a hill with other houses nearby. You'll probably have friends right next door to play with every day."

They talked about all the new things they would see and do while they ate supper, and by the end of it they had become familiar with the sudden news; the unexpected jolt to their lives became a known reflection. While Kat and Becca washed dishes, Kate and Harley went to sit outside in the chilly April night.

Harley wrapped her in a heavy quilt and tucked it in around her like she was a baby. He was quiet for a while and then asked if she had told Mel yet.

When she shook her head, he added, "Don't you think you might want to do that?"

She watched a bat dart across the clearing and head unerringly toward his supper. An owl hooted, and Kate spotted him at the top of the tallest oak at the edge of the woods. A fat coon waddled from her den to forage for food, and Kate's chest ached like a tumor was eating away at her insides.

"I want to be a bat," she said in a voice thick with emotion.

Harley looked at her strangely. "You want to be a bat? That's an odd desire."

A voice whispered to her from a place far, far away, as if the words she'd just spoken had been said before. It was a sad but comforting voice, and she heard it clearly in her mind.

"Then I'd always know exactly what to do and where to go. I'd have clear directions."

"You usually do anyway, Kate, even if you're not a bat." He patted her arm, and they sat quietly, rocking in her father's chairs. After a time, he said "I could go with you to Big Rapids, you know."

"Would you really do that, Harley?"

"Of course. One place is as good as another. I'm home wherever I am."

"Would you come for at least a while, until we get settled in? Then if you wanted to come back here, or go to Ma's, we could live with that."

Harley grinned, oddly relieved he would be with them for a while longer and that Kate wanted him with them. "Then it's done. We'll go together."

Kate breathed a long sigh, even more comforted than he was in knowing they would share the journey.

In the morning, before the sun was up, Kate slipped quietly out the door, hitched Kitty to the buggy, and let her lead them in the dark. She turned down Mel's rutted path just as the sun was peeking over the horizon and spilling over gentle hills that were Mel's fields. She led Kitty straight to the barn, knowing Mel would already be milking his large herd.

The door was open, and she saw him look up at the sound of the mare's hooves on the soft dirt, surprise lighting his face.

"Morning," she said, climbing down from the buggy.

He gave a couple more pulls on the heifer, moved the milk bucket, and patted her away before standing.

"This is a surprise," he said giving her a one-armed hug and a kiss.

"I needed to see you before I went."

"Went?" he asked. "Went where?"

Kate blurted it all out in a single, nonstop sentence before he could respond or ask a question she couldn't or didn't want to answer.

He listened and then called to the next heifer in line, and then said, "I need to finish here. Sit down and wait. Please."

Kate sat in a mound of straw and watched as he worked, his forehead resting against the warm side of the milk cow. He called each one by name as they came to be milked, patted them gently and washed the udders before expertly squeezing them to release the milk. The only sound in the barn was the rhythmic squirt of liquid into the bucket, like a snare drum softly keeping tempo for the lowing heifers waiting their turns.

Mel turned Kate's way when he patted the cow to move her on and called to the next one. Then he pressed his face into the cow in front of him and gave his attention to her, but he was processing everything Kate had told him. He knew he wasn't going to change her mind. She would do what she believed she had to.

Damned stubborn woman!

Each time the bucket was full, he got up to pour it in milk cans that sat in a large square basin of water keeping the milk cool. Then, still without speaking, he sat again and the liquid symphony continued.

When the last heifer had been relieved of her milk burden, he stood, handed Kate a bucket of shelled corn and said,

"Feed the chickens while I wash up. We're going to Big Rapids together."

They didn't talk until they had rolled down Mel's road to the hard packed one that led to Big Rapids. She looked around at the rolling, plowed fields as they left Hersey behind. Wolf, sitting in the rumble seat behind them, rested his chin on Kate's shoulder and watched with her. She breathed in the scent of freshly turned earth, relishing the way the smell deepened as the morning sun warmed it and dried the night's dew.

"Are you going to say anything?" she finally asked.

He sighed deeply, not knowing how to say what was screaming inside his head.

Marry me, damn it! Come live with me, damn it! But he knew he couldn't say those words, so instead said "You know you don't have to do this, Kate."

"Yes, I do. There isn't any other way."

He shook his head and took a long breath. "There is, if you would just do it."

She knew what he was talking about, but she wasn't ready. She just plain wasn't ready, and that would make it wrong.

"Damn it, Kate!" he said, his frustration showing in the clench of his jaws.

"Don't swear at me, Mel, or I'll just drop you off and go on by myself. Give me the reins back."

"I'm not swearing at you. I'm just . . . I don't know what," he said, keeping the reins in his own hands, knowing she'd do it, too – just drop him and drive off.

They were silent for a while, both edgy and irritated. Kate's back was stiff, and Wolf had shifted his gaze to Mel.

"Your dog is looking at me like I'm breakfast," he finally said.

"Don't call him that! He doesn't like it. I've told you time and again. Why doesn't anyone listen to me?"

"What should I call him then? What is he?"

"Wolf. He has a name and it's Wolf," Kate spit at him.

After a few moments, Mel grinned a little, "Sorry. *Wolf* is looking at me like I'm breakfast, and I *do* listen to you."

"No, you don't. You always think you know what's best, and you don't. I have to do this. Do you think for one minute that I want to go, to leave my home, my woods? There isn't any other way, and you can just . . ." she stopped, ran out of words that would adequately describe what she felt. There weren't any words. Not the right ones.

Mel drew the rig over to the side of the road and stopped. He put an arm around her and pulled her to him, but she resisted, still miffed. He waited until he felt the stiffness thaw from her back muscles as she began to relax against him, and then he kissed the top of her head. "It'll be okay, Kate," he whispered against her hair.

"Don't do that."

"What? Kiss your hair or talk?"

"Be nice! Don't be nice!"

He stifled a grin that threatened to show and asked, "Do you want to be mad at me?"

She nodded. "Yes."

Mel kissed her head again and picked up the reins, nickered at Kitty, and drove off. He knew Kate and had heard dampness choke her voice. It truly was easier for her to be mad. He understood that in her. He'd let her be mad for a bit.

They pulled onto Fourth Street to look at the house before going to Mr. Johnson's place, found the back door unlocked, and went in. Mel checked in the cellar for foundation cracks and on the roof for crumbling shingles. He banged on the walls to see if the plaster was solid and poked at the ceiling where it had turned brownish from an earlier leak.

"It looks like it's been taken care of," he told her.

"Well, what do you think?" she asked. "Will it do?"

"You'll want to fix the banister. It's wobbly, but that appears to be about the only thing that needs to be done right away. At least from this quick inspection."

Kate looked around her. The hearth in the living room was full of old ashes, and Kate poked her head up the chimney to see if it needed cleaning, too. When she did, a bat flew out, and she stumbled and fell backwards, covering her head with her arms. Wolf stood and gave a menacing growl, and Mel ran to open the door, hoping it would fly out, but it just darted across the room and back, banging into windows. Then it perched on a curtain rod and hung there upside down. Wolf stood on his hind legs to sniff at it and then rolled his eye. 'It's just a bat, silly' and went to lie in front of the hearth.

"Do something!" Kate yelled. "Get a broom!"

Mel leaned back against the wall and grinned at her cowering on the floor.

"What? Are you asking for my help?" he said, still grinning.

"Yes, damn it! Get it out of here." But when she peeked from under her arms and saw his grin, she added, "Never mind. I'll do it myself."

She eyed the bat as she crossed the room and went to look for anything to use to guide the bat out the door. She found a broom in the kitchen and stealthily edged toward the bat. Two beady little eyes in a brown, furry head watched her raise the broom. The straw bristles nudged it, then nudged it again, and it spread its wide wings like it was about to take off.

"Look at his wings," Kate said. "They're beautiful," she whispered.

The bat finally lifted from the curtain rod, made one erratic circle of the room and headed out the door. Kate watched it dart to a nearby tree, grasp a limb, and turn upside down. "Go to sleep," she told it, "outside."

"I wonder how many more little friends are up that chimney," she said going to the hearth to peer up, more cautiously this time. All she saw was soot in the black hole, and she breathed a sigh of relief when she stood and told Mel it needed to be cleaned before she would light a fire in it.

"I'll help, Bat-woman – if you want my help, that is. You'll need a tall ladder to reach the roof."

"I accept your offer, Chicken-man, afraid of a little old bat."

Mel grinned, remembering Kate cowering on the floor when the bat was flying around the room. "I'm just afraid of bat-woman, not the bat, and I recall it was you with your head covered."

"I was just protecting my hair. I didn't want it to get messed up before seeing Mr. Johnson. Speaking of Mr. Johnson, we'd better go buy this house before we plan what to do with it."

Kate had warned Mel about how crotchety Mr. Johnson was, but he was still unprepared for the ferocity of it. He was stunned speechless when the door opened and the grizzled man snarled, "Got the down payment?" through the screen door.

Kate smiled and said, "Good morning, Mr. Johnson. It's a lovely day, isn't it?"

He harrumphed and opened the door for them to come in.

"Mr. Johnson, I'd like you to meet my friend, Mel Bronson." Mel extended his hand, and Johnson merely turned away and shuffled off to his chair. Mel queried Kate with his eyes, shrugged his shoulders and waved his empty hand toward Johnson's back.

This should be interesting, at least, he thought, watching Kate deal with the old curmudgeon.

They followed him inside, and this time Kate sat in a chair next to his. She wouldn't be left standing again like a child about to be punished. "I have the down payment, Mr. Johnson. Do you have the papers for us to sign?"

He pulled a folded document from his pocket, spread it out and handed it to Kate. There was silence in the room while Kate read. It was fairly straight forward. He would hold the title to the house and property until the entire amount was paid, and if she missed a payment, he would reclaim the house. Kate handed the paper to Mel and asked if he would look it over.

When he finished reading, he said, "Isn't repossession of the property for missing just a single payment a little unusual?"

The old man squinted at Mel. "It's my house – my deal. She can buy a different one if she doesn't like it."

"That's fine," Kate said. "I won't be missing any payments."

She gave him the money and hoped she was right as she signed the document. Mel witnessed with his name below hers, and they took the key and left.

Kate skipped down the steps saying, "I own a house!"

"And I'm hungry," Mel responded. "Let's find something to eat."

"I know just the place. Letha's Diner, if it's open on Sundays. That's where I'm going to work,"

It was open, and Mel saw that Letha Cross was the total opposite of Mr. Johnson when Kate introduced them. She smiled broadly and looked Mel up and down with intentionally obvious appreciation.

"Nice choice, Kate, big and strong," she told her. "When you're scrawny like you and me, you need a big man around."

Mel just grinned.

Letha asked "Did you get to see old man Johnson's house? He's a dilly, the old fart."

Kate told her she had and that she had just bought it and would be moving in on her first day off from the diner. Letha joined them at the table and they got to know one another. When she found Kate would be traveling all the way to Big Rapids to work each day until she settled into the new house, she told her to move first and then start work.

"No sense in spending all that time on the road going back and forth."

"Are you sure you don't need me for the next couple of days? It will probably take two at least."

"I'll get by. You just get moved in. Now, what do you want to eat?"

"Everything," Mel said. "I'm starved."

"That is one big body to fill up. I'll get to it," she said, getting up and squeezing Mel's shoulder.

When Letha left, Kate grinned and said, "I think she likes you. Should I be jealous?"

"I think she just likes having big, strong men around, unlike some people I know."

"She doesn't know you're afraid of bats, Chicken-man."

"Bat-woman."

Before they left the diner, Kate told her she'd stop in during the next couple of days to let her know how the move was progressing and when she'd be there for her first day of work. The ride back to Hersey was a lot more comfortable than the ride to Big Rapids, and Kate was glad Mel had gone with her. She rested against the back of the seat with Mel's arm around her, and thought about everything she had to do. Wolf crawled over the backrest and squeezed into the seat by Kate, and she moved closer to Mel to give him space.

"I like that dog . . . I mean, I like Wolf," he said.

Kate just raised her eyebrows and peered up at him.

"See, I listen," Mel said.

It was late afternoon when they pulled into the clearing. Mel had come with her saying he'd take Kitty home and bring her back in the morning after chores. He'd bring his wagon and team, too, and help load up the furniture.

"How long do you think it will take you to pack up?"

"I don't know, maybe a day?"

"Then we could figure on hauling it to Big Rapids on Tuesday?" he asked.

They sat in the buggy talking about the move, and Kate tried not to look around the clearing, tried not to see the woods and the critters scampering. She stiffened her spine and Mel saw her struggle.

"It's not too late to change your mind," he said, rubbing her shoulder gently.

"Nope. I won't look back. I refuse. I am bat woman," she said in a whisper, and took a deep breath. "Let's go tell Harley and the girls we've bought a house." She started to climb down, and then suddenly stopped.

"Oh, my God, I forgot to stop at Eldon's to tell Rachel!"

"You can do it tomorrow, Kate. One day won't make any difference, and you've had a hard one today."

"Well, just this once – you're right," she said with a grin.

Harley and the girls were waiting for them at the door when they went in, and they all asked questions at the same time. Kate told them they were proud owners of a new house, and Harley went to the cupboard for the jug and jar of cordial. He poured a glass for Kate and said, "Sit, tell us everything."

"Well, where do I start?" Kate sighed. "The house is walking distance to town and the school. It has three bedrooms; one down and two up, and I found out Mel is afraid of bats."

"No, he isn't," Kat said.

"He sure is. One flew out from the chimney when I looked up it, and Mel just stood there, frozen with fear. He didn't even try to help me get it out of the house."

"I couldn't," Mel told them. "I was laughing too hard at Bat-woman here who was curled up in a ball on the floor."

"Were you, Ma?" Jeannie asked.

"Absolutely not. I fell because I was momentarily startled and covered my head to keep the bat from messing up my hair."

"I find this all very interesting," Harley said. "I think I feel a toast coming."

Kate groaned, and he went on. "Here's to bat-like abilities and Kate's desire to be a bat."

Jeannie looked at her mother strangely. "You want to be a bat?"

Harley stood so he could command total attention and raised the jug to continue the toast. "I wasn't finished with my toast, little one. There's so much more to this bat thing."

Kate groaned again, and Mel joined her this time.

"Here's to knowing where you're going when you're blinded by circumstance. Here's to flying straight when it's the darkest part of your night and using your innate power of direction – even if you don't realize you have it. It is there, deep inside all of us." Harley grinned broadly, taking his time and looking at all of them one by one. "Here's to being a bat." He tilted the jug, took a long sip and handed it to Mel.

"Here's to Bat-woman," Mel said and tipped the jug.

"I think you're more than a bit daft," Kate said with a fond grin back at Harley, "but since I'd like a sip of this lovely cordial, I'll toast to whatever you said."

Mel left shortly, and Kate walked him out. "Thanks for going with me today. I'm glad you did," she told him as he unhitched Kitty from the buggy and put a saddle on her.

"You're not mad at me anymore then?"

"I never really was mad at you. Well, maybe a little bit. I was just mad period – at everything. Sorry I took it out on you."

Mel put his arms around her, and Kate rested her head against his chest, closed her eyes and soaked up his strength. It was comfortable in the sturdy nest of his arms, safe, warm. She tried not to think of tomorrow and the next day. He kissed the top of her head and said goodnight.

"I'll be back in the morning, right after chores," he said.

Kate fixed supper, and while they ate, she planned and doled out work for the next day.

"Do you think I could borrow this table? It doesn't really belong to me. It was here when I found the cabin," Kate asked Harley.

"I'm thinking the man it belongs to wouldn't mind at all."

"I'll bring it back when I can get one."

Harley nodded at her and said, "Let's go for a sit outside for a spell."

"I can't, Harley. I need to keep moving."

"The forest isn't going away, Kate, remember that. It will always be here for you to come back to. And you can't run from it either – or this place."

"Maybe tomorrow I'll go outside with you, on our last night. Is that alright?"

"Whatever you need to do, Kate."

She had to wait for Mel to come back with Kitty before she could drive into town to see Rachel, and she still hadn't made up her mind if she would agree to leave her with Mr. Woodward. She was torn. She left as soon as Mel pulled into the clearing and came back soon after without her.

Rachel had been adamant, and Kate had little choice, to leave her or drag an angry young woman along by the hair. She thought it best to acquiesce, temporarily. Maybe when she came to visit them in Big Rapids, she'd like the bigger town and all the new people.

She stopped at her mother's and Ruthie's to let them know what was happening and to ask them to check in on Rachel as much as possible, and headed back to the cabin, her back stiff with determination.

"One foot in front of the other. Don't look back," she said to Wolf.

It was difficult to figure out what to pack and what they would need to use before leaving on Tuesday morning, but by afternoon, crates were piled with clothes, pots and pans, cleaning supplies, and almost everything else they owned. Rakes, shovels and hoes leaned against the cabin wall, and the wash tubs were stacked outside, ready to be loaded. The chairs her father had made still sat by the steps. They would be put on last, along with the blankets they would need to sleep in that night.

Mel looked around at all the crates, beds and furniture sitting in the clearing, looking odd and out of place outside in the sunshine. He rubbed his face and ran a hand through his hair.

"It's going to be quite a load," he said. "Should I start putting it on the wagon now?"

Kate grabbed one side of the table to help him carry it. "Sit," he said. "I can get this."

She nodded gratefully and sat watching him carefully stack the furniture and crates. Harley came out of the cabin with a steaming cup of tea, handed it to her, and began helping Mel load the wagon.

Two deer eventually came to the edge of the clearing and watched, curious about what was going on. It was their time of evening to drink at the creek and nibble at the fresh grass. They skirted the clearing and walked along the far side of the creek, alternately drinking and keeping an eye on the strange activity.

When they were done loading, Kate let the coons out of their cage, and they ran around crazily, climbed on the wagon and over the top of everything on it.

"They'll be alright by themselves, won't they?" she asked Mel, sitting next to her.

"They're plenty old enough," he said, "and if it makes you feel any better, I can check on them every once in a while, keep some food in their cage and leave the door open just in case."

"That would help. I'll worry."

She filled bowls with stew simmering over the hearth fire, and they ate outside, the girls on a blanket on the ground since all but three chairs had been put on the wagon. It was a silent group, each lost in private thought, each leaving something different behind that was to become their personal memory. It could be shared, but couldn't be viewed through identical eyes.

She washed the bowls and pot, tucked the girls into their blankets on the floor in their rooms and went back outside to sit with Harley and Mel. They rocked and watched the moon rise and light the clearing. Wolf sat next to Kate, and she stroked his head.

She thought of the way the cabin had looked when she first found it, barely visible under the foliage covering it. Scrub brush smothered the clearing from the woods to the cabin. The door hung crazily from one hinge, and rodents had homes inside. Kate cleaned up the interior and eventually whacked away at the brush, all the way back to the forest edge.

It was her refuge, hers and Bug's, a place she could escape to where no one could find her. Later, it was her home with Mark. And now wildlife and nature would reclaim it without them there to civilize the naturally encroaching forest.

This is killing me, she thought. *I think I will certainly die if I leave.*

She waited for the raccoons to scramble from their den, hoping they would come out on this last night to say goodbye. She listened for the owl and the flutter of bat wings. When Kate saw the coons scamper out and heard the owl's hoot, she said goodnight to them and went in to curl up on her blanket on the floor.

"One foot in front of the other, Kate," she said out loud, and Wolf gave her a loving Wolf-slobber at the side of her face and curled up next to her.

Chapter Eighteen

Spring 1914 – Big Rapids

They rolled out of the clearing early, a small caravan with the buggy leading the way in front of the wagon. Harley drove the buggy with Jeannie on his lap and Becca and Poochie beside him. Mel drove the wagon team, Kate and Kat on the seat next to him and Wolf lying behind them on a thick bed of their blankets. When they turned onto the path that led to the road, Kate didn't look back because she couldn't.

It was a long time getting there. They went slowly so the load wouldn't tumble, so no bump would upset the precariously perched pile. She heard the girls' excited chatter in the buggy in front of her, but she and Kat were quiet as the miles crept by.

"Are you alright, Sweetie?" Kate asked after a while, peering at her stony-faced daughter.

"No. I'm not," Kat told her mother, her back as stiff and immobile as Kate's.

"It's okay to cry when you're sad, you know."

"No, it isn't, damn it! I hate tears," Kat said, and then, like Kate, she added "Sorry." She turned to look at her mother when, after a shocked moment, Kate began to laugh.

"You cussed!" Kate gasped between giggles.

"So, do you, Ma."

As Kate continued to laugh and repeat "You cussed!" Kat couldn't help but smile a little, and Mel watched them out of the corner of his eyes. It was good to hear something besides birds singing and horse hooves hitting the dirt.

He thought the load was going to topple off the wagon and bounce off in all directions when they drove up the long Fourth Street hill that led to their new house, but they made it without losing anything. Kate climbed down, unlocked the door and the girls ran in, looking for their rooms. Poochie followed, sniffed at the floor, stuck his nose into every corner, and ran in circles.

Mel and Harley started unloading the wagon while Kate showed the girls their rooms. Kat would take the small one, and Becca and Jeannie would share the larger one at the top of the stairs. Kate went to look for the crate with the curtains they had made and the rugs Mel had given them. She wanted the girls to have something to do that would instantly make the rooms look like home to them.

When she got to the top of the stairs with the crate, Kat said, "Bring it in here, Ma, and tell Mel to take my bed into the large room when he gets to it. I'll share with Becca and Jeannie."

"Why would you want to do that, Kat?"

"So Harley can have a real room."

"Are you trying to bribe Harley with a room so he'll stay with us?" Kate asked.

Kat grinned and took the crate from her mother. Kate smiled at her retreating back and shrugged her shoulders. She wanted him to stay, too, and maybe Kat was right. Having his own room might help make it more permanent.

She directed Mel and Harley with the furniture and the remaining crates, and it wasn't long before everything was at least in the middle of the right room. Kate and Mel drove Kitty to the stable, arranged to have her boarded there, and then walked to the diner to tell her new boss she would be in for work in the morning. They went back to unpack and begin putting the house in order. Towards late afternoon, they had just about everything in place when a knock startled them.

Kate was on her knees sweeping old ashes from the hearth into a bucket and turned her head to look at the door like it was a strange object to be making such a noise. Wolf moved stealthily near, stared at it, and growled.

Harley, who was putting the table back together in the middle of the room, said, "Did you want me to get that?"

"Who would be coming here?" she asked with a puzzled look on her smudged face. "We don't know anybody."

"I'll bet if you open the door you'll find out the answer to your question," he said, amused by the way she was staring. Then he shuffled over and opened it.

Two people he didn't know stood there, a tall man holding a basket that smelled like food and made his mouth water, and a thin woman carrying a large bowl.

"We're looking for Kate Ramey," they both said at once and then looking around Harley, spotted her still kneeling at the hearth.

"And I was most definitely waiting for you and your bounty," Harley said, moaning in delight and peering into the basket. "Well, I must be honest – your bounty only because I don't know you, but please come in. I'm Harley, and you can see that your search for Kate has ended at the hearth."

Kate looked at the man by Letha's side and knew she recognized him, but couldn't remember from where. She'd met too many new people lately. Wolf sniffed at the basket, then stood on his hind legs and put his paws on the man's shoulders and his nose in the man's face.

"Get down, Wolf. Sorry," she added, then introduced Letha to Harley, searching her brain for memory of the man. He was tall and rangy, giraffe-gangly. His longish, dishwater hair straggled to his shoulders, and a crooked smile splintered his face. He danced back and forth on his feet like he had too much energy and didn't know what to do with it. She knew that face!

"I'm Frank," the man finally said, seeing Kate's confusion. He patted Wolf who had ignored Kate's command and whose nose was still in his face.

She smacked the side of her head. "Just Frank! That's it! The man who doesn't like shoes!" Wolf got down then and wandered lazily back to the hearth by Kate who stood and went to shake the hand that didn't have a basket hanging from it. She introduced him to Mel and Harley.

"Just Frank is the one who told me about Letha's Diner. What are you doing here?" she asked Frank.

"I was in Letha's for supper, as I usually am about this time of day, remembered meeting you on the street a while back, and asked if you had stopped in to see her. She told me you were moving in today, so we decided to bring a welcome basket of Letha's fried chicken and coleslaw."

"And it's a good thing you did. Kate was about to starve us, and as you can see," Harley said, rubbing his round belly, "I am wasting away for want of proper nutrition. Can you find the jug, Mel, to serve our first guests a little refreshment?"

Mel brought the jug and cordial, plus several glasses. "How did you meet Kate?" he asked Frank as he poured cordial for Letha and Kate.

"On the street. I told her I didn't like shoes either, and I don't," he said. "I like the feel of grass and dirt beneath my feet."

Mel looked confused, but Harley interrupted further questions by going on about the healthy benefits of going barefoot.

"It's better for your back," he told them. "Mother Nature didn't intend for us to encase our feet in leather. She gave us padded heels of our own." Then he lifted the jug, and Kate was afraid he was going to begin a long toast to Mother Nature or going barefoot or anything else his bizarre logic could connect to shoes. She forestalled it by asking if Frank would like his drink in a glass. When he nodded, Kate took the jug from Harley, handed it and a glass to Frank who poured and then lifted his glass.

"Here's to going barefoot and feeling good earth under your feet; and here's to all the natural wonders of the world, like grass and dirt and worms and crickets and bats; and here's to . . ." He stopped when he saw the girls come down the stairs and stand on the steps staring wide eyed at him. They hung on to the stair rail like it was a lifeline, and it wobbled precariously.

Then Frank continued, "beautiful young ladies and . . ."

Kate groaned and started laughing. Mel groaned, too, and slowly shook his head. Harley looked affronted. His place had been usurped by this stranger, and then he began

laughing too; his round belly jiggled, and his chubby cheeks pinched his eyes closed.

Frank looked around the room, saw Kate holding her sides, tears leaking from her eyes, heard Mel's deep guffaws and wondered what he had done to cause such mirth. Then he shrugged and gave them a crooked grin.

"Damn! Sorry," Kate gasped. "Are you and Harley related?" Kate asked when she could breathe again.

"Is anybody thirsty?" Letha asked, laughing with them, but not understanding why, either.

Mel ran a hand through his hair and down over his face, then took the jug from the table and lifted it.

"Here's to us," he said, took a long swig and handed it to Harley. "Just take a drink, Harley."

Kate sipped to cement all the toasts and called the girls over to introduce them to her new boss, Letha, and their new friend, Just Frank.

They ate ravenously, and afterwards, the girls were thrilled by water coming right out of a spout over a large sink. They didn't have to draw it from a well! Kate filled a pot with water to heat on the kindled stove, then poured it into the sink, and left the girls washing the supper dishes to sit outside on the small porch with her friends – old and new.

"Where do you live, Frank?" Mel was asking when she came out and got up from his chair to give it to Kate.

"Just at the edge of town. I have a small holding there and like to think I'm a farmer, although I don't have enough land for that, so I tinker around in town, helping out here and there. How about you?"

"I farm."

"Big spread?" Frank asked curiously.

"Big enough," Mel said, reluctant to talk about the size of his farm; how much he had increased his holding over the years. It was like discussing how much money you had in the bank. It just wasn't done.

"What brings you to Big Rapids, Kate?" Frank asked. "Where are you coming from?"

"I'm here for work," she told him, "and I lived around the Hersey area. It will be a real change for us, living in town. We're used to the woods."

"Ah, so you were a nymph running naked through the forest. Now I understand the comment about your feet," Frank said, turning his crooked smile on Kate.

Mel shifted where he stood leaning against the post, uncomfortable hearing Frank talk about a naked Kate.

"No. I did wear very unladylike trousers when I was in the woods, but not in town where I would shock all the Hersey matrons," she added.

Harley saw Mel shift again and wondered how long he'd just stand there. A twinkle lit his eyes as he looked from Mel to Frank, and then back again. Then he looked at Kate who was blissfully unaware of the skirmish going on around her.

Mel needed to get home for chores, but was reluctant to leave for a variety of reasons. It would be hard to think of Kate being here in Big Rapids and not in her cabin in the woods. He shuffled again and tried to think of a reason to put off going.

Harley was here. Nothing bad would happen to Kate, and you're just being a fool. He grunted, pulled himself away from the post he was leaning against. "I've got to go," he said gruffly.

"Is everything alright?" Kate asked looking up at the handsome man towering over her. She started to get up from her chair, but he leaned to put a hand on her shoulder, pushing her gently back down.

"Stay put," he said. "I'll just go say goodnight to the girls."

He came back out a few minutes later and said his farewells to everyone. Kate stood and put an arm around his waist to walk with him down the steps. At the sidewalk, he kissed the top of her head, and she felt his breath hot against her hair. "I'll miss you," he whispered.

"I'll be right here. Come as often as you can." Then Kate stood on her tiptoes to reach his lips for a quick kiss. From the corner of his eyes, Mel saw Harley grin and nod before her lips met his, and he breathed a little sigh of relief. He waved goodbye to the rest and left.

At the stable, he hitched his work horses to the wagon wondering how he was going to deal with Kate and the girls so far away. He had become placidly contented with them nearby, even if they weren't in his house where he wanted them. Now they were three hours away, and he was chained to his farm chores morning and night.

He didn't know what to do about it, and not finding a solution to a problem troubled him. 'Life is simpler than this – or at least should be, shouldn't it? You work hard. You treat people fair. You stay honest in your heart. That's the way the world works – what goes around comes around. Reap what you sow.' All the old clichés strolled through his brain as the horses led him home. None of them made him feel better.

He was late for night milking when he got there, and his herd was complaining about the time, would have pointed to a clock if they had fingers. He sat on his milk stool and laid his forehead against the first heifer's warm, milk swollen side. "Sorry, Dorothy. I know it's late. Won't happen again," he whispered to her.

He stretched out the chores, needing to be in the barn where he knew exactly what was what. He didn't need to think about it. His hands knew what to do; they had done it for many years. It soothed him to be with his cows, feel the steam in their breath as he rubbed his hand over their wide, velvety nostrils and listen to their contented lowing. He smelled the syrupy, pungent odor of straw bedding and molasses-corn mixed feed.

"Now this is simple and sweet," he said to one as he patted her away and called another to take her place. "This is how life should be."

When he went in the house, his mother was at the kitchen table and looked up from the shirt she was mending in a circle of lantern light. "You're late," she said, but as an observation, not a criticism. "Did you get Kate and the girls all moved?"

He nodded, took off his shirt, and began washing his arms and face at the sink. "They're all in."

"You hungry?" she asked, watching his deliberate movements. Her oldest son was so like her husband, buried long ago, that sometimes it was hard to look at him; the broad, thick chest, the long legs, the brown hair curling at his neck and forehead when it was damp and had grown too long. Her husband had been such a large, vital man it was still difficult to think he wasn't here. How could someone so alive, so imposing, fade into nothing? Simply be gone. He was too impressive for nothingness.

Mel had his father's way of thinking, too; determined, plain spoken and quiet, but emanating strength. You couldn't disregard either one of them. The mere fact they were there was enough to garner recognition and response. Right now, she guessed there was a battle going on in her son's mind because he had the same clenched jaw his father did when he was troubled, and she wished her son would talk about it.

"No. We ate. I think I'll just go on up to bed."

"Did I tell you one of the Jackson boys came by the other day looking for work?"

"No, you didn't."

"Well, he did. I believe it was the youngest one. Nice young man, strong and polite. We had cookies," she said, picking up the shirt she had been mending when he came in. "I was thinking you might be able to help them out if you hired him to do chores a couple of days a week. We can afford it, can't we?"

Mel wiped his face dry and stared at his mother. "Why would I hire out something I can do?"

"It was just a thought. It would help them . . ."

He looked at her oddly. His mother didn't interfere with the running of the farm. She hadn't since he'd taken over after his father's death. She took care of the house, and he ran the farm. That's the way it was.

"I'll give it some thought. See you in the morning," he said and left a quick kiss on his mother's cheek.

"Goodnight, Son" she said with a knowing smile. "Sleep well."

Kate went to bed in the strange room. She'd tucked in the girls and sat with Harley for a few more minutes before falling exhausted into her bed.

"This is home, now," she said to Wolf who'd followed her, "but it surely doesn't feel like it."

Wolf groaned and stretched. He gave her a half-hearted Wolf-nose, turned three times and plopped down next to the bed.

She lay stiffly, looking around, trying to feel comfortable in the bed she'd used for many years. But it felt different. Her mind restlessly examined the day, from the long trek to Big Rapids to moving in and entertaining new friends. Then it tried to go even further back, but she adamantly refused to let it go there. Instead, she repeated an old prayer over and over, a heartfelt but monotonous litany, until her breathing slowed and eyes closed in sleep.

When Kate opened them in the morning, she was startled by the strangeness, and it took a few moments to remember where she was. She jumped out of bed, threw on her good dress, and ran to the kitchen to rekindle the fire in the cook stove. Then she bounded up the stairs, two at a time, to rouse Harley. She had to go to the diner today! She couldn't be late on her first day!

Oatmeal was bubbling on the stove; her hair was brushed and tied at the back of her neck, and she was ready.

"I've got to go," she called up the stairs. "I'm not sure when I'll be back, but if you walk down to see me, I'll probably know by then. Bye."

She flew down the front steps. The sun was just rising, and Kate looked around her as she walked to the diner. None of the shops were open on Main Street. It seemed Letha was the only early bird in Big Rapids. When she got there, Letha was fitting the key into the front door lock.

"Good Morning!" Kate said to her. "I was afraid I would be late."

"Well, you're right on time. I like that."

"I don't even know what I'll be doing for you. I guess I should have asked, but it doesn't matter. I can cook or wash dishes or wait tables – whatever you need me to do."

When they went in, Letha gave Kate the grand tour. A single room for hungry guests held ten square tables with red checked oil cloth on top; each held a tray for condiments. Letha explained Kate would refill the condiment bottles first thing each morning to be ready when people started coming in. A long, polished wood counter held similar trays and had six red padded stools standing in front of it.

The kitchen area was small, and filled with two huge stoves they rekindled as they went by. Letha showed her a large walk-in pantry at the end of the kitchen and two big iceboxes where she would find everything she needed to refill the table trays.

She gave her a white apron, a tablet and pencil and said, "You'll wait tables today, and generally just do what I tell you, when I tell you. Ask what they want to eat, write it down, and give me the paper. When you see plates in that window," she said, pointing to a rectangle opening between the kitchen and the dining area, "pick them up and give them to the customers who ordered them. They'll tell you if you got it wrong," she said, smiling. "And you will, but that's okay. Just fix it."

Kate began filling catsup and mustard bottles, then salt and pepper shakers and arranged them neatly on the trays. She was piling paper napkins in their holders when the first customer entered.

"Hey! Who's this pretty little thing?" a dapper, slender man in a gray suit said as he walked to one of the tables.

"This – is Kate," she responded with a nervous grin.

"Just sit down and order, Bill," Letha yelled from the window leading to the kitchen. "Then leave the woman alone."

He held his hand out to Kate and said, "Bill Samuels. I own the Responder. That's the Big Rapids newspaper – the only one in town," he said proudly. "You must be new to the area because I know everyone around here, and I didn't know you. But now I do."

Kate nodded, and asked what he'd like to eat, holding her pad of paper with the pencil poised over it. Two others came in before she'd taken his order, and within moments the door opened again and again, and the bell it banged against continued ringing until the room was full of people wanting coffee, eggs and ham, pancakes and sausage.

Kate scribbled orders, gave them to Letha, and tried to remember where the food went, which person got the scrambled eggs and which got the sunny side up. She laughed nervously when she got it wrong, quickly picked up the plates to switch them and said, "Sorry. I'm so sorry."

The diner grew hot and noisy with chatter as people greeted each other and bantered back and forth in the way people do when they have known each other for a long time, and she began to find it hard to move between the chairs to get to the back tables. Sweat moistened her brow and tendrils of her hair came loose from its tie and stuck to her face.

She punched in the numbers for Bill Samuels' check, took his money and counted back the change as Letha had shown her. He put a nickel back down on the counter and pushed it at her. Kate stared at it, wondering if she had counted wrong.

Noting her bewilderment, he said, "It's for you, Kate, because you smiled. It's a tip. Put it in your pocket."

The table at the back had six men wedged around it who began yelling for more coffee, and Kate wormed her way around the tables with a coffee pot in her hand.

She heard, "Bye, Kate." It had felt good to have someone know her name, and she smiled as she yelled "Thank you," back at Bill.

The room was packed with men on their way to work, and Kate wondered why they ate breakfast at the diner instead of at home. She must have served fifty breakfasts and two or three times as many cups of coffee. She lost count after the first hour. The place had filled not long after the door opened, and just as quickly, it began to empty. They were going off to open the doors to their own shops.

Her legs tingled from running back and forth on the wooden floor with the added weight of trays of food. She didn't think she'd done a terrible job, even if she had mixed up some of the orders. They smiled with her when she apologized and hadn't been angry when she took the plate from one and gave it to another.

When she found time to think about the morning, she remembered her worst mistake. A sausage link slid off a plate. She saw it slide, and in her mind, it floated in the air for a full minute. It slowly twisted in the space between the plate and its landing place before it settled in a man's lap, right between his legs. She embarrassed herself by reaching for the sausage, and then stopping when she saw where it was. She automatically reached again – she couldn't just leave it there – and then stopped again. He sat grinning up at her, his eyes daring her to pick it off his lap. His companions leaned in to look and then guffawed loudly at her predicament.

Kate turned red, steeled herself, and quickly grabbed the sausage. "You'll have to wipe the stain yourself," she said grinning and turned away with a still flushed face. She went to the kitchen with the errant sausage, and brought back a fresh one on a small plate along with a damp cloth. When she cleared the table, several coins were left by the man's plate, and Kate wondered if she should drop sausages in all their laps.

When she had all the tables cleaned and refilled the condiment trays, she went into the kitchen and started washing dishes. Letha was clearing away the breakfast supplies and preparing for the lunch crowd. A few people straggled in, and Kate dried her hands and went out to wait on them, then went back to washing dishes. She asked Letha what she should to with the coins left on the tables.

"They're yours to keep," she said. "If people like you, you'll make some good money in tips."

Kate was amazed people would give money away like that, but the thought of earning more than her salary made her giddy. She had payments to make and a family to feed, so she still needed to find some laundry income, but tips would be a real help. Kate found out she would work until after the lunch crowd thinned out – usually around one o'clock, six days a week. Nettie, the other waitress, worked the supper hours. They were closed on Sundays.

Harley and the girls came in around ten. Jeannie and Becca were in awe of the diner and tried out all of the stools that spun around when you pushed with your foot against the rail. Kat appeared silently unimpressed. Poochie and Wolf waited outside, anxiously watching people as they walked on by or came in. Poochie looked eagerly for a pat on the head, and Wolf sat erect and poised, ready for evil on two legs.

"I should be home around one-thirty," Kate told them. Then she asked Becca and Kat to make some signs to post around town asking if anyone had laundry they'd like to have washed and ironed, "Just like you made before," she told them, "when we put them around Hersey."

Letha came out of the kitchen with a plate of doughnuts left over from breakfast. She put one in front of each of them, and Harley gave her his 'I love food grin.' He took a bite, shut his eyes, and moaned with pleasure.

"You are a goddess to all big bellied men," he told her, holding the doughnut to his nose to sniff.

"I'm a goddess to all men." And when Harley's eyes widened, she added, "because I cook, and all men think with their bellies, big ones and little ones. And now I've got to go make lunch chili and put together meatloaf for the supper folks."

When Letha left, Kate sat for a few minutes with her family. "Everything going okay at home?" she asked.

Harley told her all was well, and they were going to walk down to the school and look it over. Jeannie and Becca were excited at the prospect of meeting new children, but Kat sat with her back stiff and taut.

"I don't know why Harley can't teach me," she said irritably. "Let Becca and Jeannie go to school."

"You might like it, Kat," Kate told her.

"No. I won't. I like Harley teaching me."

"Can we talk about this later?" Kate asked. "After I get home?"

Kat nodded, but she didn't look happy about the whole world.

They left and Kate went back to the kitchen to help Letha.

Lunch hour was as hectic as breakfast – with many of the same men who'd been there earlier. The only difference was in what they ordered. Kate was growing used to whipping around the room, keeping the orders straight and the pot of coffee constantly glued to her hand. She refilled cups on the way to taking orders from new groups of hungry people at other tables.

"Hey Kate," she heard from all directions. She smiled, said, "Be right there," and hoped her feet would hold out until they left to go back to their jobs and she could take a needed break.

Curtis Taylor, from the Emporium, came in during the middle of the lunch rush and found an open seat at the counter. He watched Kate race around the diner, balance plates on her arms and banter with the customers.

She's good, he thought. Pretty, too, and wondered if he was right in thinking there might not be a husband in her house. He remembered her well from when she'd asked for work at the Emporium and wished again that he had been able to hire her. When Kate got to him, he reintroduced himself.

"I remember you, Mr. Taylor," she told him. "What can I get for you?"

"I'll have some of Letha's chili. Have you moved to Big Rapids?"

"Yes, I have. We bought Mr. Johnson's house on Fourth."

Kate took him his chili and ran off to take money from several people lined up at the register. The room emptied again as customers returned to work. Kate cleared the tables and washed them.

Curtis, still at the counter eating his chili, was wondering how to find out if Kate was married. He remembered she had daughters.

She probably has a husband, too, he thought wistfully. When the last person left the diner, Curtis was still nursing a cup of coffee. "How do you like the job?" he asked her. "It's hectic, but I like it. It's good to be busy. I'm just not sure my legs like it as much as I do," she said, smiling at him. "And feet have a way of letting you know things."

"Well with a job on top of a family, you must like being busy very much," he said, his bald head growing rosy as he awkwardly tried to probe. "Didn't you say you have children?"

Kate nodded and started clearing the counter. "I do – four daughters." She took the dirty plates to the kitchen and added them to the huge pile already there waiting, and went back out to wash the counter.

Curtis lifted his coffee cup so she could wipe under it and then reached out to put his hand over hers. "Why don't you sit a spell – take a rest?"

"Mr. Taylor, I'm sure you mean to be kind, but please take your hand from mine. I need to finish up here and get home." She stared at his hand as he abruptly removed it and then heard a noise outside. When she looked up, she saw Wolf with his paws on the window, his nose pressed against the glass.

"What the hell?" Curtis said, as he followed Kate's gaze and saw the huge black head pointed menacingly at him.

"That's Wolf. He must have come looking for me."

The rosy glow on Curtis' head deepened and spread to his ears. He stammered and jerked his hand further as if it had been slapped. "Sorry. I didn't mean to be brash. It's just . . . I . . . You're working and . . . well, you're pretty and I thought you might be alone. I've been alone a long time and . . ."

Wolf's head disappeared from the window, and people walking by saw a large, black beautiful animal sitting erect by the diner door, his ears cocked forward in the listening position.

Kate felt sorry for his embarrassment and relented, sitting on the stool next to him. "I'm not alone, Mr. Taylor. I have my family."

Curtis was a short man whose stomach fell over his trouser belt and strained his shirt buttons, and in his nervous state, his feet swung back and forth not touching the rail underneath. Kate continued, watching the rhythmic swinging of his legs, "In fact, maybe you can help me. You know everyone in town, right?"

He looked up from his cup, suddenly pleased he might be of help to her. "Sure. What do you need?"

"I need laundry – dirty laundry that needs to be washed and ironed. Do you know anyone who might pay me to do that?"

"Well," he said, thinking about what she'd said and drumming his fingers on the counter. "I might. I hate doing laundry. So might several others I know." And even though he was enamored with Kate, Curtis was a businessman first and added, "What would you charge?"

She told him, and after a thoughtful moment, he told her he'd drop it by her home every Saturday afternoon, if that was alright with her. He also gave her the name of three others he thought might be interested. She wrote them down eagerly, thanked him and got up on tired feet to wash the pile of dirty dishes.

"It seems I'm always washing up after someone," she said to Letha as she plunged her hands into the hot water. But a smile was on her face. Things were moving along in the right direction.

"When life hands you dirt, you just sweep it up, cause if you don't, it piles up around you," Letha told her.

Kate laughed at Letha's philosophical words and told her she was right and that she didn't want to sit around in a pile of dirt. "You sound like Harley," she added.

"You did just fine out there today. There were no broken dishes, and I listened; the customers seem to like you.

"Thanks. That's nice of you to say. Is there anything else I can do for you before I leave?"

"Nope. Go on home to your girls. See you tomorrow."

When Kate stepped out the door, Wolf stood, put his paws on her shoulders and looked her in the eyes. Satisfied, he got down and they walked home, Wolf hugging her legs with each step.

"You're gonna trip us both if you don't get over a bit," she told him.

Wolf rolled his eye at her. 'You might trip, but I never do, and I'm not sure I like you being so long at that place.'

At least, that's what Kate heard. She might have read it in his eyes, but she wasn't quite sure he hadn't actually said the words. "I speak wolf," she told him with a little giggle. A gentle breeze dried the sweat from her brow, and the sun massaged her stiff muscles.

'No, I speak human, silly woman,' he told her with another eye roll.

When she got home, Jeannie and Becca leaped at her, both wanting to tell her about the school. Kate said, "Can I at least come all the way inside first?" she asked them.

"There are lots of kids there," Becca said, "and they were nice to us."

Jeannie told her about the teacher, Miss McLaughlin, who showed them around the school, "and they have desks that open at the top, and you can put your lunch and stuff inside."

"What did you think, Kat?" Kate asked.

"It's okay. I liked the mouse they had in a cage and the bird, but I still want Harley to teach me."

Harley was standing on the steps watching and listening. "I don't mind, Kate, if that's what you and Kat want. In fact, I'd like to." He turned toward Becca and Jeannie. "You know Kat's going to be way ahead of you, don't you?" he teased. "With a smart teacher like me, she'll learn a whole lot more."

"Both of you are sure about this?" Kate asked.

Kat nodded her head firmly, and Harley came down the steps to hug them both.

"Thanks. I didn't really want to lose all my students at once."

"Did you find out what time school starts and ends?" Kate asked.

"We did. It begins at quarter to eight and lets out at two-thirty."

"Let's walk down there. I want to meet the teacher. Want to go, Harley?"

"Nothing would suit me better than a little more exercise," he said, rubbing his belly and grinning. "Then I can eat more at supper."

"I want to stop at a couple of houses on the way. Mr. Taylor gave me some names of people who might hire me to do their laundry, and I want to get started as soon as possible."

"Mr. Taylor?" Harley asked.

"Yes. He owns the Emporium across the street from the diner. He'll be dropping his laundry off every Saturday, so it looks like I just might be able to make the first payment on this house," she said with a satisfied grin.

"I never doubted it for a moment," Harley said, linking his arm through Kate's. "Let's go."

They walked down the long, steep hill their house sat atop, the girls skipping and running ahead, with Poochie following and Wolf by Kate's legs. On Main Street, several people said "Hello, Kate," and Harley looked sideways at her with raised eyebrows.

"You seem to know a lot of people already. You're taking this town by storm."

"They're all customers of Letha's. I think no one cooks at home here."

Kate introduced Harley and the girls to Bill Samuels who was standing outside the door of the Responder Newspaper.

"Your daughters are just as pretty as you are, Kate. Welcome to Big Rapids, girls, and you, Mr. Benton."

The girls and Harley responded and they moved on.

"Have you been out capturing the hearts of all the men in town, Kate?" Harley teased.

"Well, they give me tips if they like me, so I guess I'll just have to make them like me, right?"

"What's a tip, Ma?" Kat asked.

"It's money they leave for me by their plates if I do a good job waiting on them."

"Really? That's strange," Kat said, "Doesn't Letha pay you?" Her forehead puckered trying to figure out why people would just give you money for doing a job you're already getting paid to do.

"Yes she does, and I think it's strange, too. But I'm not going to stop them from doing it."

When they got to a large, grey shingled house, Kate told them to wait while she walked up the steps to see if Doctor Crow was home. That was one of the names Curtis Taylor had given her. "You stay too, Wolf."

No one answered the door there, but the next person was home. Mrs. Worthington was the widow of the man who had founded Big Rapids. She was a sweet looking, plump woman with blue-gray hair and asked if they would come in for milk and cookies. She smiled, smelled like flowers and was happy to see them. She wanted company. When Kate told her they would certainly enjoy that some other time, her smile held, but the sparkle in her eyes dimmed.

They chatted on the porch for awhile, and it soon seemed they had known each other for a long time, not just a few minutes. Even Wolf and Poochie stretched out in the shade of the porch and closed their eyes. Kate liked her. She had a ready smile, and her blue eyes grew soft and tender when she talked with the girls.

"I have a daughter," she told them. "She lives in Grand Rapids so I don't get to see her often, but I surely do like the company of young folks."

"What about old folks?" Harley asked, hooking his thumbs in his suspenders. "Not that I'm old, but I can be good company. In fact, I'm downright entertaining."

"Indeed Mr. Benton. I would enjoy visiting with all of you."

"Another time then, Mrs. Worthington, we would love to visit," Kate told her.

"I'll count on that. I think you'd enjoy a tour of this old house. It's quite something – way too big for just me."

"It's lovely," Harley said, "and so are you, Mrs. Worthington."

Pink suffused her almost unlined cheeks, and she told Kate she would have her laundry ready by Saturday – she'd have it brought to Kate's house.

They left Mrs. Worthington's porch feeling good. "She's a sweet woman, isn't she?" Kate said.

"Yes, she is, and I'll bet her cookies are just as delightful," Harley said with a grin.

"Your belly's talking now. After today, I'm beginning to believe all men really do think with their bellies. A full one makes a happy man; an empty one makes a grump."

At the last house, an imperious, mid-forties, dark haired man answered the door. "Yes?" he said, looking them all over one by one and then keeping his eyes on Wolf. "What can I do for you?"

"I'm Kate Ramey, Mr. Stern. Curtis Taylor told me you might need a laundress."

Ralph Stern was the polar opposite of Mrs. Worthington, but they left with a promise of his dirty laundry – at least temporarily. His housekeeper had recently quit, and he hadn't been able to replace her, so he reluctantly agreed to send his clothes to Kate's house on Saturday.

"Although I don't know why you can't do it here," he said gruffly.

"Because I have other work, Mr. Stern, which must be done at my home." Kate stiffened her back, wondering if it would be worth it to work for him. He was a younger, male Agatha Pennington.

I'll probably end up stomping his shirt into the ground like I did Agatha's, she thought, and a little smile danced at the corners of her lips.

Wolf stood close to Kate, glaring at the man who glanced nervously down at the black head in front of him. She thought about telling him Wolf was friendly, but decided to just let him stew in his own irritable juices. It would do him some good.

They came to an agreement and she turned to leave. Wolf looked back at Stern one last time and pulled his lips back to show him how big his teeth were. He could have been smiling, but Stern knew better and quickly shut the screen door.

"You are naughty," Kate told Wolf, patting his head. "Thanks."

Wolf looked up at her, 'I don't know what you mean,' but he pranced down the path to the street like a show horse and practiced his fake smile on unfortunate squirrels that swiftly scampered up trees to get away from him.

Chapter Nineteen

Fall 1914

Kate jogged to the diner in the brisk early morning air. Michigan falls could be anything from freezing cold to summer, and this morning it was somewhere in between cold and colder. She pulled her wool wrap tighter around her shoulders and quickened her step, thinking about autumn in the forest as the leaves grew red-gold and whispered ancient tales of wood sprites on their way to the earth.

She could almost smell the wood smoke leaking into the cabin from the hearth fire and the spicy scent of apple and pickled beets simmering on the stove ready to be ladled into clean, hot jars – welcome treats when winter's sparse fare dulls the supper table.

She nodded to Betty Hall as she waddled by tugging her small son along behind her. Betty smiled at Kate, bid her a good morning, and then good naturedly chided her son for being a laggard and slow as molasses. It was nice to be recognized, and almost everyone either nodded hello or spoke to her as they passed by. Her thoughts moved from the forest to the town of Big Rapids.

Kate earned enough from her wages and tips, supplemented by the laundry work, to get by – just. She washed clothes for five households, which kept her busy day and night, but she was able to make the payments to Mr. Johnson and Eldon Woodward, plus board Kitty at the stable.

She didn't need the mare in town, but had to keep her for trips back to Hersey to see her mother and Rachel, all her friends and family. Mel had suggested building a shed for her at the back of the house, and she thought she'd do that eventually.

Kate had visited with Rachel several times over the summer, and it got harder and harder to leave her at Eldon's, but Rachel was still adamant. On the last visit, Kate stopped at her sister's house to talk with Ruthie about it.

"You can't take her back with you; I would just miss her too much," Ruthie had said, her hands folded tightly in her lap, her face grim. "Besides, it's what Rachel wants, too."

Kate was torn. She wanted her daughter with her, but she'd have to break both their hearts to do it, and she knew it. "For now, . . . then we'll see," she said, and left it there.

Ruthie nodded, but wasn't appeased. "She's like my child, Kate, and besides, I don't think she'd ever leave Hersey with Charlie here."

Kate was startled and had been going to ask what Ruthie meant, but Jack came in about then, his face lit in a wide smile. "Kate! So good to see you!"

"You too, Jack. I miss you all so much."

Jack sat with them, and they chatted about everything that had gone on in Hersey since Kate had been gone.

"Pretty much the same things all over again, right?" Kate said with a grin. When Kate left, Jack walked out with her. He helped her into the buggy and stood with his foot on the step looking at her with a question in his eyes.

"What?" Kate asked.

"Are you okay?"

Kate nodded, but her eyes said no. "I just miss you; and Hersey, my family, my home. That's all."

"Yeah, I know. We all miss you, too."

He patted Kate's arm, then took his foot from the step and put up a hand to ward off an enthusiastic Wolf-slobber. Wolf had missed him, too. Jack gave her a kiss on the cheek and told Wolf a proper kiss came without excessive moisture.

Kate drove off to pick up Harley and the girls who were visiting Ellen and Verna. She hadn't stretched the truth; she missed Jack. He always knew exactly how to be there for her and to be by her side without encroaching. Jack was a bond to her past and present. He was a bridge and she missed the connection.

Kate thought about Rachel and Ruthie as she walked to work. She hadn't been able to ask Ruthie about Rachel not wanting to leave Charlie. What was going on that Kate had missed? What should she know that she didn't?

She reflected on the conflict in Europe everyone was enthusiastically and energetically debating, and she was afraid ... glad she had daughters. Then she felt ashamed for thinking it.

'Where is the forest peace?' she questioned. 'And here I am worried about Rachel being silly, acting out a bit, while other mothers are worried their sons are dying.' It made no sense to her, but she knew she couldn't change what was, couldn't stop caring about what Rachel was doing, and it wouldn't help the sons and mothers and fathers if she did.

Wolf tilted his head to look at her. "Was I talking out loud, Wolf? Or are you reading my mind again?"

On June 28th, Archduke Ferdinand was assassinated, and Austria-Hungry declared war on Serbia near the end of July. Then, according to the news, a great big snowball rolled through Europe as Germany went to war against Russia and then France. Bill Samuels' Responder described it all, and every morning the diner was full of war talk. Young men wanted to run off and sign up for the fight, puffing their chests and boasting how they'd beat those Krauts once and for all, even though the United States was determined to stay at home and out of it.

"The world has gone mad, Wolf. People are shooting at each other; automobiles puff smoke and noise up and down the street. I miss the woods. I miss our forest."

Wolf nodded agreement, and when Kate went in the diner, Wolf sat sentry outside for a while before he ambled on home to escort Becca and Jeannie to school.

They had started in September after the long summer break, and two of Kate's girls had been attending for over a month. Before it began, they had all met at the school, and Miss McLaughlin tested them to see where they were scholastically. She was amazed at what they knew, and Harley had unabashedly taken credit for their knowledge.

"They've had the advantage of my professorial expertise," he told her, a satisfied look on his chubby face.

"Well, I must say that I'm impressed, Mr. Benton. Their composition is excellent, and their understanding of mathematics and geography is outstanding. However, what I am truly amazed by is their grasp of the physical world. I'm not sure I can compete with them," she said with a grim little smile.

Miss McLaughlin was a tiny, frail looking woman who had been teaching Big Rapids children for over twenty-five years. Her brown hair showed threads of silver at the sides where it was pulled tightly back from her face and tucked in a small, netted bun at the back of her neck. Her green eyes could smile in pleasure, dazzle the receiver, or shoot darts when she wanted to impale a misbehaving student and awaken fear, but at the moment she was enjoying Harley, and her eyes showed it.

"The world is a classroom, Miss McLaughlin. Everywhere you look there is something to learn from how it works. I simply look and listen and wonder about its nature. And if you do that, you'll find it ready to teach about human nature as well. Why just the other day I was noticing . . ."

Kate groaned and interrupted as gently as she could. "Harley has taught the girls well and has taken them far beyond where I could have." She smiled at Harley and linked her arm through his saying without words, 'let's go, now.'

"I would be happy to share my knowledge of applied physics to all your students," he told the teacher, peeking up at her coyly through the gold curls falling over his eyes. "Say, once each week?"

Miss McLaughlin brightened and seized the opportunity. "How about Wednesday mornings?" she asked.

"Done." A smile scrunched his blue eyes almost closed, and he rubbed his belly like he'd just eaten a large, satisfying meal. "I will have a lesson plan all prepared."

"And where did you learn about lesson planning, Harley?" Kate asked as they walked away from the school.

"Ah, Old Harley just knows about stuff," he told her. "Things just seep into my pores and make their way to my brain."

Kate looked sideways at him, her brows arched in a question. "Are you ever going to tell me who you are, where you come from?"

"I come from everywhere, Kate, and I am simply Harley."

She filled the condiment trays and napkin holders and surveyed the room for anything that might be out of place. She had her own key to the diner now, and Letha was not due in for another half hour. Kate liked to be there ahead of time, have the place to herself when it was quiet and she could get everything done well before the breakfast rush. She kindled the stoves, made the huge pot of coffee, and filled the creamers.

Letha came in when she was piling thick slabs of bacon in one of the iron skillets and fat sausage links in the other. She set them on the stove near the end where they wouldn't get hot too quickly and said good morning to Letha.

"I sure do like this," Letha said. "You're spoiling me."

"Well, I'm out of bed early. I might as well be doing something productive. Besides, I like it when it's quiet like it is right now."

Letha looked at Kate quizzically and put on her apron. "You miss the peace of your cabin in the forest, don't you?"

Kate nodded that she did and went to get the massive basket of eggs that would be cooked that morning.

"Have you been back since you moved here?" Letha asked.

"No. It's too soon – too hard. I will one day."

Over the months, in bits and pieces between the rush of hungry customers, she had told Letha about the cabin; how she had found it and lived there with Mark and then with her daughters and Mark; about the raccoons and deer that came to the clearing; about the sounds and smells of the woods.

"Maybe you should take an extra day off, Kate, and go visit your cabin. Take that strapping man, Mel, with you and just relax. You work damned hard. I can get Nettie to fill in for one morning. She can do a double shift; it hasn't killed me yet."

"Well, you're tough as nails, Letha. Elephants, tigers and bears couldn't kill you."

"Think about it," Letha told her just as the bell over the door rang in the first hungry man of the morning.

Kate went to greet him, and the rush began. Half an hour later, the room was full and Kate was racing around taking orders, sliding steaming plates in front of people, and teasing with customers as usual when Curtis Taylor slammed the door open violently.

"Kate!" he screamed. "You've got to come!"

Kate looked up, stunned by the assault of his voice. "Why? Where?" she asked, her face instantly white.

"Down the street! She's been hurt! Come on!"

Kate dropped a plate onto the nearest table and ran out the door with Curtis. "What happened?" she demanded on her way out.

A block away she saw a crowd of people around an automobile and knew. She ran towards them, shoving and pushing her way inside the group. When they realized who it was, they parted to let her in.

She saw Wolf first, sitting erect, his head rotating from side to side, growling and glaring at everyone, and then Poochie, stretched out beside the girl on the ground. He had his head on her chest and was whining mournfully. Jeannie lay motionless next to Harley who sat with his head bowed, shoulders slumped, immobile and holding Jeannie's hand. Her foot was twisted backwards, and blood was seeping from it. Her eyes were closed. Wolf stood when he saw Kate, and the crowd backed up.

"She ran out right in front of me," a man said, reaching for Kate's arm. "I couldn't help it."

Wolf growled and crouched low. Kate jerked her arm free, pushed the man away from her and yelled, "Get away! Go get the doctor!"

"They've already sent for him," Curtis said, following behind Kate. "If he's in town, he'll be on his way."

"That dog won't let anyone touch her," a woman snarled. "He's a menace – should be shot."

Kate kneeled down by her daughter and touched her face, tears streaming down her own. She felt her wrist for a pulse, but couldn't tell if what she felt was her own heart pounding too hard or Jeannie's faint pulse coming through her fingertips.

"Jeannie," she groaned. "Please be alright, please, please. Momma's here." She put her face in front of Jeannie's and felt a small breath on her own cheek coming from Jeannie's lips. "Thank God. Thank you, God."

Doctor Crow loped down the street, and the gathered crowd parted to let him in. Kate looked up, recognized him. "Help her, please."

Wolf immediately sat back on his haunches. The doctor ignored the animal, set his black satchel on the ground, and kneeled on the other side of Jeannie.

"Should I get Poochie off her?" Kate asked.

"No, leave him."

It seemed to Kate that he just knelt there looking at her daughter forever. She watched his eyes travel from Jeannie's head, down her body, to the foot at the end of Jeannie's straight leg, and then they went back up and passed slowly down the twisted, bloody one. He picked up her hand and held it in both of his, touching the skin of her wrist tenderly and then gently pressing each of her fingers, watching the pink flesh intently as he did so. He touched Jeannie's closed eyelids and left his fingers there for long moments, then pressed his long fingers on her abdomen and laid the side of his face on her chest.

Kate was beginning to wonder if he was a real doctor when he finally said, "Nothing is hurt internally. Her leg and ankle are badly broken and will heal."

"But you haven't even looked at her foot," Kate cried, getting angry.

"No, not yet."

"Well . . . do something!"

"In time," he said quietly. "Her body is doing its work at the moment." He ran his hands slowly down Jeannie's thin arms and then placed his hands on her abdomen, let them lie there immobile. Kate could see them rise and fall with each breath Jeannie took. Then he put his large hands under her, and Poochie moved off his tiny master to let the doctor take her in his arms.

Kate ran beside him as he strode back to his office, just down the block, his long stride eating up the yards and causing her to run to keep up. Jeannie stirred, and Kate heard a small moan.

"You'll be fine, Sweetie," Kate told her in a strangled voice. "Doctor Crow will take good care of you."

He laid Jeannie on the table and put a small pillow under her head, then covered her with a blanket. Harley followed them in and stood at the head of the table, stroking Jeannie's copper curls, tears streaming unchecked down his cheeks, and his lips trembled uncontrollably. He bit at them in an effort to keep them still.

"I want her to wake up before I set the bones," the doctor told her.

Kate argued with him, said he should do it before she woke up so she wouldn't feel the pain, but he just shook his head.

"She won't feel it," he said and pulled up two chairs by the table. "Please sit."

When she started to argue again, Harley touched her arm. "He'll fix our girl, Kate."

She whirled to face him, her face contorted in pain and fear. "How do you know that, Harley? What makes you so damn sure?" Kate snarled, angry her baby girl lay broken on a wooden table, angry she hadn't been there to protect her, angry about everything she could do nothing about.

"Have I ever spoken an untruth to you, Kate?" he asked softly, his agonized eyes begging forgiveness.

She looked at Harley, saw the pain in her heart mirrored in his eyes and slowly shook her head. She sat then, and in the quiet room, her gaze alternated between her daughter and the man who sat on the other side of her.

Eventually, she noted his long, black hair and olive skin, high cheek bones that led down to a firm chin and up to wide-set eyes almost as black as his hair. He was still, serene, holding Jeannie's hand and Kate began to wonder if he was sleeping. But his eyes were open, watching.

When Jeannie's eyes began to flutter, he stood and leaned close to her. "I'm John Pierre Crow, Jeannie, and I want you to be well. Will you do as I ask?"

Jeannie, startled by his face, opened her eyes wide and gave a sharp moan as she tried to move away from him.

"Jeannie," he said, speaking softly, almost crooning to her. "Your leg is hurt, and I need you to help me fix it. Will you help me?"

She stopped shying away and carefully searched his face. Then she nodded, and he began talking to her, telling her what she could do to help. He talked about pastures and deer in them, grazing in the sunshine. He talked about how the Muskegon River flowed through the land to unknown places, rippling in the sunlight, and the fish that found their way home each spring to spawn and create new life.

Kate listened and watched, mesmerized, and felt her own breathing slow. Peace fell over her like warm sunshine, like being snuggled in the arms of someone who cherished her. When he stretched her broken leg straight, Jeannie didn't even whimper. She lay still and relaxed, free of stress and pain. He splinted it and then spoke to her again. "Come back, Jeannie," he whispered.

Her eyelids fluttered, and she reached for Doctor Crow's hand. "Did I help?"

"You did. Thank you." He told Jeannie he wanted to talk with her mother for a few moments, and they walked away.

"She must not move her leg about. It's broken in many places. In order for it to heal properly, she must give the small bones time to knit together properly. Do you understand?" Kate nodded.

"Also, the open wound where the bone has come through the skin must be watched and the bandage kept clean."

"Can she come home?" Kate asked.

He nodded and Kate rubbed her hand over her forehead, squeezing the throbbing at her temples with her thumb and fingers. He looked at her silently, his aquiline face immobile, and then repeated, "Her leg must remain still. Do you have a wagon to move her?"

"A buggy, at the stable."

He shook his head. "I will carry her. You are nearby . . . on Fourth Street, right?"

When they were preparing to take Jeannie home, Kate asked him how he had set her leg so painlessly.

"I learned in the woods," he stated, "from my grandmother."

They moved Jeannie into Kate's bedroom so she could be downstairs near people, and made her as comfortable as possible given the shattered leg. Doctor Crow gave Kate a bottle of liquid he had prepared for Jeannie's pain and cautioned her about using it too frequently.

Kat and Becca stood white-faced at the side of Jeannie's bed, too afraid to speak. Doctor Crow put one hand on each of their shoulders and told them their sister would heal, and they believed him, letting out long held breath in relief.

"Damn, I forgot all about the diner," Kate said. When she saw Doctor Crow smile for the first time all morning, she added, "Sorry. I didn't mean to cuss."

"She does that all the time, Doctor," Harley said. "And she always apologizes. Pay her no heed."

He still wore a small, almost imperceptible smile when he took his leave, saying he'd stop by some time that evening to check on Jeannie.

They brought chairs into the room and settled around her. Poochie understood he couldn't leap on the bed as he normally did and instead crawled little by little, inch by inch, to lay stretched beside her. When she finally drifted off to sleep under the effects of the medicine, they left her.

In the kitchen, Harley and Kate talked quietly. He suggested wires be sent to Ellen or Willie to let them know what had happened. Maybe Mel, too. He'd do that and stop in at the diner to explain to Letha, too.

"God, what am I going to do? I have to go to work to-morrow," Kate said in frustration. "How can I leave her here – broken?"

"Don't you think I can take care of our girl?" he said, starting to tease as usual, but then stopped. His face turned white and his eyes closed tight.

"I should have seen . . . should have had a hold of her hand . . . I won't let anything happen to her, Kate. I promise you. Never again. I'm so sorry. You can't know how sorry."

"Of course, I think you can care for her, Harley. It isn't that . . ."

"Kat will stay with her when I walk Becca to school, and I will be gone only for a short time. We'll both be here with Jeannie while you're at work," he pleaded, trying to comfort her and himself at the same time. "We'll do schoolwork here in Jeannie's room or close by when she's sleeping. It will work out, Kate. I promise."

Harley's face screamed anguish, and Kate's heart consistently and repeatedly broke for him, for his shattered sense of responsibility. He turned away, tried to leave the room, but Kate stopped him with a hand on his shoulder.

"Harley, I know you'll take care of them. And I know you're beating yourself up right now. What happened wasn't your fault. It could have happened with me right beside her. You know that, right?"

Possibly for the first time in Harley's life, he couldn't speak. It was physically impossible. His eyes and throat flooded in agony. He put a hand over his quavering mouth and nodded.

"Tell Letha I'll be there in the morning. Will you do that please?"

Harley nodded again with a choked sigh of relief that filled Kate's heart.

Chapter Twenty

When she got off work on Saturday, she was surprised to come home and find her house filled with people. They came to see for themselves how Jeannie fared. Harley had wired Willie, who filled in everyone else. Mel brought ham, bacon, casseroles and cakes, and Kate's mother was bustling around the kitchen organizing all the food, a contented, sated look on her face. She was in her element in the kitchen making sure no one went hungry.

Willie came with Mary, Verna and a load of scrap lumber. He and Jack, were already at the back of the small lot trying to figure out where to put the horse shed they were going to build, whether she was ready or not. After a brief hello to everyone, Kate hurried in to see her daughter. She abruptly stopped to stand quietly at the door and watch her small daughter with the large man at her side.

Mel sat by the bed balancing a checkerboard perched between him and Jeannie. He moved a game piece across the board, an evil grin on his face as he took three of Jeannie's black pieces. Her daughter squealed in agony, and then a gleam came to her eyes as she saw an opportunity to take some of the red ones. She took her time doing it, gloating and grinning wickedly as she cleared a path with her king, and Mel leaned back in his chair, letting her glory in her victory.

"I think you cheated," he said with a grin.

"I did not – well, not when you weren't looking," she told him.

He messed up her copper curls and tugged at a handful. "You beat me fair and square then, if I'm not smart enough to catch you cheating."

Kate cleared her throat, and they looked up to see her leaning against the door jam, watching them.

"I didn't hear you come in," Mel said. "Hello and welcome home. This rascal is beating the pants off me at checkers."

"Don't get up," Kate said as he began to rise, "especially if you're no longer wearing pants. I didn't know everyone was coming today. This is nice."

"Sit," he said. "Take a rest."

"How are you feeling, Sweetie? How's the leg?" Kate asked her daughter.

"It's okay. Dr. Crow came by this morning and told me I'm a cookie."

"You're a cookie? I don't understand."

"Yup. He said I'm a tough cookie, but I'd rather be a chewy, molasses one like Grandma makes."

"I get it, and you definitely are a tough cookie. I suspect you're a bit of a cheater, too, from what I heard a minute ago."

Jeannie tilted her head at Mel, her wide blues eyes sparkling, "I cheated fair and square, didn't I?" she asked him.

Mel nodded, agreeing with her.

"It's not really cheating if you do it right in front of people so they can catch you if they can."

"I see. It sounds like you have cheating rules, or is it rules for cheating?"

Jeannie grinned, her copper curls bobbing, and lay back on the pillow.

"Did Dr. Crow give you some of his medicine? You look a little sleepy."

"Yup, and he's going to come back later."

Kate leaned to tuck the blanket around her, saw a brown mound of fur curled up in a basket on the other side of the bed, and jumped back with a sharp yelp. "What? What on earth?"

"It's Mildred. Mel brought her," Jeannie told her.

"Sorry," he murmured, his head drooping like a boy caught dipping a pigtail in the inkwell . . . red handed. "I couldn't help it. I told you I'd check on all the critters." He went on nervously, trying to explain why the woodchuck was here. "The coons are doing fine, they're happy rascals,

but Mildred, here, seemed to be mourning, and she doesn't get around like she should on that bum leg. What could I do? Help me out here," he begged.

"She wants to be with me, Ma. She needs me," Jeannie pleaded, her blue eyes beseeching. "And Mel brought a cage, too, so she can stay outside in the back yard or in my room when I get better . . . or now?"

Kate slowly shook her head, but what could she say? Mildred was here. Forever. Mildred was part of the family. She had Wolf, didn't she?

"Dr. Crow says some people believe if you save a life, you're responsible for it. Isn't that right, Mel?" Jeannie said. "You heard him say that."

"He did, and I've heard that before."

"And we saved Mildred, so now we have to take care of her. We're responsible."

The animal looked up at Kate as if she knew they were talking about her, stretched, curled up contentedly and closed her eyes. Kate was sure there was a smile on Mildred's face -- a grin or at the very least a self-satisfied smirk. Whatever it was, Kate was sure the animal was mocking her. She felt mocked.

"Thanks a lot, Mel," Kate said. "What's next, a bobcat? Maybe a coyote?"

"Hey, I only brought the coons to you, not Mildred."

"Yeah, I know. It's my fault."

Kate told Jeannie Mildred could stay, and they left her to sleep for a while. Outside, Jack and Willie had a horse shed well under way, their comfort work, something that would keep their minds and hands occupied while their hearts were troubled.

The four corner posts were sunk into the ground and stood erect, braced across the top by two-by-fours. Verna had nailed together the triangle trusses on the ground and asked Mel to put his height to good use to heft them up where they belonged.

"If the top of my head came higher than your belly button, I'd do it myself," she told him. "But it doesn't. I'm short, damn it, and it's more than just my temper."

Mel easily lifted one over his head and held it there while they nailed it, and Kate watched as the lumber grew into a shed. 'How many times over the years have I watched this same group build something for me?' she mused, 'the cellar, the first horse shed, the addition to the cabin . . .'

Mark had been there for some of those times. A lump lodged itself in her chest, right next to her heart, hugging it tightly. Pictures of the past obscured the present, and she saw them as they were ten years ago. She sat on the ground with her back against the trunk of a huge oak tree and allowed her mind to wander.

Harley left off directing the construction and went to sit by her. "I guess the way to do something for you is to not ask permission – just do it while you're gone," he told her with a grin.

"Did you know about this?" Kate asked.

"Nope. I think Mel planned it, with your brother's help."

"Well, it's awfully nice. I won't have to pay the stable each week, but I'll need to find hay for Kitty."

"I'm betting Mel has that one figured out, too."

"Most likely. I should expect that by now, shouldn't I? Did you talk with Dr. Crow this morning? Is there anything new?"

"He said he's going to put Jeannie's leg in a plaster cast so she can get around on crutches."

Later the same day, Kate heard Dr. Crow's voice as he came up the front steps with Frank who had joined him somewhere near Third Street and was proclaiming by every analogy he could think of that they had similar vocations.

"The only difference is that you fix people and I fix things. We're the same. It's perfectly clear."

John Crow nodded solemnly, but his black eyes were shining as he let Frank ramble on.

"Bodies are just mechanical things. They work just like automobiles, don't you see? And gasoline is just food that gets pumped through the engine like a rutabaga in a person."

"Well, I can see that I will have to grow a large crop of rutabagas then, Frank. Maybe I'll get rich off the automobile owners."

Frank stopped, speechless for a brief moment before he realized the doctor was making a joke at his expense, but he didn't have time to recover before Kate saw them through the screen and opened the door.

"So, you're planning on becoming a rutabaga farmer, Dr. Crow? Big Rapids will surely miss having you to tend to their wounds, but it sounds like you want to tend vegetables instead of people."

"Frank seems to think that rutabagas are the crop of the future – something about being able to use them as auto fuel. Perhaps he's right."

"I'm sure that Frank knows what he's talking about," Kate said feeding into the doctor's joke. "Rutabaga must be good for something other than eating, I've always thought. They're not all that easy on the tongue."

Frank danced around on the balls of his feet with energy his body didn't know what to do with. "You're making fun, now, but I'm here to help so that's okay," he declared.

"And they will appreciate your help . . . and your knowledge, Frank. Why don't you go on back there and let them know you're available?" She turned to Dr. Crow. "Thank you for coming. I'm told you might be able to put a cast on?"

"If the wound has not reddened," he told Kate and led the way to Jeannie's temporary room. She brightened when Dr. Crow entered, adoration melting her eyes.

"You're here," she crooned. Jeannie trusted whatever he said was gospel and Kate hoped her daughter was right. His methods were different, even unorthodox, but Jeannie was on the road to healing, and that was what mattered.

"Told you I would."

"Yes, and we keep promises, don't we?"

He went through motions similar to when he first saw Jeannie laying broken in the street. He touched her fingers, pressed his palms on her abdomen, looked searchingly over the length of her small body and watched her face. Jeannie reached to touch a pouch hanging from a cord around his neck.

"What's this?" she asked, touching the pouch reverently. "Is it like a locket with a picture in it? I've seen those."

"Something like that," he said. "It holds things that help me remember what is precious in my life, in all life."

"What is precious?"

"Well, you are," he said solemnly. "And so is grass and the sun and stars, and birds and . . . woodchucks," he said after spotting Mildred in the basket by her bed. "So, I have tiny bits of what reminds me of them in my pouch so I can revere them."

"If I am precious, do you have a piece of me in there, too?" she asked him, wondering briefly if a finger would come up missing in the morning. "You wouldn't cut off a piece of my finger to put in there, right?"

"I don't think I need a whole finger," he said, grinning at her. "How about one tiny little red hair? Would that be okay with you?"

Jeannie quickly plucked one and held it out to him. He carefully coiled it up, opened the pouch and pushed it in. "Thank you," he said. "I am honored. Would you mind if we put your leg in a cast? Then you'll be able to move around–you'll be like your woodchuck," he said, noting the animal's bent leg, "but you'll be mobile and your leg won't be bent."

"That's Mildred. She's my responsibility now because I saved her, and nope, I don't mind. It'll be fun."

"I like fun, too," he said with the first real grin Kate had seen on his face.

After Jeannie's leg was encased in plaster from thigh to toes and it had dried enough to set firmly, Dr. Crow showed her how to maneuver the crutches he'd brought. The three of them made their way slowly through the house and out the back door where they were greeted with shouts of surprise, alarm, fear, and praise.

Jeannie swung her encased leg as if she'd been hauling it around that way for years, and she balanced on the crutches like a circus performer. She made her way through the group, carefully hopped over lumber, did a little twirl for applause and then landed in Mel's arms which were miraculously there as she started to tumble. He lifted her in the air and swung her around – plaster leg and all.

"You're back, Copper Top. You're back, and I'm glad!"

"I am, too. Can I help?"

They built the shed, ate massive amounts of food hauled out by Ellen and Ruthie, and later Kate walked with Mel to the stable in town to bring Kitty home. It was dark when they left the stable, and autumn's nip was beginning to make itself known.

On the way home, Kate rode in front with Mel's arms snuggled at her sides. She leaned against him, warmed by tranquility as much as his body heat and allowed her mind to take in the day and evening. They didn't talk. They didn't need to. It was enough to be where they were, in the quiet of the night together.

Within two months of wearing the walking cast, infection from the open, but hidden sore on Jeannie's heel began to spread. If she had told someone about the pain, it may have been controlled, but she hadn't wanted to be a problem, so she kept it to herself. She wanted to be a tough cookie. She wasn't a complainer. That's how she saw herself.

But disease didn't hear that desire, and it ate into the bone of her heel. It couldn't be seen and the only time Jeannie gave in to the pain was when she believed no one was around. Kate finally knew something was wrong when a neighbor watched Jeannie limping out in the yard one day and told Kate about it.

Twice since then she'd had to spend weeks in the Grand Rapids hospital where they tried to stem the bone disease – to contain it with cleansing and medications. Jeannie spent those weeks alone much of the time with brief visits from her family and Mel. To Kate's abhorrence, it was simply too far away to be there every day, and there was work. Always, there was work.

"It's rare that I have ever hated being poor, Harley," Kate said the first time she had to leave Jeannie in the hospital. "When Mark needed medical help, we didn't have money for, I hated it! Desperately hated that money could dictate such things. When we had to move from the cabin, I hated it! But I felt wrongful in that hate both times. Right now, I hate it again, and it's not feeling wrong any more. I hate it! I hate with a vengeance, and I hate that I can't be with her! And I'm not sorry to be so hateful! The world is a stupid, stupid place, and Jeannie shouldn't be without her mother!"

She and Harley were driving back from Grand Rapids, and Kate was snapping the reins against Kitty's back with each angry outburst. If Kitty hadn't been an old mare and determined to move at her own pace no matter the driver's wish, the buggy would have been clattering down the road in hair-raising speed by the time Harley took the reins out of Kate's hands.

"I'm thinking you go right ahead and spout off while I drive," he told her once the reins were firmly in his hands.

"You think I can't drive and talk at the same time?" Kate sputtered, her empty hands now fists planted on her hips. "You think I'm not capable of doing two things at once? I'll have you know I've spent my life doing two things at the same time. Three things, maybe four things! Always have, and you know it!"

"I know you have, Kate," he responded in a soothing voice.

"Don't placate me, Harley Benton. I know what you're doing, and I hate that, too!"

"I'm thinking you don't hate all that much. You're just a mite frustrated right now," he drawled slowly.

"So now you know me better than I do? Is that what you're saying?"

He tried not to smile. He loved to see Kate when she was riled, and sometimes he really did know Kate even better than she knew herself. But he certainly wasn't about to tell her that at the moment. Silence, he thought, might just be the better move.

"Well?" Kate prompted, still eager to do battle, "aren't you going to answer me?"

"No, Ma'am, not at the moment."

"I hate it when you get all wise and silent," she spit back at him. She heard her own words and stopped. Then he heard a small, very small, giggle. Harley peered sideways at her, and Kate glimpsed his grin. She punched him in the shoulder and giggled louder. It wasn't long before they were both laughing, and the night was brighter, poverty wasn't nearly so hateful, and Jeannie's condition was perceptibly improved.

The second time, Kate stayed with her when operating became the only choice. They cut off the back of Jeannie's heel in order to stop the bone disease from progressing up her leg. They took her . . . wheeled her away, bright curls covered by an ugly net, her tiny body under a starched sheet. She held Jeannie's hand until a nurse forcibly separated the mother from the child.

Kate felt the salt tracks of her tears as they dried on her cheeks. The room she waited in had a sick-sweet smell that screamed hospital and ether and sickness and death and Mark. It invaded her brain through the pores of her skin. Her face was stiff; the skin would crack if she smiled or frowned or spoke. Breath was a struggle.

In the waiting room, Ellen and Mel sat silently, each praying in their own way and impatient to hear word that Jeannie had not lost her leg, that they had been able to arrest the disease before it spread.

"This wouldn't have happened if they hadn't moved to Big Rapids," Ellen whispered harshly to no one in particular. But Mel was the only other person in the room, and so he assumed her words were meant for him. He wished that, too; but Kate had moved, and she'd had her reasons.

"Perhaps," he said, "but we don't know."

Long minutes of silence echoed in the room and bounced off institutional green walls, careened off them, almost physical in the intensity. Mel sat erect, hands placed firmly on his knees as if he was ready to sprint down the hallway when they called his name.

Ellen rested her hands quietly in her lap, fingers laced together to keep them from fidgeting. Periodically, she turned the ring on her left hand around and around – her gold wedding band grown thin from years of wear – and then she deliberately tied her fingers together again, trying to steal calm from the pretense of their repose.

"Thank you for bringing me here," Ellen murmured, embarrassed she had spoken harshly.

Mel nodded, not wanting conversation, only wanting to hear that Jeannie was safely out of surgery and she could still run around the woods, slide down his hay stack, swing from the rope in his barn and with a deep, throaty giggle, drop into the soft straw bedding. He concentrated on that vision, thinking if he kept that picture in mind, somehow it would come true. Being helpless to make things happen did not suit him, and he chafed at the confines of inability.

They wheeled her into the recovery room and Kate leaped to the door, hammering the nurses with questions. "How is she? What did they have to do? Is she alright?"

"She'll be fine, Mrs. Ramey. The doctor will be along shortly. He'll fill in the details."

Kate's eyes bored into the nurse and her voice was a sharp knife. "Can't you tell me?"

"The doctor will be in soon," she said, and left the room.

She looked under the sheet, saw two feet and breathed again. Kate waited, she looked at her still-sleeping daughter covered in a white sheet, her copper hair encased in a white cap, her fragile foot propped on a pillow. Small, bright freckles stood out prominently against the pale cream of her face and were brilliant spots of orange on milky alabaster.

Kate blanched when she thought what might have happened if the neighbor had chosen not to say anything. Jeannie could have lost the whole foot, even her leg – or worse – and the thought brought Kate's hands to her face to cover tears she couldn't help. Jeannie could have died from the bone disease.

"It would have been my fault," she whispered harshly to herself. "I was too damned busy to notice, too damned concerned about the loan and the mortgage and every other damned thing!" She reached her hand to cover Jeannie's and let her tears splash onto the sheet, not bothering to quell the flow, not caring about tears. "I'm so sorry, baby. I failed you. I'm sorry, Mark. I'm so damned sorry."

Then she took deep breaths, determined that when Jeannie woke, she would not see her mother sobbing, would not know her fears.

In time, an eternity, she saw Jeannie's eyelids flutter briefly and then fly open. She slowly smiled at her mother, and in that instant she looked like Jeannie, not like a patient in the hospital who had just had part of her foot cut off.

"I want ice cream. They said I could have ice cream," she demanded softly with a sliver of a grin.

"Then I guess we'll get you some ice cream, but it might be just a little bit too soon. Any particular flavor?" Kate asked, her voice throaty with moist strain and turning her head so Jeannie would not see the water pooling dangerously. Her smile cut into the brittle brine on her face, and she whispered "Thank you, God."

"Tell Jack. He'll make them get some."

For a moment, Kate thought Jeannie was still out of it and hallucinating, but when she followed the trail of Jeannie's gaze, she saw Jack's face in the window of the recovery room door, his nose pressed flat, and his mouth opened in a wide, white toothed grin. He winked, and then he was in the room kissing Jeannie's face and hugging Kate.

"How did you get in here? No one is supposed to be here but me. Ma and Mel are still cooling their heels in the waiting room."

"I didn't ask," he said nonchalantly. "I just came. How're you feeling, Copper Top?"

"Fine. Can you get me some ice cream?"

"I sure can. How about moving you into a real room and letting me talk to your Grandma and Mel first? Is that okay?"

"Sure, I guess," Jeannie told him, and he left after a second hug for Kate.

"I love Uncle Jack," Jeannie said sleepily after he left, still struggling to come out of the ether.

"So do I, Sweetie. He is special."

They all had ice cream when Jeannie was settled in her room. It was a grand party with Doctor Crow and Jeannie at center stage. Before leaving, he told Kate he would be at her house every evening for awhile to remove the bandages from Jeannie's foot and inspect it for signs that the disease had returned. She could see guilt crowd the joy in his eyes and felt it echoed in her heart.

"You couldn't have known, John," she said, touching his arm and sensing him pull away from any comfort she would give him. "And if anyone should have been aware, it's me."

"It is I," he responded, and long moments later the tiniest spark of humor lit his eyes. "And, yes, I meant that in both ways, for I am the man of medicine. Not me or you."

"And the professor of language as well, I see."

"You may hear it, but I doubt you can see it."

"Are you trying to be quarrelsome, John Crow?" Kate asked, a small but real smile parting her lips, the first since learning of Jeannie's disease.

"Perhaps it is my nature, Kate Ramey." He turned to touch Jeannie's hand, and she wrapped her fingers around his and held on. "I will see you tomorrow, Tough Cookie."

Jeannie was released later that week. Jack insisted on staying to drive them home, and Kate was glad to have his company. It always felt like Mark was nearby when she was with Jack, and sometimes she needed that comfort, especially times like this.

By Saturday, they were home. Jeannie was tucked into Kate's bed once again, her foot propped up on pillows, Dr. Crow by her side, Mel at the bedroom door waiting to be allowed in, and Jeannie feeling like a princess.

Kate was out back – behind the horse shed. She sat on the ground with her back against the wall, her arm around Wolf's shoulders and her face nestled into the fur of his neck. She murmured to him as his head turned from side to side, watchful.

"I'm so tired, Wolf. Just so tired . . ." She sat silently for a long while, holding her friend, watching the night fall around her, hiding from the reality of food to be made, people to talk to, responsibilities.

She felt Wolf's low growl rumble through his chest more than heard it; it was so slight a sound. Then Wolf got up and moved to Kate's other side, eyeing the man as he stood in front of her, then knelt.

"There are wounds from bullets and knives and broken bones. Those I can heal with medicine, and they leave small scars. But first the wounded must want to be well. They must want the injury and the scar to become small, insignificant and free of inflammation and pain."

Kate stared at his face as he talked. She saw his lips form the words, his brown eyes pierce through the darkness. She saw the earthly body of John Crow, but on him was no trace of emotion, no worry or overt joy, just peace, and she wondered how he came to be in that place. But at the moment, she was too tired to do more than lightly, perhaps just curiously, ponder why he was squatting in front of her.

"Does Jeannie need me?" she asked.

"She needs nothing at this moment. She has many helpers."

Kate nodded, wondering again why he had followed her to the back of the horse shed.

"Do you need me then? Should I be doing something besides hiding out with Wolf?"

John Crow appeared not to have heard Kate's question such a long time passed in silence. He turned his face to the yellow-white sphere rising in the sky just above the distant trees and roof lines, then back to Kate. He placed his hand over hers, the one that still gripped the thick fur at Wolf's neck.

"Yes, there is something you should be doing – healing your own wound." He stood, his long, lean body looking gigantic silhouetted by the golden glow of the moon. "It won't heal unless you wish it to."

"I am not wounded. I'm just tired."

"You are tired because you are wounded."

"You're speaking in riddles to me, John, and I'm too addled to figure out your puzzles."

"Your body is working hard to heal your injuries, Kate, and doing remarkably well given your resistance, but your spirit is not engaged in helping. Many love you – some as friends or family, some in the ways of a man for a woman. Don't drive them away because you're struggling with an old wound."

"I'm not driving anything away," Kate said, rising and turning to walk away. "You're talking nonsense, John Crow, and I need to go take care of my daughter."

Kate stopped halfway to the back door, feeling remorse for having spoken harshly to him. What he said nagged at her, and Kate tucked it away, far at the back of her brain. She would consider what he'd said later, when she had the time, not so much to do.

Turning back, his face told her he recognized her quick escape and understood it was a flight from his words, not him. Well, that couldn't be helped. Right now there were things to do, children to take care of, work to be done, bills to be paid. You couldn't do all that just sitting around thinking about your injuries no matter how damaged you might feel.

"I'm sorry, John," she told him sadly. "I shouldn't have spoken to you like that. I know you never talk nonsense, and you've been a wonderful friend. I just . . . I need time, and I haven't had enough. I don't know if there will ever be enough."

He stood erect, shoulders back, hands motionless by his sides. He could have been a statue. Kate began to think he was not going to respond, that she had insulted him and he would merely walk away, but eventually she heard his soft words.

"All people have the same amount of time, Kate. We choose to use it differently. Some wisely."

312

Chapter Twenty-one

1916

Kate beat at the wad of linens in the wash tub, taking her anger out on them instead of screaming or punching a wall. "It's stupid!" she mumbled, hammering a fist into the wash water and splattering suds over her chest and face.

"It's just plain stupid! When will they stop this madness?"

"What's stupid, and whose madness are you smacking around?" Harley asked as he shuffled into the kitchen pulling the now worn, red suspenders up over his shoulders.

"This war is stupid, and our Jamie going off to fight is stupid. It's madness!"

"And what would you have men do, Kate, let countries be overrun by tyrants?"

"Men should listen to women, damn it! That's what they should do. If just one of them ever gave birth to a child, instead of merely providing sperm for it, or suckled a babe at their breasts, they wouldn't be sending boys off to fight and die," Kate sputtered, turning an angry face toward her friend.

"And Jamie's signing up again. Mark's son, Harley, and I can't stand it . . . he's already put in four years, and now he's doing it again and going to war this time! He doesn't need to. It's stupid, stupid, stupid!"

"You heard from Jamie?" Harley asked. "When?"

"Yesterday. I got a letter from him. He's going to try to come by before he ships out." She nodded toward the end of the table, pointing with her chin to Jamie's letter. Harley held the envelope by its corner and looked quizzically at Kate, asking permission to read it.

She nodded and he read silently for a few moments, then carefully folded the pages and put them back in the envelope. He pushed his hands into the suds in front of Kate, lifted an indistinguishable, white cloth and began shoving it through the wringer. He cranked the handle, turning the rollers that squeezed out wash water, and tablecloths and sheets dropped into fresh water. Kate turned her attention to the rinse bin and began punching again.

"Well, aren't you going to say anything?" Kate finally asked him.

Harley grinned sideways at her, continuing to turn the rollers. "Just that he sounds a lot like his father, and I'm happy I'm not a tablecloth."

Kate was quiet; she'd heard Mark's voice in Jamie's letter, too. She swallowed the wet heat that was thick in her throat, trying to find an opening for words to come through. She'd been doing a lot of that lately, and she was getting mighty sick of it -- of everything, come to think of it.

"I'm going to send the girls to stay with Ma for the summer, as soon as school is out."

"And why would you do that, Kate?"

"They need to be busy, and they can help Ma. She's getting older. She could use some help. They should be in the country, breathe fresh air and . . . I don't know. It just seems right. Jeannie and Kat need to be out of town for a while, Becca, too."

"And you? What will you do without your girls around?"

Kate stabbed at the shirts she had thrown into the wash tub. "I'll work -- just like I'm doing now. Kitty and I will go to visit on Sundays, maybe even on Saturdays after the diner closes, and I'll be back for work by Monday morning – seven o'clock sharp."

Harley was unaccustomedly quiet as he ran linens through the ringers. When they were piled in the basket ready to be hung outside, he turned to Kate.

"Is something going on that I don't know about, or are you just being female?" he said with a sly smile and thoroughly expecting an outburst.

Kate didn't disappoint him. She whipped around to face him, quick anger sparking her eyes.

"Just what do you mean by that, Harley Benton?" Her fists were firmly planted on her hips; her chin jutted out toward him.

"Well, there you are. I wondered where Kate was."

"What are you talking about, you crazy old coot? I'm right here in front of you," she answered with a stomp of her foot. "You're always saying something to rile me up, and I'm not being female. I'm being logical. I mean . . . being female *is* being logical, which is something most men know nothing about. Logic, that is – not being female. Of course, they wouldn't know about that – even though many claim they know women's minds even better than women!"

Harley smiled more broadly at her and remained silent, letting her scramble around for words that would say what she meant. Kate finally threw a handful of soap suds at him, and he ducked, but a frothy glob landed on the side of his head and nestled in his hair.

"You're messing up my pretty hair," he said, pretending hurt. "And I was just trying to help."

Wolf rolled an eye from the corner of the kitchen and then turned his eyes to the wall as if he couldn't bear to watch.

"Now look what you've done. Wolf is afraid you're going to throw soap at him, too, just because he's male," Harley admonished.

"No, he isn't – afraid that is. He is male, and he's the only truly intelligent male I know, and he is quite aware of that fact."

Kate picked up the basket of linens, and Harley followed her out to the lines in the backyard. They were almost finished hanging the whites before Harley spoke.

"Do you want to tell me now?"

"Rachel is sixteen, and she hardly knows her sisters anymore. Kat and Becca long for the countryside. Jeannie, too, and her leg has healed enough for her to enjoy being at Ma's."

"What does Dr. Crow say about this?" Harley asked, knowing the pain and guilt Kate still felt over her youngest daughter's struggle with bone disease.

"John says there's no sign of it. Her foot has healed where they scraped the bone, and the scar is clean of infection. Ma would keep a close eye on Jeannie. You know her. She has an eagle eye for anything involving the girls, and she's fiercely protective."

Harley nodded agreement. "That she is. I wouldn't go up against her. But I don't have to worry about that because Ellen loves her Harley and would never find fault with me."

"True, you egomaniac. She does love you. Speaking of love, how is Verna?"

Harley blushed at her question, and Kate wondered for the hundredth time when Harley and Verna would tie the knot – or at the least become common law husband and wife. Regardless of Hersey's small town, puritan standards, Kate never believed a couple had to be blessed by the church to be united. Love did that, and as strange as Verna and Harley both were, Kate knew there was unquestionable and irrefutable love between the two of them.

"She's fine, Kate. Quit playing cupid," he said, but his eyes sparkled and his chest puffed out as he sucked in his ample stomach.

Kate was silent as she hung the last of the whites on the line. She was daydreaming about being back at the cabin for a day or two each week throughout the summer. Could she manage it? Could she drive to Hersey Saturday afternoon and be back for work on Monday morning?

If the girls stayed with their grandma, there wouldn't be a lot of packing and unpacking. She'd just get up early on Monday– in the middle of the night actually – hitch Kitty and be gone. It would be worth it just to soak in the feel of the cabin, the forest. It would be a peaceful drive, and Wolf would be with her, so she'd be safe.

She might even go straight to the cabin after work on Saturday and go get the girls early on Sunday. She'd have the place all to herself for a night. It would be heaven! Just like when she had first found the cabin and it was all hers –

well, hers and the man. She wondered again who he was, where he was. Was he even alive? Then she dismissed the pondering. It was useless to guess.

"And you're going to get them up in the middle of the night on Sunday – or Monday morning really – so you can drop them at Ellen's on your way back to Big Rapids?" Harley asked when she told him her idea.

"Well, everything isn't worked out just yet," she said, biting her lip in thought and anticipation. "But it can work; I can make it work."

Kate turned to him, her face lit and eager. Harley couldn't help but grin at her. She looked like she had years ago, when she was so much in love and determined to marry Mark – regardless of his reputation and the roadblocks in their way. Her eyes sparkled, her cheeks were flushed with eagerness, and the years fell away. The polished copper freckles speckling her nose stood out more than they had moments ago, and Harley adjusted his initial reaction to Kate's wild plan. This could be just what Kate needed – the girls too.

"Okay," he said. "Let's do it. But I'll probably ride with you and divide my time between the cabin and your mother's barn. I have a fondness for my old home. Hope that'll be alright with you."

"It's perfect, and thanks. I will appreciate company on the long trips."

As it turned out, they were able to leave on Fridays after Kate was done at the diner. With so many men going off to war and money and food in such short supply, business at the diner had slowed, and Letha was forced to cut Kate's hours back to five days a week. She'd been putting off doing it because she knew how much Kate needed the money, but when Kate told her about her summer plans, Letha figured the time was right.

"I'm really sorry, Kate. I don't know what to say or what else to do. I'll have to handle Saturdays alone just like I do on Sundays. It's so slow on Sunday's now that I'm almost bored, and you know that Saturdays aren't much different. Maybe it will pick up soon, and I'll be able to give you the six days again. Will you be able to make it?"

Kate was quiet, wondering if she would be able to pay her loan and her house payment, but she wasn't going to tell Letha. Letha had been good to her, and Kate considered her a friend.

"We'll be fine, and it will be a nice break for the girls and me. I've missed the woods, and it appears it's a good time to fix that."

They were taking in the last warmth of the sun on a spring night, relaxing on the front porch when Kate told the girls her plan. Jeannie squealed in delight at the idea of spending the summer back in Hersey, and Kat, in her understated way, showed her pleasure by asking Harley to help her make some repairs on her traps. Becca wondered if the Tate boys would be around to pick up the music lessons again.

Harley sat back in his chair smiling at his girls, all of them. While he wasn't sure it was a solid plan – it was a lot of driving back and forth and a long, long Monday work day for Kate – talking it over picked up everyone's spirits.

Kate got up from her chair and started pacing, excitement lighting her eyes.

"What about putting in the garden? Do you think we could do that on the weekends?" she asked, then perched on the railing in front of them, her bottom hanging over the edge and her legs swinging back and forth like a little girl.

"I don't know why not," Harley responded, "but do you really want to work all weekend? Why not just enjoy the forest for once, and if you fall backwards off that railing, you're gonna crack your head and we'll have to call for Dr. Crow, then none of us will get to go."

"Pshaw, you're a worry wart, and it won't be like work. It'll be fun, especially now that I can leave here on Friday after work instead of Saturday, and we could use the food from a good-sized garden."

Harley nodded, watching with eager anticipation as Frank stealthily crept up behind Kate. Frank put his finger to his lips to silence the girls, tugged lightly at Kate's shoulder, toppling her backwards, and then caught her in his arms before she hit the ground.

Kate's screech sent Wolf flying over the rail, straight at Frank's shoulder. Frank fell under the force of the attack, and Wolf, his front paws planted firmly in the middle of Frank's chest, bared his teeth way too uncomfortably close to Frank's nose.

Kate heard Frank's shallow breath and wondered how long she should let him suffer under the weight of her on his belly and Wolf on his chest.

Skinny rat deserves it for pulling me over.

"Uh, do you think you could do something?" Frank whispered, trying not to move his lips and prompt Wolf to sink those huge teeth into them.

"Like what?" Kate teased. "I'm quite comfortable; aren't you?"

"Uh, Kate – teeth – big teeth . . ."

Kate crawled off and knelt next to them, giggling at the sight of Wolf's lips drawn back in what could have been a full-fledged grin. On him, however, it looked exactly like Wolf meant it to – a warning, but a lighthearted one, like it could go either way depending on his mood and Frank's moves. But Kate knew Wolf wouldn't hurt Frank. He actually liked him. This was just a little fun on Wolf's part. Wolves get bored, too.

Kate grinned and giggled. "Yes, I can see that they are very large teeth – the better to eat you with. Why don't you say pretty please, and then I might call him off?"

"Forget it," Frank whispered through clenched teeth, just loud enough to be heard. "Frank doesn't beg."

Wolf moved closer. He knew well how to play this game, and it had been such a long time. The inch that separated hunter and prey was gone. Frank felt the cold damp of Wolf's nose on his own, smelled hot wolf-breath as it mingled with his, but it was the low, throaty growl that caused him to reconsider his manly ego.

"Except when he wants to or really needs to – pretty please call him off?"

Kate waited, enjoying the situation more than quite a bit, crossed her arms and tapped her foot in thoughtful consideration of the situation.

"Pardon me? Did you say something, Frank?"

"Mmmmph, priffy prease?" Kate heard as Frank tried to talk without moving his lips, then she called to Wolf who immediately sat back on his haunches, cocked his head, let his ears droop forward in a lop-eared rabbit pose, and gave Frank a real grin.

Friday felt like a holiday, like the circus had come to town, like it was Christmas except with beautiful, balmy weather and the sun warm on your back. It was still high in the sky when they loaded the buggy with as much luggage as it could hold and still have room for them to sit. No one cared about the cramped space. They were too excited to be going home.

"I could stay here and come with you next weekend," Harley offered when he saw the girls stuffed in the small back seat with Poochie stretched out over their legs and Wolf taking up the middle of the front. Mildred stretched lazily in her cage nestled on top of luggage strapped to the back of the buggy.

"Nonsense. Get in, cause we're going home!" Kate shouted with a wide grin.

Harley hiked up his pants and snapped his suspenders, an answering grin spread over his face. He didn't want to stay behind even if they had to sit on top of each other.

"Get over, Wolf. My big old butt needs lots of room." Wolf and Poochie decided to get out and walk for awhile, and that worked for everyone.

By the time they reached Hersey, they were exhausted from laughing at things that were unreasonably but unbelievably hilarious. The world had never been so golden, a day so bright, a tomorrow so filled with delight.

They passed Nestor's General Store, and John raced out to shout a welcome home to them as they passed. When they reached Sadie's Saloon, Harley asked to stop for a moment so he could just run in and tell Verna he was in town and would be by later. Kat jumped down to follow him into the saloon, but was halted by Kate's "Whoa, girl. We'll wait for Harley here, if you please."

"But I want to see Verna," Kat explained wistfully.

"I know. So do I. We'll just have to wait." But a mere moment later she thought of herself as a young girl peering through the dust streaked windows of that same saloon wondering why she must always be on the sidewalk looking in.

"Aw, heck with it. Go on in, Kat. Hurry up and catch him. And don't wander around. Straight in and straight out," she added to Kat's back as the door swung against it.

"Times are changing," she said, nodding to Wolf and then Becca and Jeannie who were bouncing eagerly on the back seat. Poochie had escaped to the floor and was staring anxiously at the door of Sadie's as if some mysterious creature had swallowed Kat and Harley.

"They're changing, but not fast enough. I have half a mind to go in there, walk up to the bar, and order a shot of whiskey. What would they all say about that, huh, Wolf, my friend?" she said, ruffling the thick fur at his neck. "Dumb rules, anyway. Really, really dumb. I might order one for you, too, and you can stand at the bar with me and glare at anyone who looks strangely at us."

"What are you talking about, Ma?" Becca asked. "Are you going into the saloon?"

"Not today, Becca. Not today, but someday."

Ellen was eating supper when they opened the door. Her fork was raised mid-air and her mouth opened wider than was necessary for the small morsel perched at the end of the fork tines. Jeannie threw her arms around her grandmother in a huge hug, and eventually Ellen lowered the fork and returned Jeannie's hug.

"What in heaven's name?" she stuttered. "Is everything alright?"

"Everything is perfect," Kate said, reaching around the girls to give her mother a hug.

Becca moved to the stove and sniffed the air. "Is there enough for us? I'm really hungry, but I'm probably not supposed to say that, am I?"

"My leg is good now and so is Mildred's, and we're gonna stay with you, won't that be good? I can jump now, and Mildred only has a little limp." Jeannie said without taking a breath.

Ellen stared at her granddaughter, and even though she had put her loaded fork on her plate, her mouth was frozen in a sphere that grew larger as the moments wore on. Her head circled the room, eyes fixed first on one then another like she might find answers to the sudden invasion in the faces around her.

Harley rescued them all by sending the girls out to inspect his room at the back of the barn. When they left, he went to the cupboard where he remembered the moonshine was kept and poured three small glasses. He held his out toward Ellen and expansively decreed it good to be home, "and here's to having your granddaughters with you for the summer," he added, clinking his glass firmly against hers.

A stunned Ellen lifted her glass to sip at the clear liquid because she didn't know what else to do, but Harley put his hand on Ellen's shoulder and said in 'Harleyesque' style, "Wait. I'm not finished. Here's to having your lovely and much loved Harley around for some of the summer, too."

When he grinned at Ellen, she responded as she always had to Harley. She accepted what he said, breathed again, and finally took a long sip of her drink.

"Well, goodness gracious, you could have given me a little warning don't you think?" she sputtered, then took a bigger drink and uncharacteristically passed the glass back to Harley for a refill.

When they had talked and she understood the plan for the summer, Ellen's eyes said it all. She got up, paced the kitchen with quick Ellen-no-nonsense-steps, and talked, as much to herself as to them.

"We need beds, and rugs for the loft. It gets chilly at night even in the summer, and I don't have any of that stuff

322

up there anymore." She moved to Harley, "I don't know what's left in your room now either. We'll have to check." She marked items needed and things to do off on her fingers as she talked, totally involved in the needs of her family. Her house would be full again, and she was happy. She was more than happy. She was needed.

"Does Mel know you're coming? He might have some things we could use."

"No. No one knows. It was sort of sudden."

"Well, don't worry. We'll figure it out. Right now, we need to feed the girls."

They moved out to the porch to call the girls just as the sun was passing over the tops of the trees. A stray cloud hovered near the edge of the evening horizon, picked up the sun's rays and sent back a vivid red-orange streak in the ebony silk of growing night. It wasn't a menacingly black sky, but velvety soft like the deep, dark blue-black of a kitten.

"Sailor's delight," Kate said. "Red sun at night. May we all be sailors."

Ellen touched her daughter's shoulder. "I am delighted - sailor or not" she said, quietly, "I am so very delighted that my family will be near for a while. Thank you."

Kate nodded, still staring at the red-tinted cloud, distracted by thoughts of the cabin, how it had looked when she first found it, and how it might look now after so much time abandoned – if it was even still empty. Maybe the owner had finally come back to claim it. She'd been taking a lot for granted. Maybe it had been overtaken by animals. Maybe – who knows what the maybes might be . . . It could have been hit by lightening and burned to the ground.

'Damn, you're a fool, Kate Ramey,' she said to herself. 'You're a sentimental old fool. When did that happen?'

She stole a look at her mother, wondering if she had heard her daughter cussing once again, and Kate saw a much tinier woman than she remembered. Wasn't her mother taller than the woman who stood beside her now? Wasn't she broader in the shoulders? Whose wispy, white hair covered her mother's head? And when did this happen?'

Kate's breath caught in her chest, and she held it there for a moment gathering her feelings together, pulling them inside where they'd be safe, secure, hidden.

When did my mother grow old?

She put her arm around her mother's shoulders and was silent for a moment, then said softly, "Thank you, Ma. It is I who am thankful to you."

"Who finally taught you to speak properly" Ellen asked, a small grin crinkling the corners of her lips, "when you're not cussing, that is."

Kate didn't respond, but a matching grin etched the corners of her own lips.

They ate a quick meal and then scoured the house and storage shed for usable bedding. Kate followed her daughters up the ladder to the loft where she had slept so long ago, but it seemed merely days, or at the most weeks, past. And yet, again, forever ago. They spread blankets on the floor, and Kate lay in the dark thinking about eavesdropping on her parents in the kitchen below.

She felt a familiar hot lump grow in her chest when she thought about her father, how much it hurt to think of him even after all the years he'd been gone, how much she still missed him. She wrapped her arms tighter around Jeannie who had snuggled up against her.

"I used to spy on your grandma and grandpa from this very spot," she whispered in the dark. "I'd slide right up to the edge so I could hear better, but not so close your grandma would see me."

"Grandma said you did that," Becca whispered.

"You said you didn't." Kat admonished. "So, why did you?"

"I'm not sure," Kate told her. "I just always wanted to know what was going on, and that seemed one way to do it. I hid behind the pickle barrel in Nestor's, too, just to listen to the men talk."

"Did you ever get caught?" Jeannie asked, her eyes wide with fear of some unknown punishment from the strange men.

"No, but I don't advocate you three doing it. It's not right to spy on people, and you just might hear something you wish you hadn't."

"Like what?" Jeannie prodded.

"Like what a rotten little sneak that Kate Hughes is."

"You're not Kate Hughes. You're Kate Ramey," Jeannie corrected.

"Yes, but when I was a girl – like you – I was Kate Hughes, before I married your daddy." They were quiet for a moment, listening to the night sounds and darkness fold around them. "I wasn't much older than you, Kat, when I first met your daddy, right here in this house."

"How old were you, Ma?" Becca asked.

"I was sixteen. It was my birthday and your grandpa brought him home to dinner that night. We sang songs and I played the piano. I came up here to my bed afterwards and thought about what a handsome man he was, like a prince, and I thought about what a silly girl I was because I couldn't go to sleep for thinking about him."

"I miss daddy," Jeannie said, and Kate was glad not to hear tears in her daughter's voice, simply a statement of fact.

"I know, Sweetie. So do I, and I still can't go to sleep sometimes because I'm thinking about him, about what a wonderful man he was. He was my prince. I was younger than Rachel," Kate continued, a dreamlike quality in her voice. "We'll go get her tomorrow, and Mr. Woodward can just do without her for a day or two whether he likes it or not."

When they showed up at Woodward's house, Rachel was surprised, a bit withdrawn, but excited to see them all. Kate told both Rachel and Eldon that his live-in housekeeper was leaving for a few days, period.

"Pack a few things, Rachel, and let's go," Kate told her. And she did, with little argument. Her face lit in eagerness.

They found Mel outside the barn hitching his team. His face lit up, a bronzed summer sunrise, when he saw them. "What on earth?" he asked. "What are you all doing here?"

He looked good. His hair, only lightly silvered at the temples, glowed warm brown in the sunlight, his face already tanned by early summer sun. He crossed the yards between them in two quick strides and hugged the girls and then Kate, twice each, he was so excited to see them.

"Get down. Come on in the house. Ma will want to see you."

Kate quickly explained their plans for the summer, and Mel's face lit even further hearing they would be nearby – at least for the summer.

"We can't stay. We have a lot of work to do, but, well, Ma suggested that you might have some things we could use for the summer because the girls will be staying with her most of the time, and sometimes with me, and there isn't anything at the cabin anymore, or at Ma's place, and . . ."

When Kate wound down and suddenly stopped talking, Mel crossed his arms over his chest and grinned at her.

"You really find it hard to ask for anything, don't you? It just refuses to roll smoothly off your tongue."

"Well . . ."

"What things do you need, Kate?" he asked, still grinning and holding Jeannie's hand. She had immediately attached herself and stood staring up at the man by her side.

"Maybe a bed or two, blankets, quilts, a pot or pan, things like that? Spares you might have – nothing you need."

Mel waved his hand toward the large, white house. It was two stories, and six windows faced the front yard. Six more were at the back. Kate had been inside many times during her lifetime, and knew there were six bedrooms upstairs and at least one downstairs. The house had held all of Mel's brothers and sisters at one time. Now it was just his mother and him.

"Unless I am mistaken, there are beds in every one of those rooms, and only two of us use them. I'm betting Mother would love to see them used."

"You think?" Kate asked.

"Let's go make sure," he said, and grasping Kate's hand, he made a beeline for the house, dragging Kate and Jeannie and shouting for the rest to follow. "Ma, Ma, look who's here!" he shouted. "Get the cookies out. We've got company!"

Mel's mother, rosy-faced from the heat of the oven, was just taking a tray of oatmeal cookies out to cool.

"Excellent timing," she said, putting the tray on a cooling rack and then turning with a warm smile. "As soon as the milk is poured, these will be ready to eat. Have a seat."

After they caught up with each other and news of the families had been shared, Mel explained Kate's needs to his mother who was eager to help out. In fact, she was happy that the contents of bedrooms that had been vacant for years would finally be used.

"It will be just for the summer, Mrs. Bronson. We'll make sure your things are back in their proper places by fall."

"Nonsense," she said with a little typical Bronson no-nonsense. "The proper place is where they will be used. And now that is where your lovely girls are."

"That's it then," Mel said, grabbing Kate's hand. "Let's go see what you can use," and dragged Kate from her chair. Like the pied piper, he led Kate and four stair-step girls to the upstairs bedrooms.

Mel wanted to dismantle the beds and load them on the flatbed wagon immediately, but Kate stopped his headlong rush with two hands on each side of his happy face.

"Whoa, big boy. Not so fast. I haven't even been out to the cabin yet. Haven't cleaned or even checked to see if rodents have moved in and taken over."

"They haven't. I've made sure of that."

"Well, I need to clean and get things ready, and I, you know . . . get ready . . ."

Mel's arms dropped to his sides, and he tilted his head to look at her. He was quiet for a couple of moments, watching her face, reading the meaning behind the words.

"How about this," he said thoughtfully. "I'll take two beds with their linens to your mother's house today, and I'll get blankets and mattress ticks ready to go to the cabin

when you say you're ready. How's that? You say when. I'm
good at waiting," he added with a grin.

Kate anxiously ran her fingers through her hair and
pulled at it so her head tilted back as she looked up at him.
"Am I being a pain?" she asked.

"Certainly. Why would you think otherwise?" he asked
with a wry grin.

They folded blankets, sheets and quilts; moved mat-
tresses; dismantled bed frames; and lugged it all to the
wagon. By the time they were done, Mel's mother had a cas-
serole prepared for baking and wrapped to go with them.

"Give my best to Ellen," she said as she hugged Kate,
"and please – let your girls spend some time here with me."

Her look was suddenly hollow and wistful. Kate felt she
had somehow robbed her of something, had neglected this
woman in some way. She inwardly shook her head to clear
it of those whispering thoughts and responded that they
would certainly visit as often as possible during the summer.

Mel grasped Kate's elbow as she stepped up into the
buggy and leaned in to whisper in her ear.

"She's just lonely, Kate. She's getting old, that's all. You
look like you just kicked the family cat."

Kate thought for a moment, and a heavy breath escaped
on the wings of memory – just hours ago, time had driven
home its passage as she stood side by side with her own
mother, the slender shoulders, the frail body that was once
a source of maternal power. And was it just hours ago she
had told her daughters about her own youth; how she'd
been close to Kat's age when she had fallen in love with their
father? Truth had slapped her in the face. Her girls were
now the generation to move the world, according to their
directions, their desires and needs, their determinations.
Not hers. Not her mother's.

In a sprinkling of time three generations of women
crossed paths; their wishes intermingled and clashed. So
did their loves and their memories and their needs. And the
oddest part of it all is the separate generations are not unlike each other, not in the past, not now, nor will they ever

be dissimilar because no matter the surface discrepancies, no matter how world functions diverge economically or politically, academically or socially, some things about women will not change. They will love. And all the rest of life simply fills in around the tiny crevices and crannies that are left.

"Where are your brothers and sisters?" Kate asked, wondering if they visit their mother, respect and care for their births and beginnings.

"They come when they can," he said. "They're not neglectful. She just wants things to be as they were long ago – with all of us here – you know how that is. This was a noisy house once, full of laughing and bickering and all the things families do. She'd just like it to be as it was," he repeated softly.

Kate nodded. She knew that feeling.

She only thought about the way things were half the way back to her mother's. The sun was shining. In the morning, she'd be going home. But she'd go alone the first day, like she had the first time she saw the cabin. She wanted badly to do this by herself, perhaps selfishly, but she wanted to go home alone.

Chapter Twenty-two

Wolf's ears were laid back and his head whipped from side to side as he peered into the woods for real and imagined menace. He might be a grown wolf, but he knew how to pretend like a pup. A deep, low rumble rolled from his chest. Kate glanced at him briefly as she maneuvered the buggy over ruts and around the low branches hanging over the muddy, makeshift road and slapped at her head if she wasn't careful to ward them off with a defensively raised arm.

Kate smiled at her guardian. "You look pretty fierce, Wolf. Do you think something's hiding behind a tree -- about to jump out and get us? The big, bad, boogeyman?"

He looked at Kate, rolled his eye, and went back to craning his neck to peer around trees for evil forest gnomes and other sneaky creatures.

"We're almost home, Wolf. I'm betting you've missed this place as much as I have. I'm a little scared to see it. Not sure it will feel the same . . . be the same. You know?" She was quiet then, nearing the turn to the clearing. Her heart beat heavily, her breath erratic and harsh, and then she saw it. She pulled Kitty to a halt and sat with her mouth hanging open.

"What the . . .? Damn. Sorry."

The yard had been cleared of brush. It was totally clean. No vines grew wildly over the cabin and horse shed as she had expected. Even the ground level door leading to the earth shelter had been cleared of brush. The horse shed had bright, new shingles on it, and the small fence around her garden showed fresh white paint and new chicken wire. The grass, all the way to the woods, had been cut recently and smelled like new-mown straw.

Kate sat motionless except for the movement of her head as it swung from one side of the clearing to the other. Memories battered her, stormed and assaulted her senses, and she fought to overcome the need to surrender to them. New thoughts and old fought for a place in her mind.

She heard Kitty snicker and felt Wolf's nose nudge under her arm. She automatically put her arm around him and pulled him close.

"We're home, Wolf," Kate whispered, and as she began to climb down, the words became reality and happiness exploded within her. "We're home! We're really home!"

Kate leaped to the ground with Wolf right beside her. He bounced around the clearing, leaped into the air and then sniffed with his nose to the ground, checking to see if it still smelled the same, but he would say he was sniffing out bad guys.

Kate turned in childlike circles, her arms held out from her sides like she was making snow angels, but in the air. Taking in the whole of it, all at once, she turned her face to the bright sky, her chest filling with the fragrance of forest, tasting the damp scent of earth in the air on her tongue. "God I've missed you," she murmured to it all.

When she was dizzy from spinning, Kate stopped and watched Wolf circling the yard, then called to him.

"Let's check out the cabin, Wolf. Maybe the cleaning fairy went inside, too." Once her eyes adjusted to the dim light, she let it soak in.

Kate wandered from room to room, touching the memories in each and letting the dust of time lay lightly on her skin, breathing in the days and nights when Mark was young and healthy and the darker days when he was sick; the loving days and nights with him and the times with family and friends; building the underground shelter, the horse shed and later the bedroom addition.

She ran her hand over the rough wood mantle and saw herself sitting in front of the fire, just her and her red dog, Bug, and then with Mark and each one of the girls as they joined the family, with Wolf and Harley with Jack and Mel, all of the loves of her life. Her father was here, and the rest of her family, too.

"This hearth has seen a lot of love," she whispered, and she realized the hollow place in her chest had been filled with memories and joy. It no longer ached with loss. She felt the patter of excitement flutter in her chest much like she had known before it had been buried in grief.

She stood still, breath held, afraid the feeling wasn't real and would fly away on gossamer wings of illusion. When she couldn't hold her breath any longer, she expelled it quickly and sucked a little back in, looking around wide eyed as if she might actually spy wings soaring out the door, taking flight with her joy. Then she twisted her head around to see if anyone was watching because she felt really stupid and laughed out loud at the silly picture she made.

"Damn, Kate. You're a silly twit."

She spent the morning washing the shelves and scrubbing the floors. It was easy to do without the encumbrance of furniture. She cleaned the windows and swept out the horse shed. She checked the earth shelter for critters and found it clean.

"Mel has been a busy, busy boy," she told Wolf who had given up chasing around the woods to follow her into the shelter. She didn't hear his wagon pull in, the shelter was so deep in the ground and was shocked to see him sitting on the wagon bench in front of a huge pile of furniture. He grinned when she poked her head out of the ground level door.

"Okay, I lied. Sometimes I'm not that good at waiting."

Kate climbed out and walked around the wagon, staring at the load the wagon carried. "Is there anything left in your mother's house?" she asked.

"Lots. You know how it is when you've lived some place a long time. You collect stuff, and some of this came from Jack and Ruthie's house and some from John Nestor's. Just – you know – some stuff," he said, winding down now and wondering if he'd stepped out of bounds.

Kate nodded slowly as she peered in between table legs and bed slats to see what all was there. "Are you just going to sit there and let me unload this stuff?"

"You're not going to yell at me?" Mel asked, astounded she would let him help her without a fight.

"Now, why would I do that?" she asked with a deceptively sweet smile. "I'm just going to say thank you and that's all. Just go about the business of life and not fight the gift horse. You know – be accepting and humble," she said with a twinkle. "Why would I ever yell at you?"

"Uh, because I . . . never mind. Let's just get this stuff in the cabin," he said, then whispered "Thank you, Harley."

He jumped down and began lifting a kitchen chair off the top of the pile, but he stopped midair, put it back in place and quickly turned to Kate, grabbed her forearms, pulled her against him, and kissed her. He held her there, moving his warm lips on hers lightly and then more firmly when he felt her lips open and respond. A groan escaped his throat.

Kate raised her arms to put them around his neck, and his hands slid around her back, pulling her tighter against his chest. When he took his lips from hers, he buried his face in her neck and listened to her rapid breath. It matched his own and he smiled, nuzzled her hair and set her away from him.

"We've work to do wanton woman. Work first, play later," he said grinning at her with joy that spread from his eyes to his mouth, to the swell of his chest down to the jaunt of his step.

"And it's fairly plain that either you or a fairy has been doing a good bit of work here lately. Was a little bird telling tales that the Ramey family would be coming home soon?"

"Nope, no birds, just hope."

By the time the wagon was unloaded, the small cabin was pretty much filled with everything they would need. Beds were in each bedroom, a small chest was in the main room, the kitchen held a table, two chairs and three stools that would serve as chairs. Two rockers sat in front of the hearth, and a rocker sat outside the door.

Kitty had straw for bedding in her shed and hay for snacking when she wasn't feeding on fresh grass. There was a small pile of wood next to the hearth and some outside the door.

"I'll bring more next time," Mel said as he unloaded the wood.

"Is there anything you've forgotten?" Kate questioned. "I'm surprised you didn't stock the pantry."

Mel held his hand up, palm out in defense mode. "This is all just extra stuff people had, Kate."

"Well," she said, kicking her foot in the dirt and grinning. "You probably should have checked with me first, and I guess you're forgiven – this time, but don't make a habit of it." She stretched on tiptoes to kiss his cheek, lingering just long enough to feel the heat of his breath on her neck.

"Thank you," she said quietly. "For everything."

"But this isn't all," he said, grinning almost impishly and incongruously for such a giant of a man. He almost skipped to the seat of the wagon and reached under it, pulling out a hamper and then hauling it and Kate inside with him.

"Sit," he said, pointing to one of the chairs in front of the hearth. She did, and Mel put the hamper on the table, unfolded the top, and brought out two small stemmed glasses, into which he poured an almost black liquid. He handed one to Kate, touched hers with his.

"To your return. I love it and you. Now rest a bit."

Kate stared at him, mute. She sipped the sweet cordial and rested her head against the back of the rocker. He carefully placed kindling and then logs in the fireplace, lit the small pile and then blew on the flame. She watched it spread and light his face in a rosy flush.

The toe of her foot touched the floor rhythmically, tilting the rocker back and forth in a soothing motion. She sipped again and rolled the liquid around on her tongue before swallowing, savoring the sweet taste of blackberries and the even sweeter taste of Mel moving casually about the room, lifting things from the hamper, setting the small table.

He whistled softly, a melody she didn't recognize, and she wondered aimlessly if he was creating the tune as he went, if the tune was a reflection of his mood at the moment. It was at once soulful and joyful. She let her mind fill with the wonder of him, his strength, his determination, his love. Kate did not even think of fleeing from the joy of it.

When he was finished, he brought his glass and the small bottle of cordial, refilled Kate's and his own, and then sat in the rocker next to her. He didn't say anything; nor did she. The muted click of his rocker matched hers and they silently watched the flickering flames. After a time, he broke the comfortable silence.

"I'm going to marry you at the end of the summer," he said quietly. "We can live here or at my place. It's your choice."

Kate rocked some more, seeming not to be surprised by his words. Eventually, she spoke. "Don't you think you should at least ask me first?"

"Nope. I've done that. I'm telling now," he said, tilting his head to grin at her.

"What makes you think I want to marry you?" she asked with a matching grin.

"You," he responded. "Your face. The angels in the room are joyful."

"For a strong silent type, you're quite poetic. Did you know that?"

"Yep. Come here."

She did, and as she snuggled on his lap, she sighed in sweet pleasure and felt the stirrings of excitement flutter again in her chest and stomach. She felt unencumbered happiness and looked around for those ethereal wings.

"You need to kiss me now, Kate, because your family will be here soon."

In the middle of the kiss, she heard the unmistakable sounds of her girls, Harley, Verna, Jack, Ruthie, Ellen and Poochie. She tried to block out the noise. She wanted to just nestle into Mel's chest, feel the touch of his lips. But that wasn't going to happen.

They bounced into the room with great peals of laughter and obvious delight in being there. They had missed their home almost as much as she had. When they had checked out the rest of the cabin and returned, Harley brought out his moonshine jug, took a deep breath and opened his mouth.

There was a collective groan, even from the girls, except for Becca who would listen to Harley all day long if he wanted to talk. He closed his mouth, looked around at all the faces watching him, waiting for the beginning of a long, long philosophical toast, one with deep meaning, perhaps two or three deep meanings which he would gladly explain in depth if desired.

"Here's to a great fall harvest," he said. Then he lifted the jug to his shoulder, put his lips to the mouth, leaned slightly forward, tipped it, and sipped briefly at the moonshine.

As much as there was a collective sigh when he mentioned a toast, there was an even louder group gasp at his six-word toast, almost all single syllables, too!

Harley had never been known to complete a simple sentence in six words, let alone an entire toast. Every head turned in his direction and each face wore a profound look of puzzlement, shocked amazement. No one moved or spoke. Wolf picked his head up off his paws and stared, a low growl seeping from his chest. Poochie sat up and tilted his head. Kate was sure she'd even heard an owl's 'Whoo, Whoo?' screech through the fading afternoon light.

Everyone looked to their neighbor for some sign the earth had not come to an end or for an explanation of the past few minutes, but no one had an idea that would explain the phenomenon of Harley's short toast. Harley pasted on an ear-to-ear grin and looked from face to face with his natural enjoyment of a situation he had created. He truly loved being the center of attention.

Jack, propped lazily against the sink and taking in the group as a whole, began to put together the pieces of Harley's short puzzle. He saw Mel's relaxed stance positioned close to Kate. He saw Kate's peaceful repose, a kind of leaning in to Mel's shoulder when he put his hand on her back for a moment, her obvious pleasure in Mel as he picked up Jeannie to hold her close and hugged the other girls.

He noted Kat's ease as she stood near Verna, glancing now and then at her idol in non-conversational agreement, but regarding Mel with apparent approval. Rachel stood near Ruthie, not a part of the group but not separate either. It was more like she was poised for flight, ready to accept her place in the family, but ready to flee it, too.

He saw Kate's rosy cheeks and noted the cabin full of furniture Kate could not have brought with her.

Jack finally said to the group, "Perhaps Mel would like to tell us about his fall harvest? Do you think so, Harley?"

Harley nodded his bushy head. Gold curls bobbed, and his hands pulled on the worn, red suspenders. "

That might be appropriate," he said, to the sound of suspenders snapping back into place with a dull thwack on his stomach.

Someone in the group said, "My God, only four words now?" And the rest giggled restlessly. Other than Jack, no one could figure out what was going on, but something was, and the absence of anything concrete was making everyone a bit jumpy.

Harley finally spotted the two cordial glasses and the cordial, poured a generous amount into each and told the ladies they would have to share glasses. They nodded agreement and continued to look around the room, confused.

"Do you have a toast, Mel?" Jack said, and it finally occurred to Mel what Harley and Jack were talking about. He flushed, gently scuffed the floor with the heel of his boot, then kicked at the table leg as boys and men will do. Boys and men kick things. It's some kind of rule.

He stammered unintelligible words, then took a deep breath and said, "Yes. I do."

He looked over at Kate with a question in his eyes.

Tell them? he asked conspiratorially. She nodded.

"Come fall," he said, "with the Ramey girls' blessings, I'll be marrying their mother. I'll be harvesting the best crop ever."

There was a collective roar of approval. Hands clapped together and clapped backs. Multiple voices shouted

"About time!" and "Finally!" and "Why'd you tell the old coot first?"

"We didn't," Mel and Kate said together. "Really, we didn't," Kate repeated.

Mel looked Jeannie in the eyes then tilted his head down to Kat and then Becca.

"What do you say ladies? Can I marry your beautiful mama?"

Jeannie, who was still in his arms, squealed and hugged him tighter; Becca ran to throw her arms around him, and Kat nodded and said, "That'd be fine. Where will you live? Are you moving to Big Rapids?"

He laughed, knowing and loving her direct thought process. They all laughed, and Kat looked around her wondering what was so funny.

Mel put his hand on her silky blonde head and told her they didn't have the details all worked out, but by fall they would.

"I'm pretty sure we won't make any plans without consulting you girls first," he told her.

He sought Rachel out as soon as he could separate himself from the group. She leaned against the door away from rest, watching faces and listening to the banter. Her face was a confusing mixture of sorrow and irritation, with some longing thrown in for good measure. Mel tried to figure it out as he casually moved in her direction, wanting a private word with her. He just didn't know what that word would be.

"Good to see you, Rachel. I'm hoping you'll tell your mother how happy you are for her," he said when he drew near.

Rachel met his words with silence, but Mel could see a battle raging in her eyes and spoke again. "I love her, Rachel. I want her to be happy."

"I know," she answered.

"It would help if you could be happy, too."

"I'll be happy for Ma, but that doesn't mean I have to like you. Fair?"

"Try pretending . . . for her. That's all I ask," he said and turned back toward the group. He noticed Ellen, who was standing alone, her back stiff, her face unfathomable and unreadable.

'Was she angry?' he wondered. Suddenly, a jagged edge of doubt and worry gnawed at his stomach. This was not the way it was supposed to be, damn it.

He left Rachel's side and moved across the room toward Ellen. He touched her shoulder gently, and Ellen finally looked up at him, tears gathering in her eyes and then spilling down her leathery cheeks.

"Don't be upset. I should have said something to you first, Ellen. I'm sorry to spring it on you like this. May I have permission to marry your daughter, please?" he asked formally.

Ellen couldn't speak, but she unabashedly let the tears flow in a torrent of salt water joy. Rivers ran down her beautiful, weathered skin, and she pounded a fist into her open palm. She rolled her eyes toward heaven and groaned a little. When words finally came, she swore at him and then at Kate.

"I've been planning this wedding since Kate was fifteen. It's about time," she sputtered through the sobs. Mel put his arms around her and picked her up in a huge bear hug.

"You have done your damnedest to keep me part of the family, you sneaky woman," he whispered in her ear. "Does your daughter know about your duplicity?"

"No, and don't you open your mouth, either. If you're going to be my son in law, I have the right to cuff your head," she whispered back.

Chapter Twenty-three

Summer and fall, 1916

The garden flourished in a summer of perfect sunshine and warm, gentle rains. They planted together on the weekends and hoped it would survive the critters and weeds during the week. It did, and so did Kate endure the drive back and forth to Big Rapids each week.

Sometimes Harley made the trip with her on those early Monday mornings, and on others he stayed to tend the girls and the garden – and Verna. Kate enjoyed the solitude of the ride most of the time, but it was strange being in the Big Rapids house without Harley and the girls. The seclusion and privacy she relished at the cabin was replaced here by quiet and loneliness. But she was working most of the time anyway, so she told herself it didn't matter.

She talked frequently that summer with Letha; about her cabin, about Hersey, about Mel and his farm. She hadn't had a female friend before, other than her sister. It felt good, and she'd be sorry to leave her.

"Will you visit?" Kate asked her. "We would love to have you come stay at the farm with us for a couple of days. It's huge. Six bedrooms!"

Kate hoped her eyes didn't express what she was feeling -- loss of a good friend, one she had come to love and would miss more than she had realized.

"Or maybe you and I could go stay at the cabin for a couple of days, alone, a woman's time away from everyone else."

Letha listened and heard the mixture of sadness and joy in Kate's voice. "Sure, I'll come," she teased. "Just try to keep me away from that big man of yours."

Kate stopped by to see Ralph Stern and Mrs. Worthington to let them know she would be leaving the area in the fall. Mr. Stern was true to his name and thought it was Kate's responsibility to come up with her replacement. Kate told him she'd try, but he might want to figure out how to do laundry himself for a change. He sputtered and said, "That work is something females do, young woman. Not gentlemen." She'd known he would be angry, but she didn't care. It was a glorious day.

Mrs. Worthington, however, was a different situation. She grew teary eyed and grasped Kate to her ample bosom.

"My dear girl," she crooned. "I am so happy for you." She asked to be invited to the wedding, and Kate could do nothing but agree and walk away feeling oddly like she was abandoning the woman.

Frank stopped by periodically, and she had to shoo him away when she tired of his chatter. He took it well each time she banished him; he danced back and forth from foot to foot and grinned his funny, toothy grin. She was careful with Frank because she knew, as sometimes women do, that deep down he would have liked something more from her, but he also knew she would never give it. That, too, oddly enough, was okay with him. He was an inexplicable man, and a friend.

Kate had made good friends during her time in Big Rapids, and she was beginning to understand it had become a second home. It wasn't home like the cabin, but it was what she had made it, and she smiled when she realized that fact.

Okay, she thought. I'm not a bat who homes in automatically without benefit of sight, but I can take a direction and make it work. I can zone in and find a home. I can . . . Alright, you're being silly, now, Kate.

Dr. Crow visited to inquire about Jeannie, and in a more subtle way to see how Kate was doing. He didn't come right out and ask, but Kate could see him watching her attentively, looking into her. She wondered how he did that. In fact, she asked him if he saw things others didn't when he looked at people.

He smiled his slow smile and said, "If you look, you see. It's the same for you, Kate, and others, too."

She shook her head and said, "Must you always speak in riddles? Is that an old tribal custom?"

John shook his head at her, ignoring her question and asking another with a cynical grin.

"Do you think I should dance around a bonfire with a tomahawk in my hand?" Then more seriously, "You look well, Kate. I'm glad."

"I'm getting married, John, come autumn. Mel and I will be married."

John shifted slightly and leaned against the porch rail. He tilted his head to listen like there was more she had to say. Kate waited for his reaction while moments turned into minutes.

"Well?" she finally blurted, too uncomfortable to allow further silence. "Shouldn't you congratulate me or something? That's usually what people do when they hear that kind of news."

"If you are ready for marriage, then I congratulate both you and Mel. He is a strong man."

Kate's head jerked up, startled by his strange response. "Why? Because he puts up with me? Is that what makes him strong?" Kate argued irrationally, for some reason irked by his attitude and words -- or the paucity of them.

John's white teeth glowed in the growing darkness as his lips spread in another grin.

"No, he was already strong. Perhaps loving you made him stronger."

"Well, that makes me sound like . . . like something you have to take because it's good for you, like cod liver oil!" she sputtered, looking for the right words that wouldn't come. She stamped a foot and rose from the swing where she'd been sitting.

"Damn, John, that doesn't make me sound very inviting! Cod liver oil, my eye!"

"You are never bitter on the tongue, Kate," he said soothingly, and after awhile added. "Is your heart no longer angry? Is your wound healed?"

342

Kate looked at him a long time, a beautiful, still man, so quiet within himself that you wondered if he took breath like normal mortals. She couldn't see his eyes in the dusky light of evening but knew they would reflect recognition of an untruth if she told one in her answer. Her words were soft when they came, hidden by the warm summer night sounds.

"There's a corner of my heart that I can't do anything about," she told him, hoping he'd understand and tell her it was alright. For some strange reason, John Crow's blessing was important to her.

"It holds tears, John, for my father, for my Water Bug, and most especially for Mark. I . . . loved them . . . desperately, intensely, in such different ways." She paused, looking for a way to describe feelings she knew were powerful, feelings that couldn't be defined by simple words.

"I know you told me some time ago that I was not trying hard enough to heal from my loss, that I was keeping raw wounds in my heart. But my loves are part of my heart. To cut them out would be to cut my heart in pieces and I would die. Does that make sense to you? I can't do that. They're part of who I am."

John listened carefully and heard Kate plead for something only she could tell herself, only she could know. He watched Kate's mind work in the flickering of her eyes and tightening of her brow,

"I've brought you something, a pouch like mine that holds a piece of Jeannie's hair, only it is much prettier. Your pouch, not the hair. The hair is inordinately beautiful," he added with a small, slanted grin.

He reached into his pocket for a package. "Put a piece of your father, your Water Bug, and Mark in this heart. It isn't an ugly, old pouch like mine, or an albatross. It's a pretty satin heart that holds treasures."

Kate took the heart from him, and he showed her where it opened to accept small tokens.

"It's a simple custom of my people, Kate. We believe if we hold pieces of loved ones close to us, symbolically, then our hearts are free."

"Why do you wear yours, John? Why would your heart be burdened if you didn't wear one of these around your neck?"

"One reason I do is mine alone. The other I'll share. I must be open to the pain and sickness in my patients. I heal with my spirit as well as with my knowledge. I can't do that with a heart full of sorrow ... for patients I couldn't help, for the pain of their suffering. I put it in my pouch, and I am free. Make sense, Kate Ramey?"

Kate nodded. "Is this why you came here tonight, John Crow? To give me this heart?"

"I came to check on the Ramey family. I'm a doctor," he said in his quiet, straightforward manner.

"Well, I think you're more, John. You're a friend, and I'm blessed to know you."

John Crow's long legs moved him from Kate's porch down the road and into darkness. She watched him go and was still not sure exactly who he was, nor was she sure of his unorthodox medical practices. But he healed people. She'd seen that, and he had uncanny powers of observation. She'd miss John Crow, too.

Bells rang in the Congregational Church, its steeple shimmering white against verdant emerald hills surrounding Hersey. The church was full on a warm, late September Saturday, and Mel stood in the back room listening to the lively chatter around him and fiddling with his tie.

His mother straightened it six times. But Mel could not keep his hand from yanking it right and then left, tugging at it like it was a lifeline that might save a drowning sailor or a noose choking the breath from his body.

"Leave it alone!" she reprimanded. "Leave it!"

"What time is it?" he asked for the fourteenth time.

"Why don't you go out and sit down Mrs. Bronson? I'll take it from here."

Laura sighed in relief, muttered invectives unusual for her and fled through the door. When Jack saw her back recede, he pulled a flask from his pocket and held it out to Mel. "I think you could use a nip, a big one."

At that moment, Harley pranced in looking dapper in a new suit, complete with tie. He strutted once around Mel, nodding in appreciation and then pirouetted for their approval of him.

Jack was suitably in awe. "My God, Harley, I wouldn't know you. Look at those gold curls, Mel! They're glowing. I think they're iridescent!" He handed the flask to Harley and asked that he hold the toast for later. Harley nodded and took a reasonably small sip.

"You look a might scared, Mel," Harley crooned after he swallowed.

Mel nodded, shifted his weight from one foot to the next and then froze when the preacher leaned into the small room and motioned for them to follow him to the altar. He grabbed Jack's arm, stark terror in his eyes.

"I've waited a few decades for this. I've loved her for more. What if I don't do this right? What if I can't?" he begged, his voice cracking in fear.

The big man's terror was amazing to Jack who had watched Mel tackle life without a nod, brushing off blight and defeat, holding up others when their losses were too great, lending his broad shoulders when others needed to lean. He looked at him and grinned.

"You afraid, boy? You afraid of a little bitty girl like Kate?"

Mel nodded, then croaked, "I am."

"Good, maybe that will keep you in line," Jack told him, grinning and punching his arm. "I love that woman. If you do anything – I mean anything -- to hurt her, well . . . you know the rest. Hear me?"

When Mel nodded again, Jack handed him the flask. He took another sip and felt more stable.

"Let's go see the reverend," he said, and led Jack to the side of the altar where they would wait for his bride.

Where Kate was getting ready, Jeannie and Rachel fussed over their dresses, looking in the mirror, puffing and pulling at their hair. Kat sat with a frown on her face because she'd had to wear a dress and Becca continued to peek out the door to see who was out there.

"The whole place is full, Ma! Everybody in Hersey is here!"

"I don't know why you have to wear that funny neck thing," Ellen said again. "It doesn't really look right."

"It's blue, Mother. I like it. It's a blue heart. Something old, something new – you know." She held the heart to her breast and patted it lovingly.

"I hear the organist starting up. It won't be long. Are you all ready?" Ellen said, looking at the girls and then at Kate.

"I need Harley," Kate said suddenly. "Please. I need Harley. Just for a minute."

Ellen left the room and returned with Harley in tow. He beamed at Kate, wiggling his eyebrows in appreciation of the vision. Taking her hand in his, he stopped the silliness and looked at her.

"Will you girls wait in the hallway, please?" he asked and turned back to Kate. "You are beautiful, Kate, as beautiful as the last time you walked down this aisle."

Kate's eyes nearly filled, but Harley lifted the satin heart by its ribbon and dangled it in front of her face.

"What do you know about that?" she asked, puzzled he would even notice it.

"Enough. You will never lose him, Kate. There's no need to be sad. Becoming another man's wife doesn't lessen being Mark's. You're fortunate to be so loved by two wonderful men–plus me," he said, grinning now and pulling her along with him.

Kate took a deep breath, patted the heart and knew his words were right. She was calmed.

Harley walked her down the aisle, and with his usual great flair, but no words, gave her hand to Mel who was waiting for her . . . as he had done for thirty years.

"I love you so much, Kate," he said as the ring slid on her finger. "I always have. I will treasure you always."

"I love you, Mel, and I . . . always have."

Kate didn't know if Mel believed it, but it was true. She had always loved him, in a way that was as special and different as other loves she had known, and she would spend the next decades showing him.

A brief reception in the basement of the church followed for the large group who had attended the wedding. Almost all the residents of Hersey were eager to witness the event and munched cookies, balanced coffee cups, and discussed the bride and groom. Each person knew a better story; each thought they had something new and more interesting to add to the last one.

"She taught my kids, you know. She was good but crazy. Stood on the desk to get their attention. I think my Ethan brought her some frogs."

"I heard that. Did you hear that she kept a switch by the desk? That Mel gave it to her on her first day she taught school?"

"Did you know that she stared down Agatha Pennington when she was a teacher and won?"

"Yeah, and Kate and that red dog used to go wandering in the woods a lot. I worried about her then."

"We all worried then, and when her first husband was . . . well . . . that was a sad time."

"Mel has really made something of that farm since his father passed."

"He has always known what to do and how to do it. Remember when he made the fire department happen cause no one else would?"

"Every momma of every young girl set her sights on that young man, but he wouldn't even look once, let alone twice."

Everyone knew the story of Mel's determined wait for the love of his life. And everyone wanted to own a small part of the tale, have something personal to add to the perfect day, to be a little special because they'd been there in the beginning of the fairytale. Perhaps they wanted to boast of a hero in their own world.

Everyone knew Kate's story, too, all the highs and lows, from childhood to widowhood. And those who loved her wanted to share their private memories with others who loved her, to ride on the coattails Kate's unique personality, her ability to stride doggedly through whatever life threw her way.

Mel was highly respected; Kate was admired even though they shook their heads in curious speculation. And the girls were adored. It was the wedding of the decade and no one would be anywhere else.

Mel and Kate made the rounds, greeting folks together, making sure no one was left out. Having her next to him, truly with him, was indescribable. He couldn't let go of her and kept patting her hand where it lay on his arm. And Kate's face radiated happiness; the glow was without equal.

Kate was eager to leave the church for what she thought of as the real reception at her mother's house where dinner and drinks were to be served. Where she could kick off her new shoes and wiggle her toes.

"Have we talked to everyone?" she whispered to Mel. "Please say yes."

"Yes," he answered. "And then some."

"Happy?" she asked.

"I repeat . . . and then some," he said quietly, a wide smile spreading like morning sunshine on his face.

"Then let's go."

Best wishes and rice were tossed at them as Kate and Mel, like two young newlyweds, ducked and ran up from the basement reception and then down the steps from the church to the decorated buggy waiting for them.

At Ellen's, family and almost family gathered: Jack and Ruthie, Willie and Mary with their two children, Harley and Verna, John and Esther Nestor, John Crow and Letha Cross, and of course, the four Ramey girls and Mel's brothers and sisters. Ellen and Laura Bronson bustled around the kitchen, putting the finishing touches on the wedding dinner.

The table had been extended as far as it would go; a long, long way thanks to Harley's ingenuity many long years ago. It had been beautifully set the night before and was waiting for the wedding party to arrive. All that needed to be done now was to make toasts to the bride and groom, which Harley immediately set out to do.

The jug emerged, glasses of cordial were handed out, lemonade poured, and a circle was formed.

"Get in the middle, you two," Harley ordered. "We all want to look at you when we toast your health and happiness."

Embarrassed but willing to acquiesce on this day, they obeyed. Mel held Kate's hands and rolled his eyes.

"He's yours, you know. I don't claim ownership."

"Yes, I know, and I do. He's mine, all the crazy parts of him."

Harley's eyes misted when he raised the jug. Many times he had done this toasting work. Many times he had looked at Kate, but the picture at this moment might have been his undoing.

Kate looked like a doll, her honey hair flowing down her back, her cheeks flushed with excitement. She still had her slender frame, and her blue eyes still sparkled -- her father's eyes -- those that had sweet talked Ellen and made her blush.

Mel was the handsome prince, the knight in shining armor, his suntanned face weathered in all the right ways, his broad shoulders proclaiming strength, and his gentle expression taming the meanest tongue.

Harley looked at them and wondered how he was going to make it through this toast.

"Friends," he said, "raise your glasses . . . to love . . . to fairytales and . . ."

"Nooooo," Kat yelled. She stood in front of him, faced him head on, one fist on her hip, and said, "This one's mine." She turned to the center of the circle, raised her lemonade and said, "Here's to Ma and Mel."

After everyone recovered from the shock and quenched their thirst by drinking to her toast, Kat turned to Harley and said, "Okay. Your turn and thanks, Pretty Eyes. I was thirsty."

Kat's toast kindled recollections for all of them. Kate's eyes roamed to the loft and she saw herself as a fifteen-year old. Harley saw Kate as a young woman, as she'd been when he followed Mark home and he'd first met them all. To Mel, Kate was a girl, as she'd been when he first fell in love with her; and his mother saw Mel as a young man hopelessly in love. Ellen saw Kate and her pa, heads together, sharing stories from town or making them up.

A circle moved around the room that encompassed several generations, and not a single remembered portrait would be identical to the next one. They were each too intensely personal, too entangled with individual memories. Yet, at the same time, they were shared and as meaningful together as they were separately.

Not long after dark, they escaped to Kate's buggy and let Kitty whisk them into the night. They were heading to the cabin, and Kitty knew the way, so the reins lay loosely on Mel's lap, and his arm was solidly around Kate. He felt tender, protective, possessive; so many feelings crowded his mind and heart it was impossible to differentiate between them. And he didn't want to even try.

The harvest moon was brilliant, and cast long shadows across the road, taking them in and out of darkness as they traveled.

Kate had taken this road many times, but tonight it looked different. The darkness was softer, the path a little brighter. Mel, too, was accustomed to this road, but now it was both familiar and extraordinary. Both comforting and exciting. The incongruity of being on a road both well known and exotic existed for both of them, and they were quiet. Kate's head rested on his shoulder, and his arm surrounded her.

When they got to the cabin, Mel dropped the reins and hopped down. He went around to Kate's side and raised his arms, holding them out as he would if he were going to carry a baby.

"Come on, wife," he demanded comically.

"Are you really going to carry me across the same threshold we've both crossed hundreds of times?" she asked, excitement radiating from her.

"I am, Mrs. Bronson. And we've not crossed this threshold before . . . come here."

Kate leaned into him, and he lifted her, one arm under her back, the other beneath her legs. He carried her without effort and stopped twice to steal a kiss before moving on.

He nudged the door open, kissed her again and slowly set her down. Kate looked around, surprise lighting her face. Flowers brightened every space, and a fire was flickering, warming the room perfectly for a fall night. On the table, a plate of cheese and fruit sat next to two glasses and a decanter of dark liquid.

"Where did this all come from?" Kate asked, wonder in her eyes.

"I'm not sure," Mel answered, confusion in his eyes, too. "Isn't this something?"

Kate moved closer to her husband and wrapped her arm around his back, then stood on tiptoes to kiss his cheek, then his lips.

"It's nice, wherever it came from."

"Shall I pour you a glass? Do you want to sit for a bit?"

"I'd like that, Mel. That would be nice," she answered, butterflies attaching themselves to her voice.

It had crossed his mind that coming to the cabin on their wedding night might be too difficult for Kate, and he'd suggested she might want to go to the Osceola Hotel in nearby Reed City for a brief honeymoon. She'd gently refused, saying the forest was the perfect place; where she'd like to be. But the flutters had not escaped his notice.

He poured their cordial and brought them to her where she was sitting in front of the fire. She relaxed, her head against the back of the chair, her feet pushing against the floor to rock slowly. When he sat, he raised his glass toward her, searched her face for clues to her heart, to her mind, and was pleased.

"To us, Kate," he said on a deeply contented breath.

They sipped and talked easily about inconsequential things. Comfort warmed them as much as the fire. He played with her hand as it lay on the arm of the chair, ran his thumb across her palm and felt a small tensing as her fingers stretched in pleasure. At last, he stood, held his hand out to her and she rose to follow. When they moved into Kate's room, she gasped and looked at Mel.

"What? Where did this come from?"

A large four poster bed stood in the middle of the room. The corner posts were made of thick, polished pine and were delicately carved with leaves and vines. The mattress was covered in a russet colored quilt, and matching curtains hung at the window. Two soft, thick rugs lay on either side of the bed. The room resonated warmth in brown and green forest colors.

"Do you like it?" he asked, knowing the answer just by looking at her face.

"Are you kidding? Look at this. It's beautiful, and the bed is so high I'm probably going to need a ladder to get in."

"I'll be here to lift you," he added.

"Where did it come from?"

"Harley. He made it."

Tears formed, and she widened her eyes and blinked to keep them from raining on her wedding day. Mel wrapped her in his arms and kissed them away. She responded and the fire spread, the passion grew, the need that had been there for so long intensified. She kissed his neck and felt his hands undoing the buttons at her back.

Excitement ran in waves down her spine, and Mel drew her dress down and let it slip over her shoulders and drop at their feet.

TO MY READERS

I am so happy you read my book and hope you enjoyed it as much as I loved writing it. If you want to know how it all began, read *Elephant in the Room: a family saga.* The other Family Saga Series books are waiting for you, as well.

I would love to know your thoughts. You can go to www.julisisung.com. From there, you can talk to me, leave an email address so I can talk to you, or click over to Amazon or another book store to leave a review.

Struggling authors need reviews, so I thank you.

Made in the USA
Coppell, TX
06 December 2021

67316210R00197